BY

MELANIE BENJAMIN

Alice I Have Been

The Autobiography of Mrs. Tom Thumb

The Aviator's Wife

The Swans of Fifth Avenue

Reckless Hearts (short story)

The Girls in the Picture

Mistress of the Ritz

The Children's Blizzard

California Golden

The Windsor Affair

THE
WINDSOR AFFAIR

The Windsor Affair

A NOVEL

MELANIE BENJAMIN

DELACORTE PRESS

New York

Delacorte Press
An imprint of Random House
A division of Penguin Random House LLC
1745 Broadway, New York, NY 10019
randomhousebooks.com
penguinrandomhouse.com

Hardcover ISBN 978-0-593-49788-3
Ebook ISBN 978-0-593-49789-0

Printed in the United States of America on acid-free paper

1st Printing

FIRST EDITION

BOOK TEAM: PRODUCTION EDITOR: *Loren Noveck* • MANAGING EDITOR: *Saige Francis* • PRODUCTION MANAGER: *Maggie Hart* • COPY EDITOR: *Tracy Roe* • PROOFREADERS: *Jill Falzoi, Pam Feinstein, and Robin Slutzky*

Book design by Barbara M. Bachman

The authorized representative in the EU for product safety and compliance is Penguin Random House Ireland, Morrison Chambers, 32 Nassau Street, Dublin D02 YH68, Ireland. https://eu-contact.penguin.ie

To Mavis,
queen of our world

THE

WINDSOR AFFAIR

CHAPTER
I

LONDON AND ITS OUTSKIRTS

OCTOBER 1946

THE RIDE BACK TO EDNAM LODGE SEEMED INTERMINABLE. All that the former Bessie Wallis Warfield, aka the former Mrs. Earl Winfield Spencer Jr., aka the former Mrs. Ernest Simpson, aka the current Duchess of Windsor, could do was murmur, soothe, and coo. God, how she detested having to murmur, soothe, and coo. For almost ten years, since the abdication, that's all she'd done.

"And then he said—my blasted brother, my *younger* brother—he said he quite understood my plight. As if he could! When he is the one responsible for it!"

"I know, David, I know."

"And still, nothing. No job, no purpose. Polite as ever, of course. That insincere politeness my damn family has perfected to an art form. They'll smile sympathetically, pat you on the shoulder with one hand, and plunge the knife into your back with the other. My family are ice-cold bitches."

"Was *she* there?" Wallis couldn't help herself; she had to ask. "Was Cookie there, in her dowdy dress with her fake smile?"

"No. She wasn't. Oh, Bertie said she sent her warmest love

but—what a pity!—she had a slight cold and wouldn't want to give it to me. What a joke. If she really was sick, you know she'd kiss me on the cheek and hope for my tragic demise. Typhoid Elizabeth, rotten to the core."

"So. This trip has been for nothing, then. Like all the others. No mention of—" Wallis couldn't bring herself to say it. Again.

"No, dearest. I'm afraid my blasted family still won't give you your due or your official title. But you know you're the queen of my heart." David reached for her hand, but she snatched it away and barely repressed a shiver of disgust. How many times had he said that? As if his devotion—touching, pathetic, smothering, incessant—could make up for all she'd sacrificed? Oh, yes, he'd given up quite a lot too. But still. *She* was the one who had to live up to a ridiculous ideal. She was the one stuck forever in this charade of the greatest romance in the history of the world.

Because the one thing she could never, ever do, unlike the other times, was leave.

There were, however, certain compensations, and Wallis smiled while David—sensing her disgust—started in with his usual pathetic groveling. "Oh, darling, your hair looks divine! Did you enjoy your day at the hairdresser's? I've never seen you look more lovely . . ." And so on. It was easy to tune the man out when she thought of the newest bauble—their private little word to describe the fabulous jewels David took so much care in designing and presenting to her—that had arrived just this afternoon. From Cartier, via special courier under armed guard, *naturellement*. She'd opened the velvet box breathlessly and gasped at the beauty of the pigeon's egg–size sapphire set as the breast of a jeweled bird of paradise. She had entrusted it to her maid to be secured with all her other jewels. She'd brought the entire lot over from Paris for this visit. Why, she couldn't exactly say. But in this hostile country where she was still reviled, she needed them. Wallis's jewels were fit for any queen, real or figurative. Here on this cold, dreary, impoverished island—God, she hadn't realized how pervasive the rationing remained, how ugly the bombed-out buildings, the piles of rubbish, and the clothes! The clothes were pathetic, nothing fashionable; even her hosts were wearing dresses and suits purchased before the war—Wallis needed to be surrounded by her friends.

More and more, her friends were objects, not people.

"How many more days do we have to endure with the Dudleys?" David said. "God. I hate bloody Eric and his wife. All he does is talk about fishing."

"And all she does is talk about me, apparently." Wallis didn't keep the bitterness out of her voice. *Everyone* gossiped about the Windsors, even those who claimed to be their good friends. The scant handful left in this benighted little kingdom, anyway. Even Churchill had turned his back on them during the war.

"Put on the face, dearest. Here we are, back at the ranch. Because my wretched family couldn't bear to have us cross the dusty thresholds of any of their numerous castles."

Wallis smiled tightly and stepped out of the Rolls, not even acknowledging the footman who opened the door. Their hosts of several days now, the Earl and Countess of Dudley—Eric and Laura—were waiting to greet them at the top of the stairs. Their country house, Ednam Lodge, just outside of Windsor

Great Park, was filled with light, unlike most houses in London, where electricity was still spotty or too expensive.

"Wallis! David!" Laura bobbed a curtsy to them both, which was one point in her favor. Not many people in England risked curtsying to Wallis, knowing the King's decree. "Did you have a nice time in town? How were the King and Queen?" Laura's eyebrow arched knowingly as they went inside. Footmen removed and disposed of wraps and hats, and the privileged four lingered in the grand hall for a moment. Wallis was overcome with weariness, contemplating another boring dinner with these two.

"The King looks terrible," David replied as he reached inside his breast pocket for a cigarette; he produced a silver case engraved with his royal crest, offered it to the others, who declined, then lit his own and inhaled with vigor. "He's lost weight, I'm afraid. My brother doesn't look at all well."

"And the Queen?" Laura persisted, obviously hoping for something juicy to savor and share later.

"Absent."

"Probably down in the kitchen with the cook," Wallis quipped.

"Where she feels most at home," David added with a knowing wink, and they all laughed.

"Now, you two, I'm sure you're simply exhausted, so I thought we'd pass on dinner. There are sandwiches and a few other nibblies laid out for you in your rooms. We stuffed ourselves at tea with the Cavendishes—we've only just returned—so I thought a light repast would be best. Is that all right?"

Wallis could have hugged her dear friend—truly, one of the sweetest people she knew!—but refrained. She did flash her a look of pure relief and thanked her profusely. Then the

Windsors climbed the stairs to their suite: two bedrooms with a sitting room in the middle. The bathrooms were en suite, of course.

But when they reached their suite, they were astonished. All the lights were blazing, and Mary, Wallis's maid, was standing in the middle of Wallis's bedroom crying. Hysterically.

"Oh, ma'am! Oh, my dear ma'am! They're gone! They're all gone!"

"What's gone?" Wallis snapped, wanting to slap the silly girl to stop her sobs. What now? What new crisis in this godforsaken place?

"The jewels!"

"My jewels! What?" Wallis ran to her bed, knelt down, and reached for the three trunks full of jewels that she'd stored there.

"No—look! They're empty!" And Mary—stupid, stupid girl!—pointed to the small trunks, lids open and drawers all pulled out, on the floor nearby. "The only things they left are the Fabergé boxes!" Mary ran to the open window, where a scattering of small jeweled boxes gave the sill an oddly festive look.

"They? What do you mean, *they*?" Wallis turned to her maid, peering at her suspiciously. "Who did this? Where were you?"

"I don't know who! I went down to supper with all the other servants and when I came back, everything was gone!"

"Dear God, dear God!" Now David was dashing about, wringing his hands, and Wallis wanted to laugh at him. So stupid, so little. So ineffectual. But—

"The Cartier! The new one—the bird of paradise! Did they take that too?"

"Everything's gone!"

Madness. All was madness. She was Alice in Wonderland—*Wallis* in Wonderland—and everything was upside down. The Mad Hatter was ranting and the White Rabbit was hopping about and Wallis wanted to scream.

"What's going on?" Laura was suddenly by her side. Wallis grabbed the woman's shoulders and started shaking her.

"My jewels were stolen and I want to interrogate everyone in your house! Every maid, footman, scullery girl, butler. Everyone, do you hear?"

"Wallis! My staff—why, they're all loyal, they've been with me forever. You surely can't mean—"

"Everyone. I want them now, goddamn it. Bring them to me now."

"Call Scotland Yard," David was blubbering as he ran to and fro, to and fro—*Oh dear! Oh dear! I shall be too late!* "Call the palace! Call Downing Street! Call the Special Service!"

As the insanity continued to spin around her—phones ringing, servants invading, David now crying, Laura joining him, and Eric shouting, "Did they take my fishing poles?"—Wallis dropped into a chair. Robbed.

She had been robbed. Of her title, her happiness, her freedom—and now her jewels.

"I hate this place," she said, not caring who heard. "I shall hate it to my grave. I can't wait to leave and never return."

And who was the thief of all she cherished? Who was the engineer behind the venom of an entire country flung at her whenever she set foot on its shores?

That floozy—that *Cookie*.

That bitch.

THE NEXT MORNING, THE former Lady Elizabeth Bowes-Lyon, daughter of the Earl and Countess of Strathmore and Kinghorne, the current Queen Consort of the United Kingdom and all its dominions as well as Empress Consort of India, sat at the breakfast table, her dainty feet crossed neatly at the ankles. The private apartments of Buckingham Palace had a homey feel, she thought with satisfaction. At least compared to the state rooms. But in the past ten years, give or take a few months, since she and Bertie had ascended to the throne, she had done her best to turn a drafty palace with ceilings high enough for a giraffe into a home. Family photos of the two of them and their little princesses, Lilibet and Margaret, filled every available surface in the family quarters, peeking out from behind elaborate flower arrangements and fine Meissen porcelain. Cozy little lamps did their best to warm up the frigid glare of chandeliers, and needlepoint throw pillows—many embroidered by the King—were scattered on sofas and chairs.

In the morning room, where the family took their meals when there were no guests, the wireless blared popular music, and Elizabeth hummed along to Geraldo and His Orchestra.

We'll gather lilacs in the spring again . . .

"The papers, Your Majesty." Elizabeth nodded as a liveried footman presented a silver tray upon which all the major newspapers—special editions just for the royals, printed on palace paper with ink that did not smudge—were spread out for the King and Queen to peruse.

"Bertie! Papers!" Elizabeth called out in her lilting voice, and soon her husband, still in his silk dressing gown and wearing a tatty pair of slippers that Margaret had painstakingly cross-stitched for him during the war, joined her. The girls were most likely taking breakfast in bed, a privilege they both had eagerly embraced once they were allowed.

Bertie sat down with a cough and a sigh. He sighed so frequently these days! One would have thought that with the war over, everyone would be walking with a bounce, perpetual smiles and laughter and music in the air and the promise of spring—*lilacs in the spring*—every single day. But no. How could they throw off those years of fear, despair, and heartbreak so quickly? The explosion of joy when victory was declared had lasted a week. Then the sobering business of tallying up the toll of war—the lack of housing, the rationing still necessary, the empty seats at the table, the empty pillows in beds, the lost years of those youths who were spared, the lost joys of childhood and adolescence, not to mention the devastating financial cost of fending off Hitler for five solid years—descended upon the country like one of the great London fogs. It stifled all joy, all promise. It made one wonder, occasionally, if all the wartime sacrifices had been worth it, what with inflation and shortages and this unforeseen sense of isolation from their allies, who had joined hands and skipped ahead of poor, broken England to forge a new world order.

But one must not be maudlin, Elizabeth told herself with a stern shake of the head. Particularly when one's husband looked so tired and ill.

"Is your cold better, darling?" Bertie patted her hand.

"My what—oh, yes. Yes, my cold! All better now. What a pity I couldn't see David last night."

"Yes, a pity." Bertie winked at her and she laughed. She was very proud of her laugh. She'd been told, often, that it sounded like the peals of little bells.

"The jig is up, I'm afraid," she said with a teasing pout.

"You can never deceive me, my dear. But it was for the best. He was—well, David. Or at least, David since—"

"He met *her*."

"Yes. He looked very well, though. All tanned and rested."

"Spending the war in the Bahamas will do that to a person."

"We sent him there, remember, darling."

"Because we couldn't trust him—we couldn't trust *her*—here! That Woman!"

That Jezebel. That bitch.

"Darling, calm down."

Elizabeth looked at her husband, whose blue eyes were wide with mild alarm, and laughed. Normally it was the other way around, wasn't it? She was the one who had to calm him down whenever he flew into one of his "gnashes," as the family called them. All their marriage, her role was to soothe and calm, to support and help this awkward, courageous, badly broken man shoulder his many duties. Duties that devastatingly increased once his brother—

"All the bags are gone beneath his eyes," Bertie continued. "I think he's cut back on his drinking. At least she's had that influence on him."

"Yes, and who has the bags now?" Elizabeth snapped, looking pointedly at her perpetually weary husband. But her heart did give a little twinge as she thought of David looking well. For wasn't he once the most glamorous Prince of Wales imaginable? The debonair prince she'd danced with before she'd even met his younger brother? The golden heir to the throne that every girl—and the Queen of England was once a girl, contrary to popular belief, a giggling debutante with starry eyes and dancing feet—pined after. What was that song she heard so often back then? Oh, yes—

I danced with a man, who danced with a girl, who danced with the Prince of Wales!

She had danced with the prince himself, many times. He was a divine—if distracted—dancer, she recalled. So fun, so gay—yet always, she admitted, projecting the air of only stopping in before going on to a better, more exclusive, party. Her set—which should have been his set as well, peopled as it was with dukes and lords and eligible young heiresses of landed gentry—didn't appeal to him even then. He graced them with his glittering presence, danced dutifully with every nobleman's daughter who could possibly qualify as a royal wife, then went off to revels of wild debauchery with older—angular, stylish, *married*—women.

Elizabeth Bowes-Lyon, with her long hair in a twist, not shingled, with her skirts still to her ankles, not her knees, could never catch his eye for more than a fleeting dance. No matter how delightfully she laughed.

"Good Lord!" Bertie burst out, breaking through her reverie.

"What, Bertie?"

"Their jewels were stolen! Last night—must have been when he was here. Wallis and David's jewels, I mean—read it!"

Her dark blue eyes round with perfect concern, dutifully horrified sounds emanating from her rosy lips, Elizabeth took the newspaper and read the headline.

Windsor Jewel Theft! The Duke and Duchess of Windsor Report £500,000 Loss of Precious Jewels . . .

"What a pity," Elizabeth murmured, keeping her dancing eyes averted from her husband's gaze. She did hope her cheeks weren't too pink. "Who would do such a thing? Have they caught the thief?"

"It doesn't say," Bertie said, scanning the other newspapers, all full of headlines about the theft. "Poor chap. Should I call and offer help?"

"Oh, don't," Elizabeth said quickly. Perhaps too quickly. "I'm sure Scotland Yard was called and will be all over—oh, Bertie! Listen—listen to what That Woman said! When asked by a reporter what jewelry she was wearing yesterday, she said—and I quote—'A fool would know that with tweeds or other daytime clothes one wears gold, and that with evening clothes one wears platinum.' Really! The cheek!"

"I don't imagine that will go down well with the public," Bertie admitted as he started to smear marmalade on toast. "Those two have no idea what this country has gone through these past years."

"To bring so many jewels for a ten-day visit, and now the entire world knows how much they were worth. While there is such privation, such rationing, among the good British people." Elizabeth shook her head and laid the paper down beside her plate, which was piled high with bacon, eggs, sausages. She looked for her favorite oatcakes and reached for one. "One cannot believe how clueless they are."

The two ate in silence save for the scraping of heavy silver on delicate china. Behind each chair stood a footman ready to fetch or take away, whatever their need. The wireless continued to play popular music, and despite the gloomy day outside the floor-to-ceiling windows overlooking the manicured garden, Elizabeth felt as contented as the Cheshire Cat.

THE NIGHT BEFORE . . .

She had enjoyed her dinner, as always; it did not become one to pretend not to appreciate comforting food on a cold, rainy night. Yet she had had one ear cocked, waiting—even as she smiled and charmed her guests.

Finally a footman approached, bowing. "Your Majesty," he said, then bent down to whisper into her ear. She nodded. Folding her napkin, she rose.

"Please, do go on. I'll just be a minute," she said, and gracefully left the room, ignoring the wide, questioning eyes.

In the hallway, where a telephone resided upon a gilt table, another footman held the receiver out to her with a smart bow.

"Yes, this is the Queen. You did? Very well. What did she say? She couldn't wait to leave? Did the duke say anything?"

She nodded, listening.

"Ah. Yes, of course—and again, very well done. I trust you will be utterly discreet? Thank you."

She put the receiver down with a satisfied sigh. "A job well done," she said to herself with a firm little nod of punctuation. Although she couldn't prevent a victorious grin. It wasn't the first time she'd had to take matters into her own hands. If only she'd thought of this years ago—but no, it didn't do to reflect too deeply upon the past. Only commoners did that.

Royals could never appear to have regrets.

CHAPTER
2

WINDSOR GREAT PARK

WINTER 1933

"DARLING THELMA! DEAREST DAVID! CAN YOU BELIEVE THIS weather?" Elizabeth, Duchess of York, embraced her hosts, pressing her cold cheek against Thelma's warm one, laughing as her friend shivered exaggeratedly. Elizabeth then did the same to her brother-in-law and was rewarded with an impish look from the famously blue eyes of the debonair Prince of Wales.

"Oh! You wretched girl!" he scolded, but since he immediately put a cocktail in her hand, she knew no offense was taken. None ever was. She and David got on famously. She got on famously with all of Bertie's brothers; she was the honorary big sister, the keeper of confidences, the belle of the ball. Much more their sister than Mary, the princess royal, who had an abundance of the upright stuffiness so famously belonging to their mother, the Queen.

Elizabeth sipped her cocktail—something with gin and brandy, delicious; David was such an expert bartender—and nodded eagerly to her husband. "Bertie, you'll like this. It's divine."

Bertie—taller, darker than his brother, but with the same

Windsor eyes, the same Windsor pinched beak of a nose, and the same long Windsor upper lip—downed his in one gulp. "Thi-thi-this is perfect, D-David. Wo-wonderful!"

They all three smiled fondly at the Duke of York. His stutter was much less obvious of late, thanks to Elizabeth finding him a speech therapist who had worked miracles. But still the stutter lingered, especially when he gave public speeches. Among family and friends, Bertie, once he relaxed with a cigarette and a drink, spoke much like everyone else.

Except in the company of his papa. But then, only Elizabeth could charm the King of England; all of his children were terrified of him. With reason.

"Come, warm your royal bones." Thelma, Lady Furness, linked her arm through Elizabeth's; they strolled to a roaring fire and settled themselves companionably on a sofa. "Brace yourself—we're going ice-skating! The pond has frozen over, can you believe it? I can't remember that happening before."

"Neither can I!" Elizabeth shivered, although the large room was warm as toast. Everything about the Fort, as David had christened Fort Belvedere, his weekend home, was cozy, even if it was actually an ancient fort complete with a turret and battlements. This folly had been neglected, crumbling, before the Prince of Wales asked if he could have it when he came of age. And then he'd gone about turning it into a comfortable weekend retreat full of nautical touches, like navy-blue paint and whitewash on the baseboards, paneled walls, and tartan everywhere, with the help of his lover at the time, Freda Dudley Ward.

But Freda had been replaced about three years ago by Thelma ("Pronounced 'Telma,' darling, my demented mother's idea of elegance"). Both women were just David's type—dark, thin, stylish. And married.

Although Thelma had recently gotten divorced. Elizabeth wondered how David was taking it—she studied him as he and Bertie were talking. He looked as handsome and animated as usual, his blond hair still luminous as topaz. Thin and trim—he was obsessed with exercise and ate abstemiously—he looked younger than his thirty-eight years.

Even though—perhaps, if she was being honest, *because*—Thelma, as a divorcée, could never marry David, Elizabeth liked her. She was so fun but not in a vulgar way, unlike her fellow Americans. She revered the British and the royal family. She wasn't prone to gossiping about them or flaunting her intimacy with the Prince of Wales. Although she was happy to gossip about everyone else; Thelma and Elizabeth soon were trading information about their society friends like two stockbrokers swapping tips.

"Did you *see* Emerald the other day at Claridge's? She was wearing the most outlandish hat, all peacock feathers and glitter. Glitter, during the day!" Thelma laughed merrily.

Elizabeth smiled, a bit unsure. So peacock feathers were out now? She could never keep up with fashion. Thank heavens Bertie had no eye for it either, unlike David, who could be as bitchy as a woman when it came to clothes and how to wear them.

"Oh, she was a horror. Simply a horror!" A flat, harsh—extremely *American*—voice interjected, and Elizabeth turned in surprise. A newcomer had joined them; the stranger hastily curtsied as Thelma rose and introduced Elizabeth to "my dear friend Wallis Simpson. Wallis, the Duchess of York."

"Your Royal Highness," the American said, correctly, if atrociously—goodness, Elizabeth had never heard such an accent before! Thelma spoke like an Englishwoman, despite her origins. But not this creature. Who was, Elizabeth had to admit, dressed very well—surely David would approve—in a tweed suit cut perfectly to show off her youthful figure, boyish hips, and angular shoulders, with a scarlet silk scarf tied expertly around her throat that accented rather than softened her square jaw, a diamond brooch in the shape of a tree glistening on her lapel. Her hair—jet-black, suspiciously so—was parted in the middle and drawn back in a sleek chignon, not a hair out of place. Automatically, Elizabeth smoothed her flounced silk dress, perhaps not suitable for ice-skating, but she detested fitted jackets; with her bosom, she looked like the prow of a battleship in them. Then she patted her dark brown hair, also drawn back, but simply, with a fringe. She'd always worn a fringe, ever since she was a little girl. And even though she well knew that no fashionable lady wore one anymore, she refused to give it up. For hadn't she been an enchanting child with that fringe? A fairy sprite, an angel on earth? That's what she'd been told for as long as she could remember.

Wallis, Elizabeth suspected as she studied the impossibly chic American, seemed the type who would cut off a finger if it was the height of fashion.

"Lovely to meet you," Elizabeth said, extending her royal hand. Wallis shook it with her own oddly large hand, the nails square and short and painted a vivid red that matched her scarf, Elizabeth couldn't fail to notice.

"Wallis and her husband, Ernest, are friends of my sister Consuelo's. They live in London; Ernest runs a shipping company. We all see each other often in town, so I thought I'd invite them down for the weekend. You know how David is." Thelma lowered her voice and turned her face away from Wallis, who pretended to be absorbed in the gold clock on the fireplace mantel. "He gets bored so easily these days, the little man. Ever since my divorce, things—well, never mind."

"You said we were going ice-skating?" Elizabeth said brightly, as if she hadn't heard this little slip, and Thelma smiled in gratitude.

"I haven't been skating in ages! I used to roller-skate in my yoooth," Wallis said in her unpleasant drawl, but Elizabeth didn't grimace. She flashed her famous smile—wasn't she known as the Smiling Duchess?—instead.

"Then I suppose you'll skate rings around me! I'm sure I'll be hopeless."

"That makes two of us." Thelma clinked her glass to Elizabeth's.

"Ladies, come." David clapped his hands and they all followed him to the front hall, where rows of new ice skates, white for the women, black for the men, were lined up. Wallis's husband, Ernest Simpson, had joined them; he was a tall, sturdy man with a dashing black mustache. Also American, but with a much more acceptable accent than his wife's. He seemed in awe of the company and surroundings—rightfully so, thought Elizabeth. Unlike his wife, who was trying very hard to assume a bored, unimpressed manner.

"I sent someone down to Harrods this morning—there should be something that fits, try them on!" And the members of the royal party were soon being fitted—rather like a passel of Cinderellas—with ice skates by the footmen. Laughter and protests filled the air as skates were tried on and then discarded until the right fit was achieved.

"I'm afraid you don't have anything small enough for me," Elizabeth declared with her famous laugh, conscious of the envious looks on the other women's faces.

"Then stuff a sock in the toe" was David's rather ungallant reply as he knelt beside Thelma and began to tie up her skate with the solicitousness of a nanny. Elizabeth noticed Wallis staring at him, her mouth open. It was peculiar behavior for a future king, but then again, David was always this way when he was in love. There was no task too small for him to perform, no risk too great. It was rather the same with Bertie, although perhaps not quite so public. The Windsor men shared a pathetic need to be besotted with women.

Skates slung over shoulders, the royal party, bundled up in their furs and woolens, trooped their laughing way outside and gingerly tiptoed down the slick, sloping hill toward the Virginia Water, the large man-made lake outside the Fort. The trees were laced with snow, the ground hard, and Elizabeth's breath was a little cloud that she followed. Bertie steadied her with his hand—he was a natural athlete, while she was not—and she smiled up at her husband. He always looked so gay, so jolly, when he was with his brother. Not that he wasn't jolly at home, especially with their girls. But often, especially when preparing for a speech or a ribbon-cutting or one of the endless small tasks required of the lesser royals—the backbench, as Bertie called it, not the stars like the King, Queen, and Prince of Wales—he could be so tense he snapped at everyone in sight, drank too much, and had difficulty sleeping.

Thank heavens they were the backbench, Elizabeth often thought. Although she knew she was built of different stuff and would have shone had she been one of the stars. But her husband absolutely would not have. God knew what He was doing when He made Bertie the younger brother, the spare.

Today, however, Bertie was in his element, and after trying to teach his wife to skate—she did her best, but her tiny ankles were too weak, she declared with her enchanting smile—Bertie spoke to one of the footmen standing about with thermoses of cocktails.

In an instant, both Thelma and Elizabeth found themselves pushing wicker chairs in an attempt to keep themselves upright. They tried—hooting with laughter, their feet still flailing—but soon decided to sit in the chairs, where they were pushed round the ice by the gallant Windsor brothers.

"Oh, well done!" Elizabeth called to her husband, who skated with finesse, to her great pride. David did well, but Bertie did better—and that wasn't the normal way of things. Bertie was forever in his glamorous older brother's shadow. But David didn't seem to mind throwing his brother a bit of the spotlight now; his eyes were sparkling, his pipe clutched between his teeth. He looked so dashing.

"What fun!" Thelma cried out as the wintry landscape blurred by. It felt like flying, being pushed like this.

Suddenly a dervish with a dash of red whirled past, and Wallis swooped gaily across the ice. She dipped and turned and even skated backward, showing off in such a typical American way.

"My Lord!" David said, nearly dropping his pipe. "Have you ever seen such a sight?"

"No," Thelma said flatly, sharing a look with Elizabeth. "No, I haven't."

"Goodness. We have an Olympian in our midst," Elizabeth

said sweetly. "Sonja Henie herself! Do go on, Wallis! Show us what you can do!"

"Oh, it's nothing," Wallis said breathlessly as she skated up and stopped precisely, flecks of ice flying up behind her. "I used to roller-skate in my misspent youth. This is the same thing if you have any sense of balance."

"What interesting activities they do in America!" Elizabeth replied. "You did that in school?"

"Yes, among other things. I was also the star player on the girls' basketball team." Wallis laughed, shaking her sleek black head—how did she manage it? Not a hair was out of place even now! "I told you my youth was misspent!" Then she flew off again, and even Elizabeth had to admit she cut an impressive figure as she went through her bag of frosty tricks, at one point jumping with her legs outstretched and landing on one foot.

But it was a figure trying perhaps a bit too hard to impress. While the rest of them resumed their gossip and chattering, stopping for thermos cups of cocktails, Wallis didn't pause. She continued to perform as if there were to be medals handed out after. Elizabeth, try as she might, couldn't stop looking at her.

Neither could someone else.

"What an obvious display," Elizabeth said to Bertie later, once they'd said their goodbyes and were being driven back to Royal Lodge, their country home on the grounds of Windsor, in time to play with the girls in the nursery before they were put to bed. She shivered a little; despite the cocktails and the warm fireplace after the skating party, she still felt the cold from the frozen lake. Bertie pulled the rug up over her knees and drew her close. She snuggled against him contentedly; he *was* so conveniently tall and strong!

"What do you mean?" he asked absently as he looked out the car window into the twilight.

"Mrs. Simpson—Wallis. Who on earth did she think she was going to impress, showing off like that?"

"Oh, she was harmless. I talked to her a little. Not much there, actually. Although did you notice how deeply she curtsied to us when she was introduced? As if she were a debutante! It was a little much."

"It was all a little much." Elizabeth sniffed. "The wide-eyed innocence, the tales of her misspent youth. And that performance on the ice! I never saw anyone try so hard. Ah, well. We'll never see her again, I suppose."

"I suppose. Oh, I do wish D-D-David would find a nice princess and settle down. Thelma is marvelous, of course. But I feel sorry for him, not having a wife and children, with all his burdens. And P-P-Papa isn't looking well at all these days. Not since his operation."

"No." Elizabeth frowned; King George had barely survived the operation to drain an abscess back in '28. David had assumed more and more of his father's duties; his weekends at the Fort were his salvation—"Those weekends of yours," the King called them, with obvious disapproval. He could never understand the younger generation's thirst for fun after the ravages of the World War. He particularly couldn't understand his heir's proclivity for drink, dancing, and married women.

"Let's not think of it, darling," Elizabeth said, patting her husband's hand. Then she couldn't help but yawn. "I'm getting so old. I'm exhausted and you did all the skating!"

"Never, my dear. You'll never grow old to me." Bertie kissed her gloved hand. "No one is as happy as we are," he said. With no trace of his stutter.

Dear, devoted Bertie!

"No one," Elizabeth agreed. But she had to stifle a sigh.

"THELMA SAID THE DUCHESS turned him down twice! Can you imagine? And they're the apple of the King's eye, apparently. He favors them over the Prince of Wales. That's what Thelma said." Wallis couldn't help herself; she was as jittery and excited as a child on Christmas morning as she and Ernest prowled around their suite at the Fort, getting ready for bed.

The Fort—oh, how casual it sounded now, how easily it rolled off her tongue. This wasn't their first weekend at the Fort but it still gave her a thrill to be invited. *I went to the Fort this weekend,* she looked forward to saying when she lunched with Diana Cooper at the Ritz later this week. *Do you know, we went ice-skating at the Fort?* she imagined telling Unity Mitford, should she run into her at Harrods. *Oh, yes, the prince is a dear man, isn't he? Such a divine host!* That she and Ernest were now regular members of his exclusive society still seemed unbelievable to her. But she did worry about Thelma; she and the prince were definitely having some trouble, and if Thelma was banished from his royal presence, would that automatically mean that Wallis would be too?

"Oh—I must dash off a letter to Aunt Bessie!" Wallis exclaimed, spying the stationery stamped *Fort Belvedere, Windsor Great Park.* She sat down at the desk, uncapped a fountain pen, and began to scribble on the top sheet.

"I talked to the prince quite a lot, you know," Ernest

boasted as he undid his cuff links. "He's fascinated by history too—those boring old ruins, as you call them. But he's always eager to show me around this place—did you know it actually was a folly back in the 1700s? Just a little summerhouse, built by one of King George the Second's sons as a kind of lark. Nobody liked the place much until Prince Edward fell in love with it."

"David," Wallis corrected him, still intent on her letter. "His name is David. That's what the family calls him, anyway. You should know that by now, we've been around him long enough."

"Well, he's still the heir to the throne to me. I can't help it. That's how I was raised."

"You're just as American as I am." Wallis looked at her husband, amused. God, the man could be so stuffy!

"I was half raised in England, as you know," he said with a haughty sniff. "My father was a British citizen."

"Mmm." Wallis returned to the letter. *And the Duke and Duchess of York joined us this weekend. They were very nice, if a bit dull . . .*

"What did you think of them?" She didn't actually care what Ernest thought, of course. But tonight they would have to share a bed. Pretend intimacy could go a long way toward distracting a husband while you flirted with a prince.

"Who?"

"The duke and duchess."

"Oh, he's such a poor specimen, isn't he? All those nervous tics, his stammer—pity that all the charm went to his older brother. I felt rather sorry for him."

"And her?"

"The duchess? Plump, matronly. I've never understood

her popularity. Probably because she's the only young female in the royal family who counts. She's got the stage to herself and seems to like it."

"Yes," Wallis mused, tapping a perfectly manicured fingernail against the polished mahogany desktop. "There's a woman who believes her own publicity. According to Thelma, she had a thing for David back in the day. Of course he never gave her a thought until she married into the family. Still. Three times poor Bertie had to propose to her. Who turns down an English prince? I must admit, I'm a bit fascinated by her."

"Well, I'm not, and I'm going to bed. Please finish up your letter, my dear."

"Of course." And Wallis scribbled a quick close to her chatty letter to her aunt back in Baltimore, the only family she had anymore. After painstakingly removing her makeup, creaming her face, encasing her coif in a hairnet made of the finest silk, and putting on her Chinese pajamas, Wallis got into the big, canopied bed, as far away from her softly snoring husband as possible.

She turned off the bedside lamp, but her blue eyes remained open for several minutes, imagining being proposed to by a prince and turning him down. Try as she might, she simply couldn't.

"Two times she refused a prince," she whispered. "Who on earth does she think she is?"

Then Wallis Simpson closed her eyes and dreamed.

CHAPTER 3

THREE PROPOSALS

FEBRUARY 27, 1921

ELIZABETH ANGELA MARGUERITE BOWES-LYON WAS MOST definitely not looking forward to lunch with a prince.

Prince Bertie—christened Albert Frederick Arthur George—could not take a hint. She'd written, after he'd suggested stopping in for lunch, that it was only herself and her mother, who, unfortunately, wasn't well; most of the servants would be off so no one would be available to wait on them and she would very much understand if he had something more amusing to do.

How much more could she say to the man who was second in line to the throne? She could only hope he would get the hint and stay away. But no.

It had been like this for months, ever since they met at a London dance last year, a week after she was presented at court. That was the first year everything seemed "normal" after the war, although of course, nothing was ever normal after the war. No household, rich or poor, had been spared; it seemed that almost every family Elizabeth knew had lost at least one son. Her own included; her brother Fergus had been brutally mowed down during the Battle of Loos in 1915 when he was only twenty-six. Mother hadn't been the same since.

Those war years had made Elizabeth grow up quickly. Overnight she went from a cosseted young girl—the ninth of ten children, the youngest daughter and spoiled incessantly, playing pranks on her governess—to a young woman intercepting the post so she could spare her parents, who had sent four sons to France, more bad news. Glamis—the family's sprawling ancestral castle in Scotland—had been turned into a convalescent home, and Elizabeth had experienced the crushing heartbreak of growing too close to soldiers during their recovery, dancing with them, learning about their families, trying to cheer them up, only to be shattered by their deaths later, after they returned to the front.

But by 1920, society had been able to resume almost as if the war had never happened—Royal Ascot, the Derby, and presentations at court. Elizabeth, being the daughter of a Scottish earl, was to be presented not at Buckingham Palace but at Holyrood, in Edinburgh. But before that, there was the London season, and Lady Elizabeth Bowes-Lyon, just nineteen and determined to enjoy all the delayed pleasures of her privileged life, threw herself into the dinner parties and balls with abandon. There were exquisite dresses and new dancing shoes every day, evenings at nightclubs, champagne corks popping every few seconds providing a secondary percussion to the band. Rising late every morning—even later than her usual preference—to gifts of chocolates and flowers from besotted young men. Flirting, one of her favorite pastimes, with men young and old, gossiping with her friends, dancing the newest dances, like the one-step and the foxtrot. It was at one of these parties that she first danced with the Prince of Wales. It was also at one of these parties that she met James Stuart, the dashing equerry to Prince Albert.

And it was at one of these parties that she met, again, Prince Albert himself. Apparently they'd met as children, but she had no memory of that. But she did remember the second meeting because James had been there. Oh, James! Tall, dark blond, mustached like so many young men who'd survived the war (except, curiously, the royal princes), with soulful eyes that could turn devilish without hesitation. Elizabeth had her choice of suitors and she enjoyed being pursued by all of them. So far she had not given her heart to anyone, but she could, more and more, see herself giving it to James. Wrapping it up in a gay little box festooned with a blue ribbon to match her eyes and presenting it to him with one of her famous dimpled smiles.

She was dancing with him at the Derby ball when she noticed Prince Albert standing awkwardly against a wall—awkward because his tuxedo was fitted so beautifully, yet he still managed to look like he'd rather be wearing anything else—staring at her.

"Why does he look at one so?" she'd asked James, who, after all, was presumably his best friend.

"Bertie? Oh, he's harmless. Are you going to the Hardinges' for the weekend?"

"I'm not sure," she replied, tilting her head beguilingly, smiling her most mysterious smile. "I can't think of a good reason to."

"The devil you say! I can give you one right now." He bent his head closer to hers, and her heart thumped wildly, pumping that pretty flush into her cheeks.

"James! Be good."

"Only if you promise you'll come."

"I make no promises. You'll have to wait and see."

"Flirt!"

"Pot calling the kettle black!"

Then they both laughed, causing everyone in the room to turn and admire the charming couple on the dance floor. Elizabeth couldn't help but notice the dismay on Prince Bertie's face, so she threw him a dazzling smile. It never hurt to have a royal admirer, of course. She'd tried her best with the main prize but so far had failed. Second in line to the throne would have to do. There was no one who more enjoyed being worshipped from afar than Lady Elizabeth.

But apparently the ungainly prince wasn't content to worship from afar. For in the months since that dance, he displayed a dogged determinedness that rather took Elizabeth by surprise. He had a habit of popping up at almost every turn, unasked, unwanted. Although a royal prince could never simply "pop up." A royal prince, no matter how shy or dull, naturally commanded all the attention at every gathering and had a nasty way of casting a pall over the fun and frivolity that Elizabeth and her set were so fond of, like playing practical jokes such as making apple-pie beds for one another, hysterical games of hide-and-seek and sardines, that kind of thing.

No, once a royal prince showed up, everyone had to be on their best, most dignified behavior. Which Elizabeth positively loathed, for wasn't this short time between the schoolroom and the marriage bed supposed to be *fun*? She couldn't help herself; her mischievous propensity to see the joke in everything, to turn pomp and circumstance upside down, sometimes asserted itself. Though, to his credit, Prince Bertie, once he got past his initial shyness, seemed to find it all delightful. Especially when he and his sister came to stay at Glamis for a house party, and the bighearted Bowes-Lyon clan with their bighearted hospitality and casual approach to life decided to chuck all the expected protocol and treat the Windsors like any other houseguests. Then, Elizabeth had to admit, Prince Bertie, with his facial tics and his stutter and his rather pathetic air of knowing he in no way lived up to the ideal of what a royal prince should be, relaxed. Until he was rather charming.

Still not as charming as his brother. Nor as charming as James, who was the one good thing about the prince showing up like a bad penny wherever Elizabeth turned. As Prince Bertie's equerry, he frequently accompanied his charge.

Except he was not coming to lunch today, the twenty-seventh. She was expecting only Bertie—who had very much implied that he was happy to be alone with Elizabeth. Which made her nervous, which she almost never was. When a girl was born into a family of loving parents and siblings and had several homes, including a castle that Shakespeare had used as the setting of *Macbeth,* at her disposal and never had to open a book once she left the schoolroom and knew that she was delightful because she had always been told she was, what was there to be nervous about?

The moment Prince Bertie arrived, a transparently hopeful look on his face, she knew what she was nervous about.

And then he asked, "D-d-darling Elizabeth—ma-ma-may I c-call you that? Will you d-do me the honor of—" And she blurted out, "Oh, no!" before she could think of something much more kind to say to the prince, who had gotten down on one knee—horrid!—in the garden where they'd gone for a stroll after their solitary lunch.

"Oh, no—no, sir, I—oh, do get up!" And then she'd wrung

her hands, trying not to burst into tears. There was no possibility of her saying yes, and it was impertinent of him to ask her so soon after making her acquaintance anyway, but more than anything she was terrified of offending him, lest he tell his parents and they—well, what could they do? Throw her in the Tower? But still, one did not want to make an enemy of one's sovereign. But she couldn't possibly accept his proposal! Because he was Bertie, Prince Bertie, and she wasn't attracted to him in the least—how could one be, with that stutter, his nervous blinking eyes, the bark of a laugh that tended to come at the most inappropriate times? He was so pathetically eager to please! She felt sorry for him, surely. She could admit he touched a tiny corner of her heart, the same corner that all those convalescing soldiers had touched with their gallantry, their bravery. For he was brave in his own way, a royal prince shouldering his public duties, knowing that he could never perform them with the same flair as his brother or the same authority as his father but nevertheless continuing to do so without complaint or self-pity.

But marry him? *Him?*

Absurd.

They parted with an awkward shaking of hands, and once he left, Elizabeth fell into a chair with pure relief. Well, that was done, then. She'd refused a prince.

Not many girls could say that.

MARCH 7, 1922

He caught her off guard this time. She had no suspicion at all that Prince Bertie was going to propose marriage to her again when he came to call on her at her parents' London home on Bruton Street.

It was only a week after his sister's wedding. Princess Mary had married Harry Lascelles at Westminster Abbey in the first royal wedding since the war. And Elizabeth—Why? Why on earth?—had been invited to be a bridesmaid.

Despite her misgivings—was this Queen Mary's way of throwing her and Bertie together again?—Elizabeth had accepted. Of course she had! Who would turn down the privilege of being photographed for the newspapers, invited to all the celebratory parties and balls at Buckingham Palace, of riding in a carriage down the Mall, smiling and waving at the thousands of cheering Britons waving flags, a sea of red, white, and blue?

Yet for all the pomp, Elizabeth couldn't help but notice how very dull life at court seemed to be. Everyone was so old! Courtiers and family members, cousins from near and far who were all kings and queens and princes of something, but covered in figurative dust and cobwebs. Nothing happened quickly. No popular music was ever allowed—it was Handel or, if the King was feeling particularly jaunty, Gilbert and Sullivan. Even Princess Mary didn't seem to have any friends her own age.

The princess was a dull girl, old for her years, the same way her mother had always been, and her groom was equally dull and actually old, almost old enough to be Mary's father. Not that Elizabeth knew either one very well. Nor did she know the other bridesmaids—one a royal princess, the others daughters of dukes and earls like herself—who also didn't seem all that friendly with one another or with the bride. There was none of the usual hysterical laughter and gossip when they all got together. No one made sly jokes about the wedding night. No one squealed over the royal trousseau.

The only person she really knew in all the wedding party was Prince Bertie. Who looked more handsome than usual in his dress uniform.

Although not nearly as handsome as James Stuart, also in attendance at the Abbey; Elizabeth caught sight of him as she strolled demurely behind the bride and flashed him a sweet smile. Oh, James! The only man she knew who flirted as expertly as she did, but that was the problem. He flirted with Elizabeth the same way he flirted with her friends. Perhaps he danced a few more dances with her, sought out her company more than others at house and shooting parties. But at no time did he reveal any serious intentions, not one fleeting solemn expression on his face, not one conversation that hinted at a future.

Since Prince Bertie's proposal that ghastly day—Elizabeth still shuddered a little, remembering it—there had been a period of heavenly respite. No contact save for a letter that Elizabeth sent him the day after, apologizing for hurting him, expressing the hope that they could still be friends. The usual thing one did in this circumstance. And Bertie replied with the same polite *It was my fault, I quite misread the situation, silly me*. The end.

Then the weeks before the royal wedding, such a blur of fittings and photographers and parties and balls, and they were thrown together once more. And Bertie didn't act as if it was the end. There was still that pathetic, puppy-dog hopefulness in his eyes when he saw her. But he didn't dance with her any more than he did with the other bridesmaids, and he'd never tried to squire her away for a private conversation.

So she was unprepared when he sent a note that morning, a week after the happy day, saying he'd stop in that afternoon if it was convenient. She replied that it was and thought that perhaps he simply wanted to share some photographs of the wedding party or was merely calling on her before heading off to do whatever royalty had to do. There were quite a few trips he had to undertake as part of his job, which she didn't really understand and, frankly, did not care to.

"Dearest Elizabeth," he said once more, but thank heavens he did not get down on one knee! "It would d-d-do me the g-greatest honor if—"

"Oh, no!" Again the blurting, the look of horror she couldn't prevent. Again the flush of embarrassment on his face, the working of the jaw, the profuse apologizing, the fleeing.

This time, the letter came from him, apologizing for catching her off guard, for not at least hinting what his intentions were. As if he were chalking up her refusal only to that—to her not having time to prepare herself.

She thanked him again. She apologized as well. She felt she had to tell Mother and Father, in case the royal wrath led the King to take away their title or something.

She then made plans to dine with James Stuart, which perked up her feelings quite a bit. *Two* proposals from a prince!

Absolutely no one she knew could say that.

JANUARY 1923

Elizabeth was mortified. That awful newspaper article! Pure fabrication, mean gossip. Implying that a certain "Scottish lady of noble birth" was soon to be married to the Prince of

Wales! Her cheeks burned so that she couldn't come down for breakfast even though it was a full house party at Firle, the Sussex home of her friend Viscount Gage—George. But she couldn't face her friends, her neighbors. She knew her set. They would make it all one colossal joke.

Which it was! But why—why should it be? Of course she had no hope of marrying the Prince of Wales; he'd barely looked at her in ages, they rarely met. It was true that the pressure on the handsome young prince to marry was mounting. But David would surely marry a princess, although that wasn't as strict a requirement as it had been before the war. So he could conceivably marry a commoner, albeit one "of noble birth." But his gaze had never once lingered over her in that way and she knew it, but now the world thought otherwise, and she was covered in shame. Literally—she pulled the satin quilt up over her face and lay buried beneath it, racking her brain to find a way to handle this. It was a stunner, that was for sure. Elizabeth was rarely knocked on her beam-ends, but now she was.

One could not take any action in print, naturally. The prince certainly wouldn't comment on it; the royal family never commented on rumors or innuendo. Why did this bother her so? She'd been gossiped about before. Was it because she *wished* that it were true?

Yes. And no. Yes, she wished to be desired; what girl her age didn't hope for that? And by the number one catch in all the kingdom—of course! But no, she had no longing to live such a public life as Queen. To have to be so very careful, always, of how one behaved! To be caged like a bird in that drafty yet stifling Buckingham Palace, covered in sashes and medals, receiving silly old ambassadors and crusty old kings on a daily basis instead of going out to nightclubs and the theater and generally cutting loose.

But—

One couldn't, she acknowledged, cut loose forever. She would marry; she would live a nice, unburdened life in some castle with a country home for shooting, a London home for the season. She would have babies, nice happy babies cared for by a nice happy nanny, and she would have a nice happy husband who adored her—naturally!—and catered to her every whim. This all would happen. It had happened to her mother, her sisters. It was starting to happen to her friends. It was her turn soon.

But. But.

A beguiling little voice whispered in her ear that she was too darling, too full of vim and vigor, too sprinkled with stardust, to live an ordinary life. To be singled out by the Prince of Wales would have been that little extra *something* that she, Elizabeth Bowes-Lyon, deserved. And now the humiliation of having to tell the entire world that she hadn't been singled out by him—horror!

But she *had* been singled out by his brother. Over and over—and only two days ago, he had asked her to marry him *yet again*. On this occasion, she had not blurted out *Oh, no!*

She'd asked for time. To think. And while she was thinking, someone had planted this nasty gossip about her and the Prince of Wales—

Suddenly she threw off the covers and sat up straight, her heart racing. *Bertie!* Bertie would see this article. Bertie would be hurt—devastated—by the implication. And for the first time, her heart truly ached for him, for how he would feel when he read it. He didn't deserve that, not him. An unaccustomed rush of tenderness for the prince made her feel dizzy, disoriented.

She wasn't in love with Prince Bertie. Not the way she'd been with James Stuart, who had taken a job in the United States, suddenly, mysteriously, a few months ago. He'd left her blithely, not singling her out for a special farewell or asking her to wait. When he went to the States, he did not take her heart—she was too disciplined to allow that; she locked it firmly within her chest and kept the key clutched in her pretty little hand. But he had taken her notion of ever marrying for love.

But then again, she didn't really know anyone who had. Even Mother said she hadn't loved Father at first; love had grown, as it did in all good marriages, over time.

She would never be Queen of England, and she had no desire to be. But—a Royal Highness by marriage still sounded rather—

Special.

Was it possible? Did she truly care for Bertie after all this time? All she knew was she no longer saw him as the butt of a joke or an irritation. And that she hadn't—goodness, could it be true?—in quite a long while.

In the year since he'd last proposed, Prince Bertie had grown. Some whispered that he'd had a nervous breakdown after she refused him the second time, but Elizabeth could not let herself believe it. (Even as she secretly felt a bit flattered.)

Bertie had thrown himself into his work, founding camps where the sons of the lower and upper classes could mix, giving speeches (she could only assume very badly), opening up factories, inspecting workers, that sort of thing. Christened "the Industrial Prince," he was in the papers a bit more than he had been. Always, he looked rather touching to her in photographs. More serious. Slightly sad. As if his soul had been forged by fire, the fire of disappointment. Of lost love.

It was all a bit romantic and tragic, like a Brontë novel.

But the fact was, Elizabeth had had a hand in who he was now. She had made him a man. That was true power, she reflected, tracing a finger on the silk comforter, making little divots and swirls. That one could help a man become better than he had a right to be, given the circumstances of his birth and his upbringing. That one could be the prize that made him try so very hard.

Elizabeth *herself* felt changed. She was older now; more of her friends were married, and for the first time she worried about being seen as a ridiculous eternal debutante, no longer admired but mocked. And she'd found herself seeking Bertie out at parties and balls, wanting to listen to him talk about himself. And to tell him about herself, the things she and her friends didn't discuss—about her worries for her mother, still in ill health, never quite recovered from the death of Fergus. About her sadness during the war, watching friend after friend go off and never come back. About her surprising bouts of loneliness even when she was surrounded by her friends, even when she was the belle of the ball; how sometimes she felt as if she were watching herself, apart from her body, and felt so alone, so cold.

Always, when she and Bertie met during this oddly interminable year, they were so careful with each other. As if either one might break alone.

But together—

Dearest Bertie, she wrote to him later that day after she finally found the courage to join the party, enduring the teasing from her friends. They simply wouldn't stop bowing to her, calling her "Your Majesty" and "Ma'am," and she couldn't take it, these silly fools making fun of her, of the Prince of Wales, of Bertie, although they didn't know it. Making fun of her *life*, her future.

> *Dearest Bertie, Please come for the weekend at St. Paul's Walden Bury. Thank you for giving me the time I requested to think over your question. I hope to have an answer for you before you leave. —Elizabeth*

JANUARY 14, 1923

The dear boy had tears in his eyes when she said yes. But he didn't sob, as she had expected him to (she knew by now that this supposedly stoic royal's emotions were always too close to the surface—anger, sadness, happiness, no matter). He simply pressed her hand to his lips as if it were a Bible and he was reaffirming his faith.

For her part, she was touched. And exhausted! For three days, the two of them had talked and walked all over St. Paul's Walden Bury, in Hertfordshire, which was always home to the Bowes-Lyons, more so than Glamis, in Scotland.

And she'd gone to a ball! She'd sneaked out with her sister-in-law Friday night after her parents and Bertie had gone to bed. Why, she couldn't say; she was simply seized by a desire to do something unpredictable. One last little act of defiance, she supposed, before she committed herself not just to a lifetime by the side of a man who needed her so, he had spent thirty months trying to get her, but also to a lifetime of prescribed schedules and rules that would, one could only assume, leave little room for impulsive acts such as literally escaping out a window wearing an evening gown and Wellies, her dancing slippers stuffed in her bag, giggling like a twelve-year-old and then scampering down a damp hill in the moonlight.

She'd danced until one in the morning. She'd danced more gaily, more freely than she ever had; everyone was amusing, everyone was pretty or handsome. Her decision was still a secret—no, a jewel. A precious jewel locked deep within her heart. She knew it to be dazzling and so it made her—more. More herself, more Elizabeth—her laughter brighter, her cheeks rosier, her hair more lustrous.

It made her, simply, beautiful.

The next day she said yes, and Bertie pressed her hand to his lips and she was his. And his parents'—the King and Queen of England would exercise much more influence over her than her own beloved parents ever would again.

She also belonged, forever, to England. To the British people. From now on, everything she did would be scrutinized. She would be admired or reviled, depending upon the whim of the public.

But right now, presenting her rosy lips, trembling, to Bertie, who was trembling even more, she mostly belonged to him. To her shy, overwhelmed, patient, determined, valiant prince. Forever.

"Till death d-d-do us part," he said when he released her after their first kiss, until their next kiss. Forever.

She smiled, turned away. And let the tears roll freely down her face.

Forever.

CHAPTER 4

JANUARY 1934

"OH, THELMA! THE PRINCE WILL MISS YOU SO!"

"I know, Wallis. And that's why I'm asking you to look after the little man while I'm away."

Wallis smiled, kissed Thelma Furness on the cheek, and waved as her friend—her dear, dear friend—rushed out of the flat. Thelma was always rushing—to the hairdresser, into a ball, up the stairs to show Wallis her newest couture gowns or jewels from the prince. At the dinner table, she chattered like a waterfall, never pausing. She was not a restful person, Thelma. Wallis wondered how helpful she was, really, to David.

David and Thelma and Wallis and Ernest were quite a foursome now. Almost always surrounded by others of his crowd, the Coopers, the Cunards, the Churchills, the Mitford sisters. The prince was forever inviting masses of people out to the Fort for his weekends or joining them all at his favorite nightclubs after stuffy dinners with his parents and siblings at Windsor or Buckingham Palace. "And now the fun begins!" he always cried, rubbing his hands together with that jolly twinkle in his eyes when he joined his friends. He made them all feel so special, so lucky to be in his orbit, and they paid him back with laughter and songs and dance and jokes, practically doing handstands and backflips to amuse the little prince. To *remain* in his orbit. To be able to tell their other friends and relations how close they were to him, to make their enemies green with envy.

Everyone performed backflips—everyone, that is, except Wallis.

After she'd gotten over her initial giddy disbelief at being part of his charmed royal life, Wallis became determined to study the man. Why, she couldn't quite say, not at first. But she had learned that those born without money and privilege—like Bessie Wallis Warfield Spencer Simpson—couldn't afford simply to enjoy life. No, Wallis had realized at a very tender age that she had to make her own luck, that she couldn't depend upon anyone other than herself. That in order to get what she wanted—what so many people were given at birth, namely, security, a home, and money; oh, lots and lots of money!—she had to find a man to give it to her. Because as a woman, she couldn't go out and get it on her own.

To that end, she'd learned to read men more thoroughly than she'd ever read a novel. Because men were so much more interesting than fiction. Because men could provide so much. But she'd also learned that men could take away so much as well. Pride, dignity, youth. Love, laughter.

Hope.

When Thelma departed to spend three months in America with her twin sister, Gloria, she left the prince to Wallis. And Wallis had studied her man thoroughly. She knew what she could do to him—for him, that is. She knew what she could do *for* him.

The question was, what could he do for her? She suspected

he could do much, much more than any of the other men in her life so far.

THREE MEN

SOLOMON WARFIELD

1902

Little Bessiewallis hated to do it, but she had no choice. Her mother had put her in her nicest dress, made by her own hands. Bessiewallis detested it, though; it was too fussy, too many ruffles and bows. For some reason, ruffles and bows made her skin itch, made her feel like she was a circus clown.

"Now, go and ask Uncle Sol, pretty please, Bessiewallis. Do it for me." Her mother took her by her shoulders and bent down so they were eye to eye. Mama seemed anxious, more anxious than usual. Bessiewallis had never really seen her mother happy. Of course, Papa had died when Bessiewallis was just a baby and so she and Mama had to live with her Grandmother Warfield. And, most important, with Uncle Sol, Papa's older brother. Bessiewallis could always *feel* things; she could feel in her bones when Mama was sad even though she was smiling, when it was going to rain even though the sun was shining, and when Uncle Sol—

Uncle Sol was like the weather, she thought. No, he *was* the weather, affecting everyone in the drafty old house. He could be the sun and make Mama so happy but he could also be a big thundercloud and make everyone in the house want to hide beneath a bed. Which was why Bessiewallis hated the errand she was being sent on. You never could predict which he was going to be, the happy sun or the scary thundercloud. Even Bessiewallis couldn't always feel his moods.

"But, Mama, *you* should ask him! He likes you best!" And it was true. Uncle Sol watched Mama a lot. He didn't talk to her much—he didn't talk to any of them much—but he was always following Mama with his eyes. Bessiewallis sometimes thought that even when he was in his bedroom, which was right next to the bedroom Bessiewallis and Mama shared on the top floor of the big wooden house in Baltimore, he was watching through the wall. Not watching Bessie, of course—he didn't like her; he didn't like the whole *idea* of her—but Mama.

"Bessie, I—I can't. For that very reason. You'll understand someday. But when a man . . . likes you, it's not usually a good idea to ask him for money. Because it can make people think—well, never mind. But we need more than our allowance this month because you'll be going to school soon, and you'll need new shoes and books and things that the other girls will have. I can't buy them on my own; I can't even give you a house by myself. Oh, Bessiewallis, I wish—" Mama, close to tears, suddenly shut her eyes tight and gave herself a little shake. Then she opened her eyes and took a big breath.

"Please, Bessiewallis, ask him nicely. You know how he gets. Smile and compliment him on something—tell him you've never seen him look so well. Ask him about his day. Then ask him for the money. Men like it when you take an interest in them, baby. They like to feel important. Can you do this for me—for us?"

Bessiewallis nodded, because she did feel so sorry for Mama when she was like this, sad about being a widow, sad about living with her husband's family, sad about having a fatherless daughter. Mama never said that, of course. But Bessiewallis *felt* it.

"Yes, Mama. Don't worry, Mama. I'll get the money."

"And don't be sassy!" was Mama's last piece of advice, which Bessiewallis resented but then realized was necessary, for she did have a tendency to be smart, too smart for her own good, Grandmother said. So Bessiewallis nodded and headed downstairs to Uncle Sol's office.

After knocking at first timidly, then with more confidence (nobody liked a sissy), she was greeted with a loud "Who's there? Is that you, Bessiewallis?"

"Yes, Uncle Sol," she said, remembering to smile at him as she opened the door and slid inside his office. It was exactly what a man's office should be, she thought happily. She loved it when people fit into their surroundings, and Uncle Sol definitely did that. He was a tall, imposing man (president of a bank), and he looked right at home in this office full of dark brown furniture, a rolltop desk, prints of horses on the dark green wallpaper. There was an abacus on his desk and a big leather-bound ledger, and the fireplace had two dragons—Uncle Sol called them gargoyles—for grates. The room smelled of pipe tobacco, one of Bessiewallis's favorite scents.

"What do you want?" He always got right to the point, another thing Bessiewallis appreciated. But she still didn't like him, and she understood in that moment she never would. No matter that he was her own dead papa's brother. He didn't much like her either, which was fine with Bessiewallis. It made life easier when you knew how you stood with someone.

"Uncle Sol—why, that's such a nice tie you're wearing! Is it new?"

Startled, he glanced down at his chest. "No."

"Well, I think it's very nice. Speaking of nice, did you have a nice day at the bank?"

"No, it was hell. As usual. What do you want, Bessiewallis?" He shifted impatiently in his chair and glared at her.

She sighed. Apparently Uncle Sol wasn't like most men.

"Mama—we—need more money this week because I'm starting school soon. I need books and shoes and things."

"And why didn't your mother ask me herself?" Suddenly his face went soft; the lines between his eyes flattened and his mouth hung open a little. Bessiewallis suppressed a shudder.

"I don't know." Although she did know. She also knew she couldn't tell him.

"Well, I suppose." Uncle Sol went to the safe, took a key that was on a gold chain attached to his waistcoat, and knelt down, groaning a little. He opened the safe, pulled out a pile of money—so much money! It never seemed fair to Bessiewallis that there was so much money in this house but she and Mama had none of it. Rising, Uncle Sol held out a ten-dollar bill, which she took. It was crisp and new and felt like happiness.

"Thank you, Uncle Sol," she said, smiling her prettiest. He ignored her, so she turned and left and shut the door. Maybe a little more forcefully than she should have, but it served him right.

How dare he not tell her how pretty she was when she smiled?

THROUGHOUT HER CHILDHOOD, Wallis—as soon as she started school she dropped the "Bessie" because, as she told her distraught mother, she wasn't a cow—was forced to return, time and again and with hands outstretched, to Uncle Sol. Even though she and Mama moved out when Wallis was seven—first to live with Mama's sister, Aunt Bessie, then when Mama decided she had to try to provide for Wallis on her own and opened that dreadful boardinghouse, which failed, and then when Mama married again, another sickly young man with no future—Uncle Sol still held the purse strings. When Wallis wanted to go to an exclusive private school, she had to go to the big house and ask. Her uncle said yes, but she had to show him her school reports, every single term, in order to be allowed to remain.

And after she had grown up and blossomed into a young woman who knew herself, knew how to dress to make the most of her still mostly flat, boyish figure so that she would stand out among all the fluttery, creamy Baltimore southern belles, who knew how to flirt with boys expertly—no other young woman in her class had as many beaux—Wallis had to return to that house once more to ask her uncle to fund her debut into Baltimore society, a rite of passage that shouldn't have been in question at all. She was, of course, both a Warfield and a Montague, two revered old Baltimore names. Already the invitations were flooding her mailbox, invitations to cotillions, to other girls' deb parties. She had to be given one herself. It was expected.

"I can't see my way to doing it," Uncle Sol said with an impatient wave of his hand. Ever since she started having beaux, Wallis had stopped trying to flatter or charm him; she knew he was one of the few males in Baltimore resistant to her distinctive charms. The only woman she knew who could have charmed him—Mama—wouldn't even try.

"But, Uncle Sol!" Wallis would never cry in front of him; they were much the same, the two adversaries. But this time she almost did; she felt, alarmingly, her skin begin to flush, her eyes begin to water. She blinked furiously to stop the traitorous tears. She would not appear weak in front of him. She knew that was the only thing he admired in her—her spirit.

"There's a war on." It was early 1915. The war in Europe had begun last summer.

"But not here! The United States isn't involved!"

"Every extra penny I have, I'm sending to England to help. I can't be bothered to give a silly party."

"It's not silly! It's—why, every Warfield girl ever has made her debut! All my aunts, all my cousins—why not me?"

"Ask your mother" was all he said, and Wallis, for perhaps the first time in her life, was struck speechless.

Memories—of doors opening and closing in that big house when Wallis was small and trying to sleep; of Mama crying softly in the hall; of Uncle Sol's urgent whispering; of strained breakfasts when all of them, Grandmother too, couldn't seem to look at one another—came flooding back. And Mama acknowledging that Uncle Sol "liked" her, and that was why she couldn't ask for money.

Her mother was a fool, Wallis decided as she left that big house, determined never again to cross its threshold. A starry-eyed fool who'd married for love, not money. She'd married the tubercular younger brother for love when the rich older brother would have had her. And then when she was a poor widow with a child, what did she do? Cloak herself in some silly southern belle's notion of propriety, refusing to ask a man who was besotted with her for money. Refusing to marry him—if he'd asked, which Wallis was now certain he had.

She would never do that. She would never turn her back on security, on wealth. *No* man was that odious.

Wallis vowed she would never, ever marry for love.

EARL WINFIELD SPENCER JR.

APRIL 1916

"Wallis, meet Win! Win, this is my cousin I was telling you about."

"My pleasure," Wallis murmured, and for once it was the truth. It was much more than a pleasure to gaze at this tall naval officer in his gleaming white uniform, the Pensacola sun making his brass buttons and gold epaulets sparkle like fireworks. He was tall, tanned, with dark hair and mustache, square jaw, and even white teeth, and Wallis had never seen anyone as handsome in her life.

She was nineteen and away from home for the very first time. As far away as possible from Uncle Sol and Mama and the memories of poverty and strangers talking about them and, always, that disgust at what could have been had Mama been as smart as Wallis was herself. Her cousin Corrine had invited Wallis to come stay in Pensacola at the naval base where the airmen trained.

"They grow on trees down here, like the coconuts!" she'd gleefully told Wallis when she met her at the train. "Oh, Skinny! Look at you! I'm as plump as a partridge."

Wallis had silently agreed but kissed her pretty cousin on the cheek anyway. And she glowed with the compliment of her old nickname, "Skinny." She would never be as curvy and soft as her cousin; it was by now an accepted fact. During adolescence she had not filled out in that womanly way, to her mother's consternation. And even Wallis had to admit she looked odd next to her friends and classmates. But she was determined to make the most of her assets—or lack thereof—and dieted religiously to maintain the alarming slimness that she accentuated with severely tailored clothing in jewel colors, her minuscule waist almost always cinched with a belt or sash. Although the moment she stepped off the train and was assaulted by the Pensacola humidity, she realized she might have to relax her standards and wear looser clothing down here, if only to survive.

But at the party her cousin gave for her the next day, she still resolutely encircled her waist with a wide satin bow, even though she was perspiring the moment she stepped onto the veranda. Corinne's husband, Henry Mustin, was the commander of the new Pensacola Air Station, the first in the US Navy.

And here was one of his pilots, Lieutenant Win Spencer, laughing at something a fellow officer had said but fixing his lazily charming gaze on Wallis.

And she fell.

She tumbled into love, deeply, irreversibly. That night she lay in bed going over every single significant moment in an afternoon filled with significant moments, with charged electricity sparking between two people who suddenly were no longer strangers: Win's easy, relaxed attitude as the two of them maneuvered to sit next to each other at luncheon. His strong, sinewy wrists shooting out of his cuffs as he handed her platters of sandwiches and salads, made her stomach do one—just one—slow, acrobatic flip. She'd never experienced that; she'd never gone weak in a male's physical presence before and knew it was because previously she'd only dated boys. But Win was a man. A man who exuded confidence and competence. A man who would take her places, for, after all, wasn't he a pilot? One of the new dashing knights of the air who were captivating an entire nation with their bravery, their quest to defy the laws of gravity?

Win was, he told her proudly, only the twentieth navy pilot to win his wings. Her heart gave another tumble—oh, just wait until Uncle Sol heard about that!

Just wait until Win swept her away from Baltimore, from Uncle Sol's perpetually disapproving scowl, and from her mother's continuing descent into genteel poverty in a series of boardinghouses and rooms and love affairs with sickly second sons.

Wallis fell for him. She knew it for sure by the end of the next day, during which he gave her a tour of the air base and introduced her to his fellow pilots, none of whom had the dash and bravado of Win. None were half as handsome. He showed her his airplane—such a flimsy thing! All canvas and wires and she feared for him up there and that fear told her for certain that this was love, the real thing. Because she'd not feared for anyone other than herself in years, not since she was a little girl worried about Mama.

Win was twenty-seven. A good age, she calculated. Eight years between them. That seemed perfect in a way she couldn't articulate. But that she could *feel*.

During those weeks in Pensacola, Win Spencer from Chicago and Wallis Warfield from Baltimore became an established pair, seen together everywhere—dancing at parties, lunching, always with a chaperone, on patios, even playing golf on the links. Win was a passionate golfer and Wallis pretended she was.

She also pretended not to notice his mean streak, apparent especially after he drank too much. She further pretended that he didn't drink too much. His jealousy—explosive at times, like the sudden thunderstorms that could roar up from the Gulf of Mexico—when she flirted even in the slightest way with another man only made her happier. Proud, even. He would yell, he would sulk, and she would exult in her power over him. And when he came back around like a penitent little boy, she would soothe him. And the knowledge that she could cause this virile, volatile man to come crawling to her on his knees made her giddy with happiness, with the sense of her own ability to conquer.

Made her certain that this was love.

Win proposed; she said she'd have to ask her family; Uncle Sol agreed—probably only to get rid of her, but never mind—Mama wept, and they were married. In *the* wedding of the season, *The Baltimore Sun* called it, with Wallis's envious school friends (for she was the first to marry) as bridesmaids and Win's fellow officers, in full military dress uniform, as ushers. Wallis designed her own wedding gown: white velvet, perfect for an autumn wedding, and unusual enough that it caused gasps when she walked down the aisle on Uncle Sol's arm. She was so caught up in the attention, in the thrill of marrying a dashing airman, she felt affectionate toward her uncle that day and even kissed him on his puckered old cheek, which surprised him.

Then she and Win went on their honeymoon to the Greenbrier resort in West Virginia, where her new husband started yelling at everyone in sight when he discovered West Virginia was dry and he couldn't buy any alcohol. It was a good thing, then, that he had packed a couple of flasks of gin in his luggage, wasn't it?

"Win—you mean you carry your own with you?" She was so stunned, she could hardly comprehend it. Uncle Sol didn't approve of alcohol, so she hadn't grown up around it, and although of course during her debutante year she'd been to parties where there was champagne, she herself really didn't enjoy drinking—why anyone would deliberately lose control of themselves, she never could fathom. She'd seen Win drunk before, of course, in Pensacola. But she'd assumed it was because he was around his fellow aviators, all of whom drank a bit more than most people. Who could blame them when every time they saw another sunset, they knew they'd cheated death?

But to pack flasks of gin in your honeymoon luggage wasn't anything Wallis had anticipated.

"You're such a little prude, you know?" Win sneered at her, looking completely unrecognizable—disgusted, brooding, dissipated.

It was a look she was to become far too accustomed to in the coming years. Years of following her husband around the country as he established air bases for the US Navy after America entered the war. Years of watching him drink, first because it was fun, then because he wasn't sent to the front because his experience was too valuable, he was needed to train new pilots, fresh meat for the Germans. Then because his younger brother died a war hero, forever a martyr. Then because he was jealous when Wallis looked at other men. Then because he was bored with her and told her she was the worst mistake of his life.

Then because he was filled with shame after he hit her, kicked her, locked her in a room and took the key with him. Because her cries annoyed him. Because her face annoyed him. Because she wasn't interested in sex. Because she wanted a new hat. Because she asked him where the money went when she knew damn well he had only an officer's salary. Because she complained of the drab military housing she was forced to live in—she was too good for it, wasn't she? The little Baltimore princess!

He drank because she asked to move to a hotel instead. Because she told him she wanted more out of life than following him around and throwing out his bottles.

He drank. It became who he was. No longer a heroic, handsome adventurer of the air. He was a drunk. An abusive drunk.

And finally, in Washington, DC—another post, but at least an interesting one—she had had enough and told him she was leaving him for good. By then, she was numb to him, to his penitent-boy act. Anything that tied her to him—sex, in particular, mostly forced, him slobbering over her with his moist gin breath, not even *seeing* her, let alone caring that he hurt her—existed separately. Outside her body, outside her mind.

Outside her heart.

Divorce, however, was unheard of in Baltimore.

"Divorce?" Uncle Sol could barely say the word when she showed up once more—eight years older, eight years sadder, eight years more determined than ever to live the life she wanted, not the life some man forced her to live—to tell him.

"Yes, Uncle Sol. He beat me." Wallis, by now, could say it without shame. It was the fact of Win. "I can easily divorce him on grounds of cruelty."

"No Warfield has ever gotten a divorce! I won't allow it."

"Allow it?" Every humiliation, every physical and mental abuse she'd experienced in the past years, gathered together in a mighty cyclone spitting dangerous lightning and tumultuous winds, winds that made her stiffen her spine so she wouldn't buckle. *She* was the weather now. "*Allow* it? I didn't come here for permission, Uncle Sol. I came here to tell you before I head to Virginia, where I have to spend a year to get my decree. I came here to tell you before you read about it in the newspaper. I came here to—"

"Bessiewallis—"

"I'm Wallis now and have been forever. I'm a married woman. I've seen things you'll never see stuck here behind your stuffy old desk. I've been locked in hotel rooms while my husband drank himself into a stupor, never knowing if he'd drink so much he'd die and end up in a river with the key in his hand and no one would know to come find me. You have no idea who I am anymore. But *you* are the head of the family. You're the closest thing I have to a father. And it's your job to protect me. Isn't it?" She hated herself for letting her voice falter with these last words. But she was so weary. All she wanted was to be free of Win. All she wanted was a fresh start.

All she wanted, more than anything, was a home of her own. Her entire life she'd lived in other people's homes or military quarters or hotels. When would she get to decorate her own home, fill it with things of her own choosing, exquisite things so that everywhere you gazed, you saw beauty?

She was still a young woman. She'd mastered the art of survival with flair; no one ever suspected the brutality of her marriage. She could expertly camouflage her bruises with makeup, jewelry, and the right clothes. She never appeared in public with a hair out of place because she could control that, at least. Her appearance. Her style. She could look in the mirror and see perfection, strength, reflected back. It only took constant discipline and control and dieting and exercising and hours spent studying herself from all angles to determine how to make the most of her physical attributes and finding the best hairdressers and tailors she could afford and learning how to throw perfect parties and dinners so that the guests wouldn't even notice that Win was absent or, if present, drinking too much and looking at Wallis across the table as if she were his prey.

She wanted—no, *deserved*—a fresh start, had packed up her many gifts and taken them with her, leaving the detritus of foolishly marrying for love behind. She would never make that mistake again.

But Uncle Sol wouldn't give her the money she needed to pay for a lawyer.

She went back to Win one last time.

And they broke each other into pieces; Win agreed to a divorce, she somehow found the money, and, finally, she was free. She managed to feel one moment of gratitude toward Win for not fighting her, then vowed never to think of him again.

For Uncle Sol, however, she would only ever feel fury. She wept when he died, not long after, but it wasn't because she mourned him; it was because he'd cut her out of his will, leaving the millions she had assumed would be hers to charity.

Because, once again, she would have to find a man to provide for her.

ERNEST ALDRICH SIMPSON

1928

"Darling Kitty, it's not as if I *wanted* to fall in love with a married man," Wallis told her good friend. Then she smiled, an enigmatic smile, and turned her face to the sun.

She, Kitty, and Herman Rogers—the Rogerses were American friends she'd met in China; she'd spent several months with them in Peking—were relaxing on the Rogerses' terrace in Cannes. The South of France was divine, Wallis decided. If she ever had the money, she would certainly have a villa like this, perched high on a cliff with walled gardens of bougainvillea and jasmine, orange trees, olive trees, lemon trees, and a terrace like the one they were enjoying now, with endless views of the sapphire-blue Mediterranean. Her own staff to command, and she would insist on perfection—not a wrinkled linen, not a tarnished piece of silver, and the crystal chandeliers washed weekly so they always sparkled like the brightest stars in the sky. Fresh flowers in every room, vases upon vases of them, changed every other day so the blooms never looked tired.

Would she ever have such a home? For the first time, finally, in 1928, it seemed within her grasp. Because she'd met, flirted with, and grown very fond of a Mr. Ernest Simpson, son of a British shipping magnate and his American wife. And she was staying with her friends in Cannes, waiting for him to finish the ugly business of extricating himself from his marriage.

Was she in love with him? No. She'd learned her lesson well with Win. Never again would she fall for charm and looks instead of money. After what Uncle Sol had done to her, she couldn't afford to. Her mother might have been happy trying to make a living in the only ways available to her sex and her class—chaperoning, dressmaking, taking in boarders. Never quite being able to climb out of genteel poverty but at least having enough money to eat and, occasionally, take a trip to visit kind, rich relatives.

Wallis was no stranger to relying on the generosity of

friends, like the Rogerses. She happily slept in their guest suites and enjoyed their views. But it wasn't enough. Ernest Simpson was the man who was finally going to install her as queen of her own domain. He wasn't as wealthy as the Rogerses, but his shipping business did well, and he promised her they'd have a flat of their own in a fashionable part of London once they were married.

"Is he going to propose, Wallis?" Kitty asked breathlessly. She was a sweet, matronly little woman who fussed over her husband endlessly. And she considered Wallis the epitome of sophistication, which helped Wallis overlook some of her friend's more annoying traits, such as teasingly warning her husband not to run off with "dear Wallis" and making exaggeratedly shocked faces at the two of them, Wallis and Herman, whenever she saw them talking without her. It was tiring, having to play her part in this little domestic farce. Wallis liked Herman, respected him, trusted his sound advice. Had she not found Ernest, she would have been tempted to steal him from Kitty, at that—maybe her friend was more astute than she'd suspected.

Women always surprised Wallis. Men, not so much.

"Yes, I think he will," Wallis replied, glancing at her Cartier wristwatch, a gift from Ernest, and admiring the way the diamonds glistened in the sun. "In fact, he's due to telephone at three. If you'll excuse me, I'll go inside and wait for the call. You know how these trunk lines are! Heaven only knows what time the call will really come through."

And after an insincere kiss upon her friend's cheek, Wallis strode into the house to start the next part of her life. The secure, safe, stable part.

Finally.

LONDON, 1931

"Wallis, I'm afraid I'm going to have to ask you to economize a bit," Ernest said one morning at breakfast. "With the Depression, the business is going through a rough spell."

"Economize?" Wallis raised an eyebrow at her husband, then scooped a small bite of grapefruit with her grapefruit spoon.

"Perhaps we can cut back on entertaining."

"What on earth do you mean? You know how important it is that we entertain. It's the only way we'll be accepted in society. And you want that as much as I do. It's good for business."

"Then maybe cut back on clothes?"

"Now, that's just silly." She firmly put down her spoon. "You're as fond of fine tweeds as I am of couture. And it's important to look our best if we want to keep up."

"Darling, I think that's the point I'm trying to make. Maybe we *can't* keep up."

"No, Ernest. That is a ridiculous notion," Wallis said in what he called her Queen Victoria voice. Then she glared at her husband, who turned a faint shade of pink.

The brilliantined hair, parted in the middle. The neat mustache. The broad shoulders that looked appropriately commanding in those fine tweeds. The derby hat at the ready. He looked the part, certainly, the part of the successful shipping magnate, comfortably middle class by London standards. They lived in a nice flat, not quite in Mayfair but close enough, that Wallis had lavishly decorated, exulting in the thrill of perusing fine antiques stores, art galleries, of ordering table linens from Liberty, hampers of foie gras and boxes of marrons glacés from Fortnum & Mason.

Their social standing was improving; they received invitations to shooting weekends, which Ernest loved but Wallis only tolerated for the chance to rub elbows with the landed gentry. Good God, the British did love their horses! Dinner parties at the Ritz or the Savoy after the theater—this was much more her cup of tea. Their circle of important friends was growing, and now she'd become acquainted with Thelma Furness, the Prince of Wales's mistress! Meeting the prince wasn't a mere fantasy any longer. And when she did, who knew what would happen next? Perhaps one day she'd be presented at court! Married women were as well as debutantes. And think what the prince's influence could do for Ernest's business.

Now he wanted to start economizing? When they were on the very brink of social success?

She had to remind herself that her husband was a kind man, really. Patient, content to let Wallis take the reins of their marriage, drive them forward as a couple, become a fixture in a certain circle where she finally, after so many years lost in the wilderness, felt like she belonged. For wasn't she built for this? For setting an exquisite table, filling her days planning place settings when she wasn't being driven to fittings and the hairdresser, then coming home for tea, after which her masseuse came to work her over for an hour, then having her bath and dressing for dinner either in with friends or out with acquaintances who might become friends?

When the evening was over and she'd kissed Ernest good night and firmly closed the door to their shared dressing room, she lay down on her own bed with her own linens—from

Woods of Harrogate—and slept the sleep of the richly deserving. Because tomorrow she would do it all over again. She'd never have to ask Uncle Sol for more money; she didn't fear her husband locking her in a room and forgetting about her (Ernest hardly drank at all, another thing she appreciated). She didn't have to start worrying about overstaying her welcome and then face the stress of writing to some other rich friend or relative and inviting herself for a visit.

Ernest had given all this to her. And for that, she was eternally grateful, even if her heart did nothing at all when she saw him, even if the thought of sleeping in the same bed with him, of being intimate with him, was about as palatable as the idea of finding someone else's hair in her hairbrush.

"No, Ernest," Wallis repeated, even as she smiled at him with genuine fondness. "I can't economize on those things."

"Could you at least find a way to manage with fewer servants?" Ernest—shockingly—leaned his elbows on the breakfast table and rubbed his eyes, and she saw that there were new little lines surrounding them. Well. What good was he to her if he continued to look like this—weary, troubled? She couldn't sail forth into society alone; she needed her husband beside her. After all, he was the one with London roots. And single women her age in society were rare; single divorcées, nonexistent.

"All right," Wallis conceded tightly. "I'll let a girl go."

"Make it two, if you can."

"We'll see."

SOON AFTER THAT, THEY met the Prince of Wales. At dear, dear Thelma's home.

AND NOW HERE SHE was, darling Thelma! So worried about her little prince that she'd asked Wallis to take care of him while she was away. And Ernest didn't mind in the least. Ernest was a very understanding man in his own way. He well knew what the prince could do for him.

Wallis, by now, understood what the prince could do for her too. Especially while Thelma was away.

Far, far away.

CHAPTER

5

Queen Mary Interrupts

ARE YOU THE MOTHER OF SONS? IF SO, YOU WILL, I PRAY, have some sympathy for me despite my exalted state.

I am the mother of five sons, four living. I do not speak of the one we lost; his life was a pathetic tragedy and we had to keep him out of public view. After all, the royal family cannot afford to have a weak link. Our very existence is tenuous enough, what with divine right and so forth. If the public knew we had physical and emotional ailments just as all families do, the jig, as they say, would be up. So we keep it all hidden, as much as possible.

But it's terribly difficult to do that when you have *sons.*

My daughter, Mary, the princess royal, is quite easy compared to my boys. She is dutiful, docile, decorative—and that is all that is required of her. I saw to it that she married a dutiful, docile man (alas, not decorative at all). But the others, the ones who count, the heir and the spares, are an entirely different matter.

I will tell you a little secret: The Windsor men are weak. It's the Windsor women—the ones born royal and the ones we determine are fit to marry royal—who have all the strength.

Look at myself if you need an example. Although I admit to having a stain upon my heritage, courtesy of my father. Despite the fact that I am a great-granddaughter of George III and a cousin of Queen Victoria, my bloodline isn't pure, as my father was the result of a morganatic marriage between the Duke of Teck and a mere nonroyal countess.

I've never gotten over the shame.

However, despite this, I was betrothed to *two* princes of England!

And I will tell you this: It was because Queen Victoria, the grandmother of those two princes, recognized how weak they were and knew she had to arrange marriages to strong women. Because Windsor men are made—or ruined—by their wives.

The first prince, Prince Eddy, the Duke of Clarence, was the first son of the Prince of Wales, soon to be Edward VII. So Eddy was second in line to the throne and expected to succeed his father in due time. However, nervous little Eddy—quite distasteful; I shuddered to be around him but hid my disgust admirably—mercifully died before our marriage, and I was left momentarily at a loss. Until the Queen in her great wisdom decided that I should marry the younger brother, Prince George, who eventually became King George V.

And so I became Queen of England, as was quite right and good, and turned a weak younger brother—dear Georgie had never read a book until I made him—into a forceful king. And I had five sons and one daughter.

Like Queen Victoria, I see my sons' faults with clear eyes. Those of David, the eldest, in particular. So much is expected of him! He will one day be King, and I fear it will happen sooner rather than later, as the King, my husband, is not in the best of health.

(I, however, am remarkably robust for my age.)

The King and I have commiserated about him; our dissipated eldest is our primary topic of conversation these days. If only he would marry and settle down! Surely he knows that he isn't obligated to marry a European princess the way he would have been prior to the Great War. There simply aren't that many left. Our sons are allowed to marry commoners now, as Bertie did.

Ah, Bertie. And dear Elizabeth!

Now, that was a good match. I saw to it that it was. I admit I was rather annoyed when Lady Elizabeth Bowes-Lyon repeatedly refused my son, and eventually I had to do something about it. Who was she, a mere Scottish daughter of an earl, to refuse a prince of England! Even if it *was* Bertie, poor Bertie. As I've made quite clear, I'm no fool. I know my son, second in line for the throne just as his dear papa once was, has nervous habits. And his stutter is quite shameful. But he is a kind boy who tries so very hard and is the son who is most like his father, the King. But he's not my favorite.

No, that would be David.

But I digress. When Elizabeth was reluctant to accept my son's proposal, I realized something must be done. But behind the scenes. I can never be seen to exert more influence than my husband, the King. So my corridors of power are darker, hidden. But no less effective than the brilliant throne room and the sun-filled balcony of Buckingham Palace.

Once Elizabeth was taken care of and she and Bertie married, I did rest a bit more easily. At least one of my sons was paired off, apparently happily so, and soon they had two little girls and they may still have a little boy, which—again, our little secret—I pray they won't. As I said, the Windsor women are made of much finer stuff than the men.

Henry, the third in line to the throne, is a dull boy who loves the military and married women. (I trust you remember that scandal with Beryl Markham, the aviatrix? I shudder to recall it, and the money we paid to keep it out of the newspapers.) But I have my eye on several daughters of nobility for him, once he matures a little.

Georgie, fourth in line, is not a dull boy. He is quite the opposite, and his past sexual exploits are not something I can bring myself to discuss. It's quite frustrating, really, because his mind is fine, and intellectually he is superior to his older brothers. And he is most charming—I find it difficult indeed to maintain my queenly manner when he is around, playing the piano with the ease of his great friend Noël Coward or discussing literature with the passion of one of the Sitwells or imitating various members of the family with the talent of another of his friends, Laurence Olivier. But his shocking tastes kept me up at night while I feverishly looked for the right woman for him as well. That problem has now been solved in a *most* satisfactory way.

Which brings me back to David. My favorite.

The weakest one of them all, in ways only a mother can see.

What are we to do with him? He has a mind of his own, my eldest. Of course, this is because he is Prince of Wales and has had his own office, his own staff, for years. He's traveled the globe at our behest; it was vital, after the war that decimated so many other royal families. We're one of the last royal dynasties left and it's imperative that we remind all the empire how important we are. David is quite good at this; he is so charming, with his impish smile, his golden hair, his ease with strangers and the public in general. The problem is, he has a tendency to speak out on matters he has no business speaking out on. We are constitutional monarchs, and we must not get involved with politics or be seen to take sides with any one party. (Although naturally we are Tories in spirit.)

Of course I knew about his relationships with married women, with Freda Dudley Ward and Thelma Furness. But they stayed in the background for the most part, understanding that their time in the sun was brief and that, inevitably, David would marry a suitable future queen.

But he stubbornly refuses to even think about the appropriate young women I've thrown his way, the various princesses and daughters of royal dukes (displaced Russian princesses abound, as do Greek royals, who can never hold on to their thrones; I simply don't understand it, they are intolerably weak). He says he will marry for love or not at all, and sometimes I wonder if he understands his duty. He will be *King*. King of a great nation of men who sacrificed so much during the last war while he was protected, kept safe. King of a nation that stands almost alone in all the world, a monarchy surrounded on all sides by republics. King of a nation in upheaval, what with the Depression and national strikes and people demanding rights and luxuries they never demanded before, and now there's Herr Hitler over in Germany—my own Germany. I can never forget that both my husband, the King, and I are more German than British. Which naturally caused problems in the last war, to such an extent that we had to change our name, for heaven's sake! Hence we are now Windsors instead of Saxe-Coburgs. It was our own cousin Kaiser Wilhelm, Queen Victoria's eldest grandchild, who began the last war.

And now Hitler is similarly playing with his toy soldiers and battleships.

David is forty. His father, the King, is ill. He must see where his duty lies. Kings can't afford to marry for love, although if they are lucky, love will come. Eventually.

However, David has taken up with another unsuitable woman. And I am to meet her tonight *in my own home, in Buckingham Palace,* and there's nothing I can do about it.

Yet.

The situation seems different this time; he never asked me to receive his other paramours. He's off his head, my eldest. Besotted. Bewitched. I hear all sorts of unsavory rumors about this woman and her past—I never thought it possible that being *American* could be the least unsavory thing about one of David's women.

This time, unlike the other times, in order for me to do what I must, I may require reinforcements.

CHAPTER
6

LONDON

NOVEMBER 1934

"HE'S BRINGING *HER* TONIGHT, YOU KNOW. AND HER HUSband, the poor fool."

"Oh, really?" Bertie was on his knees in the nursery, playing horse with Lilibet and Margaret. In his evening clothes with the "penguin tails," as the girls called them, his chest covered with orders, a bright blue sash across his shirtfront, he was the most royal horse ever, but to the girls he was simply Papa.

"Buck like a bronco, Papa!" squealed little Margaret.

"No, race like you're in the Derby!" commanded rosy Lilibet, who was never afraid to boss her younger sister. But Margaret could take it. She was all spirit, that one.

The Yorks were about to leave for Prince George's engagement party at Buck House, the family nickname for the palace, and Elizabeth was uncharacteristically apprehensive; she sipped a Dubonnet and gin to calm her nerves. This whole engagement business of her brother-in-law's had unsettled her, and now to have to throw into the mix David's ridiculous infatuation with this Simpson woman, who had firmly supplanted Thelma in his affections, had, indeed, done so while her supposed friend was away in America! The prince refused to take Thelma's calls now; even more worrying, he also refused those of Freda Dudley Ward, the one person in his life who could talk sense into him. Without Freda's steadying hand, David was suddenly like a child's balloon, straining now this way, now that, upward, down, forever pulling at the increasingly tenuous string tying him to his family, and more alarming, to his duty. And the winds pushing him hither and yon were the whims of one Mrs. Ernest Simpson.

That Woman.

Elizabeth studied herself in a full-length mirror, turning to the right, then the left, sucking in her stomach, tilting her chin up. One was still young, only thirty-four. But decidedly a settled matron with a family; in the eyes of the public, she was no longer the darling young Scottish lass who had captured a prince's heart along with a nation's. That role now belonged to Princess Marina, her brother-in-law George's fiancée. That Marina was taking on an unenviable task—for, as handsome and charming as Prince George was, there was no denying he was also a drug addict with unusual sexual tastes—didn't matter to Elizabeth. What mattered to her was that Marina was a true royal, daughter of Prince Nicholas of Greece and Denmark and Grand Duchess Elena of Russia. What mattered to her was that the public and the newspapers had gone clean out of their heads celebrating this royal bride-to-be, using words such as *glamour, style, elegance, chic, beauty.*

Well.

"I'll show her who's a duchess," Elizabeth whispered to herself as she smoothed the bodice of her evening gown, adjusted her sash with her own royal order on it, a ribbon with a miniature portrait of the King in the center. The dress was from her favorite dressmaker, Madame Handley-Seymour, who also happened to be the favorite dressmaker of the Queen. And it was in Elizabeth's favorite style, with flounces and puffed sleeves and rows of ruffles in the skirt, all of the finest lace and satin. It was a brocaded-rose pattern, and she had always looked lovely in pink.

And to top it all off, there were jewels from the family vault: a brooch and a necklace and two bracelets and earrings plus the tiara, all dripping in diamonds. Elizabeth had layered herself in finery, *royal* finery, and thus arrayed, she felt certain that she would outshine any impoverished princess from a refugee family. No matter how much *royal* blood that princess might possess.

"Mummy, you look so sparkly!" Margaret piped up, and Lilibet nodded in agreement.

"Mummy looks spectacular," Bertie confirmed, his eyes gleaming appreciatively.

"Do you think it's—elegant? This dress?"

"The *most* elegant," Lilibet said with assurance. Elizabeth blew a kiss to her daughter, then resumed studying her reflection. Perhaps one was—petite (not short; never that dreadful word!). And, yes, her waist was no longer clearly defined without help from undergarments. Her skin, however, was still lovely, that porcelain complexion she was so famous for; there were no lines around her dark blue eyes. She had produced two perfect little girls. And as the Duchess of York, she outranked the soon-to-be Duchess of Kent.

She certainly outmatched a mere Mrs. Simpson. And if David never married—which seemed more likely with each passing year—once he ascended to the throne, who would be the highest-ranking royal lady?

Why, the Duchess of York, of course. With none of the tedious duties of the Queen but many of the perks, including the honor of presiding over royal balls like the one tonight.

One more sip—make that two; all right, three—of the Dubonnet, and Elizabeth was ready to shine. *Sparkle.*

"Bertie, it's time to leave. You know the King."

"Grandpapa is always cross when we're late," Lilibet reminded her father, helping him to his feet and even brushing some lint off his trousers. Margaret rolled her eyes at her serious sister, and Elizabeth resisted laughing; it wouldn't do to encourage her younger daughter's already rampant impishness.

"You look lovely, my dear. Not just elegant. Tr-tr-truly lovely," Bertie told his wife, sincere as always. She smiled—it was bliss, rather, to be married to a man who never ran out of compliments for one—and straightened his tie.

"As elegant as Marina? As stylish as Mrs. Simpson?"

"Never mind her. Who is she? David's current American infatuation. And she's married."

"I know," Elizabeth said irritably.

"So what's the problem with this one?"

"Twice! She's been married twice!"

"So was Thelma."

"But he's *dumped* Thelma, Bertie! Keep up!"

"Darling, I can't keep up with my brother's romances. Nor should you. So what if she's been married twice? One day he'll find a ravishing girl like I did and he'll settle down. You'll see."

"This one is different," Elizabeth muttered. She waved to her daughters as they were escorted back to the nursery by Allah, their faithful nursemaid.

"As long as she's discreet like Thelma, I really don't see the problem."

"He never insisted on presenting Thelma to the King and Queen," Elizabeth pointed out as they descended the stairs to the entrance of their home at 145 Piccadilly. She settled her white fur stole upon her shoulders, nodded to the staff who waited to see them off, and let her husband usher her into the shining black car that would take them to Buck House.

As usual, there was a small crowd gathered outside the gate, trying to get a glimpse of the Smiling Duchess and the duke and their daughters; when the duke and duchess emerged from the house, there were a few cheers but mostly cries of "Where are the little princesses?"

Her daughters, she had to admit, had rather upstaged her of late; there was insatiable interest in the golden-haired granddaughters of King George V. Her daughters, Marina, this woman—oh, nonsense. Elizabeth smiled even more fiercely than usual and waved her hand *elegantly* at the poor souls and was rewarded with a few cheers of "We love our Smiling Duchess!"

"There," she whispered with satisfaction as she allowed Bertie to spread out her skirt so it wouldn't wrinkle on the short drive. "Everything's quite all right again."

"What's that, darling?"

"Nothing."

THE RED AND GILT and crystal and polish and shine and opulence of Buck House threatened to overwhelm one, Elizabeth thought as she and Bertie entered the ballroom. Tonight was the grandest celebration other than the wedding itself, with diplomats and royalty spread out before her like a glittering sea. Tiaras had been taken out of family vaults and polished with care; every medal and order within arm's reach glittered on male chests.

And in the very center of it all stood the King and Queen, along with George and Marina.

Marina. Who looked as every paper described her. Tall, slim, wearing her own ancestral royal tiara, not one the King or Queen had given her. She was poured into a white satin dress with long sleeves, not a flounce or ruffle anywhere. Nothing distracted from her figure; every seam was designed to emphasize her slender lines. Her dark blond hair was parted on the side and stylishly waved around her face, setting off her high cheekbones. Her jewels were stunning. Simple, but stunning—sapphires matching the square-cut sapphire of her engagement ring. Her lipstick was a deep russet red, the same color as her nails.

Her nails! Painted! Painted nails on one of the royal women! The King despised women who painted their nails, and apparently when Queen Mary told her future daughter-in-law this, Marina responded with a tart "Well, your George might not like it, but mine does!"

Elizabeth would never have dared to paint her nails! Nor would she ever have dared to speak to her mother-in-law that way. But then again, she wasn't truly *royal.*

Suddenly she patted her own dress, fingering the extra fabric, designed to conceal, not emphasize, and she was aware of how she rustled, as if she were walking through piles of brittle autumn leaves. She felt weighed down by all of it—the folds of fabric, the ponderance of so many jewels; too many, she worried. As if one was trying too hard—

Which one was.

And now David—looking far too handsome, too carefree and debonair—was walking up to his parents with Mrs. Simpson on his arm. That Woman! Her dress made Elizabeth gasp; it was a purple lamé sheath with a chartreuse bolero jacket and matching sash, and Elizabeth became uncomfortably aware of the suddenly garish pink of her own dress that had looked so sweetly flattering at home. Now, confronted with the jewel tones of Wallis Simpson and the unadorned sophistication of Princess Marina, she panicked.

For the first time in her life, Elizabeth Bowes-Lyon wished to be anywhere but at a party. Not merely *a* party, but *the* party of the year. Overwhelmingly—unfamiliarly—unsure of herself, she was terrified she would do something idiotic. Like trip over her flounced hem or split a seam—oh, why was her Liberty girdle suddenly cutting into her waist, threatening to give way?—or spill champagne down the beribboned chest of the king of Spain.

"Bertie, I—"

"Bertie! Elizabeth! Come, come, say hello to Wallis!" David had spotted them and was waving them over rather desperately.

Elizabeth caught the frozen expressions of her in-laws as she and Bertie joined the family circle. King George's face was nearly purple, his eyes bulging, and she feared he would have one of his gnashes, episodes that her husband had, unfortunately, inherited. That terrifying rage that came out of nowhere, accompanied by spitting and every curse word under the sun, rage that would then disappear in the next moment, leaving one bewildered and crushed.

Queen Mary laid a hand upon her husband's arm and managed a faint, frosty smile as her eldest pushed his "friend" forward. Wallis had a smirk on her face as she swept into a bow so deep she nearly kissed the floor.

"Your Majesties, I wish to present Mrs. Ernest Simpson," David said. "She is a great friend of mine."

"Your Majesties," Wallis said in her flat American accent.

King George looked at his son as if he wished kings could still send their heirs away to fight in the Crusades. Queen Mary made a small sound that could have been acquiescence or derision; it was difficult to tell.

"And, Bertie, Elizabeth—say hello to Wallis!" David didn't appear to notice the frigid reaction of his parents.

Wallis swept into another deep curtsy; Elizabeth felt absurd laughter bubbling up but managed to keep a composed face.

"Your Royal Highness, how nice to see you again," Wallis said with a smile, although her eyes, taking in Elizabeth from head to toe, shone with something less benign. "What an extraordinary gown!"

"Thank you," Elizabeth replied as she patted some of her flounces as if for assurance. "And you—well, I've never quite seen anything like it."

"Thank you," Mrs. Simpson said with smug satisfaction, willfully misinterpreting Elizabeth's comment. "I would be happy to give you the name of my dressmaker. He can work miracles."

Before Elizabeth could sputter a reply, the King and Queen turned to greet the Yorks. Elizabeth curtsied—a proper curtsy, not a mockery of one—and kissed her mother-in-law on the cheek.

"I love your dress," Queen Mary enthused as if she hadn't heard a word Wallis had said. "Madame Handley-Seymour outdid herself this time!"

"She certainly did," Wallis whispered to David as they moved away. But Elizabeth, her mother-in-law's hands upon her shoulders, couldn't respond.

"Thank you, Mama. You look lovely."

David and Mrs. Simpson had joined George and Marina; the two women were now laughing together, thick as thieves. Elizabeth saw them looking at her; she felt their eyes take her in from tiara to hem, after which they turned to each other and giggled again.

Goodness, it was boiling in here! It simply took one's breath away! The blazing chandeliers and the packed crowd radiated heat like a furnace; sweat was racing down her back, pooling between her skin and her girdle, and her face burned like the sun. Oh, if only she could blink and be back home, snuggled in bed with a good mystery and a box of chocolates and the phonograph playing Ivor Novello records, a fire crackling, her happy daughters laughing in the nursery and her doting husband in his adjoining room, ready to tell her how perfect she was, how wonderful. All she ever had to do was turn to Bertie, and the words were already on his lips.

Never-ending flattery and attention compensated, quite a lot, for the absence of that feeling that made one's heart race and one's knees grow weak, that feeling she'd really only ever experienced with James Stuart.

"I hear, Your Majesty, that the Mall is simply packed with people already. I predict there will be bigger crowds than there were even for the Duke of York's wedding," some silly official said—too loudly, as if intending Elizabeth to hear?—to Queen Mary, who had let go of Elizabeth and turned, regally, to a new crop of dignitaries ready to be presented.

"Naturally. Marina is a true royal," the Queen replied. Coolly.

Ridiculous tears threatening, Elizabeth could only gaze down at her dress—oh, it *was* a horror, wasn't it? So much pink, confectionery layers suited for the nursery, not a royal ball—what on earth had she been thinking? How could she ever compete with Marina, a *true royal* and so elegant? Or with That Woman, with her rakish style and unnerving confidence? The Smiling Duchess hadn't a chance in the world. She was only a mother, a broodmare. The epitome of cozy domesticity, but cozy domesticity didn't make the front page of *Tatler*, now, did it? How many times had the stylish Mrs. Simpson graced it lately?

Far more than the Smiling Duchess.

"My favorite daughter-in-law." A kind, understanding voice filled her ear. Elizabeth blinked and looked up at the King. "My favorite daughter-in-law," he continued. "Always."

"Oh, Papa!" Elizabeth could have burst into tears. She would never dare to throw herself into her father-in-law's arms; her husband's family froze at any physical demonstrations of affection, unlike her own rollicking relatives. It was one of the things she'd discovered, quickly, about the royal family; *royal* outranked *family*. Sons and daughter bowed and curtsied to their parents, referred to them mainly as the King and the Queen instead of Papa and Mama.

But now she wished she could embrace the King, for her father-in-law was the only one who seemed to understand. Even Bertie hadn't registered her distress.

"A common little Scottish girl, that's me," she said, too gaily. "That's what Marina calls me. I know."

"There is nothing common about you. You are a rare flower—dare I say a rose?—Elizabeth. Don't forget that. You have made my son happier than we could ever have hoped for. And given us two beautiful granddaughters and let me spoil them to my heart's content! Never mind those two—" He nodded toward Wallis and Marina, two sleek greyhounds in a pack of dumpy little corgis. "And especially never mind Mrs. Simpson. Promise me that, will you? Promise me that you and Bertie and your precious little girls won't have a thing to do with her. I fear for David; I fear for what she might do to him. To us all."

The King's face crumpled, and he looked, all of a sudden, quite old. Ill. He'd never fully recovered from his previous illness, but on occasions like this, he could mask his weakness with the sheer impact of his majesty. But now he looked tired, sick. A bewildered father.

"My eldest has no idea how fragile the monarchy is. He doesn't think of his country—or his family. All he thinks of is himself and his own pleasure. I don't understand him at all."

Elizabeth watched as David took Wallis's arm and began to parade her around the room, introducing her to his fellow royals. As if she had a right to be on equal terms with them! Shaking hands with King Haakon of Norway as if she were his peer; putting her hand on the arm of Astrid, queen of the Belgians, in such a chummy way.

David, *her* David, her pal—they used to have such silly private jokes together, but since Wallis elbowed her way past Thelma, he hadn't had as much time for them—was preening like a rooster, a silly little bantam rooster. As proud of the divorced and remarried woman on his arm as if she were a vestal virgin. Which she most definitely was not; she was old, much too old to be a royal bride. He couldn't be thinking of that, could he?

But then he caught Elizabeth's eye and waved at her, pulling a silly face and rolling his eyes as if he was bored out of his skull, and she laughed. Because he was David. *Her* David. The Prince of Wales; the next head of the Church of England. No, she couldn't imagine it—that the man she knew would actually marry the American.

But the old King did look so concerned, she lay a hand upon his arm.

"I promise, dear Papa! We won't see her any more than we absolutely have to—one can't entirely avoid it, of course. Not as long as—but you can rest assured we'll keep our distance. The woman is still married. There's really nothing she can do in the grand scheme of things. We'll keep an eye on David for you. I know you do worry about him. Perhaps you could talk to him? Share your concern?"

"I've never known how to talk to my children," King George said sadly. And Elizabeth could only nod; it was absolutely true. He never had, not even when they were small. After one of his gnashes, Bertie often shared his worst childhood memories: Not seeing his parents for weeks on end, only to be summoned for a royally wrathful scolding for some minor infraction like wearing the wrong hat or not shaking hands properly. His younger brother Prince John living apart from the family, hidden from view due to his epilepsy, rarely visited by his parents. Always, there was this hanging over his head and those of his siblings: Only perfect royal children were tolerated. Love never entered into any of it. Let alone intimate conversation with one's parents.

"I wish—but it's no good to look to the past," the King

continued. "I'm afraid I'm the last person my eldest would listen to. Why can't you try? He's so fond of you."

"Oh, I—sir, I don't think it's my place—"

"After I am dead," interrupted the King, his voice suddenly weak and unsteady, an old man's quaver, "that boy will ruin himself within twelve months. I pray that David will never marry and that nothing will come between Bertie, Lilibet, and the throne."

Elizabeth took a step backward as if to avoid a sudden splash of ice-cold water. How—how could King George say this? About his own son, his heir? How could he want Bertie, poor, valiant Bertie, to inherit the throne—how could he even conceive of burdening his second son in that way? And *Lilibet*? Sweet, innocent Lilibet? A little girl?

"Oh, Your Majesty," she said, tears filling her eyes. "You can't mean that."

The King simply shook his head slowly, the mantle of sadness heavier than any crown. Then he kissed her on the cheek and walked away.

As the ball increased in gaiety—the orchestra playing popular tunes intermingled with Strauss waltzes; the champagne continuing to flow even as most of the men were replacing it with tumblers of whiskey and Scotch; the women's color brightening beneath the blazing chandeliers, enhanced not only by cosmetics but by alcohol and the heat of a room packed with men in uniform—Elizabeth moved as if in a fog. She forgot what people said to her as soon as they said it; she heard her own voice uttering inanities as if from a great distance. Often, she paused in mid-sentence, searching for David and Bertie. Frequently they were together, laughing easily, freely.

Mrs. Simpson swam into view, her head comically large

atop her scant body. She hooked her arm through David's as if she owned him. David gazed at her—they were precisely the same height—with such adoration that Elizabeth had to turn away. The combination of his blinding devotion and her proprietary air was too unsettling.

Elizabeth scanned the crowded ballroom; Mr. Simpson was nowhere in sight.

"Dear Wallis," Elizabeth Bowes-Lyon said; she'd rushed to catch up with the pair, pursued by the troubling words of a troubled King. "Where is your charming husband? Such an interesting man. I did hope to see him tonight. I well remember our weekend together at the Fort, with Thelma."

Wallis turned toward her. She'd been in the middle of a conversation with a terrified Duke of Northumberland, who gave Elizabeth a look of gratitude as he fled for safer company. Wallis did not appear pleased to have been interrupted—the nerve of her!

"I'm not sure," she replied smoothly, not even bothering to pretend to scan the room for her husband. "You know how husbands are. Always disappearing just when you want them!"

"No, I'm afraid I don't know. My husband, the duke, is so devoted to one." She waved at Bertie, who was standing next to David; he smiled broadly and waved back, blowing her a kiss—bless the man!

Wallis's eyes narrowed.

"So touching. And how are your little girls?"

"Very well. Safe at home in the nursery."

"They're growing up so quickly, aren't they? Soon they'll be having their own engagement balls."

"I hardly think so," Elizabeth said with her perfectly charming laugh, causing heads to turn her way. "We don't grow up so fast here in England. Not as fast as they apparently do in America."

"We're not as fast as all that," Wallis said, her lips in a thin line.

"That's not my impression. Didn't you marry quite young? The *first* time, I mean."

Wallis stiffened, studied her perfectly manicured nails, then replied, "There was a war on."

"But your husband never actually saw combat, did he? Not like Bertie did."

"His expertise was required stateside. To train pilots."

"How interesting." Elizabeth yawned.

"Doesn't Marina look lovely?" Wallis pointedly changed the subject. "So refined. David is quite besotted with her. He believes she will be a real asset to the family, since she is a true royal and *so* elegant. Much needed, he believes. Someone the public can actually look up to. Instead of—oops! The prince is beckoning—you know how impatient he can get. Your Royal Highness."

And with another ridiculous curtsy—so exaggerated, it couldn't be anything but mocking—That Woman left to join David, who took her by the hand and led her out of the ballroom. When the two of them were gone, there was a little ripple of breeze in the air, as if a collective breath had been released.

Elizabeth, however, was still holding hers, lest her rage spill out for all to see.

"Come, Bertie," she said to her husband, who had suddenly appeared by her side. Smiling her brilliant smile as people bowed and curtsied, she began to lead him out of the ballroom.

"So soon, darling?"

"Not soon enough, dearest."

"What do you mean?"

"We're in trouble, Bertie. Real trouble." Her smile disappeared; she looked up at her husband, who had been enjoying himself; his eyes were a little bloodshot with drink, his stutter nonexistent.

But she wouldn't explain what she meant when he asked. He'd had such a nice evening, enjoying his brother's company. They had no idea, either of them, what their father had said. Had prayed for. Her heart broke for them both; they each laid claim to it, but in such very different ways. And Bertie, of course, was the one who needed her most—so his claim would always be greater.

What lay ahead for these two royal princes? For the King? For the country? For them all?

After I am dead, that boy will ruin himself within twelve months.

CHAPTER
7

LONDON

JANUARY 1936

YOU ARE ALL AND EVERYTHING I HAVE IN LIFE AND WE MUST hold each other so tight.

Wallis's hand trembled as she read the letter, special delivery from Sandringham. It was here. The moment she'd hoped for. The moment she'd dreaded.

David was at Sandringham, and the King was dying. David was at Sandringham, and the King was dying, but David had taken the time to write her. *WE*—his little moniker for Wallis and Edward. He had preened like a schoolboy when he came up with it, as if he were the most clever lad in all the land, to invent something like this!

And Wallis had laughed, had said, "Oh, David, how did you think of that? It's perfect!" She'd shaken her head in admiration and batted her eyelashes and given him all he wanted, all he needed, forever and ever and ever, amen.

Love. Attention. Praise. No, make that a *woman's* love, attention, and praise. He was surrounded by subservient courtiers and servants all the time, was the object of a nation's roaring approval whenever he stepped out of a car and doffed his derby and twinkled his eyes, a pipe or cigarette always dangling from his upturned mouth. But it wasn't enough. He was a vortex of need, never able to absorb enough real affection, affection offered by one woman, one singular woman who existed only for him.

First Freda, then Thelma. Now Wallis—but unlike the others, who had come from his same privileged world, Wallis was born to play her part, had studied all her life for it. Especially now, when the biggest prize of all was so close at hand—

The crown itself.

Sometimes, after she'd locked her bedroom door so no one would see, she stood in front of a mirror and stacked tiaras on top of each other and placed them on her head to get used to the weight.

Queen Wallis—would that do for a name? They did seem to take other names when they were crowned, these royals. David would be King Edward the something—the eighth, she believed it was. An Edward just like his grandfather—whose real name was Albert—had been. It was all very confusing, honestly, but David would explain it to her. He had already started to educate her on the intricacies of his family's ancestry, all those Tudors and Stuarts and Hanovers, but she really couldn't keep them straight. It wasn't as simple as Montagues and Warfields. But there were *people* for that, weren't there? People to keep things straight so that all she had to do was be next to David—King Edward!—and sit on gilded thrones and open Parliament and wear velvet and ermine and real crowns and, for heaven's sake, redecorate that awful Buck House, as he insisted on calling it. It was hideous! All that gilt! A child's rendering of a castle, and a bad one at that.

But—

But—

Now that it was here, this moment, not merely a fantasy shared by the two of them in bed after one of their nights when Wallis had shown him quite *im*proper deference—he was a slave in her hands, a crying, grateful slave—Wallis had to sit down. She smoothed the letter on her lap with trembling hands. Glanced at the clock on the mantel in the flat she still shared with Ernest, although it was filled with flowers every day courtesy of the Prince of Wales, its larder stocked with delicacies he sent. Her jewels were also provided by him, and many of her gowns (although she was also dressed by some of the best houses for free, since Mrs. Ernest Simpson was a regular fixture at the Ritz and the Savoy and, of course, Fort Belvedere). The Ernest Simpsons were going places, it was now universally acknowledged. The Prince of Wales himself had sponsored Ernest into the mysterious society of Masons, which granted him access to the most successful businessmen and politicians in all of London. The three of them, David, Wallis, and Ernest, were such good, good friends that Wallis had too many invitations to keep track of; she'd had to hire a social secretary (also paid for by David) to help.

The letter still on her lap, she read it again. The King had only hours left, according to the physicians.

"Wallis."

She looked up; Ernest had just entered the drawing room, his eyebrows drawn together, his face inexplicably sad.

"Did you hear the wireless? The King's not got much longer, apparently. God save his soul."

Wallis wanted to laugh. Ernest was so very—British—at this moment. His king was about to expire. He was already in mourning.

Then she peered at him again. There was now an unmistakable look of relief upon his face. No longer was he the thundercloud sitting in a corner moping as his wife and his sovereign-to-be dazzled together, the perennial third wheel. He looked stronger, more purposeful, than he had in months, maybe years. He looked like the man she had decided to marry long ago. The man who would take her places, give her the stability she'd never had.

"Yes, I've just received a letter from David, special delivery. He's at Sandringham."

"Well, he's doing his duty there, at least."

"What do you mean?"

"I mean that he's where he should be as the heir to the throne and a son. Instead of cavorting with you. He's acting like the Prince of Wales instead of a damned lovesick schoolboy."

"Don't. You're speaking entirely out of turn."

"Am I?" Ernest went over to the fireplace, removed an already packed pipe from a stand on the mantel, lit it, and threw the match into the fire. "Or am I speaking like your husband finally?"

"What on earth do you mean? Of course you're my husband." How ridiculous he was! He'd always been so complacent before, understanding the privilege of his wife being the royal mistress and happily reaping the benefits.

"I'm tired of this, Wallis. Utterly tired of the charade. This, thank God, will put an end to it. Once he's King, I mean."

"Will it?" Wallis smiled down at her lap, a secret little smile.

"What—you don't seriously think he'll *marry* you? That you'll be—good God, you don't think you'll be Queen of England, do you?" Ernest looked as if he didn't know whether to laugh or cry.

"David has—hinted at it, yes." Wallis folded the letter and rose, tired of sitting. Tired of waiting. Time for something to begin, something spectacular. For, to be perfectly honest, she was tired of David too—not only of his need for her attention but of his groveling desire to be of service to *her*. One evening at the Fort, surrounded by guests, she'd torn a nail. David had positively *bolted* from the drawing room and come panting back carrying her nail case, then proceeded to file the offending nail like a manicurist. It was a pathetic display and she'd told him so, not caring who heard—which, perversely, he *liked*. Whenever she lost her temper, scolded him in public, snapped at the constant tension of his electric, all-encompassing need and love, he accepted it. Too eagerly. It inflamed him, somehow, aroused him.

He was worse than the most devoted dog. And Wallis had never liked dogs.

In the beginning, she knew it would end someday and she viewed that as a relief. He would tire of her as he'd tired of all the others, hence her determination to get the most out of him while she could—the jewels, the clothes, the social status. Marrying him had never crossed her mind, not at first. Besides, she was quite fond of Ernest, in her own way.

However. Now that the King was dying, the tantalizing prospect of being Queen of England more than compensated for the stifling devotion. And David would be busy, much busier than he was now, doing what he called Kinging, whatever that meant. So he'd need her less, give her more space, once he was King and she Queen.

"I'm surprised at you, Wallis," Ernest said. He wasn't being insincere; he looked at her with tender consternation. "You're the smartest woman I've ever met. You live your life so carefully, calibrating everything. Taking no risks unless you've calculated the odds. You would have been a marvelous battlefield general. But you're utterly wrong about this. The British public would never allow it—you. An American. A divorcée. He'll be the head of the Church of England, for Christ's sake! And the church doesn't sanction divorce. Then there's the cabinet, the prime minister—are you really not aware of the obstacles?"

"He'll be the King of England and can do whatever he likes," Wallis replied coolly, walking to the window and peering out. Rain. Always rain. Black umbrellas shielded all those ordinary citizens of London, the people whose lives were so simple and drab. She felt pity for them.

"You have no idea—"

A knock on the drawing-room door; a butler walked in. "Madam, the telephone. Sandringham."

The clock ceased to tick, the rain to fall. She looked at Ernest, whose eyes filled with tears. This look, this last look—it was the end of something precious to her. As soon as she picked up the telephone, it would be the beginning of something so enormous she hadn't been able to imagine it or prepare for it, just as Ernest had said. A great gaping void of unknown, a world of castles and courtiers and crowds and prime ministers and tradition and cold looks from a widowed queen's eyes, stiff upper lip and carrying on and investitures and coronations, rituals and rites centuries old, towers and moats and walls, so many walls. So many fortresses. Wallis's legs felt unsteady as she followed the butler out to the hall, where the telephone receiver was on its side, waiting for her to pick it up.

The King was dead. Long live the King.

And God save Wallis.

THE NEXT DAY DAVID piloted himself—he loved to fly, although that was one thing she absolutely refused to do with him—from Sandringham to London. Wallis was waiting for him at the flat, but Ernest, after having written to the new King expressing his genuine sorrow at the passing of his father, had decided to be elsewhere.

Ernest was a good man, Wallis reflected as she waited for David, unsure what to do when he arrived—should she curtsy to him? How different would he be now that he was King? King George V had looked exactly like a king should, and Wallis had always taken comfort when people and things *fit*. A rose should look like a rose. A castle should look like a castle. A king should look like—

But try as she might, she couldn't picture David with a crown on his head. Always he was a boy to her, not a man, not like Ernest. Or even Win. The little prince, he was. Peter Pan, Ernest called him. But a little prince must grow into a king and this was what she couldn't imagine. A ghostly breeze blew through her heart—and she was superstitious enough to register it. Her hands were suddenly cold, so she turned toward the fire to warm them and didn't see the moment the new King of England came rushing through her drawing-room door.

"Wallis! My angel—oh God!"

He was in her arms. He was sobbing in her arms. Like a child, a little prince, still. Not a king, and her disappointment was another thing to note, a sobering reality, revising the fairy tale in her heart and mind.

Kings didn't always look like kings after all.

"David!" She guided him to the sofa while he still sobbed.

His eyes were red and puffy, and he looked as if he'd been crying all night. Which was puzzling, for he had never once displayed an ounce of love for or affection toward his father.

"It was awful, simply awful. Papa died—we were all there except for Elizabeth, who has pneumonia, and Papa was breathing so feebly. It was all too much for one, and I couldn't be like the others, the cold fish. They were so remote! Dispassionate! But I wasn't; I cried for my dear papa, I cried for it all to end. Then finally it did end, and Mama, the first thing she did—the very first thing before shedding a tear for dear Papa—she turned to me and curtsied and kissed my hand and said, 'Long live the King!' And I knew then that I'd never been a son to her, the same way Papa was never a husband. He was always the King, and I was always the heir, these *figures*—these roles she so reveres—and I knew that I'd lost any chance of ever being simply her son forever. I couldn't take it—I ran from the room and, darling, I so wanted you there! I couldn't bear being without you; every second of the ordeal I was missing you, needing you by my side. And thank God, here you are!"

He burst into a fresh torrent of tears, and Wallis wondered if he'd gone mad. He was always embarrassingly emotional, displayed all his feelings like the many medals on his chest, polished and gleaming for all to see. But she'd never witnessed him like this, an exhausted, hysterical child utterly overwhelmed by grief.

"David, darling—now, stop. I insist. Pull yourself together. You'll get sick if you keep this up."

"I'm sorry," he said, mopping his tears with the handkerchief she presented, then folding it neatly into quarters and handing it back. "It's just so—one is aware of this all one's life, you know. That someday your father will die and you will be King. And maybe you want to be King, but that means you want your father to die, so you can't ever, *ever* say anything out loud. You can't really let yourself think it, even. It's this huge cloud of fear and want, both, far into the future but there; you always see it. No matter which way you turn. But you—Wallis, you hid that cloud from me. You made me forget my damnable destiny. And I was happy then. Happier than I ever remember being. And now—here we are. My destiny has arrived."

"Long live the King," Wallis said, smiling tightly. Bravely. For once again she was seized with terror of all that was to come. Last night Ernest had punctured the first holes in her fantasy, and now, today, David's behavior—

She was dizzy, buffeted by ferocious waves of hope chased by dread. And then she asked herself a question she hadn't asked herself in a very long time:

What did *Wallis* want? This hysterical man in her arms moaning her name over and over, needing more than she could possibly ever give? Or the solid stability of Ernest, always so cool and blessedly detached in his affection and now suddenly solvent thanks to his friendship with her lover, the prince—the King, that is. The King?

Where was safe? Where was room to breathe in air perfumed with a thousand jasmine blossoms? She had a flash of memory from her time in China, after she'd left Win in Canton and fled to Peking. A memory of sitting on that cold concrete bench up on that hill every evening, all alone. Watching, far below, the small snake that turned into the daily camel train, hearing the bells all the way up where she sat, undisturbed. There, she had no need to impress or flatter, the burden of the perpetual houseguest. And in her peaceful solitude she allowed her mind to go blank, forgetting the questions always looming about her future, forgetting that she didn't have a home of her own or even the money necessary to get back to the States. It was always the one perfect moment of her day. The moment she merely lived. Like everyone else, no better, no worse, she had a right to draw air into her lungs.

She hadn't had a tranquil moment like that in—well. Since she and David had become such good "friends."

"Wallis, my darling." David pushed himself away, grimaced at the tearstains on her silk blouse, and kissed her hand so passionately, she could feel his teeth pressing behind his lips.

"Yes, David?" Wallis pulled her hand away, patted at her blouse, stood up, and walked away to go change it.

"How would you like to witness history?"

She stopped, turned around. The prince—the King of England—was now on his feet and grinning at her, rubbing his hands together gleefully.

"What do you mean?" She had one eyebrow cocked.

"My proclamation—the public ceremony, not the privy council; that's where I'm headed next. Tomorrow is the public ceremony, when the proclamation is read aloud outside St. James's. I have it all arranged for you to witness it—and, by God, I think I'll join you. I'm not supposed to but, damn it, I'm the King! I can do whatever I want and they might as well get used to it. Starting now."

"Oh, David!" Wallis rushed back to him, took his hands. "How marvelous! Of course I can't wait—what shall I wear?"

"Something black, darling. You'll have to wear black; the court is in mourning for at least six months."

"Of course."

The court is in mourning.

She, then, was—part of the court. Of the King of England. Who was besotted with her, putty in her hands. Saving a front-row seat to history for her. History she would soon be making herself.

This was power. The power she'd first glimpsed back in China, with Win in Canton, so long ago. The power of a woman; the power behind the throne. The air in her lungs rarified now, perfumed with veneration instead of jasmine.

What did Wallis want?

Everything.

CHAPTER

8

LONDON

JANUARY 1936

"Y-Y-YOU W-W-WON'T BELIEVE IT," BERTIE STAMMERED. He reddened, swore, then yanked off his suit coat and threw it at a table, knocking over a vase; it crashed to the floor and shattered into dozens of pieces.

"Bertie!" Elizabeth—still recovering from pneumonia but stronger today than she had been—flung off her bedclothes, ran to her husband, and guided him away from the mess while simultaneously pressing a buzzer to summon someone to clean it up.

"The b-b-bastard. My br-br-brother the fucking K-K-K-King!" Bertie ran his hand over his eyes, deepening the creases already there. It had been such a trying few days, and she'd been stuck here in bed, away from all the drama.

Not that she was complaining, mind you. There was something delicious in the convenience of an illness that forced one to lie in bed for weeks on end, reading novels and doing puzzles and hiding away from the cares of the world. *Extraordinary* cares these days.

But poor Bertie had been in the thick of it. The agonizing wait by the deathbed, the acute embarrassment caused by David's ridiculous behavior—sobbing like a child, Bertie said! His brother had behaved extraordinarily badly, even considering the circumstances, alternating between cries of despair as his father struggled for breath and running from the room like little Margaret might have! Yes, it was a tragic occasion, and the Prince of Wales was naturally the person most affected by his father's death, but even so, David had been preparing for this all his life.

"Whatever is wrong, Bertie? What did he do now?" Just when she thought things would settle down. Not that she didn't mourn the dear King, dear Papa! He was always so kind to one, so thoughtful. But no one could have been surprised by his death. And despite the dear, dead King's fears—she remembered how troubled he was at George and Marina's ball, the disturbing prediction he had made—surely David understood that now he was King, he would have to behave. He could do the acceptable thing and install Mrs. Simpson in a country house far away from the court and polite society. Kings had done that sort of thing for as long as there had been kings. They did not parade their mistresses around court for all to see—well, at least not since Henry VIII, anyway.

"He brought her! M-M-Mrs. Simpson! D-D-David brought her to St. James's and positioned her in front of a big window for all to see—and then he stood next to her! And watched his own proclamation with her beside him."

"Oh, Bertie!" Elizabeth had to sit down on a chair, her legs were so weak. And not because of her illness. A sick twisting of her intestines caused a little moan to escape; her skin was clammy with dread.

"I don't understand him. He's not my brother, not the brother I looked up to all my life. To bring *her* to such a solemn, *public* occasion—and to witness it himself, like a commoner! It's simply never been done before, kings are not supposed to be there gaping at the pageantry like damn t-t-tourists. There are certain things that have to be respected. Certain ways of doing things. And I'm afraid he's going to bust them all up, starting with the clocks—did I tell you that? The first thing he did, practically, even before Papa took his final breath, was order all the clocks at Sandringham to be set back up to the proper time. Then he muttered something about modernizing things, and when it was all over, he left—flew back to *her*. And now what happened today—where will it end?"

"When That Woman has a crown on her head, I'm afraid," Elizabeth said weakly.

"N-never!" Bertie was fumbling at his tie, trying to unknot it, but his hands were so clenched, his knuckles so white, he was doing a miserable job of it. Elizabeth flew to him, untied it expertly before he could knock something else over. She'd never seen her husband so distraught and it was terrifying. She was afraid the girls up in the nursery might hear.

"Bertie, darling. Ticktock, remember? Tick—" She brushed the inside of his wrist with her index finger, gently. "Tock." She brushed it again, then repeated the words and motion until Bertie's face didn't look quite so mottled, until his breathing slowed down to a reasonable rate.

"I'm sorry, dearest. I'm sorry—I don't mean to frighten you when you're still recovering."

"I'm much better today." She gifted him with one of her famous sunny smiles, and he relaxed even more.

"I simply don't understand him at all," Bertie said, slumping into a chair to kick off his shoes. His hair was all mussed and rumpled and he looked, endearingly, like a grumpy little boy. "There were so many newspapermen and photographers. I don't know how many saw her, of course. And heaven knows I couldn't see her, positioned as I was with George and Henry. Tommy told me; he was there."

"Dear Tommy," Elizabeth murmured. Tommy Lascelles was the late King's secretary. Such a loyal retainer! And he positively hated David; he'd once worked for the prince but asked to be reassigned; Elizabeth had no idea why.

But Elizabeth didn't hate David. Did she? At one time, she couldn't have imagined it. She still felt the same delicious thrill in his company she'd felt as a debutante. And they'd become thick as thieves after her marriage, sharing their little jokes and making fun—privately, of course!—of some of the more noticeable quirks of the King and Queen. Including, she had to admit, the King's obsession with keeping the clocks at Sandringham set ahead half an hour so that he could fit in more shooting.

No. She didn't hate David; she could never hate him. But she could hate the person behind his preposterous behavior.

"Bertie, do you know if your dear papa ever *talked* to David about his—weakness? I did urge him to."

Bertie laughed sourly. "No, I don't know. But I can very well imagine that he did not. Talking wasn't exactly my father's strong suit, now, was it?"

"No. But surely the Queen—"

"That's even more unthinkable than the King."

"Then perhaps you can? Perhaps David—he's very distraught, Bertie. Like we all are. He's not thinking clearly. But he loves you, he would never do anything to hurt you. He would listen to our—*your*—concerns."

"I suppose I could try," he said doubtfully. Then his eyes lit up with relief. "But, honestly, darling, you should be the one to talk sense into him. He's always liked you. He'll listen to reason if *you* explain to him why his behavior regarding Mrs. Simpson is unacceptable."

"Oh, Bertie!" Elizabeth laughed, but it turned into a cough, and she had to drink a glass of water. After she'd caught her breath, she continued. "That's precisely why I can't talk to him about this. I'm a woman. He'll think it's because I'm jealous or spiteful."

"But that's absurd—"

"I know," she said hastily, averting her gaze as she remembered how thrillingly her heart had beat when she'd danced with the Prince of Wales before she ever knew his brother.

"I suppose we can hope that the funeral and all will remind him of his duty. Of what's proper and right. He'll be among his own kind then, with all the other crowned heads of Europe. I've been with the Queen and the prime minister today, making up the list."

"Yes, of course. I'm sure it will remind him," Elizabeth agreed, relieved at this possibility. Because as much as she despised the situation, she also didn't want to have to deal with it. It was so very unpleasant! And Elizabeth Bowes-Lyon absolutely detested unpleasantness. She had engineered her life so that she could have as untroubled a time as possible. Marriage to the second son, not the heir. Mother of two little girls, who gave her an excuse to get out of cutting ribbons and making speeches when she'd rather putter in the garden or put up her feet in front of a roaring fire and eat scones. But still with enough privilege that she could surround herself with comfort and indulgence. David becoming King wouldn't change anything much, other than providing her with more opportunities to dazzle at court balls and dinners. Really, her life was perfect. There was no reason why it couldn't continue along such enjoyable lines even now.

"It will all blow over, I'm sure of it," she said with a little nod—as much for herself as for her husband, whose troubled face smoothed into relief.

"Of course. We just have to get through these next few days, and he'll return to form—he's David! No matter how frustrating he can be, he never lets one down in the end. I should have remembered that before I blew in here like a thundercloud and upset you! I apologize, darling. Can I get you a glass of champagne? You are still recovering, you know. A glass of champagne is just what the doctor ordered."

"Lovely! Thank you, Dr. Bertie! Now, why don't you go and change into a dressing gown and have a drink also? You must rest up for everything to come. And for heaven's sake, let's not worry about David! Not tonight." She went to her husband, knelt beside him, and lay her head upon his lap. For a few quiet moments they remained like this, Bertie stroking her hair; she felt tension washing out of him in gentle waves, and then she rose and kissed him.

"Bless you, my dear." Bertie got up from the chair with a groan and headed out to his own room through the connected dressing room with its wardrobes lining either side. "I'm very sorry about the vase. Was it valuable?"

"Not one bit!" She smiled, deciding not to tell him it was a souvenir from Venice, bought when she was eight and visiting her grandmother there. He had enough on his mind, and the funeral was yet to come.

THE ENSUING DAYS BLURRED into one muddled, somber loop of memories she would replay for the rest of her life. The astonishing moment when all four of the King's surviving sons, in dress uniform, stood at attention around their father's casket as his body lay in state at Westminster Hall—this was at David's direction and she felt a rush of warmth toward him when she heard about it from the Queen, who was deeply touched by the Vigil of the Princes.

The burial was at Windsor, and the moment the vault was lowered into the floor of the chapel while a bagpipe played mournfully, Queen Mary stood like a marble statue of grief; no tears, but the lines in her face were visible even behind her black veil. Bertie kept swallowing, his Adam's apple moving up and down, and blinking hard, doing his best to prevent a sob—and succeeding, to her everlasting pride.

David appeared unexpectedly diminished and touchingly alone. Standing slightly away from the rest of the family, misery on his face. Looking perplexingly unprepared for the moment—and for all that lay ahead.

That was when Elizabeth—hiding behind her own black veil—fully realized that Bertie was now first in the line of succession. Only his brother—so fragile, his lonely bachelor status never more starkly in evidence than in that instant—stood between him and the throne of England. Her sadness for the poor King was all but forgotten in the shock of this realization; her heart began to beat rapidly, her breaths coming shallowly in the stuffy little St. George's Chapel, the cloying scent of lilies and mothballs—why didn't people have the sense to air out their uniforms and mourning clothes beforehand?—not helping one bit.

And she remembered what the King—the late King—had said to her at George and Marina's ball.

Nothing must happen to David; nothing must get in the way of him stepping into the role he was born for. And he had to marry! Certainly by now, he had to know where his duty lay. He was the King of England. He had no time to dally with married American women. If he didn't understand, if he didn't shape up, Bertie would be doomed.

And so would she. And so would Lilibet.

Queen Mary sniffed, loudly, significantly, and Elizabeth snapped out of her reverie. Looking down at her hands, she saw that she'd crumpled the funeral program until it was folded like a fan. Guiltily, she hid it behind her back.

After the funeral luncheon was over—a morose affair, although occasional bursts of laughter from some of the visiting royals, Queen Marie of Romania in particular, couldn't be prevented—Elizabeth stole away and hid in one of the private sitting rooms with a pounding headache. The room was overdecorated with the kind of bric-a-brac that Queen Mary so loved—jade figurines, ornamental boxes, porcelain bowls, wax flower arrangements.

"Your Royal Highness." Tommy Lascelles must have followed her, for he bowed, then stood in front of her, obviously wanting to say something.

"Oh, Tommy, I'm sorry—I just had to get away, what a ghastly day."

"Of course, ma'am. Ghastly for all of us. Ghastly in ways we perhaps don't yet know."

"What?" She rubbed her temples, and Tommy immediately rang for a footman.

"Whiskey and soda, ma'am?"

"Yes, that would be heaven." The footman left. "What do you mean, Tommy?"

"Were you aware, ma'am, that Mrs. Simpson was watching the funeral procession today? That the pr—His Majesty arranged for her to watch from inside a building along the route? And that many people saw her?"

"No!" Her heart sank, and the footman approached with the tumbler just in time; she took a healthy gulp and relished the warmth as it coated her still-raw throat. She would have a stiff hot toddy this evening before bed. "What was David thinking? She at least should have had the good sense to stay away today. I thought—I hoped and prayed—that all this, the funeral, everything, would put an end to that once and for all."

"So did I, ma'am. So did we all."

"I can't talk to him, I can't tell him what to do—Queen Mary should! He's her son!"

"But she hasn't, and I fear she won't. Now that he's King, and, you know—"

"Yes, I know."

"Elizabeth! There you are!"

She and Tommy sprang apart like guilty children as David strode into the room.

"Tommy." He nodded at his former aide, the man who had been the assistant private secretary to King George in the final months of his life. Now Tommy was *David's* assistant private secretary; Elizabeth hid a small smile at the prospect of them working together again.

"Your Majesty." Tommy nodded in perfectly correct obeisance to his new king and took a step back.

"Good God," David said, pulling at his tie and flopping next to her on the sofa. "What a crushing day. I'm simply wrung out. But before I return to the Fort, I wanted to invite you and Bertie over tomorrow. Wallis sends her love and sympathy, of course, and is dying to see you both. It's been too long."

"Oh, well—" Dear Papa had asked Elizabeth not to associate with That Woman, so she and Bertie hadn't, much. Did David miss them? Once again that cursed memory of a girl's infatuation flared up. Oh, when did one cease being a silly little debutante at heart?

"No, I quite understand," David interrupted, touchingly anxious, which only increased her discomfort. He laid a hand on her arm. "It was the King's wish that you not see Wallis, just as he and Mama would not. I know he asked that of you, and you were right to obey. You and Bertie both did that much for him, and it gave him comfort. God knows I rarely did. But now that—well, things are different, and I do hope we can resume our friendship. Wallis thinks so fondly of you, you know."

Say it, Elizabeth's heart cried out with a ferocity that caused her to almost spill her drink. *Say it—say what I long to hear!*

"As of course do I," he finished.

Disappointment stamped out that little flame of infatuation. He'd said it so perfunctorily.

"How nice of her, how nice of you both." From across the room, where he was gazing out a window, Tommy Lascelles cleared his throat. Elizabeth sat up straighter, taking a sip of her drink before continuing. "However, David, we are in mourning." It was as much of a rebuke as she could muster; after all, he was her king now.

"Yes, but it's only for six months—I've decreed it, did you know? None of this yearlong horror like before—and tomorrow is a private party, strictly on the q.t. No one will know, and I'd say we all need a jolly good time after all this silly, taxing pomp and circumstance."

She heard a sharp intake of breath from Tommy, and Elizabeth had a difficult time maintaining her composure herself. *Silly! Taxing!* They'd only just buried the King of England—David's own father!

"David, again, how very nice of you to ask. But Bertie and I will remain with dear Mama for the next few days. After all, one must see how devastated she is. We mustn't upset her." This she said more pointedly, but still David didn't take the hint.

"Ah, well. Another time. I'm off—don't tell anyone I've gone, not for a few minutes, anyway. Give a fellow a chance to sneak away." David leaned in and kissed Elizabeth on both cheeks. Then he leaped up and stood for a moment, scrutinizing her clothes. "You know what Wallis said to me the other day? She said she hadn't worn black stockings since she gave up the cancan! How amusing! She's wonderfully refreshing, isn't she?"

"I can only assume," Elizabeth said, acutely aware of her own black stockings, entirely proper and respectful—*dutiful and dull,* no doubt, to David's eyes. To wear flesh-colored stockings in mourning? How very American!

How very Wallis.

"Oh, I almost forgot! Wallis said you wanted to know the name of her dressmaker. I can't remember it, but you should ring her up at the Fort. Isn't that generous of her? So kind."

David sauntered out of the room as she swallowed a retort.

He was an entirely different person from the sad little figure at the funeral whose hand had shaken as he sprinkled earth on top of his father's coffin.

"Ma'am?"

Tommy was in front of her again, peering down from his great height.

"Yes?"

"I'm afraid that the new King is continuing his old ways."

"That seems to be the case, doesn't it?" She sat her glass down, rose, and held out a hand to Tommy. "Do please keep me informed, won't you? As much as you can? Let me know if there is more to be concerned about. There might—" She swallowed, her throat suddenly burning. Oh, how unpleasant it all was! But it was clear that no one but herself and Tommy had the spine to do anything about it. "There might be something I can do if he continues to associate with that—with her. Something I once heard."

"How very mysterious," Tommy said with an unexpected twinkle in his eye; she'd never seen him so much as hint at a smile before. "I'll be in touch, Your Royal Highness." Tommy gave her hand a firm shake—they were in business together now.

He bowed and turned on his heel, was gone in an instant.

Elizabeth walked to the window and peered down at the gravel courtyard. David—his top hat on, his black coat buttoned against the chilly rain—was getting into the large black royal Daimler bought by King George only a couple of years prior that was now his to use. He hated it, she knew. He preferred his own Buick, which he'd bought the previous year, complete with a drinks cabinet in the back. She wondered how long he'd keep the Daimler; how long he'd keep any of the items and people who had had anything to do with his father, and his grandfather before him, and Queen Victoria before *him*. Bertie was already alarmed at the things David was talking about, budget cuts and selling properties like Sandringham and laying off loyal retainers.

She wondered how deeply his hatred for his father ran and if it would grow to include them all, his brothers and sister and in-laws, his two nieces. His mother. The cabinet. Parliament. The British people in general.

The car's headlights blinked on and she couldn't hear but could imagine the sound of the tires crunching on the gravel in the drive as the Daimler drove out of the courtyard toward the Long Walk. And suddenly Windsor Castle seemed empty, despite the voices of all the assorted crowned heads of Europe and members of the extended royal family still echoing down the hall. But there was no king here, not anymore. King George, with his cold blue eyes and tobacco-stained beard and ridiculous blue parrot always on his shoulder—where was that bird now? Who had taken it?—and his unmistakable, unshakable respect for tradition and the very pomp and circumstance that drove his son mad, was no longer.

And King Edward VIII had left to play games and drink cocktails with his American mistress and their irreverent friends. She shook her head. Then turned her thoughts back to that afternoon at Royal Lodge, the Yorks' home on the grounds of Windsor, right before Thelma Furness went to America and ruined everything.

BERTIE AND DAVID WERE frolicking in the garden with the girls—they adored their uncle David, who showered them with gifts and was an impish playmate, forever youthful. That's how Elizabeth had seen him then, Peter Pan with a crown hovering on the horizon.

"Ah, this is bliss," Thelma said, stretching like a cat in front of the fireplace, a tea table piled high with tempting goodies. "Sometimes I get weary of always having to entertain him, you know." She gestured vaguely at one of the windows overlooking the garden. "Of trying to come up with new games or amusing people, since he bores so easily."

"Amusing people like the Simpsons?" Elizabeth, her dainty feet perched on an upholstered stool, nibbled at a scone covered in clotted cream.

"Oh, yes. Yes, Wallis has been a big hit. Ernest has too, in his own way—a more boring man I never met, but David can talk to him for hours about old palaces and stuffy cathedrals."

"Wallis seems to know her way around men," Elizabeth observed, picking up the latest *Tatler*—Diana Cooper was on the cover, languidly beautiful as always. "She doesn't appear to have any female friends other than you. And have you noticed that she always makes a beeline for the men at parties?"

"Oh, my dear, you don't know the half of it." Thelma giggled mischievously.

"What? Oh, do tell!" Elizabeth sat up, put the scone and magazine down, and rubbed her hands with glee. Gossip! Thelma was a lifesaver in this way. The domestic Yorks, however beloved they might be, were rarely invited to the fun parties anymore. They'd become paragons of respectability, *ideals,* the four of them. Without Thelma, Elizabeth would have been entirely cut off from all the juicy gossip that stirred her blood.

"Well, apparently—and you didn't hear this from me!—

our friend spent a very mysterious year in the Orient. Hong Kong, or maybe Peking—I'm a little fuzzy on the specifics. This was when she was married to her *first* husband, the aviator. And while she was there, I'm told she visited some very Oriental brothels and learned some very Oriental ways of—pleasing—men, if you understand what I'm saying."

"No!" Elizabeth nearly clapped with joy. Oh, this was delicious!

"Yes! I'm told she's had many lovers, and, my dear, we both know she's not much to look at. Oh, she has a certain style, I'll grant her that. Very chic. But that figure! Flat as a board, and those huge hands. But what she can do with those hands—"

"Thelma!" Elizabeth looked around to make sure there were no servants listening.

"Oh, don't be such a prude!"

"I'm not! I'm simply—but why are you friends with her? Why did you introduce her to David if she's so, well—naughty?"

"Naughty!" Thelma threw back her head and laughed until tears made ruin of her makeup. "Oh, Elizabeth! Only you would say that, darling. Darling, darling little Elizabeth."

"Well, I don't know any other word to use!" Elizabeth's cheeks reddened.

"Try *decadent. Sexual. Perverted.*" Thelma drew in a big breath and dried her tears, although her shoulders still shook with laughter.

"Oh!" Elizabeth was simply going to combust with embarrassment even as her pulse quickened.

"I'm told she met all sorts of unsavory characters during that time. And performed herself at some of those brothels, made up to look like an Oriental, they say. And you know she *loves* to wear those funny Chinese dresses with the little collars at parties, just to stand out! No wonder her husband always looks satisfied. And not just her husband—she has lovers. She's hinted at it. Some car dealer, I gather. How else do you think she gets those jewels and nice clothes? Her husband's business almost went bust a year or so ago."

"Why, she's a—a scarlet woman!" Even as Thelma burst into more whoops of laughter, Elizabeth vowed that the next time she met Wallis, she would try to detect signs of decadence and perversion. She'd never met a truly wicked woman before; it would be quite thrilling.

IT HAD BEEN GREAT fun to gossip with Thelma about That Woman back then, when she was harmless, just a passing—deliciously scandalous—diversion.

But now—

God bless Thelma, thought Elizabeth as she steeled herself to go back to the rest of the family, who would all be wondering where the King had gone. Just how and when she would deploy Thelma's information remained a mystery. But Elizabeth would sleep better tonight—after that blessed hot toddy, with double rum and lots of honey—knowing she was armed and loaded.

Just waiting for one good, clean shot.

CHAPTER

9

THE LOTUS YEAR

1924

WALLIS TOLD EVERYONE SHE WAS JOINING WIN AT HIS new post in Hong Kong because she had to give her marriage one more chance. After all, the heart knows what it wants. And love conquers all.

This was a colossal lie.

She joined Win in Hong Kong because she couldn't afford to divorce him in the States, since Uncle Sol had refused to give her the money. Mama, married for the third time, couldn't help. Aunt Bessie, as much as she truly loved Wallis, couldn't stomach the idea of the first Montague family divorce, so she wouldn't help either.

During the brief time she was separated from Win, while she was staying in Washington, DC, Wallis had tasted freedom. Freedom from violence, from fear. But not freedom from being a married woman concerned about her reputation. With no money of her own and living on what Win could spare from his navy salary, once more Wallis had to rely upon acquaintances—rarely friends; she didn't make friends and perhaps for the first time she wondered about that—to keep her in society. She'd brought her patented wit and flair to their parties, and in return her hosts introduced her to diplomats and attachés. So she read up on politics, learned how to flatter these ambitious men whose lives were a never-ending series of ladder rungs to climb, their eyes always on the top job.

And these men were charmed by Wallis. At first. They responded to her total absorption, her ability to make them feel as if they were the only men in the room. Then there would be long walks at night along the Potomac or the Mall, taking in the beauty of the Lincoln Memorial under moonlight while Wallis listened, bored but never showing it, to their career plans. But she would press a hand meaningfully, take an arm to steady herself after tripping on a crack. Pause and gaze at the moonlight, breath carefully held, eyes purposely soulful. And soon the talk would stop.

Always at night. Never in broad daylight; whenever she tried to arrange a date with one of the men for lunch or dinner at a restaurant, she would be fobbed off. Politely, because the moonlit walks and sometimes more were still on offer. It was puzzling; it was hurtful. Wallis realized she would never be a prize to them, only a diversion. She couldn't fund their ambitions—the number of diplomats married to heiresses was astonishing until you calculated the cost of success in Washington—with only her flattering attention and smart dressing. And she was, after all, still married, if only in name.

But divorced or married, she had no money. Flattery wasn't enough. Style wasn't enough. What you could do in a hotel room, eyes shut and teeth gritted, wasn't enough.

So when she got the telegram from Win in Hong Kong suggesting she join him, that they try once more, she had no other option. And she did have a thirst to see some of the exotic places her diplomat friends had told her about; she'd felt so provincial, never having traveled beyond Baltimore and Win's navy bases. She joined dozens of other navy wives on a ship in Norfolk and six weeks later was being greeted, tentatively, by her husband in the port of Hong Kong. Win looked as handsome as he had the first time she'd beheld him: tanned, strong, and clear-eyed. He told her he hadn't touched a drink since she'd cabled that she would join him.

Wallis had no choice but to hope that was true, and so her Lotus Year began.*

HONG KONG

Even before the ship had sailed into the harbor, Wallis was wrapped in a damp sheet of humidity, fighting to catch her breath. Win, after giving her a hesitant handshake by way of a greeting, saw her wilt—she did; she felt exactly like a fresh flower cut off from all nourishment—and told her that several baths a day did the trick. As a rickshaw drove them up a winding, snaking road to the top of a hill where his apartment was situated, she registered several first impressions: That the streets were narrow, crowded, full of signs in Chinese that, of course, she couldn't read. That the town was actually on a mountain and so most of the roads were steep. That there were nauseating smells she couldn't identify. That there were also many signs in English advertising British staples such as tea, jam, tobacco, and gin. She would learn, to her astonishment, that in Hong Kong, Americans barely mattered. It was the ruling British who made up what she would call society.

But she wouldn't be part of that society. Because almost immediately, Win began drinking again and showing alarming signs of paranoia—insisting on opening all her mail, telling her he'd heard stories of her flirting with officers on the ship. Well, of course she'd flirted! It was her most expressive language and Win knew that. But that didn't mean she'd had affairs; she'd made sure not to cross that line on a navy ship full of gossiping officers and their wives.

But Win wouldn't believe it. And when she didn't want to sleep with him—why would she? Who wants to make love to a slobbering drunk who passes out on top of you?—he reverted to type. And she was trapped, once more, in the maniacal cycle of violence, locked doors, penitent crying for forgiveness, vows that it would never happen again, and always—the bottle.

Then Win was posted to Canton.

CANTON

Where her husband took her to singsong houses, to learn how to please a man—"Because there's no woman colder than you below the waist, Wallis. You may try to look like a woman, but you don't act like one."

She felt struck with a well-aimed arrow, because it was true—she never had felt arousal like she'd heard other women whisper about; her sexual organs always had felt undeveloped or numb or otherwise unnecessary. She was shamed.

Shamed, embarrassed, appalled, to sit next to her husband, this man who revolted her but who kept a firm grip on her arm to prevent her escape, and watch him salivate over the pretty Chinese singsong girls in their sleek silk cheongsams, dresses made in beautiful saturated colors of red, green, blue, and violet, bending and turning so gracefully. Yet Wallis was mesmerized in spite of herself. With their faces downcast so their eyes seduced from an appealingly bashful angle, they sang their strange, warbling Chinese songs that bewitched and beguiled.

And their hips gracefully swaying to and fro hypnotized.

Win would grow hard, take her hand, and place it on his penis, and he'd whisper vulgarities in Wallis's ear, proposing that she join him upstairs with her favorite girl—"Pick one out, Wallis. You know you want to. Maybe that will finally get your motor running."

And even as she was repulsed—felt the bile rise and burn her throat—something flickered in her belly, twinged between her legs. Was it desire? Or merely a spark of daring, of thrill, that she was halfway across the globe from staid little Baltimore and that claustrophobic Victorian house and Uncle Sol's perpetual disapproval and Mama's eternal need and that she was in an exotic pleasure palace dotted with opium dens, with their sickly sweet fragrance and somnambulant victims, next to gambling rooms where men with long pigtails threw dice, cheered on by sailors. Where, when the girls had finished singing their siren songs, they bashfully shuffled offstage with those seductive glances, knowing that men would join them in the upstairs rooms doing things that Wallis could only imagine. Because she never once joined Win, refused his taunting to pick out a favorite girl; it was the only dignity left to her, the dignity of refusal. She never hid her disgust when he went up without her and told her to enjoy herself while she waited.

But she returned to those houses, with and without him. Obsessed with the girls onstage, marveling at their control, at their sleek figures in those stylish cheongsams, the teasing glances—they drove men to such a state before they even had to touch them that sex seemed almost superfluous.

They had power, these women. Power that Wallis did not.

Maybe if she had mastered their skills before she met Win, she would have been able to control him, to prevent the drinking, to satisfy him without demeaning herself so that he wouldn't need to punish her with his fists. Maybe she would have been such a prize that some Washington diplomat on his way up the ladder would have asked her to accompany him.

Maybe if she mastered those skills now, she would find a way to afford a divorce after all.

When she thought of Canton later, it was of those houses and all she learned from them. How to smoke an opium pipe and blow perfect rings of vapor, drums beating in the distance, always—where they were, what they signified, she never did find out. But it seemed, at least in her memories, that there was constantly this steady percussion outside, coming down from the mountains themselves, echoing the beating of her heart. Reminding her that she was alive, a person with agency. No matter how many times Win—and Uncle Sol—had tried to convince her otherwise.

She learned how to cut and deal cards, how to expertly conceal an inside straight—this she mastered after a night spent gambling with two British sailors and a Chinese horse trader. How to drive a man crazy with a look, a smile. A touch. How to feel him helpless in your hands.

And she'd remember Win, ruby red in the face from alcohol, his features bloated and smudged once more, stumbling down the stairs of those houses, grabbing her roughly by the arm, and taking her back to their rooms—but then that memory was like all the other memories of her marriage. Except for this: One night, one kick, an explosion of pain that made her vomit. That, she would never forget.

These were her final memories of Canton—waking up on

the floor covered in her own fluids, a vicious pounding in her ears that wasn't a drumbeat, her skin on fire and a throbbing in her upper back, words pouring out of her mouth that she couldn't understand, that made no sense. Nothing made sense. Then bright lights blinding her, antiseptic halls and a needle in her arm, the menthol smell of anesthesia, more darkness, and finally—

Waking up in cool, crisp white sheets. In a narrow metal bed surrounded by other metal beds, and a sober, penitent Win sitting next to her, his face and clothes rumpled.

"It's lucky you didn't lose that kidney" was all the doctor said to her. He seemed too busy for the likes of such an ordinary couple. An ordinary, miserable, abusive man and an ordinary, miserable, abused wife.

As soon as she could walk without having to sit down every three steps, she left Win. For good this time.

But she wasn't ready to leave China; there was still more to see, to learn—she heard it in those drums, pounding from farther up the mountains. She smelled it in the breeze, carrying jasmine and rain and forgiveness. So one day, all alone with only the hope of Win's monthly navy pay that he'd penitently promised to send her, she boarded a steamer to Shanghai.

SHANGHAI

"Whatever you do, don't go to Shanghai," women had warned her back in Washington when she was preparing to leave.

"Whatever you do, you must see Shanghai," their husbands had told her in private.

An intoxicating mixture of heaven and hell, a city teeming with refugees: White Russians selling the last of their smuggled jewels and, when those were gone, themselves; wandering Americans; imperious Japanese; hungry Koreans. No one needed a visa or a passport to visit Shanghai, so every lost soul seeking forgiveness or salvation washed up on its shores.

Rickety junks on the Huangpu River, rattly trams on the Nanking Road. No electricity, so vaporous gas lights lit the city, giving it a sinister look. The smell of fish and seaweed mixed with sewage. Another cacophony of warring accents and language.

More singsong houses than in Canton. An entire social hierarchy of prostitution, from male opera singers down to the lowly saltwater sisters, whose clientele were sailors. A veritable city within a city of vice, entire streets lined with bordellos and singsong houses and teahouses. The Opium Wars weren't that long ago, and gangs still fought for territories—it wasn't that unusual to see police fishing bodies out of the river.

And another city within the city: the International Settlement, where American and British citizens lived along the main thoroughfare, the Bund, as if at one uninterrupted garden party.

After checking into the Astor House Hotel with an acquaintance from the ship, a fellow navy wife, Wallis contacted an Englishman whose name she'd been given back in Washington. Robbie was a debonair young businessman, an architect.

Robbie was safe. He was harmless. He was a homosexual, the perfect companion for a woman still hobbling around with a kidney bruised by her alcoholic husband.

It was like walking out of a nightmare and into a dream, her weeks in Shanghai. The residents of the International Settlement seemed intent on pretending they weren't in the heart of one of the most exotic cities in the world. As if they were in London or New York—as if there weren't a dozen other languages being spoken just outside the gates or rickshaws in the streets instead of taxis. There were garden parties, horse races, polo matches, and dinner dances accompanied by the latest West End and Broadway musical scores. But unlike London or New York, here the air was fragrant with jasmine, and colorful lanterns lit up every terrace and path.

Wallis could relax. She was still married, but no one cared that she seemed to have misplaced her husband. No one was looking for a woman to help attain more power. No one had any ambition in Shanghai, only appetites to be sated, pleasures to enjoy, senses to indulge. For the first time, Wallis let her guard down and wasn't punished for it. Or kicked, slapped, or punched.

There would be no visits to singsong houses as long as she remained safe within the privileged walls of the International Settlement—and for a time, she was content to linger there. Robbie flattered her, was a divine dance partner, made her laugh with his silly conversation—and then chastely kissed her on the cheek at night and went off to prowl the darker streets outside the settlement to satisfy his own—exotic—tastes.

But there was more of China to see, and when she was completely strong, refreshed and recharged, Wallis was on the move once more. Aboard the Shanghai Express to Peking.

PEKING

She had plenty of time on that train journey to reflect upon why she was so restless. Between terrifying interludes when various warlords stopped the train to search for enemies (she was frightened to the brink of incontinence the first time but soon realized it was all theatrics; no one was going to harm a white woman traveling under the protection of the United States government), she burrowed into her second-class seat and wondered what on earth she was doing.

Surely a normal woman would have returned to the bosom of her family now that her marriage was thoroughly finished. A Montague or a Spencer would certainly have done that. But the ghosts of her ancestors were strangely quiet within her; she felt out of reach of the tentacles of family and good breeding and obligation to tradition that ruled Uncle Sol, her mother, and Aunt Bessie. Adrift, she had no energy to propel herself in one direction or the other. But backward motion filled her with rage, and she fought, furiously, against its current. China had awakened something in her and Wallis was newly hungry—not for food, never for food. But for something *more*. Maybe it was simply new scenery, new scents and tastes and sounds. Maybe it was power, the power of the singsong girl but packaged in diamonds, not jade. Maybe it was hunger for control, that drumbeat that had kept her alive in Canton but had receded in Shanghai. The craving to have her own desires honored and indulged for the first time in her life.

And in those months in Peking, those desires took form, crystallized, their shapes branded upon her heart, her brain.

The luck of meeting Kitty Bigelow again! Kitty, whom she'd met in Coronado, California, when Win was posted at the base there during the war, had been widowed when her pilot husband was killed in France. One night, as Wallis exited the elevator at the Grand Hôtel de Pékin (she couldn't afford to stay more than two weeks there, and she was well into week number two, desperate for Win's paycheck to arrive but hiding it), she spotted Kitty across the crowded lobby.

"Kitty! What on earth—how are you? What are you doing here?"

"Wallis!" Kitty squealed, as she was wont to do, Wallis remembered. But desperate times called for desperate measures and Wallis managed to smile lovingly and tell Kitty how beautiful she looked, how fondly she remembered their time in Coronado. How sorry she had been to hear of Kitty's husband's death.

"I'm Kitty Rogers now," Kitty said after wiping a tear for her late husband from her eye. She grabbed the arm of the extremely good-looking man beside her, tall and muscular in an exquisitely well-cut white dinner jacket. "Herman, meet my dear friend Wallis Spencer."

"My pleasure," Wallis said, and practiced the gaze she had learned from the singsong girls—head tilted slightly down, eyes trained up. Feminine but frank.

"The pleasure is all mine," Herman replied with a startled look on his face. Startled and interested.

"Where's Win—no, I'm sorry. I heard about that. We all have. News of the free-spirited Mrs. Spencer reached us in Peking even before you did, my dear. We're all intrigued by your daring. To take the Shanghai Express all alone! Were you molested by revolutionaries?"

"Alas, no." And both the Rogerses laughed at that.

"Come, you're our guest tonight—we're dining at the hotel. Are you staying here?"

"Yes, for now." Wallis didn't elaborate; she only shrugged slightly and looked mysterious.

"Nonsense. You're stopping with us. Isn't she, Herman?"

"Of course! You must, Mrs. Spencer—"

"Call me Wallis."

"Wallis. We have a little place nearby. Far better for you than staying here—this is a hotbed of intrigue, spies everywhere, coups being plotted in every corner. Not a place for a well-brought-up woman—even a free-spirited one," Herman added charmingly.

"Thank you, then. I will." And inwardly she breathed a sigh of relief. One problem solved; Win's paycheck could arrive at its leisure.

So began the real education of her life—how to live as if she were wealthy. It was the one subject she didn't chafe against learning; she absorbed each lesson like a sponge, marveling at how easily it came to her. Because the Rogerses were simply dripping in money from Herman's family. Soap, she thought it was. Something to do with soap, or shampoo; something that was cleansing. Like money itself.

The Rogerses' "little place nearby" turned out to be a grand palace near the Hatamen Gate, the ancient entrance to the Forbidden City. Their palace was elaborately old on the outside but gleaming with the most modern fixtures and plumbing within. She was given a beautiful suite with her own servant, a native woman who followed her about and anticipated her every need. There were other servants who did the household chores, another fleet who cooked and served; the house was lousy with hired help, which was *so* cheap here, Kitty said with the carelessness of a woman with a bottomless bank account. Wallis was even given her own rickshaw complete with her own driver.

There were nights dancing at balls hosted by the various diplomatic legations at the embassies. Dinners at the Rogerses followed by games of poker that allowed Wallis to steadily add to her little nest egg from Win's sporadic pay.

The Rogerses were in China so Herman could write a novel, apparently, although why he couldn't write it back in the States, she had no idea. They were taking Chinese lessons, and Wallis sat in on a few but soon gave it up. Foreign languages didn't come easily to her, and why work hard at something she didn't really need now that she'd mastered the art of seductive communication? *That,* she needed—the international society in Peking was a woman's paradise, men outnumbering women ten to one. The Rogerses gave her the respectability she wouldn't have had living on her own, which meant she was more valued here than she had been in Washington. She had her pick of men with whom to play and, hopefully, hitch her star to so that one day she could have a home like the Rogerses had and money enough to indulge herself, not to count and hoard.

Because that was Wallis's dream now. Not romantic love. Not children; she wasn't sure she could have them, as she'd never menstruated regularly before her hospitalization and after it not at all. But this—a grand house, more servants than she could count. Time to do nothing, nothing at all. No worries. She had the power now to convince a man to give it to her. All she had to do was find him.

So she looked. She took her time about it; there was no hurry, after all. Kitty and Herman enjoyed her company, and as wearying as it was to constantly sparkle and be an amusing companion, which was the only way she could pay her debt to them, she couldn't complain.

When she wasn't entertaining her hosts and getting daily lessons in living well, Wallis thrilled in escaping their walled-in little community and exploring the real Peking. Wandering the narrow streets lined with stalls, buying cheap jade objects—she loved the weighted coolness of jade in her hand; it gave her a sense of permanence, of peace. She ordered silk cheongsams like she'd seen on the singsong girls in beautiful shades, cut just for her slender figure. Entering a ball in one of those creations, she always received gasps of surprise and admiration, which was in its way as intoxicating as opium.

What she loved best, though, was watching the camel trains approach from outside the walls of the city, the little bells on the camel harnesses tinkling like music. She was mesmerized by the sight, knew she'd never see anything like it anywhere else. The trains, with the camels' humps swaying back and forth, not unlike the hips of the singsong girls, came to represent everything she was seeking, everything she was learning about the world and herself. She kept coming back to a certain bench on a hill overlooking the city's eastern gate, where, alone and unbothered, she filled herself to the brim with exoticism, so abundant that she couldn't contain it all. There was too much.

And not enough.

One day—it startled her, like a bird suddenly landing on her shoulder—she knew she was finished with China. She'd gotten all she could out of it, and out of the Rogerses too. Herman was a man she could have easily fallen for, and while normally his being married wouldn't have been an obstacle, she did, in a grudging way, like Kitty. After all, she'd been widowed in the war, volunteered in a Red Cross canteen overseas (which was where she met Herman). She hadn't come from wealth; in fact, her upbringing was much like Wallis's. That she'd landed the princely Herman with his generations of bank vaults full of money, backed up by good breeding and connections, was something that Wallis had to admire. And not begrudge—too much, that is.

But it was time to leave. Now, while she could still claim Kitty as a friend, because Wallis had so few, and Kitty could be useful in the future.

And at least it was finally all over with Win. She'd find the money for the divorce somehow; she almost had enough just from her poker winnings. Perhaps she could win more on the ship home. She wouldn't need to ask Uncle Sol; she'd never ask him for anything again.

Free from the horrors of her marriage, she was ready for the next chapter. So much more prepared this time than she'd been back in 1916. She almost wept to remember *that* Wallis, the "Bessie" still clinging to her like the stubborn stench of soured milk, so unready to take on the world.

So unschooled in the true way of wielding power over a man.

Her Lotus Year over, she returned to the United States harder, brighter, stronger—not unlike the enameled boxes she'd seen in the bazaars, those seemingly delicate wooden boxes covered in layers of smooth lacquer. They weighed nothing in your hand; they were sleek and colorful and looked as if a mosquito could scratch the surface. But the resin that the lacquer was made from was surprisingly durable, withstanding liquid, heat, cold—all the elements. No matter the weather.

That's what Wallis Simpson was when she returned from her Lotus Year. The bruises, the wounds, were covered in brave, vivid colors, shining, always shining.

And stronger than anything—*anyone*—she would ever encounter again.

CHAPTER
10

FORT BELVEDERE

APRIL 1936

"BERTIE, I DO WISH YOU HADN'T SAID WE'D GO."

"Elizabeth, I had no choice. You know how I feel about her, but David was so pathetic about it; he practically begged me—us—to come. I find that rather touching, especially now that he has the top job. Don't you?"

In the back seat of the car, Elizabeth stared at her husband, his blue eyes blinking as they always did when he was nervous. What was rather touching was his desire to think the best of his brother despite all evidence to the contrary.

Evidence freely shared by not only Tommy Lascelles but Alec Hardinge, another assistant private secretary to the King, and even Mr. Baldwin, the prime minister. And the evidence was this: The King was hardly ever at Buck House, and when he was, Mrs. Simpson was with him behind closed doors while servants listened and giggled outside. His weekends at the Fort now lasted from Thursday to Tuesday, and he didn't allow his private secretaries to accompany him. When state papers were returned with his signature, there were often rings from cocktail glasses on them, and they were crinkled and sometimes torn or dotted with cigarette ash, obviously having been left out for all to see. The prime minister was so alarmed, there was now a secret directive not to send anything of real importance to his red box. There was no sugarcoating it—the King was neglecting his duties.

"Elizabeth, please. Now that Papa is gone, we must at least *try*. He needs a steadying influence, someone from the family. I'm convinced that we can make him give her up and settle down if only we try a little harder. We owe David that much. He's my older brother and has always looked out for me."

"Bertie, you're too good." Elizabeth patted her husband's hand, resigning herself to an unpleasant evening ahead. "I'm afraid I don't share your opinion. He should know better! It's as if he's gone mad, simply mad." She thought, once again, of that glorious golden prince of her youth and waited with gritted teeth for that traitorous little debutante flare of infatuation to come over her.

Nothing happened. Oh, thank God! Gone, gone forever was her silly little crush. Now she could see clearly what must be done. "Who else will be there?" She pressed her forehead against the cool glass of the car window, then quickly removed her powder compact from her purse and vigorously dabbed at her face with the puff. That Woman would be wearing some absurd but chic dress, no doubt. And did she ever *perspire*?

"I'm not sure—I think the Churchills, but the rest are mainly David's crowd, you know. The usuals, like Emerald Cunard and the Coopers, probably some Americans. You know how David is about Americans."

"Yes, I do," she couldn't help saying sourly. Bertie squeezed her hand in warning, and she resolved to be on her best, most sparkling behavior, if only to show Mrs. Simpson how little Elizabeth cared about her; how little she mattered in the grand scheme of things. After fluffing her fur collar until it snapped with static electricity, she reapplied her lipstick and pushed a stray hair back into place, and when they got out of the car at the entrance to the Fort, she sucked in her stomach with determination and straightened her spine.

"You look splendid." Bertie took her arm and they entered the front hall; she could hear excited voices and the distinctive clink of cocktail glasses and lively jazz music coming from the drawing room.

"As do you," she assured her husband, and when they were announced, she smiled so broadly—*so authentically happy to see her brother-in-law and all his fancy friends*—that for one alarming moment, she thought she might actually have bared a molar. Nothing could dull her brilliance tonight.

Nothing. Except for a flat American accent trying to sound plummily British and uncannily like—

"Oh, everything is perfectly wonderful! What a darling little woman one is! How utterly devoted to one's husband and daughters! How marvelous and capable, oh, goody, look—a cake!"

In the center of the room stood a woman. A sleek, black-haired woman with a gown that revealed her back. And she was surrounded by guests who were laughing, none as hard as the King himself.

"One must not forget one's smile—you can see what a good job one's dentist does, can't you?"

"Wallis!" someone hissed. Everyone in the room froze as the Yorks stood in the doorway taking in the appalling sight of the King of England's mistress mimicking the Duchess of York in front of all his friends.

Bertie had a ridiculous smile on his face that lingered like the last wisp of smoke after the fire has burned itself out before fading away. But she felt him grip her arm and was thankful for it.

Her heart had escaped her rib cage and, defying the laws of science, fallen all the way down to the bottom of her feet, taking all reason and warmth and goodwill with it. Desperately did she want to flee—she was sickened at the notion of remaining—but her feet would not listen to reason. They pinned her where she stood, her *famous* smile as frozen as the rest of her; her lips felt drawn into a weird rictus, but she couldn't for the life of her make it *stop*. She ached to relax her grotesque grin as viscerally as she ached to take a poker and stab That Woman in the heart.

But one could not do that.

No, one must allow one's brother-in-law and King to come rushing over with a scarlet face and an embarrassed, downturned gaze and call—far too loudly—to his silent guests, the jazz music, absurdly, still pouring out of the phonograph's speaker with jaunty disregard for all that was happening, "Look, everyone! Look who joined us! How are you, dearest Elizabeth? Bertie?" He took her hand and kissed it and she somehow managed a bob of a curtsy to him, turned her cold lips to his burning cheek and bestowed the briefest of kisses, then allowed him to lead her farther into the room, dimly aware of all the curtsies and bows, but they were blurry. Nothing in the room was clear to her—

Except for the knifelike woman with shining black hair who curtsied deeply but kept her insolent gaze firmly fastened on Elizabeth. That Woman didn't even have the decency to be embarrassed!

"Your Royal Highness," she said in her atrocious accent.

"What a privilege. I'm so glad you were able to tear yourself away from your darling little girls for some fun. The King has so been looking forward to seeing you. We all have. You see, we were so eager to see you, I tried to do an imitation. A very poor imitation, I'm afraid. But now we have the real thing!"

"Ah. I couldn't quite tell *who* you were imitating, it really was so badly done. I thank you for that clarification. But I had no idea you were an actress. You have so many *hidden* talents." Elizabeth could have shouted hosannas when she heard her voice, steady, cool, and detached. Utterly royal.

"Wallis is a woman of many virtues," David said proudly.

"I'm not sure about *that,*" Elizabeth snapped, and had the intense pleasure of seeing Wallis stiffen. "But certainly, one is quite amused. After all, imitation is the sincerest form of flattery—"

"Speaking of flattery," Wallis interrupted, her voice dry with irony, "wherever did you get that unusual gown? It really does suit you. It brings out your many and *ample* charms."

"Why, thank you, Wallis," Elizabeth replied oh so sweetly. "I could give you the name of my dressmaker, if you like."

Wallis reddened, and someone tittered, reminding Elizabeth that there was an audience; with a curt nod at That Woman, Elizabeth turned to her host, the King.

"I'm really quite parched, dearest David. Can one have a drink?"

"Er, yes, of course, just a moment—" David steered her and Bertie away from Wallis and toward the Coopers. Duff and Diana greeted her warmly and appeared to decide, with just a look between them, that they were her guardians for the night. They never left her side.

What was a decent interval to remain at a party given by

one's brother-in-law who happened to be one's king and where one had been so extraordinarily insulted by his married mistress? Elizabeth was mentally calculating this when Winston Churchill came stumbling up to her. In one hand, he clutched a glass of whiskey as if his life depended upon it, and in the other, his ubiquitous cigar—unlit. Clemmie, his wife, smiled warmly at Elizabeth. So dignified and tall, Clementine Churchill was one of the few society beauties who did not make Elizabeth feel like a turnip.

"Don't pay her any mind, Your Royal Highness," Winston grumbled in his slippery yet sonorous way. "She's just his latest cutie. Nothing more than that. Just one more in a long line of royal mistresses who will be remembered only as a footnote in a biography a hundred years hence—"

"That's what I've been trying to tell her," Bertie broke in.

Elizabeth, Clemmie, and Diana looked at one another. Clemmie and Diana simultaneously shook their heads, and Elizabeth nodded in agreement.

"What? What's that? You women, you oracles—you Cassandras!" Winston was laughing at them; so were Duff and Bertie. "The secret language of married women. Someone must write a book about it one day—why, I'll do it myself!"

"Winston," Clemmie said in her cool, amused voice, "with all love and affection, my dear, you are an ass."

This didn't shock her husband; he only laughed harder. So did Duff. So did Bertie.

"She's much more than his latest *cutie,*" Elizabeth said darkly, sipping a martini that had somehow ended up in her hand and that she could tell, from the buzzing in her ears and the loosening of her tongue, wasn't her first. "Much more dangerous. Why don't they see?"

"Because they have no imagination," Diana said, steering them away from their husbands. "You know I can't really speak my mind due to Duff's closeness to David. But I see. I observe. She has a hold over him that can't be explained. And it won't go away now that he's King, no matter what our dear husbands want to believe."

"And he's neglecting affairs of state," Elizabeth said sorrowfully—oh, so sorrowfully!—shaking her head as she spilled government secrets with abandon. "The prime minister is most concerned; so is the cabinet. They no longer trust him and so they keep things from him. But thus far, they've done nothing more than scold and pray. Useless!"

"So what do *we* do?" Clemmie asked, her dark gray eyes shining with concern. "I love Winston but he can be such a soppy romantic at times. He believes she's good for the King and calls her Mrs. Fitzherbert—you remember, the mistress of George the Fourth, even after he married Caroline of Brunswick. But I don't think Mrs. Simpson will be content with a behind-the-scenes role, do you?"

"I heard," Diana said, lowering her voice so that the other two had to lean in further, "that David had lunch with Ernest Simpson and told him that he must give Wallis up now, once and for all."

"And I heard that Emerald Cunard is going about town boasting that she'll be Wallis's mistress of the robes," Clemmie added.

Here it was, then. The unspeakable, baldly stated. It was as if Diana and Clemmie had each lobbed a grenade into the middle of the room, and all they could do now was wait for them to explode.

Now was the time.

Draining her drink, Elizabeth made up her mind, knowing full well that these women would tell their husbands and then it would get back to the cabinet and the prime minister and she might as well set Tommy on it too, for now the gloves were off; Elizabeth Bowes-Lyon's dainty hands were soft and dimpled but she was not afraid to get them dirty, not any longer.

"Let me tell you about what she did in China," said the Duchess of York as she reached out to pluck another martini from a tray held by a passing waiter.

Immediately three female heads were bent together. Joined by three others. Then three others.

Their husbands continued to drink their king's whiskey and talk about politics (what *were* they going to do about that Herr Hitler, stirring up trouble in Europe?) and shooting (the King abhorred it so no one should count on Sandringham this season, more's the pity) and cricket (wasn't Wally Hammond a wizard?).

The only person paying attention to the growing female conclave was the King's mistress. Who, after narrowing her eyes at the woman in the middle, squared her shoulders and strode about the room with utter confidence. Smiling so fiercely, her jaw looked like it would snap.

And the King followed behind her, wringing his hands. As if afraid to let her out of his sight.

CHAPTER

11

LONDON

MAY 1936

"IT'S GOT TO BE DONE, WALLIS. SOONER OR LATER, MY prime minister must meet my future wife."

Wallis froze. She let the blossoms she was arranging for the foyer at York House, where David still lived while in London, fall from her hands. Seventeen carnations, sent to her by the German ambassador Joachim von Ribbentrop, such a nice man and *so* interested in Wallis; he sent her flowers almost daily.

Now they lay scattered all over the floor as she turned to stare at David.

"Oh, David! You know they'll never let you marry me." This was a test, of course. She was weary of pretending, fantasizing, playacting at the Fort with his sycophantic friends. If David meant what he said, this was a new development. Stanley Baldwin, the prime minister, was no mere Winston Churchill, an outcast belligerently trying—and failing—to worm his way back into the inner circle of power. The prime minister was actually more powerful than the King himself, which made no sense to her at all.

But did David truly mean it? Was this a proposal?

"Wallis, hear me now. I will not be crowned without you by my side." David twinkled his sunny smile, circled his arm around her waist, and kissed her passionately. Suddenly desperate for air, she pushed herself away and felt her heart begin to race.

In the months since David's father had died, his need for her had increased astronomically, as had his reluctance to do his duties; it was almost as if he didn't want to be King after all. And since he'd succeeded his father, David had not specifically mentioned marriage, not until this moment. Not to her, not to his cabinet or courtiers. She trembled, from either fear or excitement, she couldn't tell. She knew only that things were about to change. For better. Or for worse.

Some things already had changed, because Ernest was in love. Her old school friend Mary Raffray had come to visit Wallis in London, and at first she was a convenient houseguest indeed, keeping Ernest company while Wallis was occupied with David. But Mary wasn't supposed to *seduce* Ernest! Jealousy, unexpected but fierce, pierced Wallis's heart. Dull, devoted Ernest—she needed him. She relied on Ernest for his steadiness, his very existence. As long as Wallis was still Mrs. Ernest Simpson, there was an out, an escape hatch. Or a safety net, were David to drop her from his dizzying new perch.

But those words: *I will not be crowned without you by my side.* Now she knew that David fully intended that she be Queen to his King, no matter what the government or his family might say, and hearing it plainly stated like this for the first time helped her map the way forward. She took a few deep, calming breaths before letting her mind race ahead: She would begin by dining with the prime minister and his wife. Despite Ernest acting as chaperone, this would be a momentous occasion.

Even if the prime minister didn't know quite how momentous. Not yet, anyway.

But David would make it very clear, and soon everyone in the government would know who would be the first lady of the land.

Wallis took a deep breath, squared her shoulders, then turned to David with her head tilted down so that she could gaze up at him. A seductive smile tickled her lips. "Darling, I'm so glad you finally spoke what I'd been hoping."

"Now all you need do is ask Ernest for a divorce. There may be some rough patches ahead—I don't deny they may make it difficult for us—but together, I know we'll triumph!"

"We must, David. We must." She put her hands on his chest, smoothing an invisible wrinkle. She widened her eyes in mock consternation. "I'm afraid I've thought, lately, that there might be those who don't want you to remain King. Those close to you. I've heard things, infuriating things."

"What? What have you heard? Who doesn't want me to remain King?"

"Your sister-in-law, for one. Elizabeth. There are those who say she hopes you'll step aside because she thinks you're unfit. That *we* are unfit. She's a very ambitious woman, you know. She wants the crown for herself and Bertie."

"No—Elizabeth? Ambitious? Why, darling, you've seen her, you know her. She's perfectly content staying home and eating cakes and doing absolutely nothing. She's the laziest woman I've ever met in my life. She has no desire to be Queen, I assure you! At least, she doesn't any longer."

"Oh? What do you mean?" She knelt down, scooped up the carnations, then began to arrange the red and white blossoms again, humming a little tune. As if she hadn't a care in the world and wasn't concerned at all about Elizabeth, the Duchess of York.

"I believe when she was younger, she did set her cap for me. Of course, most of her group—all those dull, horsey young ladies of the gentry—did. She tried harder than some, but I was never interested in her that way, even when she was younger and prettier. She and Bertie are perfect together. Terrific bores, both of them. They make royalty look like the middle class."

Wallis couldn't help but laugh; David had struck the nail right on the head. The Yorks, with their two perfect princesses and their familial devotion, right down to the way poor Bertie gazed at his dumpling of a wife as if she were Greta Garbo, did manage to diminish the Crown with a coat of dull respectability.

"Hmm," she said, her eyes dancing. "Sometimes those schoolgirl crushes don't go away, you know. Sometimes they turn into resentment."

"Elizabeth has always been the sweetest of souls to me. I really can't believe that she'd spy—"

"Tommy Lascelles. Alec Hardinge. Your very own private secretaries." Wallis turned around again and folded her arms. "*They* report to her."

"Report? Report what?"

"Everything you do. Everything *we* do. She's gathering information, David, and sharing it with your mother, at the very least. I'm not entirely sure why, but it makes sense that if she wants her husband to be King instead of you—"

"Elizabeth? Cookie, a Lady Macbeth? Pure Shakespearean nonsense, Wallis."

"Cookie? I've never heard you call her that before—what does it mean?"

"Oh, just a silly nickname. Once there was a rumor, something I heard long ago, but it's nonsense. Besides, it fits, doesn't it? She does spend an inordinate amount of time belowstairs in the kitchen. And she looks like a common cook. Anyway, I don't deny she can be a bit much, but plotting to remove me from my rightful place on the throne? No, I really won't hear of it." David's eyes turned icy blue, and he abruptly spun on his heel to go back to his office, where the red box that delivered all the state papers awaited him. He often had her read them to him; he had the attention span of a gnat and couldn't concentrate long enough to read them himself. Although she would sometimes scold him that he needed to try.

"All right, David. You know her best, naturally. I must be mistaken. Silly me, we Americans know nothing about royal intrigue. We're peasants, running around with our heads up our assets." She smiled wickedly and was rewarded by an outburst of laughter as he ran back to kiss her hands.

"Haw-haw—that's a good one, 'heads up our assets'! I'm sorry I was such a beast, my angel! I'll never speak to you so frightfully again. 'Oo's the vewwy best widdle girl in the whole world?"

Swallowing the bile rising in her throat, Wallis kept smiling. "And 'oo is too sweet to widdle old me!"

With another jaunty kiss of her hands, the King of England strode off to his office.

THE DINNER FOR THE prime minister at York House came off a smash, if she did say so herself. Still denied the head of the table—David's sister, Mary, the princess royal, was the official hostess—Wallis had to sit opposite Ernest in the middle, surrounded by Duff and Diana Cooper and the Mountbattens, Emerald Cunard, other friends. The special guests, besides Stanley and Lucy Baldwin, were the American hero Charles Lindbergh and his mousy little wife, Anne, who said no more than three words the entire time but looked around a great deal, her head swiveling back and forth as she studied her fellow guests.

Mrs. Baldwin was also rather stuffy (Wallis had heard that she once told a friend that when she had to have relations with her husband, she would "lie back and think of England") and not a little curious. Wallis caught Lucy Baldwin staring at her more than once, as if she were trying to understand what David saw in her. Mr. Baldwin did the same, although in a less obvious way.

She was growing used to these stares.

After the rest of the guests had departed—including Ernest, although he left discreetly, through the back entrance—David and the prime minister had a few words together in his study while Wallis and Lucy Baldwin made polite conversation in the entrance hall about the weather.

"Where did your husband run off to?" Mrs. Baldwin inquired after a brief discussion about the forecast for Ascot the next month.

"Oh, I'm sure he's in the library. Ernest is very fond of reading up on the history of your country."

"How very interesting," replied Mrs. Baldwin. "I do wish Stanley would hurry up. But the work of the government never ends. Day and night, as I'm sure you know too well!"

"I'm sure I don't," Wallis replied with a tight smile. Determined not to give this woman one morsel of gossip to regurgitate.

Just then, the King and his prime minister emerged from the study and shook hands. The prime minister bowed to David, nodded at her. Then they were gone.

"Well, darling, you did a wonderful job," enthused David. "I'm so proud of you—you looked splendid, your conversation was sparkling, and the food was tremendous. Everyone enjoyed themselves. Shall we have a nightcap?"

"Only a wee bit of brandy for me, but you go ahead."

She followed him back to the study, where he loosened his tie and flopped on a sofa. He looked very tired. All that public charm and effusiveness he'd been trained to perform since birth took a toll, she was beginning to understand. She felt a flicker of warmth in her heart for him, taking him in her arms.

"What did Mr. Baldwin want to talk about?"

The King paused before he spoke.

"For one, he'd like me to move into Buck House now. He said it's past time. I detest that dreary, drafty place! But he emphasized that now we have the coronation date set—next May—I must."

"What did you tell him?"

"I didn't tell him the truth—that I don't wish to move in there until you can accompany me. It makes it all very official, you know, living there. I suppose that holding on to this place has kept me from having to make some unpopular decisions. It's lulled me into believing that life can go on as it has been. But with the coronation set, and now this pressure—we do need to proceed. I haven't truly let on how difficult it might get for you. Darling, the press here has been very kind to me, and the average citizen and most of the government has no idea about you—and I long to keep it that way until I can officially protect you as my Queen, and then Buck House can become our own little fortress. But until then, I'd much rather remain here or at the Fort."

"I understand, David. I do." And for the first time, Wallis wondered what the average British citizen might think of her, an American, stealing the heart of their king. "Did you tell Mr. Baldwin about—about us?"

"I didn't need to. He brought it up. Remember what you said about Elizabeth before?"

She couldn't see his face, so she gently pushed him away from her and sat up, smoothing her dress. "Elizabeth?"

"About her having spies, collecting information?"

"Yes?"

"I wouldn't have believed it, but I think you're right." David sighed, loudly, and swallowed half his brandy. "Mr. Baldwin referred to something he said I should know about. Apparently, darling, there's a document called a China dossier floating about."

Wallis's heart skipped a beat, and she studied her hands for a minute until she could control her voice.

"And what does this China dossier say? Loathsome things about me, I presume?"

"Darling, it's utter nonsense. Vile, libelous, but nonsense. Mr. Baldwin wouldn't reveal much, only a few choice items. He also couldn't say who had instigated it, but I see dainty white hands all over it."

"Cookie," Wallis said bitterly—the first time she had used this name to describe the Duchess of York. But not, she thought viciously, the last.

"Yes. Cookie." David sounded very weary, very sad. "I wouldn't have thought her capable of it, to be honest. She's always so very charming in her saccharine way. And not the brightest woman, I've always thought."

"*Aggressively* charming, David. You don't see it, but I do. Smiling and being *so* adorable in order to mask her deviousness and ambition. David, you must open your eyes—she wants to be Queen. Or at least, she very much doesn't want *me* to. Whether Bertie shares her ambition or not, I don't know. But I do know women like her. I've met women like her before, back in school. Those privileged young women, pampered, given everything they've ever wanted so that life was never hard for *them,* so that *they* never had to make decisions no decent woman should have to make, sitting in judgment on the rest of us."

She was trembling with such anger, awash in memories and humiliation, that she forgot where she was and with whom. She was back in boarding school, and in her debutante year, beseeching Uncle Sol for her very survival in society and all that it could provide. Ashamed of her mother, despising her uncle, alone with only her wits to rely on. That path had led to Win.

A hand on her arm, a smooth cheek—he never needed to shave—against her own, brought her back to her surroundings. York House, the home of the King of England. Who was whispering his adoration in her ears, calming her trembling limbs. Promising her everything those Baltimore bitches could never have dreamed of. "I'm going to raid the family vault again, darling, to find you a little bauble, something you deserve. We'll go to the Fort this weekend. I've arranged for you to have the royal carriage at Ascot next month. I'm still in official mourning, but there's no reason why you shouldn't enjoy yourself. You'll need some new dresses, so order anything you wish, I'll take care of it. And I mean it when I say I will not be crowned without you by my side, Wallis."

She nodded, banished the demons with a firm squaring of her shoulders. Then, eyes clear once more, visions of crown jewels dancing in her head, she said, oh so reluctantly, "I was wondering about that rumor you mentioned before? About Cookie?"

"Oh, darling, it's really nothing. Why bring that up?"

"Because, David," Wallis said simply, "we need to destroy her."

When he started to protest, she put one finger on his lips. Sinking down to her knees—never mind the damage to her silk stockings; there were plenty more upstairs still folded away in little white boxes with pink satin ribbons on them—Wallis began to undo his trousers.

CHAPTER
12

SCOTLAND

SEPTEMBER 1936

"THEIR BEHAVIOR ON THE HOLIDAY WAS SIMPLY DREADFUL, I'm afraid, Your Royal Highness," Tommy said in his brisk, unsparing way.

"I can quite imagine." Elizabeth's grip on her fishing pole tightened; she took a calming breath, brought the rod back over her shoulder, and cast the line into the River Muick.

Clouds were scurrying across the sun, causing the dancing rays upon the water to dim and brighten, dim and brighten. The air was that clean, Scotland brisk that brought roses to her cheeks and cleared her head; she breathed it in deeply and felt restored. She *always* felt restored when she returned to the land of her heritage. Even though she and Bertie no longer stayed at Glamis much now that they had use of Birkhall, a tiny castle on a small estate—only fifty thousand acres—near Balmoral, she still felt as if she'd returned home with every visit north. One could hear the singing river no matter where one was in the house, as it was literally right outside the door; she feasted on fresh salmon at every meal, ate her fill of oatcakes dripping with butter and honey, strode across moors for long walks that aided the digestion and whetted the appetite, picnicked with views of snowy mountains and hills purple with heather—and fished. Elizabeth was never much for sport other than riding, but she did relish securing an old scarf about her head, plunking her feet in comfortable Wellies, tying her own flies, casting her reel into shockingly cold, achingly clear water, and standing for hours at a time, waiting for that satisfying tug on the line.

One could think clearly here. And one needed to now more than ever.

She heard the treble voices of the girls and the deeper Scottish burr of Crawfie—Marion Crawford, their governess—somewhere farther along the river, and that was also satisfying. Crawfie, egged on by Queen Mary, was altogether too strict about education. Girls needed to play! They needed freedom from duties while it was still possible; being cooped up in a stuffy schoolroom while there was all this bracing air to take in and hills to climb and roll down was ridiculous. Her daughters would never need more education than she herself had received. They'd marry minor royalty or wealthy noblemen; they'd have children; they'd need to know how to entertain well and look smart and play the piano decently, and, of course, they had to be fluent in French. That really was enough of an education, wasn't it?

But Queen Mary thought otherwise, and so did Crawfie, and too often Elizabeth had to put away a mystery novel or be interrupted while fishing to hear Crawfie's exasperated plea that the girls needed more time in the schoolroom, not less.

The royal family always headed north after the Glorious Twelfth, and here in Scotland, she put her Wellie-clad, dainty little foot firmly down. This was a holiday, pure and simple. Lilibet and Margaret were not going to spend these precious weeks in the classroom.

"I honestly don't know where to begin to describe their behavior," Tommy continued, apparently less than honestly, because he plunged right in as if he'd committed a list to memory. And Elizabeth closed her eyes against the onslaught of images he evoked with his disgusting words: David, shirtless, painting the toenails of That Woman on the deck of the yacht, the *Nahlin,* that he had chartered instead of taking the royal yacht, hoping, of course—always—to avoid the responsibilities of his role. And supposedly to avoid any controversy surrounding his mistress being on board.

More images: David refusing to put on a shirt when he went ashore despite being told he looked undignified. David swimming in the buff even with other boats around, other boats upon which foreign reporters were eagerly snapping photographs and soon after publishing them in their papers under headlines such as *The King of England and Mrs. Simpson on Holiday—Royal Love Nest!* David and That Woman sleeping together in the main suite for all the other guests, including Tommy, to observe freely. Raucous parties ashore where David and Wallis and their friends Dickie and Edwina Mountbatten and Emerald Cunard asked for American jazz to be played and then danced with such abandon that Emerald lost a diamond ring. David introducing Mrs. Simpson as if she were Queen already to the inevitable foreign dignitaries, who believed, naturally, that the King of England bouncing up to their shores was an official occasion.

That Woman behaving as if she *were* Queen already, receiving bows and extending her hand to be kissed. Beaming when naval bands played "The Star-Spangled Banner" in her honor right after "God Save the King."

Elizabeth's head was splitting by the time Tommy finished

his accounting. Her stomach was roiling when he told her how the European and American newspapers were now boldly reporting the King's love affair, making it sound like something out of a fairy tale, not the nightmare that it was.

"And one more thing, ma'am. She's taken to referring to you as 'Cookie.'"

"What?" Elizabeth nearly dropped her pole in the water. "Cookie—as in *cook*? I suppose because I'm not an emaciated stick like she is?"

"No, ma'am—well, yes, ma'am, that too. Beg your pardon, ma'am, but it would appear that there's also a rumor—it seems to have originated from the woman herself, who could only have heard it from the King—regarding your, er, rather, the circumstances, it would seem, of your, um, conception and subsequent birth."

She nearly snapped her neck, she swiveled her head so violently toward a beet-red Tommy Lascelles, who looked ridiculous standing on a muddy riverbank in his courtier's suit and tie, his mustache neatly clipped, next to her more appropriate woolen jumper and tartan skirt. At least he was wearing boots, not polished shoes.

As if from a mischievous Scottish sprite, a ghost of gossip from the past whispered in her ear that Tommy was a poof in courtier's clothing. That he had a thing for younger men, although not as young as Dickie Mountbatten liked them, apparently, and the Duke of Kent. It really was interesting, the number of homosexuals within the royal circle. All leading double lives, married, sometimes obviously happily so (the Duke of Kent, George, was noticeably more content now that he was married to Marina, and Tommy always spoke so fondly of his wife and daughters, although Dickie and Edwina

Mountbatten, well, that was a marriage made in hell). But clearly they spent time in murkier shadows. Elizabeth didn't find this twisted, only alien and rather interesting. She herself was capable of being two women at the same time, the public Smiling Duchess and the private introvert who loved nothing more than nesting at home. And spying on her brother-in-law.

Tommy's face was still bright red and it wasn't merely sunburn.

"What do you mean, the circumstances of my conception and birth?" Her voice was as icy as the river babbling at their feet.

"I mean, Your Royal Highness, that among the undignified set that now surround the King and his married mistress, there is a rumor that you are not quite of legitimate birth. A rumor that, or so the King and his married mistress are prone to whispering, your father had—relations—with a cook in the household that resulted in your birth, because your mother was, well, rather late in the day for that kind of thing, but she desired more children. Hence 'Cookie.' If you'll forgive me, ma'am, but you did ask."

Tommy looked as if he would prefer to fling himself, suit, tie, and all, into the river rather than continue this conversation. And Elizabeth would have been only too happy to shove him in herself had she been able to move. But no, she was frozen in place, her hands in a death grip around her pole, the fishing line taut but not snagged on anything. And the curious thing was, one was not at all surprised by the rumor.

Growing up, Elizabeth and her younger brother, David, were always referred to as "the Benjamins," a reference to the biblical Benjamin, the youngest son of old Jacob. There was a wide gap between the older Bowes-Lyon siblings and the two of them, and then there was the fact that it took her father a while to get around to registering her birth. And when he did, he got it wrong. But exactly how he got it wrong was vague—he registered her birth as taking place at St. Paul's Walden Bury, but her mother told a slightly different story, once saying that Elizabeth had been born in an ambulance on the way to a hospital in London, another time saying she'd been born in the house on Grosvenor Square, but always adding, with a laugh, that she'd had so many children, she couldn't possibly remember where they all had been born!

But once, at a party her debutante year, Elizabeth had heard someone whispering about the cook and her father. She'd been so shocked, she fled the party and went straight home. She didn't bother her sleeping parents but she did pore over all the family photographs until her eyes were red and raw, searching for the resemblance between herself and her mother. Finally, she satisfied herself that it was there in the porcelain skin, china-blue eyes, and determined little chin. One photograph of her mother as a child looked so much like one of Elizabeth at the same age that only the clothing told the difference, her mother in a stiff dress with many petticoats from the 1860s, Elizabeth in the softer, looser white lace dress of the Edwardian era.

The rumor was nonsense, of course! Then as now. Absolutely no truth to it! She would never dream of hurting her beloved mother and father by asking if it was true; she'd never once not known she was loved, fiercely, by her parents, cherished, petted, their own. This was as true as the sun rising in the east, and she took it as much for granted. She had never given that silly rumor another thought—until now.

"She says, ma'am, that when she is Queen, Cookie will be relegated to the kitchen where she belongs," Tommy said after a long, uncomfortable silence.

"And David—the King? What does he say?" She couldn't keep the sadness out of her voice; how had things gone so wrong between them?

"I'm afraid, ma'am, that the King has never once been observed to contradict or scold Mrs. Simpson."

"Ah."

"Ma'am, I realize this has all been difficult to hear but I beg your indulgence on one last matter."

"Oh?" It would appear that all one could muster were monosyllables. The onslaught of information had robbed her of proper speech.

"You know, of course, that the King has asked you and the Duke of York to open the Royal Infirmary in Aberdeen tomorrow?"

She nodded. "He told us he couldn't do it, as he was still in mourning. As if we aren't!"

"I have it on good authority that instead of doing his duty, he will be motoring from Balmoral to the Aberdeen train station to pick up some of his guests for this weekend."

"Aberdeen?" Elizabeth was puzzled. "Why aren't his guests arriving at the Balmoral station?"

"If one wanted to keep one's guests out of the spotlight, one would have them disembark at Aberdeen. Or so I imagine."

"Ah." Fury—it swirled around her feet like the river itself, only it was hot, not cold; boiling, not babbling. It snaked around her ankles and up her calves, raced to her heart and then to her brain. So that was it! He was installing That Woman at Balmoral. Balmoral! Queen Victoria's own beloved castle and a sacred sanctuary for the royal family ever since. It was one thing to have her play hostess at the Fort or even Royal Lodge, residences that were not so firmly associated with the royal family in the public's mind. But Balmoral? The place still kept mostly as it had been during Victoria's reign, a living memorial to her?

This was too much.

"Tommy," Elizabeth said, her voice cheerful and light once more—easily so, because her feet were now on steady ground. "If one were to ring up the publisher of the Aberdeen newspaper and alert him to the fact that the King himself is driving to Aberdeen to meet a train, what would happen?"

Tommy smiled—and it was rather disturbing, that. She wasn't entirely certain she'd ever witnessed Tommy Lascelles smiling, especially not like the Cheshire Cat. "I can only conjecture, ma'am, but I believe it wouldn't be out of the realm of possibility that a photographer might show up."

"Yes, I agree, that does seem likely. Well, Tommy, I must go inside now—would you mind holding my pole? I feel certain a few unlucky trout will come along at any second and I would hate to miss them. Do be a dear." And with that, the Duchess of York shoved her fishing pole into the very unwilling hands of Tommy Lascelles, and she laughed merrily at the sight of him standing in his crisp suit and white shirt, holding the fishing pole as if it were a snapping turtle about to bite.

Striding confidently up the muddy bank to the gravel path, she wondered how one went about finding the telephone number of the Aberdeen newspaper publisher.

—

THE NEXT DAY, RESPLENDENT in a black suit trimmed with dyed-black fox fur, Elizabeth stood dutifully behind her solemn husband as he prepared to cut the wide satin ribbon in front of the door of the new Royal Infirmary. Before them was a crowd of local dignitaries and their wives as well as many wounded soldiers in bath chairs. Older soldiers, naturally, from the Great War. Those whose wounds would never heal. It was odd to see graying hair on the heads of men who had been sent into battle so young. She thought, as she always did, of her brother Fergus. He would remain young, always. That soldiers could live to grow old yet still carry the wounds of that horrible war of their youth—her youth too—was a new idea. Not a welcome one, so she immediately banished it from her head.

Elizabeth smiled her famous smile and clapped her dainty gloved hands after her husband successfully made it through a very short speech with few of his usual hesitant pauses and cut the ribbon. This kind of royal outing was her least favorite but she was quite good at it; she could chat with anyone, say the comforting inanities that these poor souls would carry with them to the end of their colorless days. She could smile and feign delight at rock-hard tea cakes and weak tea and straggly bouquets of flowers timidly thrust at her by little girls dressed in their finest and assure them she'd never seen such beauty in her life. And for the rest of their lives they would remember the moment the Smiling Duchess smiled just at them.

Today, however, as she clutched a soggy, wilting bouquet of Michaelmas daisies, her smile was brighter than usual, and people left the grand opening of the Royal Infirmary of Aberdeen marveling at the charm and sparkle of the Duchess of York, thinking how unusually gay she was, the dear soul, even while mourning the late King.

Meanwhile . . .

CHAPTER
13

SCOTLAND

SEPTEMBER 1936

WALLIS STOOD IN THE FIRST-CLASS TRAIN CARRIAGE WITH Kitty and Herman Rogers, her friends from China, peering out the smudged window and twisting a handkerchief nervously in her hands. David had said to wait until he arrived in his latest sports car, so new that no one would recognize it as his. He would be wearing goggles, he said, to hide his identity. The Aberdeen station was sixty miles from Balmoral, however, and the roads were not good. So he might be late.

"How exciting," Kitty enthused. As the oldest and dearest friends of Wallis Simpson—or that's how Kitty put it to everyone she met now that Wallis was the King's mistress—Kitty and Herman were no strangers to the King. When they were in London, they always met him with Wallis. But none of them had ever been to Balmoral, and while Wallis dreaded it—who on earth wanted to spend time in gloomy Scotland when they could be in, say, the South of France?—she wasn't unaware of the significance of this visit. David had explained it to her, how Balmoral was bought for Queen Victoria by her husband, Prince Albert, and ever since had been part of the royal progress, which was as fixed in stone as the Ten Commandments.

The royals always spent most of August and September there, shooting and picnicking and playing ridiculous parlor games. Inviting the archbishop of Canterbury and the prime minister for visits was *de rigueur*. Attending church was mandatory, not optional, as was watching a variety of Scottish field-game tournaments. David hated it, always had—the gloominess of the castle itself, the isolation, the dullness of his father's routine even more stultifying encased in tartan—and was severely curtailing the length of his first visit there as King, to the horror of his family and staff. But still, he had to put in an appearance and was touchingly eager to show the place to Wallis even as he begged her to "put your American stamp" on the entertainment.

It was all part of the inexorable march to marriage—and the throne—that had recently been set in motion, with Ernest and Mary obligingly spending the night together in a seaside hotel, where they were "discovered" by the hotel detective, establishing Ernest's infidelity. Clearing the way for Wallis to file for divorce, which would happen next month. Smoothing the path to marriage in time for the coronation, and then—

Queen Wallis, forever bound to the King. Yes, with a crown on her head and castles—even gloomy ones—at her disposal. Taking precedence over everyone—the ghost of Uncle Sol and smug little Mary Raffray and poor dull Ernest and Kitty and Herman and Win and Aunt Bessie and her mother's memory and cool, beautiful Princess Marina (a bit too cool and beautiful; she needed to be put firmly in the background) and, best of all, that grinning crocodile of a duchess, Elizabeth of York.

Cookie—oh, what a joke she was; Wallis suddenly started to laugh. The way that dumpy duchess swanned about, lording her status over Wallis! And she wasn't even born royal, not like Marina. As soon as Wallis was Queen, Cookie would be put in her place. And that loathsome China dossier would disappear. She could do that, once she was Queen. She could make anything—and anyone—disappear.

Anyone except for the ridiculous figure roaring up outside in a shining yellow car wearing—yes, he was—dirty goggles. They would fool no one, but when she stepped down from the train, there didn't seem to be anyone around. She was followed by the Rogerses, and David leaped from the car like a rabbit and ran toward her with his arms outstretched—

Click. Click-click-click-click-click.

She heard them before she saw them, the cameras—three of them, aimed right at the quartet and snapping away, disembodied things. She never did see the people they were attached to because it happened too quickly; they clicked, a *rat-a-tat-tat* like a muffled machine gun, then there were feet running away, bodies getting smaller and smaller, and the four of them—David, Wallis, Kitty, and Herman—were staring at one another with stupid expressions on their faces. Asking one another to explain what had just happened—

Then understanding what had just happened.

"How on earth did they know?" David said over and over as they shakily got in the car, Wallis in the front passenger seat beside David, the Rogerses in the back, the luggage to follow in a special lorry. "I never—no one ever comes to Balmoral from the Aberdeen stop. That's why I proposed it."

Wallis smiled grimly as she tied a scarf around her head to keep her newly set coif in place. She donned a pair of sunglasses even though the sun was nowhere in sight; she wished she could shroud herself in a heavy coat or blankets or wrap herself up with gauze like a mummy. Anything to protect herself from more cameras, more eyes. There had been photographs taken of them on the *Nahlin,* which enraged David, but he had a deal with Lord Beaverbrook and the British press, so none of them had run in British newspapers, only foreign ones. She hoped that deal held in Scotland, because she wasn't ready, not yet, for the British public to learn about the American woman who had bewitched the King. She needed time, more time, to figure out how to charm them, to captivate the average Briton, but time was running out with each turn of the calendar toward her divorce proceedings in October.

"How on earth did they *know*?" lamented David once more.

Wallis took a deep breath, tying her scarf more tightly.

"Tommy," she said. "And Cookie." Then the car tore off, and she couldn't hear what David muttered in reply.

TWO NIGHTS LATER, the weekend was in full swing. The local newspaper—the *Aberdeen Evening Argus*—had run the photo of them all getting into David's car alongside a photo of the Duke and Duchess of York opening the Royal Infirmary. No names were listed, so she was still anonymous, thank heavens. No real commentary was made other than the juxtaposition of the two photos. It could have been much worse, so Wallis soon forgot about it and turned her attention to entertaining. The usual crowd—the Coopers, Emerald—had migrated north, but so had the Churchills, Helen and Alec Hardinge, the Rogerses, Aunt Bessie, who had recently sailed from America, and various other nonroyal dukes and duchesses whose names she could never be bothered to remember. There were also some

American celebrities, like Alexander Woollcott and Alfred Lunt and Lynn Fontanne, since David found Americans so amusing. The most important point was that this was the first time Wallis played hostess without Ernest lurking in the background, and she was surprised to find that she missed his sullen but solidly reassuring presence. His perpetual third wheel had served as her training wheels; she would never fall so far or so violently with a husband ready to catch her.

Now the training wheels were off. For the first time at a royal residence, Wallis and David were openly together, just as they would be once they were married and crowned. She was the undisputed hostess, the Queen-in-Waiting.

It was startling; she felt exposed and judged by all, and now if she fell—or if David dropped her—she would be very much hurt, her reputation tarnished beyond salvation. All the gilded doors would be closed to her and she'd have no choice but to slink back to America and live in Aunt Bessie's guest room.

Yet she also felt her skin thrum with excitement, adrenaline coursing through her veins as she embraced being the center of attention, the belle of the party. The presumed next Queen of England, and while eyes did judge her and some guests did dare to pull her aside and lecture her about how to behave—Helen Hardinge had the nerve to tell her she was too brusque with the servants, that in Britain they were treated with kindness!—there was an air of acceptance in the room. No one was overtly hostile, not in the presence of the King.

So when, during Saturday's dinner party, a footman announced "the Duke and Duchess of York," Wallis giddily but confidently strode across the room to welcome her guests. Forgetting any stuffy British notion of precedence or fealty, she held her hand out in greeting as she exclaimed, "Elizabeth! Bertie! Hello! Welcome to Balmoral!"

Elizabeth Bowes-Lyon froze; her eyebrows nearly became mountain peaks, they rose so alarmingly. She was absurdly dressed, as usual—diamonds like icicles hanging from every available surface, a monstrosity of a gown in chiffon. Wallis herself was wearing a bias-cut dress by Schiaparelli, simple lines to show off her figure, although the sleeves were hugely puffed at the shoulders.

"How *dare* you?" Elizabeth's usually lilting voice was as icy as the rocks clinging to her like glaciers to a mountain. "*You,* welcoming *me* to Balmoral? I've come to dine with the King." She then brushed past Wallis as if Wallis weren't even there, leaving a vaguely embarrassed Bertie to trail after her. The crowd parted before her like the Red Sea as she stormed off in search of David.

Wallis froze. Her face burned, but not from embarrassment—from anger. Who the hell did Cookie think she was? *I've come to dine with the King*—as if Wallis were only the help! If that!

"Isn't she delightful?" said Emerald Cunard—overly made up, as usual, the foundation caking in her wrinkles, the kohl smearing around her watery eyes—as she slid up to Wallis.

"Charming," Wallis murmured sardonically.

"She feels threatened, of course. And she wants to be Queen herself—she always has! Practically throwing herself at David in her youth, such a spectacle. She married poor, dull Bertie only because he was the sole royal prince interested. She's always had her eyes on the prize."

"She despises me."

"So what? It doesn't matter, Wallis, darling. You will be

Queen. I have it on the best authority that Mr. Baldwin has all but paved the way with his cabinet. They're all royalists first, politicians second. They'd never defy the King."

"Really?" Wallis turned to Emerald—the dear! The old sage! What a good friend she was! "I'm so clueless about these things. David keeps saying he'll not be crowned without me by his side, but other people do whisper. And judge. And spread malicious gossip." She looked pointedly at Elizabeth, who was now huddled with Bertie in a corner of the drawing room, the two of them visibly agitated. Bertie kept waving at David, trying to get his attention, but the King was too engaged with helping to pass around drinks. He played the charming host a bit too literally, given the army of servants at his disposal.

"Really," Emerald replied. "Don't worry about it, Wallis. Look at you—you're at Balmoral! But, please, darling, I beseech you—*do* try to prevent His Majesty from playing those awful bagpipes after dinner, will you?"

"Oh!" Wallis laughed, relieved. She'd thought she was the only one who found David's habit as annoying as a migraine. He did love to play them, though. He was so convinced his guests loved it too, never suspecting that as his guests were also his subjects, they could never tell him the truth. The only one who could was herself. She delighted in it—she rejoiced in it. The one person who could tell the King of England what to do.

"I'll do my best," she assured Emerald, warmly placing her hand on the older woman's arm. "He listens to me." *He obeys me. I tell him to bow down before me and he does. I scold him for being a bad boy and he cries for forgiveness. He is putty in my very capable hands.*

"Thank heavens! No, wait," Emerald whispered as she

tugged on Wallis's dress; Wallis was about to take her place on David's arm to lead their guests into dinner. "Let *her*. She has precedence, and these things do matter, Wallis. It will look well if you acknowledge that. Show some modesty. It's only for a little while."

"I despise all this pomp. It's ridiculous," Wallis grumbled.

"It's British. You need to get used to it. There." Emerald nodded as dinner was announced and David strode over to his seething sister-in-law and offered her his arm. "That should mollify her. Be sure to let her be the first one up to lead the ladies into the sitting room after dinner. But it's not for long, darling. Not for long—soon it will be Queen Wallis leading the way!"

Wallis smiled, relishing the prospect of having Cookie curtsy to her instead of the other way around. She was a poisonous little woman, but how much harm, really, could she do? Wallis shrugged and was graciously deferential when Bertie—stammering as usual—came to escort her into the dining room, to murmurs of awe and approval.

Wallis wanted to slow down, take it all in—the ancient but still breathtaking splendor of Balmoral, the long dining table groaning with silver, crystal, and gold, the bagpipers (not David, thank goodness!) piping outside while they dined, footmen standing behind every seat. The tartan wallpaper, the stag's heads on the walls (rather grotesque, really; she wondered if David would mind them being removed). It was quite a different thing than entertaining at the Fort. The sense of history, majesty, was more palpable here, and for the first time Wallis wasn't frightened of it. She belonged here, truly—she alone of all the women here had the elegance and presence to outshine her surroundings.

Cookie was a dumpy, fussy little woman in comparison. It was impossible to imagine her on the throne of anything—except the porcelain throne. Wallis stifled a giggle at the thought; that was unbecoming of her.

But, oh, so amusing! Wallis would have to share it with everyone once Cookie went home. Which she did as soon as the men had their cigars, popping up from her seat like she'd just been pinched, screeching for her husband, and saying, loud enough for all to hear, "Thank you so much, dearest David, for inviting us but we are rather tired. Opening the infirmary was very taxing on one, and Bertie needs his rest. We do work so very hard these days. But it's the least we can do to carry on the legacy of dear Papa, God rest his soul. He was such a *good* King."

Then she was gone, tinkling like a Christmas tree with all her baubles, her stuttering husband in her wake. David's face was bright red, his eyebrows like thunderclouds—good. *Finally, he sees her as I do,* Wallis thought. *Finally, he knows her true nature.*

Finally.

WHEN WALLIS AND DAVID left Balmoral three days later, she was already planning her return once she was Queen. She would breathe some life into this stuffy mausoleum—dear God, they even had an old chair that Queen Victoria once sat in, set off to one side like a relic. Yes, those flea-bitten stag heads would be removed, David agreed with her on that, and all that dusty tartan replaced by modern wallpaper—silk, Chinese prints, that sort of thing. Lacquered furniture instead of the horsehair left over from Queen Victoria. David didn't like stalking, and of course she'd rather be dead than spend a day tramping about the hills, so maybe they could put in a croquet lawn, turn the gamekeeper's house into a dance pavilion.

The possibilities were endless!

Smiling, her mind full of plans to modernize with the Crown's money, she even allowed David to put his arm around her shoulders as they and the Rogerses were driven back to the Aberdeen station (she'd put her foot down about the absurd little sports car).

"Did you have a nice weekend, darling?" David asked as they slowed upon reaching the outskirts of the small town. "I'm sorry about Elizabeth—I'll have to talk to her, I suppose. She needs to be reminded of her proper place now that you will be my wife."

"I did have a nice weekend. And Cookie didn't bother me at all—I know an insecure woman when I see one. She's simply jealous."

"She ought to be. You looked divine all—good God!"

David let out a gasp, and Wallis looked at him. His eyes were trained on a wall at the station. She didn't see it at first; she was about to ask him what was wrong when she saw the white paint, the words sloppily done but clearly readable.

Down with the American harlot!

Her throat closed; for a minute her vision wavered and everything turned blurry. Kitty made a strangled sound. David said nothing, not until they were on the train in their private car. Then he summoned brandy and piled blankets on her and fussed about the temperature and ran around closing the window shades, shutting out the world, shutting out those words.

But it didn't matter; every time she closed her eyes, they

appeared, as if illuminated by electricity, ringed with light bulbs, like the signs at the Savoy and the Ritz.

"I'll contact the Aberdeen police right away. They must have some idea who did this—there must be some punishment involved—"

"No, David." Wallis put a hand on his vibrating arm. "No. That will only make it worse. We mustn't stoop to that level. You are the King."

"I'm a man, and I'm going to protect the woman I love."

"But you are the King. First and always."

David peered down at her, the most inscrutable look on his face. Not puzzled, not bewildered. Angry—and perhaps a little sad?

"You are the most wonderful woman in the world, Wallis." He pressed her cold hand to his warm lips. "But sometimes, I don't know if you understand me at all."

Then he smiled. But it wasn't a sad smile. It was the smile of a man who had just figured out the solution to a problem that had plagued him for a very long time.

CHAPTER
14

LONDON

OCTOBER 1936

KING TO MARRY WALLY! WEDDING NEXT JUNE!

THE NEW AMERICAN QUEEN!

KING'S MOLL STAYING IN WOLSEY'S HOME TOWN WHILE AWAITING DIVORCE!

CUTIE SIMPSON CAPTURES KING'S HEART!

"GOOD LORD," BERTIE SAID AS HE SURVEYED THE AVA-lanche of newspapers that Alec Hardinge had fanned out on the drawing-room table at 145 Piccadilly after the breakfast dishes were cleared. Elizabeth, literally clutching her pearls, soothing herself with their cool graciousness, sat next to her husband and tried not to vomit.

"So far it's only the foreign and American newspapers that are covering her divorce," Alec calmly explained, although his left eye was twitching. "But the location of the divorce hearing—Ipswich—was simply crawling with reporters and photographers. Wallis was taken by surprise, much rattled. She and the King weren't expecting it at all—they thought she'd get a nice quiet little divorce and nobody would notice. Your little Aberdeen plot paid off, ma'am. It got the attention of the international press and here we are. Beaverbrook and the other London publishers are still playing ball with the King, but I'm very much afraid it won't be for long."

"Why afraid, Alec?" Elizabeth peered up at the King's private secretary; he was married to one of her oldest and dearest friends, Helen. They'd been debutantes together, and the memory of tipsily laughing in the back seat of taxis after dancing with James Stuart at a ball seemed like a memory of a different person's life. From a different, untroubled time.

"Oh, I don't know." Alec ran his hand through his hair and looked frightful; he probably hadn't slept in days. "Because it's all so sordid. So unbecoming—and I'm afraid, I'm deeply afraid, for you both. Because the King met again with the prime minister, who asked him to stop the divorce, and he flatly refused. Because he's stubborn and childish and must have his way—you know how he is. Because I think he might actually abdicate if he's not allowed to marry her. And if he does abdicate, who's to say he won't take the entire monarchy down with him? Will the people still want it if it's been tainted so? What good is making a case for divine right if one can just chuck it all when it gets too messy?"

The words that Elizabeth both feared and hoped for had finally been spoken aloud. She'd not been able to bring herself to discuss the possibility of abdication with Bertie; he was too fragile these days, too bewildered by his brother's obsession, his recklessness, so she had no idea if the thought had occurred to him; she reached for his hand, gave it a squeeze, refused to let it go. She felt his pulse racing and automatically ran her index finger along his wrist to calm him down.

Then she steeled herself to look at his face. Bertie was pale, his eyes wide and terrified, and he kept swallowing like he was drinking in the air. The idea of David abdicating truly hadn't occurred to him, then. This was a complete surprise—and a horrifying one. To her consternation, his eyes suddenly filled with tears, and he broke down sobbing. She jumped to her feet and flung her arms about his shoulders as he put his head upon the table and wept. Alec hastily removed the newspapers, lest the ink run.

"Oh, my dearest!" Her heart broke for her husband. So quietly determined, always, to do his duty but never once coveting more; in fact, relieved at being the second son and not the first. Happy in their cozy domesticity, loving their daughters, devoting all his free time to them in a way his own father never could have or even desired to. Loving her forever—longer than she had loved him. For love had come, but it had come later in their marriage for her. Always she had admired him and his courage, his doggedness at taming his cursed stammer. His efforts to control his temper. But love—it had crept up on her, melding seamlessly with the admiration and quiet comfort she had always found in his company.

But now she knew it, claimed it—she loved him. As much as *she* was loved, and this was a first for Elizabeth Bowes-Lyon.

That love now caused her grief, as she realized how utterly devastated her husband was by the prospect of becoming King. How it might break him, the burden of the crown heavier on his head than on his golden-haired brother's; David, after all, had trained for the job his entire life. Bertie hadn't. And it was hardly a job one could learn on the fly, was it?

That *she* could rise to the occasion was not in question, and for now, Elizabeth successfully tamped down the little sparks of excitement that she had entertained as of late when she contemplated all the many ways her brother-in-law's affair with

That Woman might end. That David might abandon the throne *had* occurred to her; she was smarter in that way than her husband, could acknowledge this and love him still. Bertie's mind did not work like hers, anticipating all outcomes. He chose one path and plodded down it, undistracted, until he reached the end. Only then was he able to think of another path.

Nor was he prone to believe the worst in people. Never could he have imagined his beloved brother would be so treacherous; Bertie believed in the King much the same way his subjects did, seeing only the good, not the bad. Admired the way the King, particularly when he had been the Prince of Wales, championed the common man, was interested in their plight, outraged on their behalf. Impressed with the way David had traveled the world as no other Prince of Wales had ever done, bringing the Crown directly to its scattered subjects, bringing romance to the monarchy. That was what Bertie saw and remembered—and why he was terrified now. Because no matter how courageous Bertie was, he was not a romantic figure. He had no dash, no élan. That was not why she loved him.

But love wouldn't be enough now. It would help, yes. But it wouldn't be enough. He would need every bit of her polish and cunning and strength if David did what Alec was afraid he would. If he abandoned his family, his country, his throne.

Alec respectfully waited for his potential future monarch to stop crying and pull himself together before he spoke again. "There is, of course, the hope that he won't marry her, that he'll be content to keep her as his mistress. But I fear that hope has all but vanished now that she's divorced. I hear he put her up to it—that she would have been happy to remain married to Mr. Simpson and have things stay the way they were."

"I highly doubt that," Elizabeth said. "She's wanted to be Queen all along and deluded herself into believing the British people wouldn't object to a twice-divorced American slut in Buckingham Palace."

"Elizabeth!" Bertie, his eyes still red, looked shocked, although he couldn't help laughing. "That's unlike you, dearest."

"No, it's exactly like me. And thank heavens for that! We'll need all the humor we can get from now on. Not to mention a *touch* of bitchiness occasionally."

Both men laughed, obviously enjoying, for the moment, some relief from the tension that was going to be weighing every conversation, every look, every thought from now until—

Well, *until.*

"Has the King spoken to you about any of this, Your Royal Highness?" Alec once again looked troubled. There was a decanter of whiskey and a siphon of soda on a tray in front of them, and he reached for both without asking permission. Bertie already had a tumbler in his hand, and she worried about that. He was prone to drinking too much when he was upset. And all she saw from here on out was worry, stress, and strife.

Still, a good belt wouldn't do her any harm right now. So she poured herself a neat glass, forgoing the soda.

"No, he doesn't talk to me at all anymore," Bertie said. "Ever since Papa died, he's kept his distance. I haven't spoken to him since Balmoral."

"Where is the twice-divorced floozy now?" Elizabeth asked calmly.

"He's installed her in a flat here in town. Of course they have to wait several months for the divorce decree to become final—next May."

"Coronation month," Bertie noted miserably.

"Yes."

"Do you think it's possible he'll wait until after the coronation to marry her?" Elizabeth hadn't thought of this before—that he'd be crowned the bachelor King, beloved by all his subjects, and then betray them by marrying the whore *after* the crown was on his head. Worse still, she'd have no choice then but to accept That Woman in her life, to spend holidays with her, to take precedence after her. To watch her Americanize everything—why, she'd probably serve hot dogs on silver trays at Buck House! Install a baseball field in the gardens! Wear shorts and chew gum and play the radio too loudly, awful American jazz, banish Handel and replace him with Sousa, celebrate American Independence Day on the Mall itself!

She grew lightheaded as horror after horror flashed in front of her eyes. How had she not anticipated this?

Think, Elizabeth. Think.

"As long as the British papers keep their silence, she's protected, isn't she?" she asked Alec. "I mean, the people won't know what hit them if the King waits until he's crowned and then springs her on them. And for the moment, she's free to keep swanning about and not be worried one bit about anyone doing her real harm."

"Yes, ma'am. For the most part—although after Aberdeen, there have been more signs the public is aware of her. Graffiti here and there. Not much; enough to outrage the King but not enough to loosen her grip on him. They both seem to be under the delusion that once he's crowned and they're married, the British people will be as enamored with their love story as the rest of the world apparently is. Particularly America."

"What do you think, Alec? Do you believe the British people will tolerate her?"

"Frankly, no, ma'am. They may not mind adultery, but they won't tolerate bigamy. And with two husbands living, that's what she is in the eyes of the Church. A bigamist."

"Then the British people need to know. Now." Bertie straightened his shoulders, and his eyes were cold and clear. Elizabeth had never seen him this way—commanding. One could almost say—

Kingly.

A little thrill tickled her spine as she witnessed her sweet, troubled husband assume, however briefly, the demeanor of a monarch. It wouldn't be this easy, she knew; there would be many more gnashes and tears and melancholy spells spent with a bottle if the worst actually happened and David abdicated.

No. The worst thing that could happen was that he wouldn't abdicate and would marry That Woman.

"Kings—or future kings—shouldn't sully their hands with such matters," Elizabeth said brightly, stroking her husband's arm. "You concentrate on the task at hand: Preparing yourself, should David truly go mad. Using what influence you have with him, trying to make him see reason, although, frankly, I believe that ship has sailed. I'll take care of Mrs. Simpson."

She said it so sweetly, so lightly, the way she might have said, *I'll take care of arranging dinner* or *I'll take care of the Christmas cards*. Any typical female task. Which, really, this was.

Because men always underestimated an alluring female.

CHAPTER
15

LONDON

NOVEMBER 1936

THE FIGURE SMOTHERED IN A VELVET ROBE AND AN ENORMOUS ermine collar was seated on a gold throne. Surrounding him were noblemen resplendent in red tunics with gold braiding, some with staffs in their hands, others with curled wigs atop their heads. Trailing them were little page boys in scarlet tunics with white ruffled cravats, and Beefeaters with flat black hats and meaty legs. The gilt throne completely dwarfed the slender, golden-haired King as he read his prepared speech to open Parliament.

Another invitation to witness history—"What do you say, Wallis?" he'd asked with that twinkle in his eye. It was a present to her, a balm to her jittery nerves after the dreadful ordeal of Ipswich, where she'd been hounded by the foreign press and outraged locals, unable to leave her shabby little hotel except to go to court. Where she was forced to testify to her husband's adultery, outwardly tearful but inwardly seething, for the whole charade had become no charade at all. Ernest and Mary Raffray were now planning to marry; Wallis had lost her safety net forever.

And what had she gained in return?

Well, there was the new flat in London, courtesy of the King, lavishly decorated and filled with fresh flowers daily, a royal car and chauffeur at her command. As well, there were the requests that kept her social secretary busy day and night—would Mrs. Simpson consider being on the board of the Orphans' Institute? Could she put in an appearance at the Royal Opera House on behalf of the Red Cross? Not to mention the invitations to balls and dinner parties from social climbers she'd never heard of and had no wish to.

And there were the charge accounts at Harrods and Selfridge's and Fortnum's. The baubles that arrived in their precious velvet boxes almost weekly. And now this—

The opportunity to sit in the House of Lords and watch her fiancé open Parliament.

Still, Wallis hadn't slept well in weeks. Not since Aberdeen and especially not since Ipswich. One night she would lie in bed imagining her coronation—that priggish Tommy Lascelles bowing to *her,* Wallis! But the next, she would toss and turn, determined to leave David and his eternal, everlasting *want,* flee to freedom and start again. But where would she go? What would she have then for all her troubles? Once she left Britain, she would be a notorious figure, known to one and all as the King's moll. Or former moll. The woman who had broken the heart of the King of England instead of the woman who had captured it. She'd never desired notoriety, only social respectability. And power. She would be the least powerful woman in the world if she left him. She'd have nothing *except* notoriety. And pity, from some.

But was she strong enough to stay?

Wallis heard the whispers when she slid into the Royal Gallery above the floor of the Upper House. She felt the glances branding her skin; she might as well have been wearing a scarlet *A* upon her chest. A scarlet *A* adorned with the royal coat of arms. David had branded her; sometimes she felt as helpless as a calf being brought to slaughter. She hadn't planned any of this five years ago—*five?*—when she was happily introduced to the Prince of Wales by her friend Thelma Furness (now a stone-cold bitch who spread rumors about her). Wallis was entirely blameless! All she'd wanted was to have a little fun, see how the truly rich and powerful lived, be part of that world, help Ernest grow his business. How on earth could she have predicted that the Prince of Wales would become entirely besotted with her?

Oh, no one had as many troubles as she! Wallis shifted uncomfortably in her seat, stroking the pearls at her throat; they'd arrived that morning from Cartier. Oh, well. Once she was Queen, she could lock all those whisperers in the Tower!

When David—the King—entered the House of Lords, she had thrilled to the pageantry in spite of her woes; none did it as well as the English. All eyes were watching her watch the King, and she had held her head high and smiled. Smugly. Because everyone knew that beneath that pile of robes and ermine was the little man only *she* could make weep with ecstasy.

But then the murmurings began again. Did she hear a hiss? She saw the disapproving looks from members of Parliament, after they were summoned, cast upward and landing upon her. The grimacing face of fat Stanley Baldwin, the prime minister. The sickening sweetness of his wife's smile fading as soon as she spied Wallis across the gallery. The ghastly pallor of the Duke of York in his uniform down below—where was Cookie? Wallis looked but didn't spot her. She was not a woman who could hide behind a pillar, not with that figure, so at least Wallis was spared that sight.

Down with the American harlot, the graffiti in Aberdeen had said.

Two days ago she'd walked, as usual, to the hairdresser. For the first time, people stopped and stared at her in the street; she had shivered, despite an unseasonably warm temperature, and hurried on, head down.

Yesterday evening at dinner, David had been as jubilant as if he'd bagged a stag as he planned when they could marry after the decree was final. It would be a spectacle worthy of his Queen—Westminster Abbey, a choir and trumpeters and page boys and little flower girls, a red carpet. All eyes on her, Wallis. Who should design her gown?

"David," she'd said, after allowing herself to visualize it all—the cheers, the trumpets, Cookie forced to witness it in a horrible dress with a sour look upon her face—"I don't know. How can it be like that? I'm not a blushing virgin. Are you sure they'd allow it?"

"I'm King," he'd said with that cocky grin. "I can do anything I want."

Now David was rising; the ceremony was at an end. Parliament could go on doing—whatever it was they did; she had no idea. She supposed it was like Congress at home. But then, she had no idea what they did there either. Make laws. Debate issues. Declare wars.

Little men with big egos, all of them. Just like every man she'd ever known, with the exception of Tommy Lascelles, who was more like a woman than a man, with his exceptional devotion to holding grudges and tallying mistakes and slights. She didn't fear any of the men.

Their wives, however—

As she gathered up her cloak to leave—Chips Channon, David's dear friend, had appeared out of nowhere to escort her, bless him—she heard a woman's whisper, so sharply aimed, it expertly pierced its target's heart:

"What a nerve, to show her face only days after getting her divorce."

Trembling, she clutched Chips's arm and begged him to hurry. She had to get out of here quickly; she had to return to the new flat, where it was safe, where no one would harm her.

Where the King would join her. And remind her of all she had to gain.

IT WAS ONLY DAYS later that David showed up at dinner with a rather determinedly jaunty expression and a letter in hand.

Aunt Bessie had loyally remained by her side through the divorce proceeding—"I promised your mother I'd take care of you when she was gone. And, Wallis, you need taking care of right now." So it was just the three of them at the table when David put the letter next to her plate and said, "Darling, I wanted to keep this from you. But we're a team, aren't we? I think it's damned impertinence! And of course I'll sack Alec Hardinge for writing this. But—well."

Wallis scanned the letter, written in that peculiar combination of obeisance and imperiousness common to the courtier's language.

> *The silence in the British Press regarding your friendship with Mrs. Simpson is not going to be maintained . . . the government may resign if you*

insist upon marrying her. The effect will be calamitous. I urge Mrs. Simpson to leave the country now for the good of all.

Yes! her heart cried out in agreement. *Yes! I'll leave now!* She was half rising from her chair to bolt upstairs and pack when David's petulant voice stopped her.

"Of course you'll do no such thing. I think it's a bluff. This is just one member of my staff talking. I doubt he speaks for the entire government. But even if he does, the people are very fond of me. I've been the most popular Prince of Wales in history. Everywhere I go, the public approves of me, and I know they'll support me—support *us*. This letter—it's just typical of the old-fashioned ways I mean to eliminate when I modernize the monarchy. That scares Hardinge and the others to death, you know, far more than the thought of you. But I'll allow nothing to stand in the way of our love—of we two, forever. They think I'm a king and not a man—goodness knows, that's how my father comported himself, so little wonder. But they don't know *me*. They don't know *us*. And if—and I can't imagine it—but if the government does react this stupidly, I'll abdicate. Pass the salt, please, will you, Aunt Bessie?"

"Pass the salt, please"?

"You fool!" It tore out of her throat, hard as diamonds, sharp enough to pierce flesh. "*Abdicate?* And then where would I be?"

She couldn't believe she'd said it, the one honest thought in her head, the seed of her existence: self-preservation. Always, she'd tried to make their time together all about how she could serve *him,* help him, soothe his aching head and provide rest and recreation from a job too onerous, from a family too scheming and pompous, playing the singsong girl transported to London. She'd hidden her true self from him; she'd hidden it from everybody all her life. Aunt Bessie was probably the only one who suspected the magnitude of her selfishness, which was just the most obvious form of self-preservation, anyway. She was ashamed of this part of her character but also would never apologize for it. And now she'd served it to David on a platter—*pass the salt!* So that he could finally understand her, the real Wallis.

So that he could let her go—with full payment for services rendered, of course—if she couldn't be Queen.

"Why, you'd be with *me*, darling. We'd be together. That's all that matters." David smiled at her so sweetly, so idiotically. Not for the first time, she questioned his emotional maturity. He'd never been told no, not in his entire life, so he couldn't really believe it would happen now—and, more important, he simply hadn't the imagination to envision the hard truths of a former king in exile. How impotent he would be, how purposeless. Always drifting, never in control.

But she could readily imagine it. She'd lived like that, hadn't she? All her life.

Her stomach was roiling; she couldn't bring herself to eat a morsel. David, normally so abstemious, was shoveling food into his mouth with uncharacteristic gusto.

"Wallis," Aunt Bessie said worriedly, "do eat something. You're wasting away to nothing."

David, his fork halfway to his mouth, peered at her, puzzled.

"Not hungry, darling? You're worried, are you? Don't be. I'm still the King. They can't very well behead me. A government in turmoil only means there will be an election. Maybe some will try to advance the cause of my brother—as Shakespearean as that sounds, it could happen. There have been rumblings. But can you imagine Bertie locking me in the Tower and storming Buckingham Palace? Timid little Bertie with his stammer and his tics?" David laughed, and Wallis realized she'd never seen him in so jovial a mood.

"No," she said with a shaky voice. "But I can certainly imagine Cookie storming the barricades."

"In pursuit of an éclair, no doubt!" David guffawed, while Wallis allowed herself a small smile and Aunt Bessie hooted with laughter.

"No, David. You underestimate her."

"Well, I certainly am disappointed in her after her behavior at Balmoral. Now, darling, don't worry. Churchill is with me, and so far Mr. Baldwin has only expressed concern at your divorce; he's not threatened to resign. And Lord Beaverbrook and the other publishers will continue to cooperate with me—it's how the game is played here. They know I'll give them something later in exchange for their silence now. I could always tell them that my youngest brother, Henry, impregnated Beryl Markham before he was married—that's a juicy morsel they'd be grateful for. So grateful, they'd keep you well out of any press. Now, don't worry, darling. My dearest girl—that little line between your eyes is getting too pronounced. Don't trouble yourself further, my Queen."

"I'll try," Wallis said. Because he *was* King. And the people *did* love him. And the smart set all but curtsied to her now when she entered a room. Lavished compliments on her. Sought favor. Jockeyed for position at her court. She'd already ordered lingerie embroidered with the royal arms, as it took some time to get that right—nuns were embroidering them in

Switzerland. Although she'd held off on ordering stationery. For now.

Aunt Bessie suddenly raised her wineglass.

"To the King! And Queen Wallis!"

"To Queen Wallis," David said heartily, leaning over the table to clink his glass against hers.

She smiled. One of her special smiles—head down, eyes up. A promise of ecstasy later.

Anticipation of more baubles tomorrow for her to wear as she sat for one of David's favorite portraitists; it was to be for the wedding announcement, he said. First the wedding, then the coronation; he'd speak with the cabinet about the dates.

AND THEN IT ALL unraveled, so quickly.

One day, David was storming around complaining about some clergyman denouncing him for not being a "godly" King—there was no mistaking the underlying meaning of the attack. "By God, I'll not have some minor rector casting aspersions on my character!"

The next day, the British newspapers broke the story of "The King's Love Affair," complete with Wallis's photograph and name and a timeline of their relationship. Ernest was mentioned. So was Win. And she grimly read all the papers calling her a temptress, a siren, a floozy, describing what was happening as a "constitutional crisis" and blaming her, although she was pleased, at least, to find no unflattering photographs of herself. Still, one name kept screaming in her ears.

Cookie.

Who else? Who else would have fluttered her lashes and promised photos of her darling girls in exchange for the press releasing the hounds? There were ample articles and photographs of the perfect Yorks mixed into the coverage, along with opinions about the line of succession, the suitability of a childless king marrying a divorced American. While some of the coverage was as breathless as a young girl starry-eyed over romance, most of it was downright hostile.

Now David kept disappearing into meeting after meeting with Baldwin, Churchill, and Walter Monckton, David's own lawyer. He rang her in between to assure her of his devotion in an increasingly panicked state. He returned to her in London at night or whisked her away to the Fort for weekends, where they attempted to entertain as usual—only now, a sizzling tension, like electric wires, hung over everything. Their loyal friends—Emerald, Sibyl Colefax, Chips Channon, Walter Monckton, Fruity and Baba Metcalfe, and Duff and Diana Cooper, who had somehow managed not to incur the wrath of the rest of the royal family with their continued friendship—all valiantly tried to distract them from the crisis at hand. Still, David was growing weary of Duff's plea that he wait until after the coronation to marry Wallis.

"No, I've said it and I mean it. I'll not be crowned without Wallis by my side."

There was, apparently, something called a morganatic marriage that would allow Wallis to be his wife but not the Queen—and this was something David appeared to consider, after initial reluctance. But it wasn't what he wanted.

What did Wallis want? That old question, the one she was rarely allowed to pose. No one asked her what *she* wanted in all of this. And she was mired in quicksand, unable to move in any direction lest she be sucked under and suffocated, never to feel fresh air upon her face or in her lungs again.

One day while she was upstairs in the new flat waiting for her masseuse—and thank heavens she was coming; Wallis was so tense, her neck sent sharp lightning bolts into her brain whenever she moved—she heard a loud crash downstairs followed by the sound of glass shattering. She ran down the steps and met the butler, also on his way to investigate, and they both froze on the threshold of the drawing room. An enormous rock had been thrown through the window. Outside, through the gaping hole in the glass, she heard taunts and jeers, saw big signs on wooden sticks.

WALLY, GO HOME!

—

LEAVE OUR KING ALONE!

—

HANDS OFF OUR KING!

—

Every limb trembling, suddenly looking at all the servants with a suspicious eye—would one of them kidnap her? Poison her tea?—she ran to the phone to call David at Buck House.

"David! My God—they've thrown a rock through the window! There are hordes of people outside, and I'm frightened, David. Do something!"

"What? Wallis—hold tight. I'll send someone to fetch you and Aunt Bessie. You'll go to the Fort—pack your clothes, I don't know how long you'll have to stay. But you'll be safe there. Don't worry about a thing—I am still the King."

Still? What did he mean by that—oh, she didn't have time to parse it; she flew up the stairs to bark directions at her maid and yell at Aunt Bessie to pack.

And then she and Aunt Bessie were ushered out to the waiting car, ducking their heads as the furious crowd—red faces, snarling lips, the prim and proper British inflamed with frenzied hate—chanted *Whore! Harlot! Go back to America!* Fists pounded the car windows and she was terrified someone would throw a rock at her, or worse. Finally they pulled away, driving into traffic, unpursued—or were they? She twisted around to look out the back window—was that car following them? Or that one?

They made it to the Fort unscathed but imprisoned. For her own safety, David assured her.

THREE NIGHTS LATER, A miserable, cold, damp Wallis was on a boat heaving up and down on the choppy Channel, bearing her away from England. David's latest meeting with Mr. Baldwin had not gone well; he'd returned to the Fort with a grave expression, no trace of his determined jauntiness or his blithe arrogance. He'd taken her hand and they'd walked up and down the slick flagstone terrace overlooking the Virginia Water, which was partly obscured by fog. Did she see a flash of red out on that water? A memory of the time the pond had frozen over and she and Ernest, along with Thelma, David, and the Yorks, had skated on it filled her vision. She'd been so young then. So carefree—so thrilled at being in the Prince of Wales's orbit. Would she have been content to remain there, one of many?

She knew herself well enough: No, she wouldn't. But how on earth had things come to this?

"Mr. Baldwin said the morganatic marriage is not an option, as the dominions, it appears, won't accept it. Whomever I marry will be thought of as Queen no matter her official status. And since the church doesn't recognize divorce, they say they can't countenance you as the wife of the King. So it comes to this, my darling—I must either give you up or abdicate. And I don't intend to give you up."

The fog seemed to creep in closer and closer until it wrapped itself around her windpipe, strangling her. Just when it was all within reach—she stretched out her hand, groping wildly for something wrenched from her. All she felt was damp air.

"No," she'd managed to choke out, then she took a deep breath and nearly shouted the word: "No! David, you must not abdicate. You cannot. Your place is here. Your people love you. Don't let Mr. Baldwin tell you otherwise."

"Hmm." He'd been lost in his own thoughts, scarcely hearing her. She had to break through to him; she had to buck him up. She had to remind him she was worth the fight.

"David, I'm leaving." She hadn't quite come to the decision until she heard her own voice affirming it. "I'm leaving England. I ought to have left long ago, before things came to such a state." She waited for his cries of protest; she steeled herself for his sobbing embrace.

Instead, he'd turned to her calmly.

"It will be hard for me to have you go, but harder still to have you stay. Who knows what the newspapers will say tomorrow? And the day after that? I'd be frantic about you."

"David, without me to worry about, you'll be able to concentrate on the most important thing. You *must* stay strong and remain on the throne. You must take your case directly to the people—oh! David! You must broadcast your side of it!" It was a flash of inspiration, pure brilliance. "Let the people hear it from *you* and not the newspapers or Mr. Baldwin. They love you. I know they'll be on my—*our*—side."

"I'm not sure the government will allow it."

"How can they prevent it?"

"I'm afraid they can, my love. I'm only a constitutional monarch, you know."

"No, I don't."

"Don't they teach you anything in American schools?" He'd smiled sadly, and she had, for an instant, felt her heart, which had been focused only on herself and her own survival, reach out toward him. "But you are correct, I need to handle this in my own way. Alone."

Standing with him on the terrace of this home they'd shared, where she'd been treated like a queen already, the servants answering to *her,* obeying *her* wishes, where the crème de la crème of society had begged to sit by *her* side, Wallis had wanted the fog to remain. It was like a fairy tale, this setting. Here, right now, she'd thought, they were untouched by the press. She wasn't reviled.

She was Queen.

But tomorrow the fog would dissipate in the sun. Reality would intrude once more. And she would be the harlot who caused a constitutional crisis. No, she knew she must leave and give him time, give the British public time, to find a way to accept her. She wasn't a brave person, she realized with a shock. She'd always prided herself on her self-awareness, but this was a new observation. Bitter, perhaps, but honest. She'd always run from danger and unpleasantness, flight instead of fight. No matter what Ernest had said about how she should have been a military general, she knew she would never lead anyone into battle if real bullets, not figurative ones, were coming her way.

Already there were real rocks.

So she'd packed her bags, hastily. Phoned Herman and

Kitty Rogers and asked for shelter at their home in Cannes, hastily. Kissed Aunt Bessie goodbye, hastily.

And said goodbye to David. Not hastily.

"I don't know how this is going to end, Wallis. It will be some time before we can be together again—now that it's all public, we'll have to wait until your divorce decree is granted. We have to keep up appearances—everything must be perfectly aboveboard. You must wait for me no matter how long it takes. I shall never give you up!"

David kissed her hand, tears in his eyes, as he settled her in the car. One of his closest aides, Perry Brownlow, was accompanying her, along with his chauffeur, Ladbroke, and an Inspector Evans from Scotland Yard as protection.

"You must not abdicate! You must make your case to the people," she'd urged him, even as her fevered mind sorted through various checklists—had she brought her passport? Enough clothes? All her jewels? She'd left her little terrier dog, Slipper, to stay with David to comfort him. Comfort she was no longer capable of giving him herself.

Or that she was too cowardly to give him, absorbed as she was in her own dilemma.

"I will try," David had answered, leaning into the car door for one last kiss. As she met his lips—chastely; there were too many others present, and God only knew what photographers might be lurking in the trees—she'd felt detached from the entire scene, observing it as if she were watching a film. The touching parting of the lovers, one of whom would sail into the unknown. Would they ever meet again?

How could they? The entire scene was so fraught with meaning, so absurd in its melodrama, that it had to be final. If they met again, it would render all this drama ridiculous. It would render *them* ridiculous. Not big enough for the moment. Yet what would happen to her if they weren't reunited? But there were rocks, so many stones and boulders and precipices and hills of granite, in England.

So, dry-eyed and cowardly, she had left.

Later on, she would see it for what it was—her biggest mistake.

CHAPTER
16

LONDON

DECEMBER 1936

DECEMBER 8

PROPPED UP ON SILK PILLOWS, HER HAIR TIED IN A PINK ribbon, and cozy in a quilted bedjacket with a hot-water bottle at her feet, Elizabeth read the *Daily Express* from the comfort of her bed at 145 Piccadilly.

MRS. SIMPSON AUTHORIZES DRAMATIC STATEMENT FROM CANNES

—

I AM WILLING TO WITHDRAW

—

I AM WILLING, IF SUCH ACTION WOULD SOLVE THE PROBLEM, TO WITHDRAW FROM A SITUATION THAT HAS BEEN RENDERED BOTH UNHAPPY AND UNTENABLE . . .

—

The photograph accompanying the dramatic text was of Wallis Simpson wearing a deep-cut evening gown, sleeveless, posing with her arms crossed and a wistful expression upon her face. She looked beautiful.

And devious.

Elizabeth tossed the newspaper onto the floor, pushed herself up, reached for a handkerchief, and blew her nose. She felt her forehead—a little warm, possibly a fever. A reason to remain in bed reading the papers.

Releasing the newspaper hounds had proven to be the right tactic, as they'd chased That Woman clear across the Channel to Cannes, where she'd released this "statement." Meanwhile David, on the rare occasions he remembered he had a family and deigned to grace them with his presence, smiled his Prince Charming smile but remained tight-lipped, refusing to talk about the mounting crisis, the growing outcry in the press, the shouting matches in Parliament as his private life—the private life of the King of England!—was parsed and probed and the very future of the monarchy itself debated.

And always, the specter of the once unthinkable—the idea that took root and then grew alarmingly fast, like a freakish tree: abdication. It now was talked about in the press, debated in Parliament, discussed on the street by costermongers and sweeps. But David refused to reveal what he was thinking. Oh, he'd nodded during one of his meetings with Bertie, so understandingly, when Bertie poured out his fears, his frustrations. Bertie even burst into tears and sobbed on his brother's shoulder, but David did nothing but pat him on the back. When Bertie told Elizabeth that, she had cringed but understood. The appalling realization that he could soon be King, and not only King, but King of a country torn in pieces, for there would always be those loyal to David along with those who increasingly questioned the need for a monarchy at all, had completely undone her dear husband. Even now, no one despised *David;* they only despised That Woman. Bertie knew how the public perceived him—as the slower one, the awkward one, the one who tried so hard, but wasn't that simply a backhanded way of saying that one *needed* to try harder? That one wasn't born with all the gifts one's elder brother possessed in spades?

How could Bertie ever take his place?

He was smoking entirely too much; his fingers were stained with tobacco. And he was drinking more than ever; his temper had a short fuse. While he was never angry at the girls, who had started tiptoeing around their parents with wide, questioning eyes, with Elizabeth he wasn't so careful. He was never angry *at* her. But he didn't hide his fury at his brother's behavior in her presence; indeed, he seemed to find her the only suitable audience for it. It was like sitting in the first row of a fireworks show on Bonfire Night, never knowing if the sparks would reach one or if they'd shoot up harmlessly into the black sky.

During this time, Baldwin found his way to 145 Piccadilly to meet with the Yorks. Churchill did too; although he was firmly on David's side, he was wily enough to stay in Bertie's good graces—that man was a survivor. They dined regularly with Queen Mary, with Bertie's siblings and their spouses. But always the Yorks felt apart from the others, who treated them with wariness, as if preparing for the moment when they would no longer be one of the lesser royals.

So it was Bertie and Elizabeth, together, weathering the storm of uncertainty. She found her mind racing down all sorts of snaking little paths—how on earth would they prepare Lilibet for her new role? Would they need to separate her from Margaret for that preparation, which was unthinkable? They'd have to leave 145 Piccadilly for Buck House, of course, and that was a hideous prospect, residing in that place among all the courtiers and secretaries in their offices, on display like animals in a zoo. This home felt so quaint and cozy, protective. What new protocols would they have to learn overnight? Would she bow to Queen Mary still? No, one wouldn't do that. How would her own family react? Would they still be able to live their quiet lives, all her siblings, her parents, who were getting older, frailer?

And the press—the furies she had summoned with promises of photos of her little girls—would they turn on her someday? For saying the wrong thing or wearing the wrong dress or smiling too much or too little? As Queen, she'd be much more visible; she wouldn't be able to take to her bed—like now—when the world got too complicated. When she didn't want to think of unpleasant things.

All these worries were creating new lines in her porcelain complexion; she slathered her skin morning and night with face cream, trying to prevent them. And had she spied a gray hair today?

But now it was nearly over. This ridiculous article in the newspapers—this "statement." Hollow as a rotten log, it was. Designed only to make That Woman look sympathetic, one last ploy to gain the admiration of those she hoped to rule over. Had she known, when she released this statement to the press?

Did Mrs. Simpson know that David had already decided to abdicate, that he had, the previous evening, summoned Bertie and told him his intention?

The unimaginable was soon to be reality. David would abdicate and leave for France and That Woman. Bertie would be King—King George VI, it was decided.

Elizabeth Bowes-Lyon would be Queen.

DECEMBER 10

Still conveniently in bed with influenza—a mild case, but it did wear one out so!—Elizabeth was listening as Bertie described the signing of the abdication papers at the Fort earlier that day.

"W-w-we were all th-th-there, his brothers, Georgie and Henry and myself, we were the witnesses who had to sign along with David. It was very short, he renounced the th-th-throne for himself and his d-d-d-descendants."

His stammer had come roaring back these past few weeks, unsurprisingly. Bertie already looked ages older than he had before this all had started; Elizabeth quailed to think what the ensuing years on the throne would do to him. He hadn't been eating well, so he'd dropped weight; his collars were too big. She'd have to make sure he had some new ones made up. The King couldn't go around looking like a scarecrow—

The King. Her husband was King—or would be tomorrow. Bertie was saying that Parliament would pass the instruments of abdication *tomorrow*.

"I'm t-t-terrified, Elizabeth." Bertie sat on the bed and lit a cigarette. She normally didn't like him smoking in her bedroom, but today she didn't say a word, only watched as ashes fell on her bed linens, tried to flick them off before they could do any damage. "Terrified. How can I step into his shoes? You should have heard him last night at dinner after we signed the thing. How easily he spoke about the poor, how something must be done. He was so passionate, so determined! I c-c-can't imagine being able to speak like that. The people love him—how will they ever accept me?"

"Bertie, darling. You'll have to give them time! They've

been used to the idea of David as their king ever since he was born. He's had forty-odd years to earn their love and respect—and look what he did with it in the end! Do you think they still love him now that he's betrayed them for *her*?"

"I d-don't know," Bertie said. He looked so miserable, so small and weak. She smiled, patted the mattress, and he curled himself around her so he could lay his head in her lap.

They remained this way for several long minutes, minutes where they heard only the comforting sounds of their home going about its usual business—the steady tick of the bedroom clock, the squeak of a stair step that never would remain fixed, the rustle of servants tidying and straightening, laughter as they passed each other in hallways, the creaking of a rocking horse in the nursery above. All the sounds of their sweet house within earshot. Buck House wouldn't be like this at all—she wouldn't be able to hear it living and breathing the way she could 145 Piccadilly, not with all those great unused halls and enormous ballrooms and warrens of smaller rooms, like offices and package rooms and rooms for the silver, rooms for the china, rooms for their dogs, probably—poor Dookie and Jane, their sweet little corgis! She'd have to ensure they remained in the family quarters and were not fobbed off to staff. The girls were in charge of feeding and exercising them. They would remain so; they must not get absolutely spoiled, one must make sure of that.

Elizabeth was almost nodding off, Bertie's breathing steady and soft, comforting, when she became aware of an unusual sound outside her window. At first it was only a murmur, a little throat-clearing, but then it grew more intense, louder, until it was most definitely the roar of a crowd. A large crowd, by the noise of it, gathering outside 145 Piccadilly.

"Bertie, Bertie, wake up!" But he was still softly snoring, so she slid out from beneath him and, pulling her bedjacket tight to her throat, padded to the window. The curtain was closed, so she pulled it aside a sliver so she could see.

Below her, the street was full of people. All kinds of people—bundled-up children with yellow lollipops and nannies with prams and policemen with nightsticks and businessmen in heavy black topcoats and bowler hats, happy young women wearing bright red lipstick arm in arm with each other, workers in denim coveralls, matrons with old-fashioned hats unmoving on unyielding hair. The British people, she realized with a shock; the good British people, ordinary citizens, not politicians or royalty. The people who were now—even more of a shock!—their subjects. All gathering outside their home; the crowd was filling in at the edges, spilling around the corner of the street.

God save the King! Dear ol' Bertie—God bless 'im!

"Bertie!" she cried, and he rose in alarm, rubbing some sleep from his eyes. "Bertie, come quick!"

"What—what's happened now? Are you all right, Elizabeth?" He sprang from the bed, was by her side in an instant, peering at her worriedly with those troubled blue eyes. But she couldn't say anything else; her heart was suddenly enormous with cheer and hope, the same cheer and hope that the crowd below was radiating in waves, waves so buoyant they had reached her in her sickroom with her sad, tired husband. That same heart also bursting with pride and love for her husband, the King.

She only beamed and nodded down to the crowd, and Bertie's eyes grew enormous; his face reddened, and he tried to speak but couldn't.

"Listen, Bertie—just listen!"

And he did; the crowd was now spontaneously singing "God Save the King"!

"Oh, Bertie, you must go out and say something! The dear people—oh, you must show yourself to them!"

"B-b-but what on earth am I to say?" He looked at her, honestly baffled, endearingly shy. "Why would they want to hear from *me*?"

"Oh, you goose!" Elizabeth wrapped her arms about her husband, warming him—he was trembling—steadying him. "You goose! You don't understand, do you?"

He shook his head, tears making his eyes glisten, his cheeks wet.

"Bertie, it's going to be all right. I know it will—I know it now. That Woman is gone and she won't set foot in this country again, not if I have anything to say about it. And David will be gone too, and you mustn't let him come back for a long while. This country can't have two kings—there's only one, darling. *You*. We can't let David have it both ways; we must be strong. Once he's gone, he's *gone*!"

She didn't mean to say this last with so much vehemence. But David's behavior, his spreading that rumor about her birth, his cruelty (yes, cruelty!) toward Bertie in all this, never once thinking of what his abdicating might do to his younger, more fragile brother—

Elizabeth hated her brother-in-law now. Once she might have been distressed about that. But she was only animated by her hatred, coaxing it into roaring life, knowing it would be useful, this flaming fury, in the future. Whenever she grew weary of the responsibilities, whenever she wanted to retreat and take to her bed or somehow not live up to the expectations of the good people outside her window, whenever she thought of letting them down—this burning core of energy—hatred—would prevent her from doing so. It might not be very Christian; she had a child's fear of hell and damnation that reared its head now and then. But it would be useful. So she reached out, took anger in hand, and named it one of her closest friends.

"He wants to make a broadcast," Bertie mused as, hidden by the curtain, they gazed out at the growing crowd. It was getting darker, and the streetlights were turning on. She saw a young boy with the evening newspapers get swallowed up by people eager to read the latest headlines.

"What do you mean?"

"David. He wants to make a broadcast to the people tomorrow night before he leaves. We're to have dinner, the family—not you, darling, I said you're still recovering."

"Thank you." She closed her eyes, weak with gratitude.

"And after, he's going to broadcast. Baldwin said it was all right, since he wouldn't be broadcasting as King. They asked me how he's to be introduced, though—they can't say 'His Majesty the King' any longer. I've not yet decided what his title will be, but I said that he is still a royal prince, no matter what. So they'll announce him that way—as a prince of England."

"Hmm." Elizabeth took her husband's hand and led him back toward the bed; the lights in the room were on, and it wouldn't do for the crowd below to catch their new Queen in her nightgown. "Bertie, I—well, I do have a thought about all that. About titles and such. But it can wait. We can talk about it later."

"Thank you, dearest. I am rather knackered. I think I'll change and have a tray brought up for my dinner. In here, if you don't mind?"

"Not at all."

"I don't know what I'd do without you, my darling. I could never begin to do all this"—he gestured vaguely with his arm—"without you by my side."

"Fortunately for you, you won't have to!" She kissed him on the tip of his nose, then settled back into bed as he left for his own dressing room.

Outside, the crowd was still growing, laughing, singing. "God bless the Queen!" someone shouted.

Elizabeth Bowes-Lyon smiled.

Indeed.

CHAPTER
17

CANNES

DECEMBER 11, 1936

"A FEW HOURS AGO I DISCHARGED MY LAST DUTY AS KING and Emperor, and now that I have been succeeded by my brother the Duke of York, my first words must be to declare my allegiance to him. This I do with all my heart.

"You all know the reasons which have impelled me to renounce the throne. But I want you to understand that in making up my mind I did not forget the country or the empire, which, as Prince of Wales and lately as King, I have for twenty-five years tried to serve.

"But you must believe me when I tell you that I have found it impossible to carry the heavy burden of responsibility and to discharge my duties as King as I would wish to do without the help and support of the woman I love."

The voice over the radio was less confident than usual, slow, measured. A little tinny, but then it was broadcast from London, and Wallis was in Cannes. A long way away.

And yet not.

She lay on the sofa in the Rogerses' drawing room, one arm over her face so that the others—Kitty, Herman, Perry Brownlow, and members of the staff of Lou Viei, the Rogers villa—couldn't see her face. She longed to be anywhere but surrounded by people, even these close friends, but there was only one radio. And she had to hear him say it herself.

That for the first time in history, the King of England had voluntarily abdicated the throne.

She had to hear the words that damned her to history as well. She'd known what he was going to say, of course. The past frenzied days had done nothing to dissuade him.

That awful night, Wallis had been driven away from the Fort hiding her face with her handbag in case there were any press in pursuit. There weren't then. But by the time the ferry arrived in Dieppe, the King's Buick there had been recognized, and the press were all over the little group of exiles. Yet Wallis and her escorts had to stop for food and rest, and so commenced a ridiculous game of cat and mouse, Wallis hiding beneath rugs in the back of the car, smuggled up to hotel rooms in freight elevators or up back stairs. And she had to call David every day. For the first time it was she, not he, who insisted on this. At that point, in real fear for her safety, understanding what life on the run would be like (and if he abdicated, they would always be on the run, wouldn't they?), she realized her mistake in leaving.

It made her look weak and guilty of something far worse than causing the King to fall in love with her. And he would crumble without her there to prevent it; he'd do the impossible thing and abdicate. So she had phoned every day, no matter where she was, in what inn or what small town in France, and that was hell. Waiting for the operator to put in the call, then waiting for a line to become available. Sometimes she was cooped up in a hot, smelly phone closet for hours at a time, Perry Brownlow and Inspector Evans standing sentry just outside, holding off the hordes of newspapermen and curious onlookers until she felt like an exhibit in a zoo or an asylum. When the phone finally rang with David on the line, the shouting crowd grew eerily silent, listening in. And then *she* had to shout, because the cross-Channel phone lines were terrible, so they could hear everything she said. Which was always:

"You must stay strong! You must stay on the throne! You must broadcast to the public and plead your case! Whatever you do, *you must not abdicate*!"

This was the only way she would not become the most infamous woman in British history. If he remained on the throne, they could plead their case together to the people, and she would be a queen, returning to England in triumph. Or he would finally give her up without betraying his people—

And she would be free.

As the hours and days ticked on and the journey to Villa Lou Viei continued in this farcical manner, Wallis found the idea of freedom, no matter how notorious she was or how punitive her future, more appealing than the idea of being a queen. Because for the first time, Wallis wasn't sure that she could win. The only sensible thing to do was to cash in her chips—thank God she'd brought most of her jewels!—and walk away.

Which she could do only if David remained on the throne and not by her side.

Even after they got to the Rogerses' villa—Wallis again hiding beneath a rug on the floor of the car—she was under siege. Day and night, reporters and photographers and newsreel cameramen patrolled the property. She didn't have the protection of royal guards here, and the Cannes police force was a farce. The weather was cold and rainy, but even so, she would have relished being able to walk outside, to clear her head from the stuffy, hothouse atmosphere inside the villa. In a misguided effort to cheer Wallis up, Kitty had filled every corner with enormous floral arrangements, which gave off cloying, then decaying, odors.

Wallis was so terrified of the press and the deranged onlookers who might prove patriotic in the extreme that she begged Herman to sleep outside her bedroom door on a cot. And he obliged—although Kitty didn't approve, and this too increased the tension in the air of the villa.

More phone calls, more shouting down lines, more confusion when she or David couldn't hear the other, but always, always, her plea:

You must not abdicate!

She released the statement to the newspapers; it was written by Perry but she signed it. Perry—the two of them brought so close through their ordeal, perhaps he was a little smitten with her—had suggested it and, at her request, had also planned her escape. He had an itinerary sketched out: first to Italy, then Egypt, then South America. Seeing the names of these places on paper, with train lines and boat names penciled in, was like putting a key in a locked door and holding your breath just before turning it. Freedom was so tantalizingly close; all she had to do was release that breath, turn her hand. And take the first step.

But she didn't.

There were other ways out—her lawyer had shown up with the suggestion that she stop the divorce proceedings, that it wasn't too late. Then David would have to remain on the throne. He wouldn't abdicate for an unavailable woman, would he?

But she didn't.

The previous night, they'd spoken again.

"David—David? Can you hear me, David?" she shouted on the drawing-room phone—there were no phones in the private quarters, only in the most public room, where everyone could hear. "David?"

"Wallis?" That voice, faint but also shouting, she knew. "Wallis? It's done."

"What? David, what?" Oh, it was absurd! A drawing-room farce. Hadn't Noël Coward written a play with a scene like this? The protagonists comically shouting into phones, unable to hear, misunderstandings ensue until the end, and—curtain!

"Wallis? Can you hear me, darling?"

"Now I can—David, can you hear me?"

"Yes, I—"

"You must stay strong—you must not—"

"It's done. I signed the instruments of abdication. It's done."

She couldn't shout; she couldn't breathe or whimper or cry or run or move a muscle. She was frozen, one hand grasping the receiver so tightly her knuckles were white, the other hand gripping the cord.

"Did you hear me, Wallis? I said it's done—I'm yours, darling. We'll be together forever."

"You damned fool." The words slipped out so easily. She didn't shout them—they were like serpents snaking through the wires of the phone, hissing all the way across the floor of the Channel until they reached the Fort. And David, gripping his own phone and smiling that ridiculous smile of his, the smile she would have to see every day now, for eternity.

"You damned fool," she said again. Louder.

"What? What did you say, Wallis? I'm going to broadcast tomorrow, and then I'm leaving England. We can't be together until your divorce is final, but I'll be in Europe somewhere. I'll let you know. Darling—can you hear me?"

"Yes, David. I hear you." Wallis looked out the window toward the terrace, which was slick with rain from an earlier shower; the tops of the trees were even with her gaze. Were there men with cameras hiding in them, spying on her?

She knew there were ears listening in on the phone line; she'd even made a joke of it a couple of days earlier when she heard the succession of *click*s signaling the various spies—Scotland Yard, royal courtiers—listening in. "Are we all here?" she'd asked. "Good."

But she couldn't joke now.

"Wallis? Darling—"

"I have to go," she said, and put down the receiver. Her legs were weak and rubbery but they managed to carry her upstairs to her room, where her suitcases were open, had been since she arrived. She'd unpacked but kept them ready, waiting—for what?

With a strangled cry, she slammed them shut, then threw herself on the bed. But her eyes were dry; she was no longer a person who could weep.

"AND NOW, WE ALL have a new King. I wish him and you, his people, happiness and prosperity with all my heart. God bless you all. God save the King!"

Someone stifled a sob—one of the Rogerses' servants, no doubt. There was a long silence, then the radio was shut off.

Wallis remained where she was, face hidden by her arm. She looked tragic, she knew. Small and wan (she hadn't been able to eat in days) and tragic. Thank God no one said a word to her; she heard steps as everyone tiptoed out of the room, giving her privacy at last.

He was a fool. What fools they all were—herself included. Queen Wallis—she'd let the flatterers and sycophants like Emerald convince her it would happen. That she would be the Queen of England.

Now she was—nothing. Nobody. Oh, sure, she'd be given some royal title, probably—David was still a prince, that's how they'd announced him on the radio broadcast. She'd be a princess or a duchess or something. But she couldn't see what her life would be with him, the king who gave up his throne to—what was it he'd said? To marry "the woman I love."

Damn him for that, for saying it out loud to the entire world, for showing himself to be the lovesick little boy he was.

Because she could never leave him now.

CHAPTER
18

LONDON

MAY 1937

THE CROWN WAS NOT AS HEAVY AS SHE'D FEARED. IN FACT, it fit her head quite well and was lighter, with moleskin lining to protect her skin, than Elizabeth had anticipated. The coronation ceremony—all symbolism and pageantry and sacred rites, the cheers of the people, the bowing and curtsying as she'd walked back down the aisle of Westminster Abbey behind Bertie after they were crowned—those had felt heavy with portent, with divine responsibility.

But the crown? Not at all! In fact, she looked quite charming in it; her eyes seemed bluer, and her complexion was absolutely set off by the red velvet and the jewels, especially the Koh-i-Noor diamond, the size of a baby's fist, center stage. Her white coronation gown, made by loyal Madame Handley-Seymour, was a long, slim column, and the purple velvet cape, even with its absurd length, also slenderized her figure. Despite her short stature, she seemed to have grown at least a foot in her resplendent robes, the crown giving her height.

She looked—queenly.

At least that's what everyone told her, and mirrors—there

were so many in Buck House!—confirmed it. So did Bertie's eyes and those of Lilibet and Margaret.

"Mama!" Margaret had said when she saw her parents arrive back at Buck House after the long, arduous journey through central London following the ceremony. Riding in the Gold State Coach, even with its wheels and springs freshly oiled, was like riding in a small boat on a big ocean, it heaved and lurched so. It was positively wearing on one's bum, even with the extra padding of royal robes. "Papa! You look *bigger*!"

Elizabeth had to laugh, and Bertie looked as if he wished he could tear off his crown and get down on his hands and knees and play with his girls like he used to, to remind them he was still Papa first, King second. But that was impossible; there was still pomp and circumstance left to endure.

Lilibet and Margaret—perfectly sweet in their white satin dresses, velvet capes, and miniature crowns—had been in their royal grandmother's care throughout the torturously long ceremony, and even though Elizabeth, seated in the center of the abbey and staring straight ahead, couldn't always see them as she and Bertie were anointed and crowned, trumpets blaring, hymns resounding, when she could lay eyes on them, they seemed to be behaving. Of course, Lilibet always behaved, and being eleven to Margaret's seven, she took the role of big sister too seriously sometimes.

Margaret had fidgeted and was seen to yawn once or twice but otherwise made no fuss. The entire ceremony—two and a half hours long!—had gone off without a hitch, even Bertie's vows. He hesitated only a few times, knowing that the ceremony was being broadcast on the wireless.

Knowing that his brother, across the Channel in France with That Woman, would be listening. The thought terrified

Bertie, but Elizabeth had no such feelings. She fortified herself during the long service, which was particularly trying on one's bladder, by imagining the look on That Woman's face when she, Elizabeth Bowes-Lyon, was crowned Queen Consort of the United Kingdom and the Dominions of the British Empire as well as Empress Consort of India.

The girls and Queen Mary had come straight back to Buck House with all the others of the party—the ladies-in-waiting, pages, family, both extended and close, all in their own finery. But Elizabeth and Bertie—the Queen and King—had been driven through the streets lined with cheering crowds, the people undaunted despite the rain, waving white handkerchiefs or miniature Union Jacks, a sea of red, white, and blue. Bunting hung from shop windows that were filled with displays of coronation souvenirs and figures of herself and Bertie—it was astonishing to see oneself depicted through others' eyes! She couldn't help but note that every likeness of herself was a bit too flattering; was it really necessary to whittle her waist to nothing in these figurines and mannequins?

Bertie waved in his bashful way; he still didn't quite believe that he could take his brother's place, and it was Elizabeth's purpose, now and forever, to help him realize that he could not only take David's place but do the job much better.

As they wove their way through the crowded streets slick with rain and *so noisy*—not only with the cheers but the clip-clop of the horses' hooves, the jangling of brightly polished harnesses, the clanging of swords and clinking of medals on uniforms of all the regiments accompanying them—she recalled the previous months.

David had left England for Austria. Out of boredom—or perhaps latent misgivings?—David telephoned Bertie day and night. Often he begged for more money—he had misrepresented the extent of his personal wealth in the initial negotiations, and when Bertie discovered this, he had rightly reduced the financial settlement upon his brother. When not begging, David was giving unasked-for advice about how to rule. These phone calls had so wrecked Bertie's fragile psyche that Elizabeth finally put a stop to them. "Refuse to take his calls," she'd advised, and while Bertie was initially reluctant, he soon acquiesced. One obstacle out of the way, at any rate. Without his brother constantly haranguing him, Bertie gained a little more confidence. But still, not enough. Always the ghost of the charismatic young Prince of Wales seemed to be hovering over her husband, despite the fact that David was no longer that dashing figure. He had changed; he was a pathetic clown, unrecognizable to them.

Still, Bertie was hesitant and tentative, ducking his head and hurrying from car to building when he had engagements, face flushing when confronted by cheers. Even now—after the triumphant ceremony, the cries of the crowd still ringing in their ears—he seemed taken aback by the adulation. More than once, his blue eyes filled with tears.

Elizabeth, however, had no doubts at all about her ability to reign. Waving in her own signature way to the crowds, a circular motion with her raised right arm, something she had hit upon when she first became Duchess of York, she was cool, calm. Thrilled, but composed.

Long live the Queen!

Oh, bless their dear souls!

BACK AT THE PALACE, after the official photographs were taken—a grueling ordeal, having to stand so stiffly; one must not smile, apparently, for posterity, and by now the crown was beginning to feel a bit crushing on one's skull; a headache was starting to introduce itself—it was time for the balcony.

Bertie was absolutely dreading this part. He'd not been able to sleep nights, he'd confessed, dreaming about going out there and being confronted with absolute silence or, worse, hisses and jeers, and she felt him first stiffen, then tremble, as they waited for the footmen to open the glass doors to the balcony from the Centre Room, which was filled with priceless Oriental porcelain vases and vessels.

"Don't forget to smile," Elizabeth whispered to her husband, who was still shaking so much that little Margaret, standing in front of them, looked up at him and took his hand. Lilibet nodded encouragement. "Bertie, you belong here," Elizabeth said. "Don't think of him—let's never think of him again. The people love *you*. Don't be afraid."

"B-b-but, it's just so very—much," he said, his teeth clenching, his throat tense. She was afraid he might burst into tears, but before he had a chance to, she stepped forward and, each holding the hand of a little princess, she and Bertie went out on the balcony.

Elizabeth was already smiling, her hand raised, and she leaned to tell her husband to wave too but she couldn't hear herself speak. The roar of the crowd, bells ringing, noisemakers whirring, was so deafening, it took even her by surprise. For a minute she wasn't sure she could proceed to the front of the balcony; the thunderous adulation was like a tsunami of goodwill pushing her backward until she stumbled against her husband.

So it was he who had to buck *her* up, give her a little push forward, and the two of them, with Lilibet and Margaret, reached the front of the balcony, the rest of the royals—including Marina, always destined to be a few steps behind Elizabeth now—filing in behind them.

God save the King! God save the King!

Long live the Queen! Long live the Queen!

They stood there smiling, waving—Bertie did have to wipe some tears from his eyes, but it only made the crowd even more adoring—for so long her shoulder began to ache and she had to switch arms. But she couldn't have stopped beaming if she'd wanted to; her happiness, her relief, was overwhelming. She took a big, cleansing breath and released it. It was over. All over. The Year of Three Kings was finally at an end.

There was only one King now, and his older brother didn't even cast a shadow up here on the balcony. He was no longer a threat; she knew, finally, that if David did somehow manage to return—although she would do her very best to make sure that he did not—he would never have the love of the people again.

There were other shadows, even if David didn't cast one this day, shadows from across the Channel, shadows from German war planes that were flying over Spain during that country's bloody war. Blustering and posturing from the little man with the ridiculous mustache in Berlin, echoed by the fat bald man in Rome. There would be a new prime minister in only a few weeks; Stanley Baldwin, so instrumental in keeping That Woman off the throne, was resigning and had urged Bertie to appoint Neville Chamberlain to take his place until the next general election.

But those shadows could be banished for now. For this moment one had never dreamed of but welcomed with all the considerable self-assurance and charm and grace in one's possession. Even if she'd never asked nor schemed to be the Queen, Elizabeth Bowes-Lyon had no doubt that she would make an excellent one. A much more suitable one than That Woman—who was going to have a nasty surprise handed to her very soon. Elizabeth smiled even more brilliantly, thinking of it.

Because even as the new King and Queen acknowledged the cheers of their people, an emissary was preparing to sail across the Channel at their request.

Just in time for a certain wedding.

CHAPTER

19

THE SOUTH OF FRANCE

MAY AND JUNE 1937

"I UNDERSTAND WHY THE KING WON'T BE HERE, BUT—NONE of them? Neither of my other two brothers? My sister? My own *mother*?"

David was pacing back and forth on the terrace of the Château de Candé, where they were staying as guests of a new friend (they'd had to replace all their old friends, who had suddenly deserted them, no doubt at Cookie's behest). Charles Bedaux was an American manufacturer with close ties to Herr Hitler in Germany, one of the few heads of state eager to champion the newly created Duke of Windsor. And his soon-to-be wife, the duchess.

It wasn't Queen, of course. But *Duchess of Windsor* did have a certain ring to it. *Her Royal Highness the Duchess of Windsor.* She had already ordered new stationery.

But now David was smoking cigarette after cigarette, not bothering to stamp them out but flinging them about instead, littering the flagstones. Walter Monckton, the lawyer who helped guide David through the abdication crisis, had just arrived with a letter from the King. But first, he had news—news that drove David into an absolute fury. Wallis had been expecting it; David, however, still retained the hope that he would be treated fairly, respectfully, by his family.

Wallis knew better.

"The King has made it clear that none of the family will, er, be able to attend your wedding. But he and the Queen send their best wishes, naturally."

"The King? The *King* has made it clear? That's a laugh, eh, Wallis?"

"I'm sure Cookie is behind this," Wallis said, outwardly cool as she poured lemonade for their guest, inwardly seething.

"I'm certain she is. Bertie is the kindest of souls and would never do me any harm; it's always been *her* egging him on, denying me the money I need to keep Wallis in the style she deserves. And now this—not a single member of my family to attend my wedding!"

"I'm afraid, sir, that Lord Mountbatten has also declined to be your best man."

"Oh, Dickie—the weasel! The cockroach! Well, I suppose I shouldn't be surprised."

"Your Maj—I mean, Your Royal Highness, there's more."

Walter opened his briefcase and produced the letter emblazoned with the King's seal.

Wallis pulled her sweater tightly about her shoulders and closed her eyes. What more could she endure? What fresh hell awaited her?

She had just suffered through the longest five months of her life.

AFTER HIS BROADCAST, in the middle of the night, David left England and headed to Austria, where an acquaintance had offered him refuge at her mansion, Schloss Enzesfeld, while they waited out the months until Wallis's divorce became final. Keeping up appearances even after all was lost—David wouldn't countenance anything else. And Wallis wasn't complaining; her reputation was already hanging by a thread.

During those months, David called her night and day, his mood swinging wildly, one minute crooning sickening love sonnets into the crackling line (she knew they were still being spied on), the next exploding in fury at his brother's penury—"He wants me to have to beg for scraps from strangers!"

(David had, apparently, neglected to inform Bertie of the extent of his personal wealth when they were negotiating a financial settlement. Bertie had, apparently, taken great offense at that and was now threatening to ban David from England unless expressly invited by Bertie.)

The phone calls, the letters, the press stalking her at all hours—Wallis couldn't sleep at night. Could barely eat. She was shot through with jealousy; was his hostess, Kitty von Rothschild, sleeping with David? Ernest and Mary were planning their wedding and she couldn't bear to think of Ernest happy without her.

Who would make Wallis happy? Even now, after the abdication, she couldn't see David as the answer, although, of course, he had to be. But one night, eyes dry from lack of sleep, shaking like a leaf from lack of nourishment, she wildly suggested to Herman Rogers that she would have his child (Kitty could not) if only he would take her away from—

Everything.

"Eat something, Wallis. You're going to put yourself in an early grave" was all Herman said before sending her to her room like a naughty child.

A week later she left the Rogerses to stay with some new acquaintances, the Somerset Maughams, at their villa on Cap Ferrat. Still a houseguest. Always a houseguest.

Always welcomed in an unwelcoming way—a tight smile, a sympathetic tsk-tsk. Proximity to the most infamous woman of the day was the only thing these people, wandering expatriates like herself, valued. Wallis as a person with real problems, they could take or leave. Mostly leave; there was scant sympathy for what she was enduring, although David's sacrifice was much spoken about.

She read that in London, her wax figure at Madame Tussaud's was removed from the display of the royal family and had to be replaced due to vandals. For some reason this filled her with a rage that had mostly been kept simmering in the lowest part of her belly; it erupted, and she screamed at the top of her lungs, throwing a vase across the room like a bad cinema actress.

She packed her trunks and vowed to leave for some unknown destination where David, the press, the spying eyes, the world, couldn't find her.

She unpacked her trunks and wept.

She went to Paris under cover of night wearing dark glasses and a wig and bought forty dresses for her trousseau, sending the bills to David.

And then—the waiting was over. The divorce was finalized, and one day David ran through the doors of Château de Candé, weeping with joy, slobbering on her breast, ruining one of her new Paris gowns. He fell to his knees and wrapped his arms around her legs, and she was unable to move, unable to do anything but pat his head and feel the cold from the marble floor steal all her warmth, her radiance—her very youth.

She knew she would never again dream.

Then David began hopping about like a frog in a frying pan—"You can't have a coronation, darling, so you will have the most spectacular wedding possible!"—taking charge of the plans, inquiring about cathedrals and flowers and choirs and horses and carriages, putting out feelers among the monarchies of Europe to gauge attendance. He worked day and night to find a British clergyman who would perform the ceremony; it still meant something to him that they marry in the Church of England. Dickie Mountbatten promised he'd be David's best man. The Rogerses reappeared; Kitty agreed to be Wallis's matron of honor, and Herman offered to give her away.

Then the telegrams started trickling in. Evidently, this particular June, all the royal families in Europe had unexpected engagements preventing them from attending. David stopped searching for cathedrals and choirs, deciding the small chapel at the château would be perfect—"It will be so intimate, darling. Which is what we want, after all!"

And Walter Monckton, who had been acting as the emissary between David and Bertie, showed up two days before the wedding with his briefcase.

WHILE WALLIS WATCHED THROUGH narrowed eyes, Walter handed the letter from the King to David, who tore it open and began to read. It evidently wasn't a very long letter because it was only a few seconds before David crumpled it and, with a face so twisted with fury she could barely recognize him, threw it on the ground.

Walter hurriedly retrieved it—to save it for posterity? To burn in a voodoo ceremony later? She had no idea other than that it had to be saved. Everything from the royal family had to be documented. Every slight, every slur, every sting.

"What is it, David? What now?" She was nervous but not overly so. Ever since David had joined her, she'd felt as if she were encased in ice, immobilized. Even when she spoke, she felt as if her words weren't being heard. But most of the time, she didn't bother to speak. Or feel.

"My dear brother has refused you your right to be an HRH. It's not legal—it can't be, can it, Walter? Nevertheless he has issued a letters patent that says you may not be styled 'Her Royal Highness' nor be curtsied to or shown any of the deference that should be your right as my wife. He can't strip me of my rightful title, of course. You should naturally be an HRH upon our marriage. But no—no!" David's entire body spasmed with anger; it was as if he were doing a weird modern dance.

"Ah," she said. Thinking it over. With detachment and some amusement. "Ah," she said, and even smiled. She remembered the stationery she'd ordered. She chuckled.

"A fine wedding present from my brother," David spat out, his face still purple.

"So," Wallis said, her mind beginning to speed up a bit, some of that ice melting as her heart began to pound. So from now on, people would bow to David and not her? They would say "Your Royal Highness" to him but not to her? What would they say to her? "And Mrs. Windsor"? "That Woman," as Cookie referred to her?

Cookie.

"She did it," Wallis said, and she noticed that her hands were balled into fists, her knuckles white. She steeled herself for it—the hurt, the betrayal. They pierced her concave stomach, she'd lost so much weight. She'd never looked so chic. Or so haggard. "Cookie. Of course. She's behind everything. She's jealous of me. She always has been. And now she's Queen. *You should never have abdicated!*" Wallis flung herself at David, pounded his chest, grabbed his collar, wanting to tear it from him, wanting to fall entirely to pieces so that he would see, finally, what he had done in his utter selfishness. Destroyed her—ground her into bits of frothing rage and paranoia.

Allowed Cookie to ascend the throne. That fat, frightful cow!

"You did this!" she screamed, and Walter was suddenly gone and David's face was white and she could have picked him up, even in her weakened state, and thrown him over the edge of the terrace, someone else's terrace, not hers, never hers—he was such a pathetic little shell of a man. The world might see him as a great romantic hero, but she *knew* him. She knew him thoroughly, better than anyone, and the great irony was that now she didn't *want* to know him; he could never match Ernest, with his strength and stability and steady way of looking at the world, his ability to protect her.

David never wanted to protect her. Some Romeo! If he had, if he'd truly loved her, he would have set her free with a lifelong annuity and remained on the throne instead of dooming her to a life of wretched infamy and humiliation. A life yoked to him—him minus the crown and the throne and a kingdom and castles and a tower full of jewels.

Drenched in sweat—it pooled beneath her brassiere, ran down her back, stained her new gown at the armpits—she closed her eyes and slid to the floor. The world was too bright, too dizzying, and it spun round and round. Later she awoke in her bedroom—or, rather, a guest bedroom in someone else's house—and drank water as though she'd been shipwrecked, guzzling it greedily. She slept again; she had no idea for how long.

Always dimly aware of a small, broken man sitting in an armchair at the foot of her bed. Too weak even to hold her hand.

SEVEN PEOPLE ATTENDED THE "Wedding of the Century," as the newspapers dubbed it. They gathered in a small chapel that was part of the château. Herman Rogers walked Wallis down the short aisle; she was dressed in a tight, light blue crepe de chine dress with a halo hat and clutched a nosegay of flowers that David had picked out. He'd done all the flowers—there were too many; he'd obviously been thinking of an abbey, not a small chapel, when he ordered them.

When the minister—already defrocked by the Church of England for agreeing to perform the ceremony, dear *God,* these Brits could hold a grudge—asked if David would take her, Wallis, to be his lawfully wedded wife, David shouted his "I will!" like a man defiantly screaming his last words before the hangman's noose.

Wallis whispered her part of the vows while David trembled beside her. She herself was very calm. Completely resigned. Glad, after all, for what was really a clandestine wedding. Had she been forced to perform her role in the Greatest Love Story Ever Told in front of a crowd of hundreds, she doubted she could have done it.

Afterward, outside on the terrace, Cecil Beaton took the photos that would run in every publication across the globe. Understanding the photographs' importance, he begged the couple to look as though they were happy. Wallis tried—honestly, she did; she stood stiffly next to David and smiled wanly into the sun while the camera shutter clicked. David laughed and joked but he too seemed uncharacteristically awkward. When she saw the photos later, she thought she'd never seen a sadder couple in her entire life.

There wasn't a single photo in which the world's most famous lovers were looking at each other.

CHAPTER 20

Queen Mary Interjects

It truly pained me not to attend my eldest son's wedding. I'm not the marble figure they accuse me of being. I do have feelings, maternal feelings. Despite what my sons may have said over the years.

Now, I will admit, I never liked babies. Nor the business of getting them and having them—all so distasteful! So ordinary. The same act that peasants perform, required of kings and queens in order to continue the dynasty. I could never get that thought out of my head when my husband, the King, and I had relations.

Then the unpleasantness of being enceinte itself, the swelling and indigestion and inability to fit in one's gowns, the mood swings that even I couldn't always control. Childbirth—well, at least I didn't have to endure that without the blissful ether allowing me to sleep through it. But waking up with aching breasts, my stomach bound tightly with bandages to help restore a figure that could never be entirely restored, was torture. And then the crying babe itself! I was quite content to have the nannies and nurses take over at once.

Although that is another thing my sons accuse me of: abandoning the two eldest to a cruel nanny, who, they claim, mistreated them. How they can remember this happening when they were so young is a mystery. And as soon as another nurse brought it to my attention, that nanny was banished. But, really, what did they expect me to do? Hover over the nursery at all hours? I was the Duchess of York, then the Princess of Wales, when my children were young. I had duties to perform! A husband who would one day be King to attend to.

Children are always so ungrateful, no matter what one does.

Now David has written to inform me how bitter he is because I did not attend his wedding, and I do believe he has a right to be. Yet how could I be seen as approving of the marriage? No matter how I ached to see my son achieve happiness, if that is indeed what he has attained, I could not cross the Channel. I could not betray another son, my King.

My sovereign. My son. My weaker son, who might well be destroyed by his older brother's abandonment.

My allegiance is to Bertie now. No—not Bertie. I cannot refer to him as that. He is the King. And he will need all the help I can give him. Elizabeth will too, although I'm not worried about *her*. She has her faults, of course. I dislike how cavalier she is about her daughters' education, especially since Lilibet is now heir to the throne. I'm not fond of her fundamental frivolousness; she will always find a way to laugh or joke to lighten a mood. She reads too many novels and eats too many chocolates.

But she is strong and sensible. And during the crisis of the abdication, we saw each other frequently and grew closer than we were before. Women do that, of course. Instead of vying to be the leader of a situation, the commanding hero, we band together. We are born knowing we are stronger than men but must always act otherwise. But when we are together, we unsheathe that strength, taking turns to polish it, to hone it. To brandish it.

And now little Lady Bowes-Lyon is Queen. One day, perhaps, I'll tell her how responsible I am for that.

But I have another daughter-in-law now. One I cannot grow closer to. I cannot receive Wallis Simpson—no, Wallis Windsor.

Imagine.

I cannot receive her. I cannot forgive her. I can perhaps forgive my son, because I love him. Because I ache for him, for the loneliness he must surely come to know living in a foreign land. I cannot see a way in which he can return to this country, for never before has there been a living former King of England. And in spite of his disappointing behavior, his apparent eagerness to abandon his throne and his country, I know that he loves it. England is part of him; it's not just the noble blood flowing in his veins, the bloodline of King George V, Queen Victoria, King George III.

The Scottish Highlands are in how he dresses; he always favored kilts in a way the other boys didn't. The mist from the River Thames, the snow at Sandringham at Christmas, "Land of Hope and Glory" every Sunday. English roasts and bracing tea and strawberries and cream in summer, sticky toffee pudding in winter. I know these are part of him. I know he will miss them all.

And I will miss him. No more will he be part of our family; he forfeited that as well.

And I grieve.

I sent him a telegram on his wedding day, wishing him and

his bride happiness and health. I heard that he was so pleased, he showed it to everyone in attendance.

That grieves me as well, that a few barely considered words from his mother could still mean so much. Did I fail him so thoroughly back when I still had him, when the country still had him? Should I have talked to him before it all got so out of hand, back when Mrs. Simpson was merely an annoying insect and not the probable destroyer of the Windsor dynasty? Would he have listened? I believe there was a time that he would, and then one day I awoke and understood that that day was the day he no longer would. It's like that with children. You never know the last time you will be allowed to caress them, kiss them, influence them. It simply—happens.

There was a time when I would not have allowed myself to even consider these questions or reflections. This is a sure sign that I must, despite all evidence to the contrary, finally be feeling my age.

But the country needs me; Bertie needs me. Lilibet needs me. And them, I can still help. David, my former King, my son, is beyond me now. He has to rely on another woman.

God help them both.

CHAPTER
21

LONDON

OCTOBER 1937

THE QUEEN OF ENGLAND STARED AT THE PHOTOGRAPH. That Woman was beaming up into the face of Adolf Hitler, her hand extended while the führer bowed over it as if to plant a kiss upon those mannish, impeccably manicured, hands. The woman never wore gloves; the better to show off her vulgar rings, no doubt.

Elizabeth tasted acid rising up in her throat.

"How dare they?" she managed to say to Bertie, who was going through the newspapers laid out on a table, his eyebrows raised in alarm.

"How dare they act as if this were a royal tour?" she continued, the anger churning more acid; she stifled a very undignified royal belch. "He said he's researching housing conditions—researching for whom? On whose authority?"

"Not the Crown's," Bertie said. Very softly, but the anger was there.

Good. Anger was strong; anger was *kingly*. Despite the outpouring of affection at his coronation, dear Bertie often still felt like second best, worrying about the long shadow cast by his elder brother even across the Channel. Even from Germany.

Especially from Germany.

"There's really no way to prevent him from going on like this," Bertie said as he continued to look through the newspapers—*Former King Receives Enthusiastic Reception! Declares Germany a Wonder of Modern Technology! Expresses Hope that Germany and Britain Will Negotiate a Lasting Peace Through Diplomacy!*

"I don't like what this might say to our allies, especially the United States," Bertie continued, his forehead furrowed. "He didn't make an official speech, thank God. But obviously he is willing to see Germany as a potential ally, not an enemy. And that is very dangerous right now."

"Did Mr. Chamberlain have any news?" Bertie had had an audience with the prime minister that afternoon.

"Nothing in particular. But Herr Hitler is not hiding his ambitions, and to have my brother go off and have tea with him up on some damned Austrian Alp on what most will assume was an official state visit—it's embarrassing. Damned embarrassing, if not damaging. The world will think that Britain is soft on Germany. When nothing could be further from the truth. I could wring his neck!" Bertie stabbed out the cigarette he'd been puffing and immediately lit another.

Elizabeth frowned, but she wasn't about to nag her husband now. Taking his anger out on tobacco was preferable to him throwing things or having a fit. Those had been few and far between as of late, but any communication from David could set Bertie off. And David simply wouldn't shut up; he wouldn't *leave,* even if he wasn't physically in England. The calls, telegrams, and letters never stopped! He no longer gave Bertie unsolicited advice about kinging, but he still begged for money and beseeched him to give That Woman the title he felt she was due—HRH.

Now this—making headlines in Germany. Determined, as ever, to eclipse his younger brother and perhaps even worse—

To stage a comeback?

"I know why they went," Elizabeth said as she walked over to the drinks cart. It was four in the afternoon, but she needed something right now. She looked over the contents on the tray—the cocktail napkins with the royal crest embroidered upon them, the fine Irish crystal glasses, the assorted liquors from the finest distilleries in gleaming decanters—then pressed a buzzer on the wall.

"Yes, ma'am?" A footman slid noiselessly into the drawing room of their private apartments on the north side of Buck House, overlooking the gardens, and bowed.

"I think we could both use a nice martini. Don't you think so, Bertie?"

"Mmm."

"Of course." And with the expertise of a bartender at Claridge's, the footman quickly filled a small pitcher with ice, gin, and vermouth, stirred, strained, and poured. Elizabeth accepted her cocktail with a gracious tilt to her head, her most charming smile as thanks, and sipped. Delicious.

"Why d-d-d-you think they went to Germany?" Bertie asked after the lad was gone.

"Because—see?" Elizabeth walked back to the table that was scattered with the newspapers, picked one, and held it up for Bertie to see. She was careful not to spill a drop of gin. *The Duchess of Windsor Charms Munich Officials*, the headline proclaimed. And the photograph showed a grinning, pretentiously regal Wallis being greeted by curtsying and bowing "Munich Officials."

"She's being given the full HRH treatment there. He's doing this for her—to show her off and allow her to receive all the pomp and circumstance she will never be allowed *here*. And probably also to annoy you, but mainly it's for her."

"I'm sure you're right, my love. You're always right, especially about her."

"At least now you listen to me."

"She looks well, though." Bertie was staring at another photograph of Wallis in which she was wearing a chic little suit, an enormous diamond brooch in the shape of a tree on her lapel the only adornment.

"I think she looks ridiculous, although at least she's not wearing a lobster dress," Elizabeth said with a sniff; she took another long sip of her cold martini as she remembered that horrific white dress with a giant lobster on it that Wallis wore for some photo around the time of the wedding. Really, That Woman had the most absurd taste in clothing! Such garish colors, tight, tight, tight clothes that accentuated her faults instead of hiding them. Other times she wore frivolous concoctions, such as the lobster dress, that made one question the state of her mind. "That brooch! It must have cost David a fortune. I still say he stole some of the family jewels when he left. Don't those look like Queen Alexandra's diamonds only in a different setting?"

"I have no idea."

"And that suit—it looks like one of those Chanel suits, that French designer. She always did prefer French designers to perfectly good English ones. Who does she think she is? A model? She's emaciated enough, I'll grant you. That hairstyle doesn't help—so severe." Elizabeth patted her own brown hair, curled softly around her face. "And she never wears gloves, have you noticed? With those hands, I'd wear gloves to bed, even! I've never seen such large knuckles on a woman. And you know, there were rumors she had to have electrolysis to remove facial hair. I heard that from several people when she was in London."

Bertie laughed, and although she was happy to hear it, she frowned at him. "What?"

"You women! The way you gossip! I don't care if she's a hairy little ape or not. My main concern has always been that she's bewitched my brother until he's all but unrecognizable. Until he's doing—this sort of thing. In Germany. Which he shouldn't be doing at all because he should still be on the blasted thr-thr-throne instead of me!"

The brief moment of sunshine passed before she could even appreciate it. Bertie was once again blinking his eyes and lighting up another cigarette. He paced the room, not once looking out the enormous windows to appreciate the gardens in their autumn glory, the clipped lawn rolling down to the pond, which was framed with trees whose leaves were turning into muted yellows and oranges.

When would it be over? Would it *ever* be over? Would they ever be able to enjoy one moment's peace without David and That Woman ruining everything? Bertie tried so hard—*she* tried so hard! Now that they were the big show, the main event, life was much more regimented, with little time for lounging in bed reading mysteries or whiling away the afternoon in front of a fire, listening to the wireless.

No, the moment they stepped into the harness, so to speak, time was programmed down to the very second as they followed the prescribed schedule of royal progress and royal duties. Christmas at Sandringham, weekends at Windsor, August at Balmoral after a stop at Holyrood Palace. Photo and portrait sessions and factory openings and sculpture unveilings, park dedications, ship christenings. Investitures in the throne room at Buck House, smiling and shaking hands and smiling and shaking hands, shifting one's weight from foot to foot so that one's legs didn't grow numb, changing gloves every few minutes, they became so soiled. Court presentations and garden parties, so boring but one must always smile, smile, *smile,* marvel at dresses, compliment hairstyles. State dinners—well, those were at least made tolerable by the excellent wines from the royal cellars, cocktails beforehand, and brandy after. Still, one had to talk to dull diplomats and their wives after having stayed up all night reading the briefings about this country or that country, the economic situation or lack thereof, when one really would have preferred to listen to the wireless or gossip with friends.

At these dinners, Elizabeth had to sparkle ever more brightly, laugh more charmingly, focus her eyes more intently on her partner to make up for poor Bertie's awkwardness in most of these situations. The dear man only truly relaxed and charmed when he was doing something with the military—inspecting troops or launching battleships, that sort of thing. The rest of the time the King of England invariably did his best to sidle away and find a quiet corner, or at the very least, he *looked* as if he'd like to sidle away and find a quiet corner.

And Hitler! Always Hitler. Somehow that man came up in every conversation these days. What was he up to? What was fascism, really—wasn't it just socialism dressed up in a military uniform? Surely he couldn't be taken seriously? But then, the mere fact that he was discussed at every banquet, ball, and garden party meant that he already was.

But what did he *want*?

What did *David* want? And That Woman?

That part was easy, at least. Hitler might be a riddle, but David and his wife were not. They wanted to have their cake and eat it too. They thirsted for all the glamour and privilege of being royal without the responsibility he had so willingly abdicated. Look at her! Elizabeth grimaced as she turned over another newspaper. Accepting curtsies and bouquets as if she were Queen Wallis.

"It says in this one that David is planning a similar trip to America soon," Bertie said, slightly more mellow now that his martini glass was empty. She walked over and took the glass from him, pressed the buzzer for the footman again.

"Another, please."

America. She could just imagine the reception Wallis would get in her home country. The very idea made Elizabeth nauseated. *America's Queen. The Queen of Hearts*—goodness.

"Do you—Bertie, do you think it's like Tommy said? That he's trying to stage a comeback? That now he's married, he wants to return? And challenge you for the throne?" She shuddered; how on earth would that be accomplished? She pictured David and Bertie on horses, clad in armor, jousting for the crown, and suddenly she laughed. Looking down at her half-empty martini glass, she stifled another giggle.

"He can't. He simply can't return to the country without my inviting him. Can he?" Bertie's eyes were wide with distress, and his tense face showed every muscle. "C-c-could he?"

"I don't know if Tommy is trying to alarm us or not—you

know he despises David. But he has voiced this concern. I don't truly believe it. I can't imagine David wanting the responsibility of the crown; he always chafed at it, wanting to do whatever he pleased. But he's certainly determined not to go quietly."

"If this was all for Wallis, that's one thing. But to see the former King of England performing the Nazi salute! In front of giant swastikas!" Bertie shoved a newspaper in her hand, and Elizabeth glanced at the photo in question. Shuddering again, she couldn't, this time, prevent a royal burp.

"Her jewels are absolutely vulgar," she commented, looking at another photo of Wallis with enormous sapphires around her chicken throat, encircling the wrists that were entirely too scrawny to support those giant hands.

Bertie, however, was still glowering at the photos of David and Hitler, of those giant spiderlike swastika flags, the people with their arms upraised in that terrifying Nazi salute.

"I thought we were finally home free," she said with a heavy sigh, then sat down because she felt the *teeniest* bit dizzy. But she gazed at her husband, still absorbed in the newspaper headlines, and a hopeful thought pushed its way through the uncertainty, anger, and gin.

"You know, Bertie, that no reigning King or Queen has ever visited America?" Elizabeth made her voice—so musical, so delightful—even more so.

"Really?" Bertie put the paper down, considering. "David went when he was Prince of Wales. So did my grandfather. But I suppose you're right—no King."

"I imagine there are people in America—very important people, perhaps even Mr. Roosevelt—who won't be at all happy about this German visit of David's. Think about it. The only heads of state truly aligned with Hitler are Franco and Mussolini. I expect America feels much like we do about those two."

"Yes, that's the prevailing sense." Bertie shared quite a lot from his meetings with his ministers as well as the contents of his red diplomatic boxes. But sometimes he was cautious with what he told her.

"But I do imagine Mr. Roosevelt would be most excited to be the first American president to host the King and Queen of England. We've our visit to France coming up, but after that, don't we have room in our schedule? We could of course make it primarily a visit to Canada. We haven't visited any of the dominions yet, since India won't have us." She couldn't keep some bitterness out of her voice; the unrest in India against British rule, courtesy of that man in his diaper, Gandhi, was a sore spot. She had looked forward to visiting the colony and being crowned Empress at the Imperial Durbar, but Mr. Chamberlain had warned the King and Queen to expect "unpleasantness" if they proceeded.

"I can't imagine David would be very happy to hear of us going to America." Bertie looked genuinely upset at displeasing his brother. Even with a mass of those newspapers in his hand.

"Remember, *you* are the King," Elizabeth replied gently. She and the girls, despite their youth, had an understanding. They must encircle Bertie with their love, *their* strength, in order for him to succeed in his role.

In order for him to make peace with it and not fret himself into an early grave.

So Elizabeth would continue to remind him that he was the King, that he could do this job. And if an occasional article in

Tatler or the *Daily Mail* mentioned how much the King relied upon the Queen, how she was his rock, his confidante, the sparkling presence that gave his life meaning, that was only the icing on the cake. Speaking of cake . . .

"It's teatime now, dearest. Let's call the girls in, shall we?"

"Marvelous," Bertie said, and his face did finally relax, and his eyes shone when the girls came romping in. He laughed at Margaret's jokes and capers but his eyes always followed Lilibet these days. As if he needed to see for himself that even if he failed as King, he had succeeded in being the father of the next monarch.

But he wouldn't fail as King. Not if Elizabeth the Queen Consort had anything to do with it. So she swept the newspapers into a bin and rang for someone to empty it. All traces of the Windsors and even Hitler were gone. Outside, the light was fading, though in that glowingly warm, russet hue of autumn, and inside, the palace fires were being lit and lights turned on. Margaret started up the gramophone, and soon the royal family was contentedly eating cakes and scones and playing Racing Demon in their drawing room. Safe and secure in Buckingham Palace. In which That Woman would never set one Chanel-clad foot—that much, Elizabeth could guarantee.

Hitler, however—

Nonsense; she shook her head to dismiss the faint chill creeping up her spine.

CHAPTER
22

ANTIBES, FRENCH RIVIERA

JUNE 1939

"COOKIE LOOKS RIDICULOUS IN THAT GETUP," WALLIS SAID acidly as she and David sat in the darkened room, a small table filled with hors d'oeuvres and drinks between them, watching the Pathé newsreels on a portable screen. There was no sound, just the steady clicking of the film projector behind them accompanied by the gentle grunts and occasional farts from the terriers at their feet. "Look at all those frills and ruffles—she's like a wedding cake left too long in the sun. And that parasol, as if she might melt if the sun's rays touched her. How precious."

"She looks as if she's lost weight, though," David replied, and Wallis sniffed.

"She looks like a stuffed sausage. Her girdle must be gasping."

KING AND QUEEN CONQUER AMERICA

—

GEORGE VI BANISHES THE GHOST OF GEORGE III

—

BRITAIN'S QUEEN—A MOST ROYAL CHARMER

—

MRS. ROOSEVELT WELCOMES QUEEN ELIZABETH WITH OPEN ARMS

—

All the intertitles in the newsreels, all the news headlines, were the same: Cookie and her consort were triumphing back home. Back in *Wallis's* home. Where *she* should have been welcomed as America's Queen! She and David had been planning to visit after their trip to Germany, which was such a success.

Ah, Germany.

What a delightful trip that had been! What a balm to the soul. After the awkwardness of the Windsors' honeymoon—they were both so emotionally drained from the drama that preceded it, they'd barely spoken, hiding behind books and newspapers and the blare of the wireless as they'd stayed at various people's lavish homes—the trip to Germany was like a gift from the gods, the wedding gift they deserved. That *she* deserved.

And she had to give David credit for thinking of it, then planning the whole thing with the expertise he'd gained from all the royal trips he'd made as a young man.

Of course, Wallis had her German admirers; Herr von Ribbentrop, the emissary to Great Britain, had been one of her early champions before the abdication, sending her flowers every day, which he continued to do. Unlike most of their so-called friends from those months, who had disappeared like the cowards they were. Emerald Cunard hadn't even sent them a wedding gift! Nor had most of those who had clung to Wallis's hem in London, sure they were backing the right horse, jockeying for positions at the court of Queen Wallis.

Now that she wasn't even an HRH, they had deserted her like the rats they were. Except for some, like von Ribbentrop. And several German officials had sent warm telegrams or presents when she and David were married. Those, they'd kept. David had insisted on returning every present sent by his "godforsaken" family.

David was so furious about his family's continued rejection of her, particularly his brother's refusal to grant her the HRH, he devoted himself to providing her with everything he felt guilty of cheating her out of—and Wallis wasn't going to deprive him of that pleasure.

Gift boxes from Cartier, Tiffany, and Harry Winston full of delicious baubles—a diamond bracelet hung with crosses in every known gemstone; a cigarette case inlaid with a map, made of gemstones, of their trips to the Mediterranean before the abdication; platinum earrings in the shape of flowers with sapphires in the middle; feathers made of rubies and diamonds. And the clothes—she was devoted to the salons of Mainbocher (who had designed her wedding dress), Schiaparelli (who had designed that stunningly delicious lobster dress that Cecil Beaton photographed her in before the wedding), Chanel (who came to Wallis to ask how she had her jackets tailored so exquisitely to her shoulders and then copied them shamelessly).

When Wallis was named to the international best-dressed list in 1938, she considered framing the announcement and sending it to Cookie. Wallis might not be a queen, but she at least dressed like one.

And lived like one! Glancing around the sitting room that linked their bedrooms in the château they had leased in Antibes, Château de la Croë, Wallis sighed with satisfaction. Here and in the Paris house they leased on boulevard Sachet, Wallis finally was able to live the life she'd been deprived of for so long. No longer a houseguest but the chatelaine of her own home. Make that *homes*.

How David got the money—beyond venomous calls to Bertie back in London—she really didn't know, nor did she care to. He was an ex-king, after all; she told herself she had to provide him a home worthy of the castles he had given up. And she was quite frugal, really! It was much cheaper to buy certain things, like Baccarat crystal and Brussels tapestries and silk fabrics for draperies, in bulk. And she could expect discounts when she prowled through the finest antiques stores and furniture showplaces in Paris and here on the coast; all she had to do was agree that they could advertise that the Duchess of Windsor patronized them. And patronize she did—crates and crates of fine *objets* were unloaded nearly every weekend both here in Antibes and in Paris, *objets* she spent long, happy days sorting through and arranging. Many things had to go in storage until she could determine just where to put them. But if she saw something she adored, she had to have it! She could figure out where to put it later.

David had arranged to have some of his things sent from London, although many remained at the Fort in anticipation of their eventual return. But they had his various official robes, uniforms, and honors, paintings of him in full regalia both as a young man and as the King, and these needed a royal setting. And royal both homes were, with their liveried footmen in knee breeches, lavish touches of gold and scarlet reminiscent of Buckingham Palace, and tartan wall hangings echoing Balmoral. Gold-plate dinner services, the finest crystal, antique china sets—but Wallis wasn't afraid to intersperse her own favorites, such as porcelain Limoges vegetables, china dogs, and jade figurines that reminded her of the Lotus Year. She balanced all the tartan and gilt that David favored with leopard prints and brighter colors, yellows and Mediterranean blues. Every inch of each house was designed, staged, and fine-tuned by Wallis herself.

And the parties they gave! Everything had to be perfect—*everything*. Each sprig of parsley on each plate the same size; even the cuts of meat or pieces of fish had to be absolutely uniform. She could spend hours before a dinner party moving forks a fraction of an inch or summoning a footman to refold napkins. Ice was a perpetual irritant—she never could get uniform ice cubes!

And Wallis was in charge. Wallis was the hostess. Wallis was the one bowed or curtsied to, the edict of Bertie be damned; in France, she was Her Royal Highness. The most enchanting seductress of all time, the most photographed—*Life*, *Le Figaro*, *Vogue*, the *Saturday Evening Post*, all had her on the cover—and talked-about woman in the world.

This, then, was what Wallis wanted:

Fame. Fortune. Beautiful objects to fill the emptiness in her heart, the carved-out portions of her soul.

Love wasn't necessary when she could surround herself with such beautiful *things*! When she could be envied for her chicness, have her baubles coveted, her dresses copied, her invitations sought. Oh, she felt affection for David, of course; they had gone through hell together, after all. And, yes, he had given up the throne—good God! The way people still went on and *on* about that! He hadn't even liked being King all that much! And, yes, there were moments that they alone had experienced in a way that no one else would ever understand. Even now, books were being written about the abdication and their great love affair. Most were amusing, but even if she snorted with laughter at some of the more florid descriptions of their romance, she need only to look around their grand houses and be satisfied. Mostly.

Sometimes, when she couldn't sleep, she left her bedroom (she and David naturally had separate suites; they weren't *peasants*) and padded around, up and down lushly carpeted stairways, in and out of rooms vast and intimate. This was *her* home. Even if it was leased, *she* was the chatelaine. And she touched her things, the fine porcelain cool beneath her fingers, the soft silk curtains like rainwater in her hands. Or she simply gazed at them, breathed them in, let their beauty please her eyes as she assured herself of their presence, and this was happiness, then. That she possessed items so fine and precious, that brought her so much pleasure to look at and touch and move an inch this way or that. They brought luxurious order to a life that had been so chaotic. And she was the one, the only one, to *deserve* them. They would always be the same, ever more valuable as the years went by, but their fundamental existence, their appearance, would never alter, would never disappoint. Looking at them would always bring her pleasure.

No matter how often people let her down.

And after she had assured herself of their exquisiteness, their *worth*—and, by extension, her own—she would return to her grand canopied bed with its Belgian linens embroidered with her insignia, intertwined *W*s beneath a crown, and she would finally fall asleep. Satisfied with herself, even proud, for creating a beautiful, aspirational life out of the ugly debris of the abdication.

But was she happy? Could she do this forever, knowing that David was snoring softly in the adjacent bedroom in his silk pajamas embroidered with a crown? Because even in sleep, he clung to what he had once had and given up. For her.

The Germany trip had been both a lifesaver and an eye-opener, because after it was over she was more mindful than ever of what might have been had David not abdicated. For the first time, she was by his side in a public role and not hidden away or watching from a distance. She was able to experience what David had grown to expect on all his royal tours when he was Prince of Wales and then King, tours he still reminisced about at dinners and parties no matter who they were hosting—Greta Garbo or Barbara Hutton or the president of France or Charlie Chaplin. Because to be cheered at every turn, to have trains and boats wait for you and you alone, to expect the royal suite in every hotel, the highest-ranking official as your dinner partner, was highly addictive. Particularly when someone else was footing the bill.

And the German officials were all so charming and flattering! They were firmly on the side of the Windsors and didn't care to hide it. They laughed when Wallis did her impression of Cookie, even if they didn't understand English, and they shook their heads when David (who spoke fluent German) enumerated all the mistakes his brother the King was now making. And Herr Hitler was the most charming of all! A truly gallant man; one who appreciated women, she could tell by the gleam in his eye.

In Germany, she and David truly felt like a team, equally magnetic and beloved, equally important. She was no longer the woman England despised. She was no longer the harlot or the seductress, depending on the point of view; to the Germans, she was Cleopatra in Cartier. She was respected, she was courted, she was feted.

And in Germany, Wallis was especially tender toward David. He sparkled as he had when she first met him as the

Prince of Wales. No longer by turns petulant and sullen, prone to hysterics, he thrived in the spotlight. He was assured, jaunty, calm. Full of interesting questions, sympathetic to the commoner but completely at ease with the highest-ranking Nazi officials. With Hitler himself.

It was simply perfect. More tours were planned, giving shape and purpose to their lives post-abdication. They would be goodwill ambassadors when they weren't holding court in France, bringing their charm and sophistication to the world as a kind of balm in these increasingly troubled times. America, they decided, would be next—even more perfect! Wallis would be welcomed home with open arms; Americans would surely come out in droves to see their homegrown duchess in the flesh. She imagined a ticker-tape parade in New York, a state dinner at the White House, a triumphant return to Baltimore, where she would play Lady Bountiful with her former classmates and friends. David was putting out feelers to some of their American acquaintances in high places when word came from Buckingham Palace that the King would not be pleased by such a visit in the light of their recent trip to Germany, which might be construed as showing support for a fascist government rattling the saber, threatening a European war.

Washington, DC, sent a similar message.

The trip was off.

Meanwhile the sun warmed them on the terrace of Château de la Croë. Wallis had a hairdresser come every day to maintain her sleek coif, even on the nights when it was only she and David dining together. Although she did her best to ensure that didn't happen often; her secretary scoured the gossip columns, was in direct touch with the concierges at the best hotels, had access to the passenger lists of all the ships crossing the Atlantic. Invitations to dine with the Duke and Duchess of Windsor were rarely turned down; two years after the abdication, they were still objects of fascination.

But the latest party thrown by the Windsors couldn't compete with the first visit by a reigning King and Queen of England to the United States; David was despondent watching the newsreels.

"They certainly look more mature," Wallis mused. One of their terriers was begging for a snack, so she reached into a sterling-silver bowl and produced a pitted olive; the dog swallowed it whole.

"*Mature* is kind," David said, frowning at the screen. "My brother looks fatigued as hell."

"Cookie doesn't—it's the fat, you know. All that fat. It keeps the face young. That's the only good thing about it. You know my mantra—you can never be too rich or too thin."

"And you are neither. You are perfection." David reached across, took her hand, kissed it. But then he dropped it and glared at the screen again. Cookie and Bertie were smiling from the front porch of the president's home on the Hudson, a Roosevelt on either side. "You know, the newspapers barely mentioned my speech urging peace. Back home they didn't even broadcast it."

"And it was a brilliant speech," Wallis said automatically. But was it, though? She honestly couldn't recall, but it was part of the game, wasn't it? They had only each other now, no courtiers or prime ministers or Parliament. So each had to constantly flatter the other, even if they didn't mean it. Forever and ever yawned before her, a great gaping maw of false praise and empty promises. With war looming—Germany had invaded Czechoslovakia and was threatening Poland—

goodwill ambassadors were no longer welcome. All the trips were off.

David sighed, got up, walked to the projector, and turned it off, then he flipped a light switch. Wallis grimaced at the sudden glare. He picked up a newspaper from an end table and thrust it at her.

"Look! It says here that the King's visit heralded a new partnership in any war against fascism. They mean against Germany! They're fools, utter fools. Germany will win any war; it's inevitable. Britain doesn't stand a chance. They should be doing everything they can to appease *Hitler*, not Roosevelt. Roosevelt doesn't give a damn over there, but Hitler is right here, and you know I don't want war, but good God! If it happens, we want to be on the winning side this time. Not like last time; it can't be like last time."

"I know, I know."

"No, you don't. Forgive me, darling, but you Americans have no idea what it was like last time—the carnage. The absolute and senseless carnage. An entire generation of men wiped out. No one was spared—even Cookie lost a brother in the war. I went to the front, I saw it—I didn't get to do as much as I wanted to, because the government wouldn't allow me. But Bertie knows, he fought on a battleship. Yet Britain is still honoring its alliances with France and Belgium and Poland and Denmark—the old alliances. And trying to drag America into it too. Good God, I wish—" But he abruptly broke off and began to pace back and forth, his hand massaging the nape of his neck.

"You wish *what*?" she snapped, turning on him in fury. "That you hadn't abdicated? For me?"

"I never said that."

"But you think it."

"I didn't say that either." Suddenly he was down on his knees before her, grabbing her hand. His eyes were wide, pleading; now she was annoyed. *God, don't let him cry.* "Dearest, my angel—my one, my only, my all. I never regret, for one minute, my actions. I will spend the rest of my life making you see that—I swear!"

Wallis allowed David to caress her hand, press it to his lips. Then she retrieved it, rolling her wrist so that he might see how slender, white—and bare—it was.

She sighed. Loudly.

"What is it, my love?"

"I was just thinking. The Mendls are throwing that party at Versailles next month, and I'm planning on wearing my new Mainbocher gown. But I'm not sure I have the right bracelet for it—do I, David? What do you think—do you think the ruby cuff will work with that shade of blue?"

"I do not, and I'm shocked to think that you do!" David sprang to his feet, sloppy sentiment replaced by energy and purpose. "The ruby cuff? With that dress? Nonsense. No, that will never do. I'll call Phillippe at Cartier this instant—there's plenty of time to find something perfect. Nothing but the best for my Wallis, you know!"

And he was off in a flash to put in that call.

Wallis smiled, reached down, and petted the dog by her side. The little terrier sniffed her hand for more food, then yawned, got up, and walked over to the newspaper that David had dropped on the floor. The crocodile-grinning Queen of England was soon forgotten—in fact, soon covered in dog mess. While the Duchess of Windsor was already anticipating the sensual caress of diamonds upon her wrist—canary-yellow diamonds would be perfect with that new dress. Or maybe topaz? Abruptly, she got up, nearly stumbled over the now-steaming newspaper, wrinkled her nose, and left it for the servants. She needed to talk to David before he made that call.

Two bracelets wouldn't be a bad idea, one of each. That would make the most sense, of course.

One had to be prudent about these things.

CHAPTER
23

LONDON

1940–1945

HOUSES.

It was the houses that seemed different to her during the war. Not only the broken houses or skeletons of houses, but all the houses, intact or not. All the houses in all of London, at first, but then also in the other bombed-out cities, like Coventry and Glasgow and Liverpool.

All the houses in all of England.

During the abdication crisis—absurd, now, to think of that time as a crisis! Quaint, actually—Elizabeth had often looked at London's countless houses and flats and marveled that inside them, people had no idea what was going on with their king. Londoners in their homes went about their normal days blissfully unaware of the upheaval that Elizabeth and her family were undergoing, the stress of the unknown, whether David would stay or leave, marry That Woman or not. They had worried that the very existence of the Crown was at stake back in 1937. But inside houses that weren't 145 Piccadilly or Windsor Castle or Buck House or Sandringham or the Fort, no one suspected a thing. The royal family was alone in their turmoil.

But in 1940, Elizabeth looked at all those houses, small and large, and didn't feel alone anymore. Inside every home in England, from Buck House to the poorest workman's cottage, the same fears now resided. The same terror, the same constant anxiety. Because when the bombs started to fall, no one was spared.

All of England was at war.

Bertie put on a uniform on September 3, 1939, and didn't take it off until August 16, 1945. The usual state robes were carefully packed away and hidden beneath Windsor Castle along with the crown jewels. Bertie himself oversaw the latter's removal from the Tower and helped the jewelers disassemble them by hand. The gems were hidden in canisters of sugar and sacks of flour and bags of rice in vast underground tunnels—Bertie kept a meticulous account of where each one went—so that if the Germans invaded, they wouldn't easily find them. These they wouldn't take away from Great Britain.

Bertie put on a uniform; the girls were sent to live at Windsor for the duration (better fortified, with sturdier bomb shelters and outside the city). Elizabeth and Bertie remained at Buck House in London, where their people were suffering so much, during the week and saw the girls only on weekends.

"Send them to Canada!" was Winston Churchill's command; he'd become prime minister when Neville Chamberlain was forced to resign soon after Germany invaded Poland. "We must protect the heir!"

"The girls won't go without me and I won't leave without the King, and the King will never leave," Elizabeth had replied. But she did agree to carry a revolver at all times. "I won't go down without taking a few with me," she said with her famous smile and merry laugh, and secretaries reported it to the newspapers and it was printed for all to see to show that the

King and Queen were one with their subjects, that they weren't going to leave them, that they weren't going down without a fight.

Although it was difficult in those years, excruciating sometimes—many times—to deploy that famous smile and merry laugh. Even though the country needed one's charm more than ever. As much as they needed Bertie's dogged determination. And the two of them—unbowed, with concerned Bertie in his various uniforms, careful never to favor one branch of the armed services over the other, and Elizabeth with her unflappable smile, wearing her furs and brightly colored dresses and coats so that she could be seen from afar—together, a team, a partnership in the truest sense, became the symbol of a people who would not give up. Along with Winston, dear Winston. All his support for David during the abdication was forgiven and forgotten as he gave stirring speech after stirring speech and came to weekly lunches at Buck House, during which the three of them planned and strategized and, yes, laughed and even cried.

Those years. Those dark, hopeless, terrifying, stupefying years.

The worst wasn't the Blitz, although that was bad. September of 1940, after the months of the Phony War, when Germany parked its tanks and guns at the border of France and waited for the world to blink, could never be forgotten. The air raids that became routine—curious how one did get used to the sirens blaring, although it seemed impossible to imagine at first. In the bowels of Buck House, former servant quarters were kitted out as bomb shelters, with rugs and curtains and gramophones with records to play. Elizabeth never moved a foot, even within the palace, without her gas mask in its sweet little case of fur designed by her new dressmaker Norman Hartnell slung over her shoulder.

In those early days of the war, Buck House was like a life raft for deposed royalty. As their countries fell, one by one, the royals of Denmark, Belgium, the Netherlands, Norway, all made their way to London, to Bertie and Elizabeth. The last ones standing. It was surreal to walk the vast, frigid halls and rooms of the palace—windows boarded up or taped, chandeliers lowered almost to the ground and covered in sheets in case of bombing, all the royal paintings carted off to various secret locations, leaving bright, unfaded patches on the wallpaper; ghosts of paintings, Elizabeth thought—and hear all the different languages as queens and kings and princes tried to marshal their scattered governments from afar. They were all desperately clinging to the notion that they still had countries that they would return to once this was over. Queen Wilhelmina of the Netherlands was like a tattered battleship, always wearing a flak jacket over her old-fashioned gowns. King Haakon of Norway, Bertie's uncle, was as determined as a bomber pilot as he planned and plotted, always accompanied by his son, Prince Olav, who was despondent at being parted from his wife and children—the Roosevelts in Washington had taken them in.

Eventually most of the displaced royals made their way to America or other homes, and Buck House was, once again, theirs, Bertie's and Elizabeth's, along with the servants and courtiers who hadn't left to serve in the army, RAF, or navy.

The nightmarish day after the first bombs fell on the East End, Bertie and Elizabeth consulted with Winston.

"Should we go there? Should we see it for ourselves, console the people? Or would we just be in the way of those who can really help?"

"Go," Winston said, without elaboration. So they did. Bertie put on one of his uniforms and Elizabeth wore one of her prettiest dresses, a matching coat with fur cuffs, and a jaunty hat.

"Darling," Bertie said worriedly, "we're not going to a garden party. You'll get filthy and ruin that pretty dress."

"I must dress up for them," Elizabeth insisted. "For if they were coming to see me, wouldn't they wear their finest?"

And this too miraculously found its way into print—after she repeated it to the press secretary—adding to Elizabeth's reputation in the eyes of Hitler as "the most dangerous woman in Europe."

One was quite tickled about that, to tell the truth.

That first trip to see the survivors—that too Elizabeth would never forget. Although there were so many of these unprecedented moments, moments she told herself would remain with her for her entire life, that she eventually wondered how long one would have to live to accommodate the memory of them all. A very long time indeed.

They were driven through the streets slowly, the car having to swerve around rubble and fallen streetlights and craters, police helpfully directing them away from streets that were impassable because of collapsed buildings. Slowly enough for Elizabeth to get used to the sights—smoke, flames still flaring up, enormous gaps where buildings had once stood so that there were odd patches of sky and sunlight. Flowers still, amazingly, bloomed, although trees were bare of leaves as if it were December instead of September. Broken glass everywhere; if buildings were intact, their windows were not. And the sounds—sirens blaring, never stopping, growing louder as ambulances and fire trucks drew near, then fading as they passed, growing louder, then fading.

She didn't truly smell the odors until they stepped from the car, and when she did, she nearly was flattened by them. Smoke, of course; choking, noxious. Burned wood, burned fabric. Burned flesh. Sewer drains exposed or broken, spewing foul vapors into the air. Gas leaking due to broken pipes—"Don't light a cigarette," she hissed to Bertie just in time. She wanted to grab a handkerchief from her handbag and hold it to her nose but knew she could not; there were photographers following them as Elizabeth and Bertie began to pick their way through the rubble to greet the people.

The survivors. The broken citizens of the East End.

There were some boos and hisses, and Bertie looked startled. But Elizabeth didn't break her stride; she knew how it appeared, the King and Queen coming here in their gleaming black car from their fortified palace. The poor people! Children grubby with soot and smoke, some sitting alone on curbs sobbing quietly, maybe clutching a toy; young women holding babies to their chests, men looking lost and useless as they sifted through rubble trying to save something, anything; old women and men who should have been in bath chairs or beds lying flat on the ground or on stretchers. They'd lost everything. And the few who hadn't—for there were some buildings that had been miraculously spared—guarded their homes or stores warily.

And just as warily, they watched the King and Queen.

"I'm so sorry," Elizabeth said gently to a young mother with a little boy by her side; the boy had a fresh bandage around his head, startlingly white compared with his soot-covered, tattered jumper and shorts. "How are you? How is your little boy? What can we do to help?"

Beside her, Bertie was doing his best—small talk never came easily to him, and under these conditions, how could it?—stammering his sympathies, asking basic questions.

It was all they could do. They could inspect and sympathize and question.

They could bear witness.

Soon they had to move on—there were countless neighborhoods that were neighborhoods no longer, more people to console; they would never be able to see them all—and they got back into the car. Elizabeth clutched Bertie's hand; she had seen a dead baby in his mother's arms, the mother not ready to give him up, not believing what she held was real. Elizabeth had seen bodies covered in gray blankets, not entirely whole. She had seen broken toys and plates and lifetimes' worth of possessions shattered and scattered. As horrible as the Great War had been and as devastating as it was to lose her brother, she had mostly been spared its sights and sounds, had seen only the memories of it in the broken soldiers in her care.

She would not come away from this war so unscathed, she understood. Shaking like a leaf—that baby; she'd only glimpsed its face but the skull had been smashed. It didn't take much to break a baby's skull, so she wondered what it had been, a brick or a picture on a wall or a piece of furniture tumbling over; how could such a tiny thing survive Hitler's bombs? Yet other babies had; she'd seen them too. But the one, that precious one, the mother's haunted eyes, the dried blood from her own head wound, but adult skulls were thicker, more protective, that dear baby simply hadn't had enough time for his to thicken and grow, and now he never would;

his eyes were closed as if he were sleeping but the top of his head was flat—

"I don't know if I can do this," she whispered shakily to Bertie. "How can we do this?"

"We don't have a choice," her husband said without a trace of doubt or fear. And so their roles, for the first time, were reversed; Elizabeth's heart faltered while her husband's steady arm gave her strength.

They were driven to the next block; they got out of the car; they did it all over again.

For long weeks, then, this was Elizabeth's life: During the week they drove through London. They climbed atop rubble—she refused to give up her high heels—and accepted cups of tea from survivors. Always, there was someone anxious to provide the King and Queen with a good cuppa, and always they drank it, sometimes sitting on the curb, sometimes on chairs in what used to be someone's kitchen, the floor somewhat intact but in the open air. When the air raid siren sounded, they scrambled for the nearest shelter with everyone else, although they were usually given the best chairs or benches to sit on. They comforted sobbing children; Elizabeth couldn't help herself—if she saw a crying child, she had to stop and console it. They listened to the stories of loss—"I had this 'ere shop for thirty years and now it's gone." "My 'Arry's at sea, what'll he come home to now?" "I don't have no place to stay, do you have room at the palace?"

This last was always said as a joke and always with such good cheer that Elizabeth wished they *could* house them all. Yet even Buck House, Windsor, Sandringham, and Balmoral combined wouldn't hold all the displaced people of London.

And always—*God save the King! Dear old Bertie! God bless the King!*

Fuck Hitler!

A sentiment Elizabeth heartily endorsed.

Then the weekends at Windsor, latching onto the girls and not letting go, feeling their strong limbs and bodies beneath their clean, warm clothes. Smelling hair that was fragrant, freshly washed, and not greasy with soot and smoke. Listening to their chatter, what they'd been up to during the week—Crawfie's classes, Lilibet's lessons with a provost at Eton about the constitution and government. Girl Guides meetings during which they knit scarves for the soldiers at the front. Every week they had a new crush on one of the soldiers who were assigned to protect them. Although Lilibet remained steadfast in her devotion to her cousin Prince Philip of Greece, whom she'd met just before the war at his naval base. But that too was just a crush; the foreign prince was far too old for her.

During those weekends, the King and Queen of England would try to relax. They'd putter in the garden—Bertie was never happier than when he was pruning and trimming and building bonfires with brush, always wearing the same tattered woolen jumper that he refused to give up. They'd listen to the gramophone, although they never missed a news program on the BBC. Bertie still received phone calls and dispatches—the war didn't take weekends off—but mostly, their time at Windsor seemed like something out of a fairy tale, surreal compared to the destruction of London.

Sometimes they'd hear the drone of German bombers passing over Windsor on their way to town, and they'd go out and look at them, marveling at their formation. They'd hear the *ack-ack* from the guns on the ground, nearer London. But so far, few bombs had fallen around Windsor, although there had been several air raid warnings.

On Monday morning they'd kiss the girls and return to London and begin the business of bearing witness, of surviving, of *leading*, all over again.

SEPTEMBER 13, 1940

"Darling, I've got an eyelash in my eye—can you get it out for me?"

The air raid sirens were blaring again, and the Queen and King were on their way down to the shelter. But first they'd stopped in Bertie's office—the windows, many broken from the last time a bomb fell near the palace, still not completely boarded up—so he could get some papers.

"Oh, Bertie." Elizabeth, her arms full of magazines and her gas mask slung over her shoulder, sighed. She dropped everything into an armchair and went to her husband, who was blinking, eyes watering. "I can't see it, move over to the light," Elizabeth instructed, after she'd peered into her husband's weary eyes. "Over here." She led him closer to the doorway, where the light was stronger. He crouched down before her so she could get a better look.

A movement outside the window, clods of earth shooting up into the sky. The air seemed to be sucked out of the room, and then—

An earsplitting concussion, windows shattering, lamps tumbling. The walls shook, the ceiling cracked, and Bertie pulled her down to the ground, where they crouched in the door frame. Servants were screaming and crying in the hall, and footsteps were running toward them; she looked up into the face of one of the pages—Johnny, his name was—who was saying something to her. But she couldn't hear him at first, her ears were ringing so.

"Ma'am? Sir? Are you all right?"

The ringing in her ears persisted, and she worked her jaw to try to make her ears pop. "What—what was it?"

"A bomb, ma'am. We've been bombed—a direct hit."

"Good God!" Bertie helped her up, and they peered into the room. Vases were shattered, furniture overturned. What windowpanes had remained were now gone, and glass was all over the floor near where they'd been standing mere seconds before.

"Ma'am! Sir! Your Majesties!" More and more people were running to the King and Queen, tense faces and hysterical voices. She clutched Bertie's hand as they said, over and over, "We're all right. We're fine."

"That was a near miss." Tommy Lascelles's dry voice cut through the hysteria, and Elizabeth could have wept when she saw him. Just the person to calm them all down! She felt oddly cool and collected but her knees were a bit weak as they all trooped down to the shelter. Bertie saw, and he placed his hand on her back to steady her.

But when Winston arrived after the raid was over, red-faced and agitated and full of questions—Did they see the bomb? What kind was it? Did they have any warning, hear any siren? Did they see the plane?—Elizabeth's entire body began to shake, and she couldn't quite catch her breath until she downed an enormous gulp of Scotch someone poured for her.

"No," Bertie said—he too looked pale and strained, his

neck muscles thick as ropes. "I didn't see anything. Did you, Elizabeth?"

"No. Not even your blasted eyelash!"

Bertie smiled, then paled and clutched her hand as they both realized that had it not been for his wayward lash, they might have been badly hurt indeed.

"I can't believe it. He actually bombed Buckingham Palace while the King and Queen were in residence. That's the biggest mistake Hitler's made yet, mark my words. Nothing could be better for the national morale!" Winston was as ecstatic as a baby after a bath. He rubbed his hands together. "Let's go out and inspect the damage—and someone get a photographer!"

"I'm glad they bombed us," Elizabeth declared as they strolled the grounds, inspecting the broken pavement and fallen stone, the shattered windows, torn-up lawn, while a few invited members of the press were scribbling notes and snapping pictures. "Now we can look the East End in the eye." Chin up, head tilted just so. A new—more determined—smile on her face.

This was printed in all the newspapers the next day, along with the photos. After that, when the King and Queen toured other bombed-out neighborhoods and towns, there were no more hisses, no more sarcastic remarks about their many homes, only cheers and defiance, and Elizabeth understood what Winston meant about this being Hitler's greatest mistake.

The war continued, year after grinding year. Those early years of absolute darkness and desolation, the threat of invasion ever looming, England the lone holdout against Hitler's armies. All the goodwill generated on their trip to the United States seemed pointless now, as Roosevelt couldn't convince Congress to declare war. In those months of 1941, even after the bombings in London had died down (although not in other towns, like Liverpool and Coventry), Elizabeth couldn't muster any optimism at all; their lunches with Winston were gloomy affairs as he numbered the loss of battleships, of troops in North Africa. It seemed inevitable that the Germans would invade.

But later came more hopeful moments—when Hitler decided to turn against Stalin and the Soviet Union. When the United States entered the war after Pearl Harbor. When Montgomery started to win in North Africa. Then more gloom—more bombings in London. Then anxious anticipation—the months leading up to D-Day and lunching at Windsor with that charming General Eisenhower and all the other American generals, an infusion of confidence and soldiers, so many soldiers, now devoted to saving England, saving the entire world.

Then the terror of the buzz bombs just when everything looked to be coming to an end. Worse than the Blitz, even. No warning, just the sudden cut-out of the engine as the pilotless little planes full of explosives fell on their unsuspecting victims.

Tragedy—Prince George dying in a plane crash. Queen Mary frozen with grief, Marina a widow with three small children, the youngest just a baby. Bertie utterly struck through with loss, mourning his younger brother who had overcome so much. They didn't have a state funeral; it wouldn't be right in the midst of so many other funerals. The Windsors mourned their dead like everyone else: Quickly, preparing themselves for more loss, but never really getting over it.

But Bertie—the war *made* him. One of the peculiar joys of those devastating years was watching one's husband finally grow into his role. Gone was the lowered head, the shy bafflement when he greeted people. The endless tours of broken cities, sympathizing with and consoling broken citizens, cured him of that forever. Miraculously, his stutter disappeared during these outings, and the same dogged determination that had seen him propose to her three times propelled a man who was afraid of heights to scale clock towers to survey damage; turned a replacement monarch who had been afraid to talk to his subjects, convinced that they would only be disappointed in him, into a king who chatted easily with those who had lost everything. He was more confident with the government, unafraid to express his opinion about appointments and military issues, although still within the boundaries of the constitution. He no longer looked up to his prime minister as a father figure, someone to teach him. Bertie could hold his own with Winston Churchill, and not many people could say that!

Elizabeth's pride in her husband warmed her during those cold—even in summer, it seemed in memory—years. She'd always been the stronger one in the marriage, which suited her just fine; after all, one mustn't hide one's light under a bushel! If she was a more natural fit for their new roles, there was no reason to apologize for it. But to be able to rely on Bertie for more than just platitudes and adoration felt like coming home, in a way. She could relax a little, not worry about him so much. And the room that worry vacated could be filled by love, reliance. Even joy, even in those years.

When he made an unexpected quip, catching everyone by surprise, he smiled like a proud little boy who had just pulled one over on his schoolmaster. Despite the burdens of his job, he always remembered minor anniversaries—the day of his first proposal, for instance—by bestowing little gifts, like a bouquet of flowers he'd plucked from the garden himself or a dried sprig of heather on her pillow to remind her of her childhood. His contentment—pure, complete—in the company of their little family, "us four," he called them, never ceased to amaze Elizabeth. This was a man who could dine with literally anyone in the world if he so desired. But he always chose home; he always chose family. He never seemed hurried or preoccupied when the four of them were together in their sitting room at Windsor on the weekend. Not even when Elizabeth knew that the red box waiting for him contained the worst of the war news—loss of battleships, setbacks in North Africa, contingency plans for Hitler's invasion.

Still, the war took its toll. Bertie lost weight, smoked more than ever. Neither of them slept well, and it seemed that every dead body they saw in the rubble, every sobbing widow who had just lost a husband, every destroyed landmark of their youth—145 Piccadilly wasn't spared; it was bombed during the Blitz—carved a new line or grayed a new hair. How much longer could it go on?

How much more could England take?

Unsurprising, then, that even during the peak of despair, David and That Woman managed to make things worse.

First, by refusing to leave France when Hitler invaded Poland and war was declared—there was a mad scramble to get them back to England, but David refused to board the airplane Bertie sent for them unless That Woman was guaranteed her HRH title and would be received by the Queen and the Queen Mother.

"Imagine, when the entire world is at war, to be so supremely selfish," Elizabeth sputtered when Bertie told her. "Of course I won't receive her. Neither will your mother."

"He doesn't understand—he's a target now. Hitler would take them hostage."

"Which is probably what he's hoping for."

"And he wants a job. He wants to be of use now, he said. He wants to be in uniform."

"Absurd. He can't in any way represent the Crown. You can't trust him. You can't trust *her*—that's the truth. Remember von Ribbentrop? The rumors of her affair with him?"

"Not proven," Bertie said calmly.

"Not unproven," Elizabeth retorted.

"But you're right, we can't give him anything that provides access to sensitive information. I'll find him a desk job for now, liaising with the French army, as long as France stands."

But when France was invaded, the Windsors lingered at their villa in Antibes, still hosting their posh parties! Finally they realized the situation was serious and they should leave, but they drove through Spain leisurely, as if on holiday, visiting Madrid before motoring to Lisbon. Their situation there took a sinister turn, as depicted in the daily dispatches that Bertie and Elizabeth read side by side. With each report Bertie read, his animosity grew, until finally it was on par with Elizabeth's. He struggled with what to do with his brother and his unseemly demands, with his meddling and worse. Much worse. Churchill agreed that they had to get him entirely off the Continent until the war was over. They knew now they could never trust him again; the dispatches saw to that once and for all. David's betrayal was complete; it wasn't confined only to his family.

He would betray the country of his birth and all the people in it, given the opportunity. And perhaps he already had.

The venom in her veins—and in Bertie's, for finally he had heard enough to harden even his most tender heart against his former king and brother—was truly poisonous. There were moments when Elizabeth knew she could have happily stabbed her brother-in-law in the heart. As for That Woman—

There were no Christian words for what one wanted to do to *her*.

Finally, she, Bertie, and Winston came up with a solution. One that made Elizabeth genuinely smile as she hadn't in a very long time.

CHAPTER
24

NASSAU, THE BAHAMAS

1941–1945

"WITH GREAT PLEASURE I ACCEPT THIS PORTRAIT OF YOUR—our—esteemed queen on behalf of the British Red Cross."

Applause, applause. Wallis smiled tightly and tugged at the gold rope in her hand; it pulled a velvet covering off a portrait of Cookie. A portrait of her head and shoulders only, with her crown and a choker of diamonds, her absurd smile showing all her teeth. The artist had generously deleted one of her chins and firmed up her jaw. Still, he hadn't quite disguised the roundness of her shoulders, the way her neck seemed to melt into them.

Wallis wanted to laugh hysterically, it was so absurdly flattering. Instead, she turned to the crowd before her.

"And thus concludes our meeting. Please join me for some refreshment on the veranda." She remained at the lectern, gripping it. Trying to slow her breathing—she was gasping in the humidity, far worse than she'd ever encountered in China. Good God, the Bahamas were the armpit of the earth. The rank, sweaty armpit. And the woman responsible for sending her here was now grinning behind her for all eternity.

Damn Cookie!

Still waiting for the other women in their linen dresses, straw hats, and gloves to file out to have finger sandwiches and tea (in this heat! Wallis would never understand the Brits, even the ones in this hellhole), Wallis worried that her silk dress—a Schiaparelli—was permanently stained beneath the arms and at her waist. She should have been in her Red Cross uniform, but if Cookie refused to wear a uniform back in England, the only royal woman not to wear one because the King had given her a special dispensation, then Wallis was damned if she would wear a uniform in the Bahamas. Besides, what could they do about it? David was the governor, and they were far, far away from anyone else representing the government.

They were far, far away from everything. Civilization and good hairdressers and fine food and decent shops. Communication was spotty so they didn't always know what was going on in the war. And even though Wallis was grateful she wasn't being bombed, she still couldn't help feeling that she and David were missing out on, well—*everything.*

They were exiles. Again. Still. Chased from France but not welcome in England. Punished by being sent to this hellhole, and Wallis had no doubt that it was Cookie who had decided on the Bahamas instead of Bermuda. Which would have been much nicer! More civilized, less humid.

Instead, she and David had to inhabit a termite-ridden house that she couldn't even decorate to their standards, given the difficulty of importing furnishings and the lack of money; the government back in London seemed aghast that they had even asked for more funds. They'd been told, for the millionth time, that there was a war on. But London had no idea how crumbling Government House was! Tragically unfit for the man who had once been their king. How on earth could Wallis entertain in such a small space, only thirty rooms or so? And the plumbing was an absolute horror! They finally wheedled money out of the government and augmented it with some of their own so they could add a wing and update most of the structure and plumbing.

And they weren't allowed to leave the islands even during the worst of the tropical summer heat! She couldn't escape to New York or even Miami except to see a dentist or a doctor. She'd asked the government if she could have a hairdresser flown in from New York, but no, they said that wasn't permissible. When David proposed that they summer at his ranch in Canada, Bertie refused to let him, expressing astonishment that he wanted to leave his post so soon after taking it up.

After all, there was a war on.

The only war the Windsors fought was with the soupy tropical air, the bugs as big as hands, the mosquitoes, the lizards, the sand, the threat of hurricanes, the lazy islanders who had no allegiance to the Crown, the stuffy government officials and uncouth businessmen and their wives who did but were so provincial, they insisted on asking Wallis how her dear sister-in-law the Queen was doing, how did the Queen Mother take her tea, was the King really as shy as he seemed to be, was Buckingham Palace as grand as they imagined?

The day the Windsors arrived, there was a telegram on every government official's desk reminding the British citizens that they were not to curtsy to the Duchess of Windsor. *Even with a war on,* Cookie and Bertie's pettiness reached across the Atlantic.

And the Windsors fought on another front: the home front.

Boredom, unrelieved—none of their friends, European or American, were going to hop on a boat or a plane to visit them in the Bahamas, war or not—caused them to snip and snipe at each other. They couldn't distract themselves with entertaining on the scale they were used to; their official receptions and dinners were as deadly dull as family reunions. Nassau wasn't exactly the Algonquin Round Table; only the most boring officials with no hope of ascending the government ladder were posted here, and they were all old, of course. Every man under forty was fighting.

Worse still, David couldn't present her with a new bauble each week. He couldn't spend as much time flattering her as he used to. He now had actual work to do: phone calls with shipping companies, meetings with the local conscription board, inspections of buildings, and endless paperwork. He complained about it all bitterly—"What an utter waste of my experience as King!"—but when she did the same about the ceaseless teas she had to host and the small talk she had to make with idiotic matrons who asked if she and the duke were planning on having children ("I'm afraid the duke isn't heir-conditioned," she'd quipped at that, and it really was very good, very funny, and she filed that away to use again with intelligent people once the war was over, *if* the war was ever over), David had surprisingly little sympathy for her.

"There are bombs dropping all over England. I think you can manage to drink tea with a few gossips now and then."

She'd been so shocked by his rebuke, she couldn't come up with a retort. So she sulked—something she was getting very good at these days.

When they did get their periodic shipment of magazines and newspapers, weeks if not months old, Cookie's smug face was on every cover. *The Brave Queen of England*, *The Pluck of Queen Elizabeth*, *A Heroine for Our Time*—goddamn it! Cookie was the most admired woman in the world, ahead of Mrs. Roosevelt, even.

But where was Wallis? Suddenly forgotten by all. She couldn't get even a mention in anything but the local paper. The Windsors were no longer front-page news, and it wasn't fair. This was not why she'd married the former King of England, not at all. Not for this—powerlessness. Invisibility.

Irrelevance.

The Windsors were being punished, but for what? They'd left Antibes once the Germans invaded France—oh, she could hardly bear to think of that beautiful villa! All her precious things; she'd had time to fill only a few crates and store them in a warehouse—then they'd had to jump on a boat and sail to Madrid, then travel to Lisbon on orders of the Crown.

In Lisbon, they were lavishly welcomed by German officials who were keeping an eye on Portugal, making sure it remained neutral. And the Germans were so *helpful* when she asked them to look after the Antibes villa in her absence; more than happy to do so, honored, even. She was sent flowers by the German ambassador every day while the Windsors lingered, luxuriously, in the beautiful villa of a Portuguese banker, who pulled out all the stops to host them. They awaited instructions from London as to where David would be posted—Churchill had refused his request to return to England and reminded them both they would not be received even by Queen Mary, and Wallis would not get her HRH, which had the desired effect of causing David to pout like a child and decide he didn't want to return after all. But all this trouble was mitigated by the many German officials, emissaries of Hitler, who hosted dinners in their honor. In this company, in this strange purgatory—all of Lisbon seemed to be suspended in time, a dreamlike place full of refugees awaiting their final destination—David finally relaxed after their flight. He became reflective and expansive under the Germans' sympathetic hospitality.

"Had I remained on the throne," he assured the German ambassador one evening at dinner soon after they'd been informed of his posting to the Bahamas, the governorship, "Britain would not be at war with Germany. And as much as I despise the idea of bombs falling on citizens, perhaps this is for the best. Bombing Britain into submission until even my idiotic younger brother understands that the only solution is to join forces with Germany. I urged appeasement with Germany and they bloody well wouldn't listen. Now look what it's got them."

Wallis inwardly froze; how stupid was he? Surely David knew that every word he uttered would find its way back to Bertie and Cookie and Churchill and then she would *never* get her HRH. But she caught a knowing wink, a secret little smile meant just for her, and she relaxed. Ah! He wasn't as stupid as all that. He was hedging his bets. Because every word would also find its way back to *Hitler.* Who was winning the war.

"The British King would do well to listen to his wiser brother," the German ambassador—what was his name? Von Hoyningen-Something-or-Other; Germans had the most ridiculous names, even worse than the British!—replied coolly. "But instead he banishes you to the Bahamas like a traitor. Unsuitable for a former king!"

"Entirely," Wallis agreed. "As if David were some minor government clerk!"

"When Germany takes England—as it no doubt will—we will need someone to govern in our name. Herr Hitler cannot be everywhere! And he himself has said that he has no objection to there still being a King of England—*if* he was sympathetic and understood the new world order."

Wallis swallowed a gasp, then linked her arm through David's. She smiled her most charming smile at von Hoyningen. Her pulse quickened as she willed her face to remain neutral, calm, and cool. But her mind, her heart, thrilled at the thought—

She could still be Queen of England after all! If Germany won the war. Which it certainly appeared to be doing while the Windsors dined at German tables in Lisbon in 1940.

And also during 1941, 1942, 1943. Those interminable years in Nassau. David dutifully accepted his posting, but now they both had hope of something bigger, brighter, awaiting them in the end as they swatted flies and hosted tea parties and pretended to be patriotic while knitting scarves and sweaters for the troops. They listened with performative worry in front of their guests when the wireless picked up a clear signal and relayed news of Britain's losses, of the bombings, and smiled broadly, presumably proudly, at any mention of the beloved King and Queen. When they did manage to escape for one teensy-weensy little sanctioned trip to America in 1941—alas, no dinner at the White House, but at least a lovely little parade in Baltimore and vital trips to the hairdresser, the facialist, and Bergdorf's—they were watched like hawks by an agent from Buckingham Palace and jeered by the locals when they returned to Nassau for having abandoned them for a couple of weeks.

Imagine! The cheek of these provincial people!

In private, they received letters from their German friends, coded messages telling them to wait. They scanned letters from the few British friends they had left, searching for signs that Britain was about to be invaded. But Hitler kept hovering in France, never crossing the Channel. What on earth was keeping him? Oh, Wallis couldn't, she wouldn't, remain in the Bahamas forever! The Duke and Duchess of Windsor were being wasted here while Cookie and Bertie were soaking up all the glory in London. Gray, bombed-out, desperate London, but somehow it still hung on. Somehow, the same British people who so hated Wallis that they drove her out of the country managed to show surprising pluck, even humor, and refused to give up.

Even—especially—after Buckingham Palace was bombed. Oh, how Wallis had to grit her teeth and pretend her devoted admiration of the Queen and King when news arrived of *that*! It was the only thing any of these stupid royalists talked about for weeks. Wallis hadn't counted on the war elevating the formerly boring Yorks to mythical status, but that's what it appeared to be doing. And it simply wasn't fair.

It should have been *Wallis* bravely consoling the public, *Wallis* welcoming Mrs. Roosevelt for a visit, *Wallis* on the cover of *Tatler*, of *Time*, of *Life*. With each passing week, month, year, she was fading from the public eye. Would she ever get back in it? None of this was what she wanted—or deserved. Not after all she'd given up.

When David received news of his brother George's death, he was shattered; he turned into a sad little boy before her very eyes and sobbed in her arms while she did her best to console him. And he cherished a letter his mother wrote him in sympathy because she asked him to pass on a kind message to his wife.

But the old battle-ax still refused to call her by her name.

By 1944, the tide was beginning to turn, and she and David no longer believed the Germans were winning the war. By then they were both so thoroughly sick and tired of those stupid islands, so thoroughly starved for the privileged and pampered life they'd been denied all these years, that they were barely speaking to each other. They left Nassau in May 1945, completely dispirited and adrift. Although they were united in some goals. One: to make Bertie give Wallis her HRH.

And another: to reclaim the spotlight and live the life they deserved. Because after Nassau, they both understood that love wasn't enough, not even for the man who had given up his throne for it. As for Wallis, well—

What was love, anyway? Love was a cool diamond against her breast. The newest Mainbocher gown designed solely for her. The freedom to do whatever she wanted, for if she was to be denied a throne—oh, how she seethed when she watched the newsreels of Bertie, Cookie, and Churchill out on the balcony on VE Day, basking in the cheers of a grateful nation!—she needed money. Lots and lots of money to buy all the things that could distract the Windsors from their disappointment in their relatives and in each other.

For David was disappointed in her; she knew it. She suspected he couldn't help but compare her to the dumpy Queen of England and her ability to put on a happy face even while the bombs were falling. By contrast, Wallis had complained about *everything* in Nassau, much more than he had, and while she told herself she was bitter on his behalf, she knew that wasn't completely true. She'd been happy enough in Antibes before the war, when the Windsors were still glamorous, romantic figures, and she'd had a beautiful villa to run. But when all the lovely things were taken away from her and the spotlight faded, she'd shown her true colors, while David, surprisingly, had done a good job as governor, working harder than she'd ever seen him. Exile hadn't brought them riches but it had brought *him* purpose.

However fleeting.

Now she had to find a way to recapture the relative contentment of their time in Antibes before the war; she had to come up with distractions to dazzle them both so that they could blind themselves to the despair, boredom, and recrimination that was always lying in wait, like an alligator lurking beneath a footbridge.

Especially after the war and their dashed hopes of returning to England in triumph.

CHAPTER 25

EDNAM LODGE

OCTOBER 1946

THE MORNING AFTER THE BURGLARY

"Yes, yes, she brought the whole lot over. Yes, I told you—a few things were recovered, those boxes, a couple of earrings. And we found one brooch hidden beneath a jar on the mantel—so strange, that. I don't have an explanation."

David was smoking his pipe, much calmer now in the light of day. Lloyd's of London had sent an agent to the Dudleys' this morning after David called to file the claim.

Wallis stroked her new brooch, the Cartier bird of paradise that had arrived the day before. She'd pinned it to her suit this morning, a talisman. Her very own Order of the Garter. How did it escape; why was it hidden beneath that jar? Who placed it there—someone on the inside? Could it have been Eric, Lord Dudley, who was still blathering on and on about his fishing poles, which had been spared, thank the good Lord? Or Laura, still glaring at Wallis for having the temerity to doubt the loyalty of her servants? Wallis studied her own maid, summoned for questioning, who did look a bit shifty; the woman was not meeting anyone's eye and kept twisting her hair up into a knot that would immediately loosen so her thin hair kept falling to her shoulders. A very untidy look for one's personal maid, and Wallis made a note to sack her once they returned to Paris.

Or could it have been David? He still seemed flustered over the value of the jewels—perhaps a bit too flustered? Wallis didn't know the value and she cursed herself for her lack of knowledge. But David had always taken care of the financial part of their lives, securing the lease of their new home in Paris (for a nominal fee, and they didn't have to pay any income taxes in France), begging for his allowance from Bertie (and bitterly complaining about it), asking well-placed friends for occasional funds in return for the Windsors' glamorous presence at their parties and dinner tables. For that was to be their life now, after the war; this trip had sealed it for her. Any hope that David had of returning to the Fort, of having some kind of ambassador-at-large job on behalf of the Crown, was dashed now. Wallis would arrange to have the rest of their belongings shipped to Paris, where they would remain in exile with occasional trips to New York City. A life of frivolous fabulousness; now that the war was over, Café Society was once again playing and partying and grabbing the headlines. At least in France it was, and in America. And in both countries, the Windsors were fashionable again.

Britain, as always, was different. Despite its victory, it acted defeated. Glamour had no place here. The dowdy Queen and King, with their dutiful daughters—what had David once said? That Bertie and Elizabeth made royalty look positively middle class? They perfectly fit the times. Queen Wallis would have been tragically wasted in postwar Britain. Or so she often told herself.

So she need never come back. That chapter was, once and for all, over. She knew it, even if David didn't.

"I'm sure my brother the King will be most anxious to have this settled as soon as possible," David was telling the detective now, and Wallis's heart did twinge to hear the former golden Prince of Wales rely on his younger brother's name to get things done. Once, he'd had the world at his command. Once, he'd convinced her that she could too.

Once.

"We'll get right on it, Your Ma—Your Royal Highness." The man, embarrassed, started to leave the room, then stopped and bowed to David, then turned to Wallis, then looked confused, then practically fled to safety.

And it would be forever thus.

"Now what?" Wallis asked her husband. Whom she very rarely referred to in that way, she realized. Never did she say "My husband thinks this" or "My husband would enjoy that." It was always "the duke." "The duke would like trout for dinner tonight"; "The duke and I would be pleased to accept your kind invitation."

Funny. She'd never noticed this before.

"Now we wait. I have to make copies of the receipts, which are back in Paris."

"Back *home*," she said firmly. "Listen to me, David. *Paris* is home now. Not here. Not this dreadful country. It will never be our home, never again."

He looked at her with the expression of someone who had just found out that there really wasn't a pot of gold at the end of the rainbow. And she felt terrible, as if she were the one who had stolen it. But it wasn't her, it was his damnable family who had destroyed his hopes, his fantasies—his assumption that the former King of England would at least have the same rights as the lowest British citizen.

But he didn't.

"I don't—I just thought it would be different. This is my home, my kingdom. I don't want to steal it from my brother but I don't deserve to be exiled from it all my life. Didn't I do well in the Bahamas? Why should I still be punished? All I did was fall in love. Is that a crime?"

David didn't seem to recall that during the war, he had voiced his support for the bombing of that kingdom. Wallis *did* recall, but she wasn't going to apologize for it. No amount of groveling would convince the royal family that the Windsors weren't traitors; she understood that now. Were they traitors, though? Hadn't they also been banished exiles, deprived of all the courtesies and honors to which they were entitled?

To whom had they owed their loyalty then?

Still, Hitler hadn't been the man they'd thought he was, that much was certain. When the news of the camps broke at the end of the war—the horrifying photos of the skeletal survivors, the piles of clothing taken from the bodies of those who hadn't survived—Wallis had stopped reading the newspapers. She simply couldn't bear to see the evidence of what had gone on in Germany, the Germany that had so welcomed her and David before the war. It was in the past, at any rate. She had more immediate problems.

What David felt about it all, she didn't know. She couldn't bring herself to ask him.

Wallis couldn't bring herself to answer him now either. Had she ever felt love for him? Fondness, certainly. Early on, she'd been dazzled by the idea of him and the golden aura that surrounded the heir to the throne. And she felt pity for him now.

But was any of that love?

Too many questions, too many disappointments. The only thing she knew with certainty was that it was up to her to get them safely back to Paris; she ordered her hapless maid to start packing, right now.

David would never stop pining for this place, this island of tradition and grudges reaching back centuries. But he needed to understand that no more should he grovel or beg for favors for her. Wallis Simpson would never be Her Royal Highness, and now the Windsors needed to recover what dignity remained to them and leave.

With visions of insurance money instead of crowns dancing in their heads. With days at the races, shopping trips a long the Champs, masquerade balls where they could hide their bitterness—and, yes, maybe even guilt—behind elaborate masks. Trips on friends' yachts—the Guinnesses were always so generous in that way. The Paleys were always good for a weekend stay at their Long Island estate. The Agnellis had that beautiful villa in Venice.

Anyone, anyplace—as long as it was grand, of course, and exclusive, naturally—to distract the Windsors from their bitter disappointment in their fate. And in each other.

Anyplace but England. When they boarded the boat to ferry them across the Channel—far fewer people to see them off than David had expected, and he couldn't hide his hurt and disappointment, and she did try to console him with plans for a dinner party upon their return—Wallis knew: Cookie had won.

Wallis would never willingly step foot in this beleaguered little country again.

BUCKINGHAM PALACE

Elizabeth, when she heard that the Windsors had left England seemingly for good, savored the victory, her third in two years.

VE Day, just over a year ago, had been sweet—breathtakingly, overwhelmingly sweet. She remembered how the crowds stretched out before them below the balcony, people clinging to the Victoria Memorial like colorful mushrooms, a sea of humanity spreading out as far as the eye could see. The roars were overwhelming, nearly drowning out the sounds of the bombers flying overhead in victory formation. Lilibet in her khaki ATS uniform was surprisingly grown up, a visceral reminder of how many years they'd spent at war. She'd been a girl of fourteen when the war began. Now she was a young woman of nineteen with a photo of her distant cousin Philip on her nightstand. Margaret was almost fifteen, a girl in an awful hurry to become a woman, her hair longer now, not held back by barrettes or ribbons anymore; a sly, almost seductive smile suddenly evident on her delicate face.

Dear Bertie in his naval uniform, still so slender—cursed men!—almost gaunt. But no longer did she need to push him out on the balcony; he strode out confidently by her side.

And Elizabeth Bowes-Lyon beside her husband, the King. In her favorite shade of blue with a matching hat and a fur stole, basking in the love of their people.

When they brought Winston out, the crowd nearly lost their heads, but that was all right, it was well earned. One was confident enough in one's position that one could afford to be generous. They appeared on the balcony four times that day and allowed the girls to go out into the night to celebrate (accompanied by armed guards, of course).

While they waited for the girls to return, she and Bertie relaxed in their sitting room—windows still boarded up, carpets worn and dirty, light bulbs missing in the still-lowered chandeliers; there was so much to do, so much to clean up, she couldn't even begin to think where to start—and they shared a bottle of champagne.

"Do you remember when I proposed?" he asked sleepily, reaching for her hand.

"Which time?"

He laughed. "The one that stuck."

"How could I ever forget? We spent that entire weekend avoiding talking about it—why, I can't recall."

"I can. You were afraid still. Afraid of marrying a poor specimen like me."

"Not a poor specimen, Bertie." She gave his rough hand a squeeze. "Not a poor specimen at all. The best of the lot by far."

"We didn't do badly, did we? Seeing the country through this? I could never have done it alone, you know."

"Nonsense," Elizabeth said, but her eyes welled up, and she had to turn away. After all these years, she was shy about showing him the true depths of her emotion. Even though he so beautifully shared his with her. But her role, ever since the abdication, was to cheer, to jolly, to support. Not to burden with soul-searching or reflection.

"Yes, Elizabeth. I mean it."

"Well." She gave herself a stern little shake and sniffed. "I return the compliment. How ever would I have made it through those horrible visits to the East End and Coventry without you? I don't believe I could have done." And she realized, with a shock, that this was the truth. For all her confidence and self-aware charm, she knew the unpleasant side of life was not her cup of tea. She would have remained inside Buck House or, better yet, back at Windsor, had it not been inconceivable for her to abandon Bertie in the crisis. And also abandon the knowledge of military secrets and battle movements—all the *access* she'd been privileged to have. But mostly, she couldn't have abandoned Bertie. He pulled her out of her comfortable inclinations and forced her to confront the devastation, and as awful as it had all been, she was grateful for that.

So that night was sweet. Victory over Germany was sweet; victory over Japan, a few months later, was also sweet.

But nothing was as sweet as the knowledge that That Woman and David were leaving England for good this time, please God.

Still, she did itch to know exactly who had stolen those jewels! Had the Windsors arranged it for the insurance money? Goodness knows, David was always pleading poverty with Bertie. Or had it been the work of a real jewel thief? But then why were Queen Alexandra's Fabergé boxes left behind? (Elizabeth knew all the details of the theft by now; Mary Dudley wasn't quite the friend of Wallis's that she appeared.) Well, one might never know.

And it didn't really matter in the end. Now she and Bertie could be left in peace. Oh, how Elizabeth looked forward to the rest of their years! A victorious England, rightfully recognized as the lone country in Europe to hold Hitler off. The empire would remain strong, despite the gloomy predictions (even if it lost India, which would be tragic but seemed inevitable now). Surely the shortages would end soon and the country would remember how Churchill had led them through the war and restore him and the Conservatives to power. The girls would marry; Lilibet and Philip were all but engaged, and there would be grandchildren to spoil, the line of succession would stretch on and on, and there would be no more scandal, no more brother against brother strife, no more betrayal.

Best of all, Bertie would relax, finally, and indulge in shooting and stalking at Sandringham and Balmoral, putting in more gardens; he'd be a peacetime king and she a peacetime queen. Instead of inspecting destroyed houses and broken people, they would resume the pleasantries of opening infirmaries and overseeing court presentations, clad in the newly polished crown jewels and robes. The remainder of the reign of George VI would be long, glorious, and untroubled. It was what they deserved, after the abdication and the war. After all, Bertie was just fifty, she was only forty-six.

They had so much time left.

CHAPTER

26

Queen Mary Reveals a Secret

Sometimes I wonder what would have happened had the line of succession held firm all those years ago, when I was Princess Mary and Queen Victoria was still on the throne. If Prince Eddy, my original fiancé, had not died of influenza, would he and I have been happy? As happy as I was with Georgie? And would there have been an abdication—or two World Wars?

It's not profitable to dwell on such thoughts, naturally. But the older I get, the more I indulge myself. One of the perks of age, I suppose. One is no longer necessary, but one has so much more time on one's hands. I never was much for frivolous things like long lunches and wine-soaked dinners. Indulging in them now would be most out of character. So instead, I indulge in imagining. Now and then.

I assume, all things being equal, I would have had disappointing children with Eddy too. Children who had minds of their own, children who didn't honor the past. But perhaps that's how it is in all families, even commoners'. Expectations are set, then met or, more likely, not. Children look at the world differently than do their parents, who look at the world differently than did *their* parents. The world changes faster than those who inhabit it. Only the young can keep up.

Only the young *desire* to.

I confess that the world has sped up, frightfully so, since the war. My granddaughters go to parties and dinners unchaperoned. They fraternize with commoners. They wear lipstick and listen to records on the gramophone day and night. Noisy, jangly records.

No one wants to wear a tiara and evening dress at dinner every night. Although *I* refuse to give it up.

Life at Marlborough House, where I reside while in London, is as unvarying and constant as a Swiss clock. I have my devoted servants, my ladies of the chamber. We play bridge, we listen to the wireless (only educational programs and classical music). I go to museums, attend theater (although it's not what it used to be, not with these new playwrights and their devotion to purveying deviant smut). I enjoy the ballet. I'm invited to state dinners and banquets by my son and daughter-in-law, trotted out to lend credibility to the monarchy, to remind all how far back it goes. I'm "the last link to Victoria," as some like to say.

The Queen rarely seeks my counsel the way she often did before the war. I admit that I've grown rather fond of the former Elizabeth Bowes-Lyon. Our unity during the abdication crisis (such an inadequate word that, really, *crisis*; more like *cataclysm*, *devastation*, *betrayal*) brought us closer than I once expected we would be. Two women against one kind-hearted man, Bertie—he never had a chance. We wouldn't have stood for it had he been inclined to give David all that he still whines for today—more money and a job representing the Crown while he continues to pursue a frivolously extravagant lifestyle. And the biggest issue of all, the HRH for his wife.

I do believe Bertie would have given in on some, if not all, of these points had Elizabeth and I not been of one mind and voice against it.

Odd, isn't it? I was not at all fond of Lady Elizabeth Bowes-Lyon when she repeatedly refused my second son's proposals. A daughter of a mere Scottish lord, refusing a prince of England? Yet Bertie was *so* besotted. I feared he might not get over his heartbreak if she didn't accept him—he had found his true love; anyone could see it. Except the young lady in question.

So I did what I had to do back in 1923. I planted that newspaper article hinting that she and David were to be engaged. I didn't name her, but the description was enough. And I knew that David had no interest in her. I also knew the young lady had a great deal of pride; you could see it in her tilted chin, her winning smile, the smile of one who is very much aware of her own charm. I had a strong conviction that once she read this anonymous little morsel of society gossip, she would be happy to accept the second son to save face. I hoped she had some heart as well, a reluctance to hurt Bertie further.

And it all happened precisely as I'd planned. While my daughter-in-law's pride and vanity are still present in abundance, so, somewhat surprisingly, is her heart. She and Bertie have had a happy marriage, and I pray to God that they are granted more years together, peaceful years after the turbulence of the past decade.

Bertie is so frail, though. Every month it seems he has a new ailment, and I fear they might all add up to something unthinkable. Yet he still works so hard!

Meanwhile, I read that David and his wife, over in Paris in a vulgar house, throw their ugly little pug dogs lavish birthday parties. Imagine! Imagine having nothing else to do but that! What a tragedy it all is, to see my eldest, the former King, reduced to being a lapdog for That Woman's lapdogs. I shudder to think of it.

I am an old lady and I haven't much time left. I've witnessed history; I've made it; I've given birth to it; I've buried it. Shakespeare could have had a field day with the royal House of Windsor. But now, dear God, finally let this family enjoy some peace. Let Lilibet, once she's married Philip, be the future. But not for a long while.

I do beseech You.

CHAPTER

27

SANDRINGHAM

FEBRUARY 1952

HE WENT TO BED SO HAPPY. IT WAS *SUCH* A PLEASANT evening, a quiet family dinner with Margaret, Bertie boasting about how many pheasants he'd shot that day. Afterward, Margaret played the piano while Elizabeth and Bertie looked at a catalog of some new paintings they were thinking of acquiring. Then they all went to bed—well, Margaret stayed up late, as was her habit, but Bertie and Elizabeth went up at their usual time. Bertie wanted to awaken early to go shooting again. He did seem almost like his old self, one could believe, as he'd been before the leg troubles and the operations and then the lung resection. The doctors never gave them a reason to doubt that he would fully recover, yet he hadn't, not really. He still tired so easily, coughed worryingly, couldn't seem to put on weight, and their planned tour of Australia was out of the question; Lilibet and Philip had gone in their place, after a stop in Kenya. They'd seen them off only a few days ago; Bertie had wept when they took off on the royal plane, which wasn't altogether unlike him, yet it had tugged at Elizabeth's heartstrings in the strangest way, and she had taken her husband in her arms once they were safely in the car and out of the public's view. He dried his tears, yet still needed consoling. It was as if he thought he would never see his daughter again, such a strange idea. Lilibet was going to be away for only a few weeks.

Did Elizabeth kiss her husband before they went to their separate bedrooms that night?

Oh, if only one could remember! Because, in the gray light of the terrible morning after, memories of other kisses—the tentative first one after she finally said yes; the less tentative one the night they were married; a million little affirmations of affection throughout the years, before engagements, after speeches, during quiet evenings when it was just the two of them alone before a fire, reminders that in the end, despite thrones and crowns and balcony appearances and curtsies and bows and trumpets and swords, they were, quite simply, a married couple who loved each other in that quiet, easy way that fortunate married couples earned.

But she couldn't recall, in all the turmoil, if they'd kissed last night.

The last night.

Elizabeth's mind couldn't accept what Bertie's valet was saying to her when he burst into her room that morning, not knocking, not whispering. He simply was *there,* eyes wild, shouting that he couldn't wake the King up, he couldn't wake the King up, she must come at once.

Finally she registered the words and bolted out of bed, forgetting her dressing gown and slippers. She felt a cry wrench its way out of her heart, because she knew, she knew even before she saw him, what had happened. The thing that they'd not been able to talk about yet was always trailing them like a shadow these last couple of years.

Oh, but he lay so peacefully in his bed! On his back, his

hands above the covers, arms alongside his body. Such a quiet, almost happy look upon his face, his eyes mercifully closed. But still, so very still, and a grayish pallor on that peaceful visage.

He'd died in his sleep—her mind quickly took that in. And she was able, for a morsel of a moment, to rejoice in that. He hadn't suffered. He'd simply gone to bed and not woken up, so he'd had no reason to be afraid or sad.

The moment passed and all she knew was her own grief. It was a monstrous thing; it roared up from unknown wells deep within, and she wailed for the enormous loss of him, of his touch and voice and smile and quiet valor, the pride in his eyes whenever he saw her, the disbelief, even after all these years, that she was his, that he'd won her—

It tore her in half. She was a widow wild with grief. Just like any widow. The Crown could not protect her from this.

Margaret's wretched sobs—when had she come in?—forced Elizabeth to quiet her own; her daughter was as broken as she was, and her instinct was to console her younger child, so the two of them somehow ended up back in Elizabeth's bedroom while the doctor was called. Ridiculous, wasn't it? A bit late for that, but who else to call? Elizabeth hugged her daughter to her breast, her nightgown awash with her tears, and let her own fall on Margaret's thick brown hair. Courtiers were scurrying about while mother and daughter huddled together on a life raft of grief. Tommy Lascelles came running in, as distraught as she'd ever seen him; Bertie's valet was full of apologies, as if he could have banished death the way he banished dust and lint and untidiness. Peter Townsend, Bertie's devoted equerry, eventually took Margaret back to her room, letting the poor girl sob all over his uniform but not seeming to mind.

Elizabeth was alone. No longer Queen of England. In the

stopping of a heart, the last breath of a man, Elizabeth Bowes-Lyon was no longer Queen of England.

Her daughter was. Queen Elizabeth—oh, Lilibet!

"How—how do we tell her? Where are they on the tour?" She sprang up, pulled on her dressing gown, and stepped into her slippers. She slapped some color into her face, smoothed her hair, and addressed Tommy Lascelles. "And one must tell Queen Mary. Oh, I can't bear to do it!" Her grief roared back after that brief moment of lucidity; she wanted to wallow in it. All these years, ever since 1937, duty had come first. Duty could go hang itself today.

Bertie had been killed by it, hadn't he? All the stress of the war followed by the bewildering political situation that chased Winston out of office, then lured him back, all the economic troubles, protests, the loss of empire—it had killed him. And who was to blame for that?

How quickly grief could be banished by anger, her dear old friend. Boiling anger, a lifetime of resentment toward the one who had left his younger brother, his more *fragile* brother, to assume the duty he himself didn't want. Because of *her*.

Then a vision of Bertie in the last days of the war: He was in the garden of Royal Lodge, their old home on the grounds of Windsor that they'd still used as an escape from the grander fortress of the castle. Royal Lodge and 145 Piccadilly were where they'd been their happiest before the abdication; once 145 Piccadilly was bombed, they clung to Royal Lodge like it was a beloved old teddy bear.

She remembered musing about how rare it was to see him out of uniform after the long years of the war. He was in that old gray jumper with patched elbows, tweed trousers, a rake in his hands as he furiously scraped it along the ground, tidying up broken tree limbs after a storm. He was happy, she knew; he hummed a little tune, paused to light a cigarette. There were no more fires, no more smoldering buildings or bombs falling from the sky. He was a man at peace since his country was at peace—or almost; it was simply a matter of days now, Winston had assured them both.

But his face was so lined. The deep pockets beneath his eyes held untold quantities of sleepless nights in stuffy shelters. He would have written a personal letter to the family of every fallen soldier and sailor and pilot had Winston not forbade him. (There was a form letter of condolence with the King's signature stamped on it.) As she gazed at him, wondering how on earth he had made it through the war—how they both had, how the entire country had—he'd waved at her and smiled. That joyful smile he always flashed when he saw her, no matter how many times he'd seen her that day. It was always as if he were seeing her after a long separation.

And she would never see that smile again. Her daughters would never be as happy to see her as her husband was, every day. No one would ever be that happy to see her ever again.

She was only fifty-one. And she was alone now.

Forever.

EVEN DURING THIS TIME—THIS achingly slow-moving march toward her husband's funeral, after the flurry of getting Lilibet and Philip home, trying to console Margaret, who did not want to be consoled, spending wordless hours with a shockingly frail Queen Mary, then having meetings upon meetings about the funeral itself—David was a problem. *The* problem. Unlike Bertie, he would probably live forever just to spite one.

"Your Majesty—"

"Yes?" Both Lilibet and she spoke at the same time, and while they tried to laugh it off, it was startling. Would she ever remember that her daughter was now Queen, head of the family? No more would anyone defer to Elizabeth first; no more would she know before anyone else all the political gossip and crises. She'd been Bertie's partner in reigning from the very beginning. He'd wanted her to know everything, he'd asked her for advice—not always taking it but always seeking it.

Lilibet, as deferential as she was, as sweet and docile, would not need advice from her mother. She wouldn't even need it from her husband—and goodness knew how that was going to play out. But Lilibet was stubborn, even more stubborn than Margaret. Most people didn't understand that about the two sisters.

"Your *Majesties*," Tommy Lascelles continued after a respectful pause. They were still at Sandringham, in the sitting room, going over the funeral details. "The Duke of Windsor has requested a private audience before the funeral."

"Of course he has," Elizabeth sputtered. "It's all about him; it always is."

"Mummy."

"Oh, don't. You have no idea what that man is capable of. The things your father and I shielded you and Margaret from during that time, the insults, the persistent whining, and worse. I suppose he wants to talk about his money—and I suppose there's nothing I can do about that since I'm no longer Queen."

Lilibet looked concerned—and a little annoyed; her cheeks flushed.

"He's already written that book," Elizabeth continued. "That memoir. To think, a member of the royal family doing such a thing! As if Crawfie, your own governess, Lilibet, writing a book about us wasn't enough. *He*'s no better than some Hollywood starlet, breathlessly telling *all*, as if there is any interest in what that man has to say."

"I believe the book has sold very well abroad," Tommy said, and Elizabeth could have cut him off at his knobby knees.

"That's neither here nor there. He has cheapened us all with his endless thirst for attention and celebrity. If he'd stayed the course, he would have been the most important person in the country. Now he has to seek attention because without it, he has no idea what to do with his poor, pathetic little life. You can be sure That Woman made him do it, and she'll write her own memoir as well. Mark my words. There is no vulgarity, no distasteful bid for attention, those two aren't capable of. Meanwhile, your poor father lies in his coffin—" She couldn't go on; anger fueled one only so long. Weeping bitterly, she left the room.

If she had to see David, she would. But without Lilibet. Let this be just Elizabeth and her brother-in-law. Alone. For the first time since 1937.

ELIZABETH MADE HIM WAIT until after the funeral. She assumed she'd need all her strength for that, but in the end it was much like any other ceremony she'd taken part in since Bertie had ascended the throne, the same rigid scheduling that didn't allow one much time to think, for one was always *moving*. Train from Sandringham to London, car to car, procession after procession, the casket looking so small despite the royal standard, scepter, and crown. The funeral ceremony at Westminster so long and, yes, boring; she couldn't bear to keep staring at the casket all that time and the archbishop of Canterbury did have a tendency to drone on and on, so she amused herself by turning her widow's gaze on various guests. She stared at Winston and Clemmie (was it true she'd had a facelift? She looked very refreshed), Mrs. Roosevelt (gained some weight, that one had, but one shouldn't throw stones), and Dickie and Edwina (what on earth had she seen in Nehru? The woman was a serial adulterer, but to have an affair with a *Hindu*?) in turn until they squirmed.

The worst moment was in the vault at Windsor, when Lilibet—very elegant and slim in her black suit—held a trembling hand full of dirt over the casket and let it drop while the archbishop of Canterbury intoned the last of the funeral service. It struck Elizabeth then, a lightning bolt illuminating the haze of her grief, that her daughter was rapidly becoming an institution, not a person, was no longer her little girl who loved dogs and used to make Bertie carry her around on his back while she played ponies with him.

Elizabeth had never seen Bertie as only the King; first and foremost he was her husband. But Lilibet was turning into the Queen before her mother's very eyes, and Elizabeth didn't entirely like it. She caught herself ennobling her elder daughter in a way she never had; always, she'd been scrupulous in treating Margaret and Lilibet as equals, even after Lilibet became the heir apparent. Now, she realized, if one wasn't careful, Lilibet's problems would assume more importance than Margaret's; Lilibet's flaws—and she did possess them—would be overlooked while Margaret's were amplified. She ought to have more sympathy for her younger daughter, who looked so miserable, so lost. She had adored her father to an extreme. But Lilibet's burden was greater, and it always would be.

Is it easier to love a queen than a princess? One would soon find out, wouldn't one?

Through it all, *he* was hovering. Walking beside Philip and the Dukes of Kent and Gloucester behind the coffin during the procession from Buckingham Palace to Westminster. Seated somewhere behind her at Westminster but directly across from her at St. George's Chapel at Windsor. Holding his mother's arm, for Queen Mary had aged decades overnight, and it wouldn't be long before they had to do this all over again, one feared.

Finally, after the funeral lunch, Elizabeth nodded to Tommy and went to the private rooms in Windsor, where she was reminded that another dispiriting task lay ahead—moving out of Windsor and Buck House so Lilibet and her family could move in. She supposed she'd move all her things to Royal Lodge here, perhaps Clarence House in town. But that would come later.

Now she sat in Bertie's office, behind his desk. Absurdly, she picked up an ashtray, hoping to find one of his stubs, some ash. But of course, it was perfectly clean. Foolish, foolish—one must guard against being maudlin, now that one was a widow.

"Your Majesty." Tommy's voice made her put the ashtray down, and she looked up to see David walking toward her with his hands clasped behind his back. He gave her a slight bow and then surprised her by moving toward her with his arms outstretched; she sat, immobile, while he put his arms around her shoulders and kissed her on both cheeks.

"Elizabeth," he said, and to her disgust he had tears in his eyes. "Such a sad day for us all."

"Yes." She watched as David took a seat in front of Bertie's desk, studying him in a way she hadn't since—

Well, since 1937.

The hair wasn't so golden but it did look artificially enhanced; he should be grayer now. Like Bertie was in the end. But despite her hopes, David looked years younger than his actual age; he was as trim as he'd been as a young man, tanned, the lines on his face merely from the passing of years, not the falling of bombs. He walked with that jaunty spring he'd always sported. Only his teeth—stained yellow from tobacco—marked him as a man in his sixties.

His accent was strange, though, oddly American; the influence of That Woman.

Yet young as he appeared, there was a dissipated air about him. Signs of a frivolous, empty life. He was too eager, his eyes too wide and earnest. His hands were exquisitely manicured, his hair freshly cut, his clothing tailored perfectly, as if he had nothing else to do in his life but play dress-up. She imagined him changing clothes constantly and preening before a mirror like a dandy for lack of any real purpose. He couldn't sit still; he crossed and uncrossed his legs, fiddled with the cuffs of his pants, and smoked incessantly. In the face of such nervous energy, Elizabeth felt herself gather her forces inward as she grew still, dignified. She sat up even straighter, raising her chin.

She'd once been a girl who had thrilled to dance with the Prince of Wales. Now she was a widow of a king. How the heart could expand and contract throughout a life!

"I'm so very glad you agreed to see me, dear Elizabeth. I thought perhaps the Queen would join us?" David looked around the room nervously, as if he expected Lilibet to pop out from behind a curtain. As if she were still the little girl who'd once adored her uncle David, playing hide-and-seek with him at Royal Lodge.

"I told my daughter the Queen I preferred to meet you alone. After all, it has been so long. And she has quite enough on her plate, as I'm sure you can recall." Icy, icy—that was the best tactic. Remind him that he once had buried a father and inherited a throne. Even for so brief a time.

"Ah, yes, of course. I do recall, most vividly. So much to do in those early days. I hear she and her husband wish to remain at Clarence House instead of Buck House? I can't say I blame them."

"She will move into Buckingham Palace, as the monarch has always done. Philip may have his ideas, but in the end Lilibet—*the Queen*—knows her duty. Unlike others I could mention."

"Ah. And here we are. Gloves off already, eh?" With an exaggerated sigh, David shifted in his chair, and the fidgeting stopped. Now his eyes were narrow with suspicion.

"I don't know what you mean," Elizabeth said with one of her most charming smiles.

"Oh, do stop simpering. You're too old for that—that blushing debutante act. It didn't charm me then and it won't charm me now."

"I never wanted to charm you."

"Yes, you did, you practically threw yourself at me. You always wanted the top dog, and you settled for my brother, poor dear man."

"Bertie required no one to settle for him!" She could have thrown that ashtray right at his Technicolor hair.

"Then why did you refuse him twice?" David had such a

smug smile on his face, she did pick up the ashtray; it was glass and heavy as a brick.

"I—"

"That ghastly newspaper article, remember—the one that hinted at our betrothal? What a laugh we all had when we saw it—Mama, Papa, my other brothers. I can't believe you had the gall to put that in the papers. As if that could force me to propose."

"What?" Elizabeth was so shaken, she dropped the ashtray on the desk. "I—*I* wasn't responsible for that! I was mortified, humiliated—oh, do be quiet!" For David was laughing merrily now, and she felt as if the tables had turned and she'd lost her footing. How had this happened?

How old did one have to be before one stopped being rattled by a charming man?

"Poor Elizabeth."

"I am the *Queen Mother*—that is how I will be styled. I've talked to the Queen about it and she agrees."

"Very regal. Can't let go of the crown just yet, can you? Ambitious as always."

"I will remind you that neither I nor Bertie desired the crown. The last thing either of us wanted was for you to desert us for That Woman."

"Wallis. She has a name, for God's sake."

"That Woman."

"So you can't even say her name. After all this time."

"Never. Never will I say it, nor will your mother. Bertie may no longer be with us, but some things won't change. I will never receive That Woman, and as long as I'm alive, your wife will never be Her Royal Highness."

"And?" Not entirely to her surprise, David merely shrugged

off this once all-consuming grievance of his, his wife's lack of an HRH. After all, he had reason to be cynical about her, if one believed everything one read in the newspapers and magazines these days. He was more concerned about the money. Of course. It was always about the money with him.

"And—there is nothing I can do to prevent Lilibet from continuing your allowance from her own funds. I know my daughter. She is dutiful; she is kind. You were once her favorite uncle and she—for some reason—still remembers you fondly. Even though behind her back, you call her Shirley Temple. Your own niece. The Queen of England."

"Oh—how—you've heard. Spies all over the place, I imagine. Just as always."

"Of course. We knew what was going on in Germany, in Lisbon. Why do you think we sent you to the Bahamas? Because we couldn't trust you anywhere near Europe and Hitler. Why do you think we still give you that allowance despite your traitorous behavior? To remind you that you're on a leash, that you have to beg for our scraps. You, once the King of England, have to rely on the charity of your relatives. *That* is the most satisfying aspect of all this distasteful begging for money and titles."

"Ice-cold bitches—you and my mother both. My dear brother would never have been so cruel had it not been for you."

"Cruel?" Elizabeth leaned back in the chair and closed her eyes. The chair still smelled like Bertie—his cigarette smoke, his aftershave. The entire room still smelled like him. But too soon it would be filled with Lilibet's scent, Guerlain's L'Heure Bleue. She opened her eyes. "Who started that awful rumor about my family, David? Who calls me Cookie? You—you broke my heart. Oh, not when I was a young woman, but later, after we'd been such good friends, the four of us—Thelma, you, Bertie, and me. When I thought I was a *sister* to you. That you could spread such a filthy rumor about one—" She couldn't finish because suddenly she was awash in memories of the past, when she and Bertie were young, the girls were young, everyone was young. Memories of parties and dinners with the gramophone playing David's favorite jazz records, picnics on the lawn of the Fort, swimming parties in the pool he'd installed. Bertie was always so relaxed around his elder brother; they had all looked up to David then as the protector, the progenitor of fun and excitement. The hope for the future.

Too many memories, too many reminders of how it might have been if That Woman hadn't come along—Elizabeth's eyes filled with tears, and she dabbed at them with her sleeve. The sleeve of her widow's weeds; the sleeve of the dress she'd worn to her husband's funeral.

"What rumor? What on earth are you referring to?" David rose from his seat and came around to her side; he put his hand on her shoulder, and it was gentle. Concerned. She felt an unexpected moment of pure contentment—but it was rooted in the past. Not the present.

She gazed up at his eyes. Watery, the tiny red veins like a cross-stitch pattern. The eyes of a man who drank too much. The eyes of a man who had reason to drink too much.

Like brother, like brother.

"Tommy told me. Oh, ages ago, right after your papa died—right after that cruise you took with *her*. He said you called me Cookie because there was a rumor my mother was—well, not my mother. A cook was instead. Oh, David—how *could* you?" She grasped his hand, clutched it too tightly. But he didn't pull away.

"What—Tommy? That bitter old queer? Elizabeth, I promise you, I never said that. Cookie—well, yes. I am ashamed to admit that has become our nickname for you, but it has nothing to do with your parentage. Only your—well. Tommy Lascelles once propositioned me, if you must know, on one of my royal tours as Prince of Wales. I turned him down, and he's despised me ever since."

"So—you never said that?" Elizabeth recalibrated everything she'd known in the years since. Was Tommy really capable of spreading such loathsome gossip, just to make David look even worse? It had been in the middle of all the angst concerning That Woman and David's determination to marry her. Could Tommy have been *jealous*?

"I did not. I promise you."

She dropped his hand, turned away. If she looked into his face one more time, she was afraid of what she might see. Who was the liar?

They were all so very *good* at it. That was the problem. But it didn't matter, none of this mattered, for she opened a drawer in her agitation and found Bertie's cigarette lighter, a present from her one Christmas, and it was engraved *To my husband, who warms my heart.*

Liars, saints, sinners—what they were didn't matter any longer. The most important person was gone. Forever. Had worked himself into an early grave.

And there was only one person responsible for that. No, there were two.

"I understand your wife is in New York," Elizabeth said, smiling her most winning smile, the smile that Hitler had been so afraid of. "With a friend of yours—what *is* his name? James, Jim, something or other?"

And she had the satisfaction of seeing David's face drop into an expression of total despair.

"Jimmy. Jimmy Donahue. A very good, uh—a very good friend to us both."

"Yes, but isn't he rather more of a friend to *her*?"

"I don't know what you're talking about."

"Was she worth it, David? Was she worth it after all? Or has it all turned out to be a bitter disappointment? How do you fill your days now? Watching your wife and her lover make a fool of you? It's such a shame, really it is. My heart absolutely *bleeds* for you." Oh, anger, blessed, blessed anger, her dear old friend! Now she could find her tongue again.

"Same old Cookie. If your loyal subjects could see you now. Always the little hypocrite."

"Does she know, David? Does she know that you despise her as much as she despises you?"

The strangled look on his face, now beet red, the garbled sounds coming from his throat. She was correct; her arrow had hit home.

Finally he was able to stammer, "My p-poor dead brother—he's better off now, I'm sad to say."

Fury pushed her out of the chair. "Don't you dare pretend you were ever concerned for Bertie! You were never concerned about anyone but yourself. You did this—you killed him. Back in '37, *you* pulled the trigger. Now get out."

"I was just leaving—"

"No. You are *dismissed*." And Elizabeth pressed the buzzer on the desk that summoned someone to escort him out.

David, who had turned to leave the room, paused. "Give my best to the Queen. Don't bother a footman. I'll see myself out—I once lived here, you know."

Breathing heavily, Elizabeth watched him head to the door, where he was met by the footman she had summoned. So the former King was escorted out of her presence just like any common minister or clerk. A smaller man than she remembered. A defeated man.

A cuckolded man, if the newspapers were to be believed.

But her triumph was as brief as the flame she ignited with the lighter in her hand. Tracing the inscription, she gazed around at Bertie's office, still full of his favorite things—framed photographs of the two of them, the four of them, one of Lilibet and Philip on their wedding day, the grandchildren, Charles and Anne sitting with Elizabeth on a bench in the garden of Royal Lodge. A sweet little watercolor of the River Muick painted by Margaret when she was about thirteen. While the mourning country might have been remembering their king with a crown or in military uniform, the way he was depicted in all the black-edged newspapers, *this* was the Bertie she knew—father. Husband.

Friend.

Elizabeth felt her rage desert her, leaving her alone with only the vast nothingness that yawned before her now until the end of her days, the loneliness, the missing person for whose voice she would always be listening.

Drained, exhausted from all the emotion of this day and the day before it and the day before the day before, Elizabeth sank into the chair, still clutching the lighter.

And she lay her head on her arms and wept, her heart crying out her husband's name over and over.

Bertie.

CHAPTER
28

WALDORF ASTORIA, NEW YORK CITY

APRIL 1952

WALLIS WAS IN HER ELEMENT.

Wearing a Mainbocher white satin gown with a black overskirt, gold feathers in her perfectly coiffed hair, and an amethyst necklace, she danced the foxtrot with David who, she had always been proud to say, was a divine dancer. The Windsors, cutting a stylish rug, were the center of attention even among all the other high-society figures—Bill and Babe Paley, Gloria and Loel Guinness, Woolworths and Rockefellers and Astors by the dozen, and movie stars like Marlene Dietrich and Greer Garson. She had Edward R. Murrow at one elbow, asking them to appear on his television program, Walter Winchell at the other, begging for a quote for his column.

Just minutes before, Elsa Maxwell, a sight to behold in acres of lace covering her ample figure, had ridden in on top of an elephant to open the April in Paris Ball at the Waldorf Astoria, ostensibly a benefit for various organizations and a celebration of relations between the United States and France, but in reality, just another opportunity for the rich and famous to outdo one another, to be photographed and envied, all in the name of charity.

This was Wallis's kingdom now. Who needed dumpy little England when you could rule the jet set? Giddy with the power of international celebrity, Wallis smiled as someone tapped David on the shoulder to cut in. Ignoring David's sour expression, she fell into the arms of Jimmy Donahue, who was soon spinning her around like a top. He was *not* a divine dancer, but Wallis didn't care.

How could she? Because he was *Jimmy*.

Jimmy Donahue was nineteen years her junior. He was a Woolworth, fabulously rich—he never allowed the Windsors to pick up a bill when they were together. Which meant that they were together frequently. He was also gay. That is, until he met Wallis—he said it solemnly, crossing his heart, his wide-set impish eyes gleaming with sincerity. Then he'd pinched her ass to bring the point home.

He also pinched David's.

For a while, after they first met at a party in Paris, they were a merry threesome. Jimmy was so divinely outrageous, telling smutty jokes that made David laugh until his eyes watered. He didn't treat the Windsors like collectibles, the way most people did (always with care, always displayed prominently, seldom handled with warmth or affection). Jimmy acted like they were his chums, like they were all naughty schoolboys in on the prank. And while this was at first shocking—he refused to call David anything but "the Dook," with an exaggerated American accent—soon it felt refreshing. The Windsors' carefully regimented schedule, designed by Wallis to give some kind of meaning to their lives (they met at eleven in the morning to discuss their day together; had luncheon; David went off to play golf while Wallis had her hair and nails done; tea at four; drinks at seven; dinner—with guests, almost always with guests—at eight), was entirely upended when Jimmy decided to drop in.

Prior to Jimmy, Wallis and David had had to resort to little games to trick themselves and the public into believing they were still the fairy-tale Windsors. Even if alone they barely spoke to each other, in public they always had to appear to be deeply—excessively—in love, blowing kisses across rooms, holding hands, babbling endearments. When the two of them dined out alone, Wallis refused to let anyone see them sitting in silence; if they ran out of conversation (meaning if Wallis couldn't bear to hear one more word about David's latest round of golf or if he shut down when she told him about her latest hat), they recited the alphabet to each other, punctuating it with occasional laughter.

When Jimmy entered their lives, the alphabet was no longer necessary. Conversation never stalled. Even David—dour ever since the war—seemed witty when Jimmy was around.

Did Wallis grow a little concerned when David and Jimmy seemed to be a bit too—chummy? When Jimmy's ass-pinching wasn't playfully slapped away as it had been before? Yes. Yes, she did. So she stole Jimmy from him. It was really very simple—gay or not, every man liked to be flattered and told he was the most interesting person ever.

Gay or not, every man had the same equipment in the bedroom. Equipment that Wallis was very adept at handling.

Soon Jimmy was her constant companion. Squiring her to dinners and balls and luncheons on both sides of the Atlantic. Staying with them at their home in Paris, Villa Windsor. She and Jimmy swam together in Antibes, skied together in Switzerland, shopped together on Fifth Avenue—oh, he was simply the most divine person to go to Bergdorf's with; he never allowed her to pay for anything and he could sit for hours watching her try on dresses and gowns and coats, oohing and aahing his approval, unafraid to groan exaggeratedly when something didn't suit her. Unlike David, who held her purse with a grumpy expression, sighed loudly every fifteen minutes, and reminded her every five that he had once been King of England.

Jimmy never scolded, never whined, never sighed loudly. Jimmy was always thinking up new pranks and adventures; he sparked something long missing in Wallis's very soul.

Fun.

Ever since the abdication and especially ever since the war, fun happened only because of Wallis's steely determination to *make* it happen through her carefully curated parties and dinners. She'd accepted it as her role in the marriage, just as David was in charge of securing funds and showering her with baubles.

But Wallis hadn't had anyone plan fun for *her* in so long—in forever. She hadn't risen in the morning wondering what delightful thing might befall her today since before her marriage.

Heavy, heavy, heavy was the Windsors' life together; the weight of unrealistic expectations, of eternal disappointment, of secret shame and guilt (no longer did they display their photos with Herr Hitler), of pretense and charades and excruciatingly good manners. Of constant companionship, cloying, cloistering. The war had changed him and, while she didn't show it as much, her as well. So she *must* cram her schedule with invitations and soirees; she must ensure that neither she nor David had much time to think about the fact that they would have gladly thrown open the doors of Buckingham Palace to Hitler if they'd had the chance. She and David were damn lucky they hadn't been summoned to those tribunals that scarred France after the war, where anyone suspected of collaborating with the Germans had been imprisoned, sometimes executed. David always told her they would never dare do that to the brother of the heroic King of England, though it had been weak assurance, at best.

Jimmy was a bubble filled with champagne who came along at the perfect time. And he *adored* her. Jimmy rose every morning wondering how he could amuse her, flatter her—and make her feel like a desirable woman, not a statue on a pedestal symbolizing love's greatest sacrifice. Or love's greatest disappointment, depending on one's point of view.

Now David was the third wheel—just like poor Ernest had been. Look at him! Sitting grumpily at a table adorned with silver and gold balloons. Beatrice Lillie was talking to him, but he didn't appear to be listening; he was watching Wallis and Jimmy with an intensity that caused her to flash a brilliant smile his way before turning to gaze at Jimmy with that certain softness in her eyes, tilted up while her head was lowered, that she had mastered so long ago.

"Shall we dip?" Jimmy asked, his voice full of laughter and promises he would never keep.

"I'm too old to dip," Wallis protested. Smiling.

"You're eternal. You're a sprite, a nymph. You'll never grow old." And Jimmy proceeded to bend her over until her supple back nearly touched her heels, and she felt young and strong and vibrant; all the rust of over ten years of the hated, admired, endlessly scrutinized Duchess of Windsor fell off her like sand. When Jimmy pulled her back up, she was breathless, giddy, and had to hide her face on his shoulder lest anyone see.

Oh, hell. Let *everyone* see. She raised her head and let her heart show on her face in a way it hadn't since she was a girl. Since she'd met Win Spencer on a navy base in Pensacola, Florida, and knew what it meant to be a woman.

"I'd like to dance you up to bed," Jimmy growled in her ear, and she giggled. *Giggled!* Wallis Warfield Spencer Simpson Windsor giggled.

Cookie would be shocked. They'd all be shocked, all those stuffy Windsors on their stuffy thrones in their dreary castles. Ridiculous, that David still pined for all that no matter how much he protested otherwise. But why else did the man keep putting on his kilts and playing his bagpipes until one wanted to brain him with a scepter?

Cookie wasn't Queen anymore, and that was another bubble of delicious champagne. Sad that poor Bertie had died, of course. But Cookie had been put out to pasture, was sitting in one of her fabulous homes reading magazines with *Wallis's* face on the cover. Watching her daughter—simpering little Shirley Temple—get all the glory now.

While she, Wallis, was being seduced on the dance floor by the young heir to the Woolworth fortune.

"Jimmy, we can't," Wallis said demurely—even as she knew her cheeks were flaming. David was watching them with the expression of a hound dog but with the determination of a German shepherd. They couldn't sneak off, and besides, the ball was still going strong, photographers snapping away and, outside the ballroom, throngs of common people straining to get a glimpse of the stylish Duchess of Windsor.

"What if," Jimmy said, whispering in her ear, "we meet for a midnight snack in my suite? I'll go charm the Dook formerly known as the King, throw him a bone or two, you know. You go be charming to, oh, why not Aly Khan? Go sit with Elsa for a bit too—she is the hostess. Then we'll meet up. And over. And under."

Even though she did not possess the equipment that Jimmy was familiar with, he had proven surprisingly good at handling it. Wallis felt her legs grow liquid, and she nodded. With a kiss to her hand, Jimmy sauntered off toward David.

But Wallis stood on the dance floor a moment longer. Couples swirled about her; the orchestra kept blaring "Begin the Beguine"; the expensive perfume of a hundred wealthy women filled her nostrils. She nodded at each and every one of them as she saw her name on every person's lips, heard it from every corner: *the duchess, the duchess, the duchess*—

The queen of the ball.

THE NEXT MORNING, AFTER Wallis rose completely refreshed, even humming a little tune, she was confronted with a morose David at breakfast in their suite.

This five-room suite at the Waldorf was now their home in New York during the social season. She had furnished it with her things—her jade, her lacquered boxes from China, paintings of her, the one of her and David in their wedding costumes. They had their own linens with their royal crest on them, their special brand of tea in its own wooden box, also embossed with the Windsor crest. The rooms were painted in Wallis blue and the furniture upholstered in that same shade, trimmed with gold, and the heavy curtains were gold as well. The pugs, of course, always sailed over with them, and the Waldorf politely overlooked the ruin to their carpets. The duke and duchess were good publicity.

"Well, you certainly made a fool of yourself last night, my darling," David said as he sipped his black coffee.

"I'm sure I don't know what you mean. The ball was a success and our photographs are all over the place." She gestured at the newspapers in a careless heap on the floor. "We're already flooded with invitations and opportunities." She held a thick stack of envelopes and started to go through them. "Tea with General Eisenhower and Mamie—she is so plain, that woman. I long to take her to Antoine's so she can get a new hairstyle. Cole Porter wants us to stay at his place on Long Island—he's so witty! Perhaps he'll put us in one of his songs. Here's one you'll like, an invitation to shoot in Scotland from—"

"Oh, for God's sake, don't. I'm sick of it, sick of it all."

"Sick of what?"

"All this—oh God. All this. This foolish frippery. I had a miserable time at that ball last night. I have a miserable time at all of them—what a waste."

"Now, David, you know I only do it for you—"

"Goddamn it! For once in your life, be *sincere,* Wallis!"

Startled, she looked across the breakfast table. David was glaring at her, for the first time in their marriage unafraid to wound her. And in spite of herself, she was impressed—and intrigued.

"All right. Yes, I do it for myself too. Of course I do! And *I* had a marvelous time. Jimmy is a divine dancer, you know."

"And a divine lay, I would say. Judging from the roses in your girlish cheeks. What time did you return to the suite last night?"

She giggled but didn't answer. Directly.

"Wallis, you know, I don't really mind," David said. She

raised an eyebrow; of course he minded. Why on earth would she pursue this affair if she didn't think it wounded him? What other pleasure did she have in this world? And she needed to hurt him, really flay him, after the war and the jewel theft and the reality of their situation set in, after he still had to go begging to Bertie for a job, for her HRH, for more money, for the right to return to the Fort. She hadn't been able to bear it any longer, seeing him do exactly as she'd had to do to Uncle Sol all those years ago. His constant prostration at the feet of his relatives turned her against him more than anything they'd been through; it crumbled the candy shell of their occasional spells of contentment with only each other. She despised his family, yes—good God, yes!

But over time, she'd grown to despise David more for going to them, hat in hand, again and again and again. Even as she knew he did it for *her*.

So when Jimmy came along—all flattery, but with a sarcastic edge, a wit that matched her own but that David had never been equal to—she seized the chance to hurt David. Not that she didn't get quite a lot out of it, of course; blushing, she remembered last night, and Jimmy in her hand, and she in his. But the former King of England's total despair when he realized what was going on was too delicious for words. What was power if it wasn't that?

"But, Wallis," David continued, not able to look at her directly, "this has been going on for two years now. I'm beginning to grow weary of it. You're—we're—too old for such games. Too settled."

"Too stagnated, you mean," she replied, spearing a slice of grapefruit, rejoicing in its acid bitterness. "And speak for yourself when it comes to growing old. Jimmy told me I look like I'm in my thirties. There's something to be said, darling, for not dwelling in the past and pickling yourself with alcohol. Just a little advice."

"What the hell am I supposed to *do*? Be your lapdog the rest of my life? Watch while you try on hats and applaud like a trained monkey? Go from party to party like a pathetic clown so that people can say they shook hands with an ex-king? People like Jimmy Donahue don't like us for ourselves, Wallis. They like us for the notoriety. For the publicity. But they don't truly know us, nor do they want to. I thought you of all people understood that." Abruptly, David got up and threw his napkin across his plate. He started pacing back and forth, pausing now and then to gaze out the window, taking in New York City, all the honking cars and crowds of people, Grand Central Station just a few blocks away, the Chrysler Building peeking around a corner.

She knew he hated it here. At least in Paris, he continually reminded her, he had gardens he could walk through, and when he did, she knew he was pretending he was back at Balmoral or Sandringham or any of the places he'd been so eager to shed in 1937.

But he'd spent the intervening years trying to replicate them, hadn't he? Designing gardens exactly like the ones at the Fort. Demanding that there be at least one room in each of their homes full of tartan. And she'd obliged him, turning their homes into palaces, training staff to behave as if he were King and she Queen. Allowing him to play those goddamn bagpipes after dinner.

In New York, however, she could take a break from the stuffiness and truly enjoy herself; the Waldorf staff was marvelously accommodating and the shopping even better than in

Paris. And she didn't have to pretend to like the outdoors; she'd never even strolled through Central Park.

But David detested everything she loved about New York, even though he acknowledged it was the epicenter of the social season and avoiding it was not an option.

"You're wrong about Jimmy. He likes me—he likes *us*, David. He's really quite fond of you."

"Said the lover to the cuckold."

"Oh, stop whining." She was in no mood to placate him this morning; she was due at Elizabeth Arden in an hour for a facial and manicure. Jimmy was taking her—*them*—to Twenty-One tonight, a place she adored. So much energy, all the newspaper columnists and stringers eager to snap their photos or quote them on some issue or another. Celebrities dropping by their table to say hello or introduce themselves—movie stars and politicians and, once, the winner of the Miss America contest. Of course, Jimmy always secured the best, most visible table in the house. Woolworth money and the Windsor name was an irresistible combination. If only she could convince David not to sit there looking like he'd just eaten a pickle; the newspapers invariably ran photos of him looking bored while she smiled with animation. It wasn't the image she wanted the public to see, but what could she do? Stay home with him?

God forbid.

"Whining? I?" David turned from the window, genuine surprise on his face.

She laughed.

"You've been whining since 1937. Annoying anyone who was ever your friend. Going on and on about that ridiculous HRH thing—you know I never cared about that, don't you?

How could I care about that when you promised I would be Queen? What a disappointment you are. What a disappointment I must be to you. I suppose, after all, Cookie was more to your taste. A nice, solid—in every sense of the word—English lady, dull as dishwater."

"I had quite a talk with her after Bertie's funeral. While you were here in New York doing God only knows what with Jimmy for all the world to see."

"Oh, did you?" Wallis yawned, pushed away her grapefruit. She had put on five ounces in the past week; she needed to be careful. She had a fitting at Bergdorf's in two days; Jimmy was going to escort her and take her to lunch at La Côte Basque after. She'd already had her press agent alert the papers.

"Yes. She's lost weight—grief, I suppose. She actually looked better than she had in years. Rather dignified, even."

"How fortunate for her that her husband died," Wallis said coolly.

David glared at her, then continued.

"We had quite the nice talk, she and I. Cleared the air about a few things. She is quite fetching, really, in her own way. Odd, I never could see that before. But she has such sympathy. One feels as if one could confide the most scandalous secrets to her."

Wallis froze. "And then she would tell them to Tommy Lascelles and Winston and all that bunch. She's not discreet."

"Precisely." David turned back to gaze outside; a flock of pigeons streamed by, surprisingly graceful. "I was thinking. Biblically, it makes sense, you know. One brother taking the place of another. I wonder, if I were to come crawling back, would she have me now? She wanted me once. Then I would be not only the uncle of the Queen but the stepfather. They'd have to find a place for me then. Welcome me back with open arms."

"And where would that leave me?" Wallis snapped, standing up so suddenly, she jostled the table, and her coffee spilled all over the snowy white tablecloth.

"That would be nasty for you, wouldn't it, my darling? To be—let's see, it does take some calculating. Oh, yes. Thrice divorced. Jilted by the man who gave up his throne for you. Cast out into the wilderness. I can't imagine Jimmy Donahue would have much use for you then. I can't imagine anyone would. All those invitations would disappear. Then where would you be? Without me?"

"You wouldn't—you couldn't! It would be just as mortifying for you. Imagine the headlines: *Turns Out I Was Wrong After All, Says the Ex-King*. But really, now that you mention it, I could see the benefits. I'd be rid of the most morose man I've ever met. And the stupidest, for abdicating instead of standing his ground and doing what he *said* he would do, *promised* he would do, which was make me Queen of England. Yes, I can see. It might be the best solution for us both. No need to pretend any longer. And of course, I'd manage a nice fat settlement from either you or the Crown—Jimmy could find me the best lawyer in town. Your dear relatives would surely pay me to shut up and not tell tales about how their former king likes to be treated in the bedroom. It would be positively *shocking*, were the truth to come out about *that*."

The atmosphere in the suite was electric; the little hairs on her arms stood up. They'd never said such things before; they couldn't afford to, and those unsaid words were part of the stultifying atmosphere that pressed down upon her chest every day. But this—this was *fun*! Exhilarating, liberating, to finally tell David what she really thought rather than going through the endless charade of the greatest love story ever told. To hear him tell *her* awful things, truthful, painful things, but at least they weren't platitudes, they didn't make her cringe.

They made her hate him. As much as he hated her. And hate was a real emotion; it sparked energy instead of ennui. In the absence of love, mutual hate was the next best thing, she decided. It finally made her marriage *interesting*.

Grinning wildly, Wallis was about to shoot more flaming arrows his way when, to her horror, his face crumpled. Utterly—like a little baby's face, unable to comprehend the cruelness of the world. He wrapped his arms around himself and started sobbing, rocking back and forth, his face red, his shoulders heaving. Burying his face in his hands, he slowly walked toward her, then fell down on his knees and threw his arms around her legs. She was too horrified to move. Or speak.

"Oh, my angel, my queen of hearts, what have we done to each other? To speak to each other in this way—what have we done? What have *we* done? Don't ever leave me, my precious, promise me. And I'll never leave you—I was only trying to wound you as I have been wounded myself. I didn't mean a thing I said, I didn't, I didn't!"

Now he was sobbing convulsively. She remained still as a statue, pondering her life. The fact that she was in the most luxurious suite at the Waldorf, her photo in all the papers, only because of *him*. That deep down, in the recesses of her soul she had never cared to explore, she was, despite Jimmy Donahue, despite Walter Winchell and Edward R. Murrow and Aly Khan, as miserable as she'd ever been. And as defeated.

Because none of them would ever know her the way David did. For better. Mostly for worse.

She held out a hand; it hovered over David's head as he sobbed and sobbed. Stifling her own sob—*Goodbye, Jimmy. Goodbye, Wallis*—she finally let her hand drop. She patted him while he tried—and failed—to stop crying.

"Don't ever leave me," he burst out again, so explosively, her knees nearly buckled. He looked at her with his red eyes, lacerating her with desperation. "Don't ever, *ever* leave me!"

"I won't," she whispered, feeling her heart hold still long enough to be captured in plaster like a death mask. She wondered if ever again it would feel love—or if it ever had. If it would ever know joy or any other emotion except pity. Pity, for the rest of her life.

Only pity, for them both.

CHAPTER
29

Queen Mary Makes Amends

ONE REACHES A POINT WHEN ONE MUST TAKE LEAVE OF this life.

I've lived longer than the biblical span. Longer than my husband, the King, longer than three of my sons. When Bertie died last year, I stood it. But I couldn't bear it, and there's a difference. The public didn't see that part of me died on the inside. As part of me had died with my husband, the King, with Johnny, with Georgie. Bertie took the last bit I could spare and still remain on this earth.

So now I lie in bed. Finally! I do see the appeal of it after all. (Elizabeth is quite fond of indulging herself in this way, and now that she's no longer Queen, she'll have much more time for this luxury.)

I never could see the appeal of it before. One's duty must always come first, which was the thing I could never understand about my eldest. But now that I'm two generations removed from ruling, and Lilibet has produced an heir and is safely on the throne, I can say that there were rumblings about some nonsense concerning a regency with David in charge while Bertie was ill, but it was all rubbish and I made it very clear to those involved. Thank heavens, they were minor idiots, no one of influence. And to my great relief, David appeared to have had no real role in it and dismissed it outright when he was made aware of the plot.

David is here now. He came over not to plan and plot and beg but to visit me. Which is how I know that I am, finally, after many months, dying.

Lung disease, they say. Respiratory. Not quite what killed Bertie or my husband, the King, but close enough. They blame the cigarettes—the very same cigarettes Bertie was encouraged to smoke because we thought it helped with his stutter. Now the things are poisonous, evidently.

Most things are, I've learned; words, thoughts, deeds. The trick is to build up an immunity to them, a tolerance to the toxin, even if the toxin is a person. Unfortunately cigarettes appear to be an exception to the rule, and my lungs are filling with fluid, and I can't breathe without the help of oxygen. Still, I allow myself one cigarette every evening. The nurses have promised not to tell my doctors or the Queen, who visits her old granny almost every day despite her many duties.

Margaret, however, does not. I never really did like this granddaughter, nor she me. She's too sly, that one. Too headstrong. Too unwilling to stay in her sister's shadow. And I have it on good authority she has referred to me as a "common old bitch." *Bitch* I may be. *Old* I certainly am. But *common*?

Absolutely not.

David, meanwhile, is here, and he sits beside me when he's not visiting old friends, those who still grieve the day he abandoned the throne. There are still some subjects who come to greet him when he arrives, I'm told, who are at the airport or the dock waving the Union Jack, calling him the King. But not many. Not any longer.

Bertie was a good King. A better one than David would have been. A mother can say these things. A Queen cannot, so I never told Bertie this. He died not knowing how his mother felt; it's a pity, but it couldn't be helped. We are not a normal family, a family that expresses love freely. We cannot afford to be or we would get *soft*. We need to remain vigilant; too many people want us gone. I'm not old enough to remember Marie Antoinette, no matter what people say. But I am old enough to remember the Romanovs.

I do hope Lilibet—the Queen—remembers that. She is young, of course, and of this new generation that is a bit sappy about their children, in my opinion. In my day, one did not get silly and slippery just because a child took a first step or uttered a first word or drew a picture that looked like a cross between an elephant and a dog. One did not constantly shower praise upon one's children simply so that they would be encouraged. *Character* mattered, and one differentiated between the children who possessed it and the children who did not.

Bertie had character. David did not.

"You know, it was I," I believe I said to David this afternoon. I was rather drowsy; apparently oxygen is not flowing to my brain as it should, according to my doctors. So I don't always know or remember what I have said or thought. I do remember this conversation, however amorphous it might be around the edges.

"You? What do you mean?" He was sitting in a chair beside me, a book in his hand. I assume I had dropped off into one of those startlingly deep sleeps I sometimes find myself swimming out of these days.

"It was I who put that article in. Long ago—Bertie, remember? When you asked Elizabeth to marry you and she kept refusing?"

"I'm David, Mama."

"Of course you are." Really, how impertinent! As if I didn't know my own children! "Of course you are David."

"You put what article in?"

"In the papers. Hinting that you were going to be engaged to her. I thought that might shake some sense into her. He loved her so, you know. He had such valor, Bertie. She just couldn't see it yet. But she did eventually. I was right."

"Yes, Mama," David said, and he reached for my hand. I smiled; one forgets how very nice it is to be touched by another human. Especially one's own children. My little boy blue, I used to call David when he was small, for I fancied he resembled the famous Gainsborough painting. But only in my heart did I call him that; never did I say it out loud. It wouldn't have been becoming of royalty; he was the heir apparent, after all. He outranked me even then. One always had to remember that, how one fit into the line of succession, who had precedence over whom; it was much more important than familial relations.

Do I have to remember it now, however? Is it not the time for taking off the crown, if only for a moment?

"I'm sorry." I turned my head to look at my eldest. He looked so old. So weary. So sad. I don't believe his life has turned out the way he hoped it would when he betrayed us all.

"For what?"

"That you—that you aren't happy."

"Of course I'm happy," he said sharply, so I knew that I was correct.

"If you say so," I replied. "I'm sorry, though. Perhaps if I'd been—more amenable to—" But the words were harder to find, obscured by an unsettling fog in my head, and my chest felt tight; breathing was hard, too hard, and that drowning sleep was beckoning.

When I awoke—hours, days?—later, David was gone.

I'm told he'll come back soon, that he only stepped out for some air and a walk. He always did love a good, brisk walk. Just like his brother the King. They are passionate gardeners, both of them. They really have so much in common. They both married strong women, for example. If only they all could see themselves through the eyes of a dying old woman.

"Where is David?" I ask. There is a nurse hovering. There is always a nurse hovering.

"I told you, Your Majesty. He will be back soon."

"Good." I'm relieved, because there is something else I want to tell him, something about the jewels. Oh, yes, that's it—the jewels. Is this what they mean by a deathbed confession? It would appear that I am as overflowing with contrition as a prostitute at Christmas.

How revoltingly *ordinary*. But shouldn't I tell someone that it was *I* who arranged for the jewels to be stolen? So David would get the insurance money and stop pestering Bertie? I've left instructions to have them returned after my death. I need to tell him so he won't be surprised.

And there's something else. Some thought I didn't finish before. Perhaps I'll remember it before he returns—because that fog is creeping in again, that vise around my chest tightening as I try not to struggle against its grip.

Oh, my son, all my sons. I do hope they come back soon.

CHAPTER

30

LONDON

JUNE 1967

ELIZABETH THE QUEEN MOTHER SAT IN HER POLISHED Rolls-Royce, the picture of calm and assurance. She arranged her face into the famous smile, chin charmingly uptilted. Once the car door was opened, she stepped out—not as nimbly as she once had, but still very spry; she did not need the arm proffered to her—and waved at the crowd roaring its love.

Look, it's the Queen Mum! Good ol' Elizabeth! Don't she look grand for her age?

This last made her smile even wider, even as she took a deep breath. Heavens. One would think one was Methuselah, the way people talked. One supposed it was because one had been in the public eye for so long.

Glancing ahead, she took another deep breath. There *they* were. For the first time since the abdication, she was meeting That Woman. And for the first time since Bertie's funeral, she would be face to face with David. When Queen Mary died, she'd managed to avoid him. Now she could not.

She almost trembled with all the thoughts unexpressed, the words unspoken. Decades of a drama played out in the public eye, and now here it was, the touching reunion. Oh, she'd read the newspapers! Hopes for reconciliation and all that rot. Perhaps now the royal family would bring their black sheep back into the fold; it was appalling how many newspapers framed the moment in that way. As if they'd forgotten all that had happened thirty years ago.

Thirty years ago! Heavens, how could it have been that long? Three decades in which she'd lived with her hatred for That Woman and David. It was an old friend, her enmity. She was at an age when she was starting to lose friends by the buckets; this one she would clutch to her breast.

The Windsors had arrived the day before at the invitation of the Queen. Lilibet had insisted that they be present for the unveiling of a plaque honoring Queen Mary on the centenary of her birth. After all, Lilibet pointed out reasonably, only David and Henry, the Duke of Gloucester, were left of her children, since Mary, the princess royal, had died two years ago. The plaque was to be unveiled outside Marlborough House, where Queen Mary had spent her widowhood. And where she'd died.

"Oh, Lilibet, but why do you have to invite them both?" Elizabeth couldn't stop herself from asking when her daughter broke the news over lunch. She really did try not to interfere in state matters or with her daughters' lives. Although they accused her of doing so. Constantly.

But really, how else was one supposed to pass the time? Once she'd been one of the most important people in the kingdom. Now she was merely a figurehead, a memory of those valiant times when Britain had, despite the odds, triumphed. She was a revered granny, that was all. And while long, wine-soaked luncheons with friends followed by naps, followed by drinks, followed by wine-soaked dinners were perfectly pleasant, they didn't possess quite the same *élan* as lunching with Winston in a bunker during air raids, tin helmets on their heads as they listened to the BBC on the wireless.

And, yes, she had grandchildren, six of them now. And, yes, she had managed to steer Lilibet down the right path when Margaret wanted to marry Peter Townsend—what a betrayal that had been! Bertie's favorite *divorced* equerry, having the gall to believe he could marry a princess! The absolute cheek. And then Margaret—headstrong, passionate—never forgave her or Lilibet and married Tony Armstrong out of spite, purely. But Tony was really such a charmer, and he introduced one to so many interesting artistic types. Why Margaret persisted in being so deeply unhappy, she had no idea.

Raising daughters was *so* exhausting. But the grandchildren were quite delightful.

So, all in all, she was lucky. Still, being a *former* queen for much longer than one had been a queen was rather depressing. When one allowed oneself to dwell on it. Fortunately, a stiff martini helped prevent one from doing so.

"It's time, Mummy," Lilibet had said firmly at luncheon, pulling one of her Queen Victoria faces; honestly, the resemblance was astonishing. "Mummy, you will behave, won't you?"

"Darling, I would never do anything to embarrass you or let down the family. You know that." Elizabeth pouted prettily.

"Yes, but I thought it prudent to ask. It's been so long, can't we let bygones be bygones?"

"No," Elizabeth said with a sweet smile as she patted her daughter's hand. "You'll understand someday. But there are some things one can't—one shouldn't—forget."

"Were it not for That Woman, as you insist on calling her, I would not be Queen," Lilibet reminded her as she speared a pat of butter, embossed with a crown, and placed it on a bread plate. "And I rather like it, you know. Lots of perks." She laughed, trying to get her mother to join in.

Elizabeth sighed instead. Her daughter was a very good ruler. Different than Bertie had been; she was more at ease in front of her subjects, more adaptable to the times than her father. When television came in, she'd done her Christmas message in front of the camera with no hesitation. The ability to appear to be genuine in public while withholding, protecting, one's truest self came naturally to her, as it had to Elizabeth but not to Bertie. Bertie had been born with no protective layer; Elizabeth had been born with several, in all the colors of the rainbow to accent her wardrobe. So had Lilibet. Thus accessorized, Lilibet had presided over the crumbling of empire but had knit together the commonwealth, proving herself to be more politically savvy than most had expected. Including her mother.

"So perhaps you and Uncle David and the duchess can bury the hatchet. Finally." Lilibet beamed at her mother with the assurance of a queen, then changed the subject, and that was that.

OH, BUT IT WASN'T. A lifetime of pent-up words bubbled inside Elizabeth the Queen Mother as she made her way to where *they* were standing. She'd never really had it out with That Woman. She'd never even written her a letter, because if she had, surely the American tart would have done something common with it, such as selling it to a magazine or including it in her distasteful memoir. Really, this need to tell one's side of the story in public! So pathetic. So craven; every word those two said, every action they took, was in exchange for money. They were as common as dirt.

And she'd had only that one moment with David after Bertie's funeral, when they'd come the closest to truth-telling they'd ever managed. It had felt wonderful to let her venom out, positively cleansing. Her hatred of them both—of what they did to Bertie back in '37, of how they upended Lilibet's life, of how they'd treated the crown and the succession as if they were *optional*, an invitation to a dinner party one didn't want to attend, and how, in politely declining, they'd opened the door to those questioning whether Great Britain should even have a royal family, questions that only grew louder with each passing year—

And the slings, the arrows! That Woman mocking one's appearance, laughing at one, always. Perpetuating that awful rumor, no matter who had started it—

When would Elizabeth get *her* chance to sharpen her arrows and let them fly at the only target that mattered? But it couldn't be here. Not in public. She'd promised Lilibet.

There they were, on the dais, alongside the Kents and the Gloucesters. It was a bright sunny day, June, but That Woman was dressed for Siberia! She was in a bright blue coat with a white fur stole around her neck—absurd. And she alone of all the women in the family did not wear a hat. Her jet-black coif—surely she dyed her hair, how pathetic—was bare for all to see, teased into a pouf but not a hair out of place.

Elizabeth patted her own chapeau, a bubbly lilac creation full of flowers and net, the same color as her summer coat. Was her hat *too* big and bright? Her coat and dress cut too generously (she did so dislike having to suck in her stomach all afternoon)? She'd always dressed so the people in the crowds could see her no matter how far away they were; she'd started doing that during the war, when she and Bertie visited bombed-out neighborhoods. But now, was it too much? Too frumpy or frilly or—

Once again she was back at the engagement ball for Marina and George, feeling like a lumpy corgi, all swirls and ribbons and flounces. The dumpy dowager. As Elizabeth approached the dais, That Woman looked at her, taking in her entire outfit from shoes to hat. The duchess's mouth fell open, then she quickly smoothed it into an amused smile.

Elizabeth wanted to run away and hide. Curse That Woman! How did she always make one—the former Queen of England!—feel this way?

But David saw her then, and he smiled. A genuine smile, and she was reminded that it had been a long time since they'd last met, however bitterly they'd parted. He'd finally aged, although his figure was as trim as ever. But the hair was white now, thinning, the lines in his face deeply etched, the eyes bloodshot. As she approached them, she held out her hand to him with her own almost genuine smile. He kissed her hand, then bowed.

"Dear Elizabeth, what a pleasure."

"David, I'm so glad you could come."

Elizabeth then turned to That Woman. The entire crowd seemed to hold its collective breath, and she was keenly aware that every eye, every camera, was watching, hoping to catch a glimpse of—what? Reconciliation? Not if she knew the press. Despite the platitudes they'd printed, they were hoping for a cat fight, pure and simple.

Elizabeth Bowes-Lyon held out her queenly hand.

Wallis Simpson did not take it.

Nor did she curtsy.

Elizabeth smiled her most charming smile and moved on without a word to her enemy as the cameras clicked. Swallowing her venom, saving it for another day. Turning her face to the cameras as they snapped away. Serene. Not in the least bit perturbed, as far as the public could see.

Really, she wasn't. So That Woman hadn't curtsied to her as she ought to have, hadn't shown her any deference at all, even though she was currently bowing to Philip and curtsying to Lilibet, who had just joined them on the dais—so what? Once again David's tart had shown her true colors for all to see; she needed no help from Elizabeth. Who, after all, was the delightful Queen Mother. The savior of the nation. The mother of the Queen.

And That Woman was nothing but a shriveled-up shrew.

COOKIE LOOKED ABSOLUTELY RIDICULOUS in that hat. What on earth was she thinking? The woman was dressed like a meringue. Wallis had almost forgotten how terribly Englishwomen dressed, especially the women of the royal family. Even Shirley Temple looked absurd in a hat that resembled a bathing cap. It made her look far older than her years, but then again, she always had looked older than her years.

Nobody in England had any *style*.

Wallis had taken great care with *her* appearance. Givenchy had designed her coat in Wallis blue, and she'd paid for one of Antoine's assistants to come over on the boat with them to do her hair. (Dyed black, of course, and augmented with some pieces. There were some age-related indignities she couldn't entirely prevent.)

Wallis had been shocked when David received the invitation addressed to them both. Shocked and suspicious; her first inclination was to decline. Why now? Why after all this time did they invite her back? Although, she noted wryly as she scanned the invitation, it was just for the ceremony. There was no offer to stay at Buckingham Palace, no mention of any family gathering before or after.

But David, seeing her name on the invitation next to his, had been so giddy, so pleased, she'd had to smile. And say that of course they must accept.

She smiled at him more these days. She allowed herself to feel his pain as well as her own, and wasn't that love, then, after all? Or a type of it? Finally, it seemed they'd achieved that most ordinary of things: a companionable marriage, now that the times, it appeared, had passed them by.

John, Paul, George, and Ringo; Liz and Dick; Warren and Julie; Twiggy and Penelope and Jane and the Shrimp—these were the unlined faces on the magazine covers. Music was loud and obnoxious; no one foxtrotted. Jimmy Donahue had died alone (pills and booze, it was whispered) last December. And the Windsors were yesterday's news.

Wallis, however, wasn't giving up without a fight; she'd had her face done, tried something with her neck, although that hadn't been satisfactory. She dyed her hair every week and still dieted fanatically, as did David. She'd even tried on one of the new miniskirts, but one look at her legs in the mirror told her this was one fashion trend she would not be following. Even David couldn't bring himself to compliment her.

The younger set didn't even know the Duke and Duchess

of Windsor existed, and the older set was dying off or staying home with their feet up. The latter was something that, more and more, the Windsors did, and with the ebbing of the hot flame of their notoriety, they kindled a gentler warmth. She could listen to him go on about golf now without wanting to stab him with one of his knitting needles. He didn't fear she would leave him, so he didn't try to lasso her with endless declarations of his love. They dined together in silence, and it was comfortable; not a defeat but a victory.

When they watched television at night in their shared dressing room, cozy in their robes ordered from the Ritz, they sometimes held hands. Because in the end, all they had, all they were, was this: Two people who had come together under the white-hot glare of the most intense public interest and managed to stay together despite the odds. Whether that was because of convenience, self-preservation, money, or true love didn't seem to matter anymore.

They were the only two who knew the whole story. And even they didn't know the whole story. They were too good at lying to each other. And to themselves.

Not even Cookie knew everything; she had only her side of the story to tell, her singular part to play, which she had done very well in the ensuing years; Wallis had to give her that. Look at her now! Meringue or not, she was the beloved grandmother of a nation, the beaming mother of the Queen, the enduring symbol of British pluck and courage during the war. A national treasure, Cookie was—and she knew it. Look at the way she mugged for the crowd!

And the way she greeted David with that crocodile smile! And he, embarrassing them both, met her with the same enthusiasm; oh, Wallis *could* stab him with one of his knitting needles right now.

All she could do then was stand her ground. Maybe David was willing to perform the reconciliation bit for the public. But Wallis would not curtsy to her; she wouldn't let Cookie have that triumph. Cookie could spare a victory, couldn't she? She'd had all the rest. And Wallis was, after all, an American. Americans did not defer to royalty, she reminded herself as she stood stock-still. She heard gasps and cameras clicking.

Cookie looked her in the eye. Wallis met her gaze. They appraised each other in an instant. Wallis had no doubt that Cookie knew the essential emptiness that Wallis had always tried to disguise with designer clothes. Just as Wallis knew Cookie spent her nights in front of her telly drinking too much and reliving the past.

The moment passed; Cookie moved on down the line to greet the rest of her dowdy family, and the much-heralded opportunity for reconciliation vanished.

But not the bitterness. Never the bitterness. There was a family luncheon planned after all; David's brother Henry—always such a stupid man!—let it slip. But she and David were not invited. Once the photo op of the ceremony concluded, they were no longer necessary. Wallis wasn't surprised.

But David, gullible, pathetic David, was. As they were being driven back to Dover to catch the boat for France, Wallis patted his arm as she watched him study the rolling English countryside; the day remained sunny, so the green of the grass and the blue of the sky met in vivid, crisp lines of stone walls and hedgerows. David's eyes kept filling with tears that he tried, in vain, to hide from her.

"I do miss it all so," he whispered. "I never meant to leave it. But they gave me no choice."

"I know," she replied, and took his hand in hers. "I'm sorry, my love."

David laid his head upon her shoulder and sighed.

CHAPTER
31

LONDON

JUNE 1972

ANOTHER FUNERAL FOR ANOTHER KING. PRINCE EDWARD Albert Christian George Andrew Patrick David had been King of the United Kingdom and the Dominions of the British Empire and Emperor of India.

Once. For so brief a time, so long ago. But when Elizabeth beheld the coffin holding his body lying in state at St. George's Chapel at Windsor, it seemed like only yesterday. The emotions she'd thought long suppressed came rushing back: the anger and resentment, the fear and the shock, and, yes—the joy. For, once, when they were all so young, David had meant joy.

Like all coffins, it looked too small. Why was that? She remembered thinking the same about Bertie's. As if the body, only a shell, shrank once the spirit left. Maybe it did, at that.

Elizabeth the Queen Mother accompanied the Queen and Prince Philip to pay their respects. The coffin was draped with David's royal standard, but no scepter, no crown. David had never actually been crowned, which was something one tended to forget.

Instead of a crown, there was an arrangement of lilies in the shape of a cross from That Woman.

Wallis.

How extraordinary, the way hate can dissolve like sugar. Like salt. Like vinegar. Ever since Elizabeth had been informed of David's death—not unexpected; Lilibet and Philip had seen him in France only weeks before and told her how frail he was—she'd occasionally slipped and used That Woman's Christian name. Was she getting soft in her old age? Or was widowhood a sorority, albeit one no one desired to join? Perhaps. All Elizabeth knew was that for the first time, she felt the tiniest bit of kinship with Wallis Simpson. Wallis *Windsor*. She knew instinctively that they had now felt some of the same emotions, had experienced the same dreadful but necessary details of death: making funeral arrangements, transportation arrangements, guest lists.

And loss. Always, loss. Even if the marriage wasn't a happy one, and Elizabeth could never be convinced that the Windsors' had been (unlike her own), there was still loss. So many subtractions—one less place setting at the table, one less opinion to consider, one less person who remembered your best and worst times. One less person who could tell your secrets.

One less person who looked forward to seeing you. One less hand to hold. One less person to hate, if that was the case. Or love.

One *less*.

Elizabeth hadn't said a word when Lilibet informed her that, for the first time, Wallis would be invited to stay at Buckingham Palace. Elizabeth had even offered not to go to the interment, out of respect; a widow didn't need former enemies studying her every move as she watched her husband's coffin disappear into the ground. (Naturally Elizabeth had to attend the funeral service; there would have been a public uproar if she didn't.)

But when Charles, who accompanied Wallis to view the casket the night before the funeral, told Elizabeth how frail Wallis was, how seemingly bewildered by all that was happening—"Granny, sometimes it was as if she didn't realize he was dead"—she decided to attend. She had to see her for herself. She had to—

Speak her piece. Finally. After all these years.

"She said," Charles told her, shaking his head, "she said, over and over, 'He gave up so much for so little.' "

Elizabeth had gasped to hear that. Was That Woman really that self-aware, finally? Was she ready to apologize to Elizabeth after all these years, apologize for nearly toppling the monarchy, for upending all their lives?

Would it matter if she was? Once, Elizabeth would have said yes with absolute certainty. Now she wasn't sure—all she knew was that this was her last chance to have it out with her. With David gone, That Woman would never return to England alive.

However.

When Elizabeth first saw Wallis at the funeral, she was beyond shocked; the always thin woman was positively emaciated. She looked as if she subsisted on liquids only. Her dress was beautifully cut, simple, very much in her usual style. Behind her heavy veil, the face was made up, the hair still charcoal black. But the eyes looked bewildered, the veiny limbs were unsteady, and she clutched Charles's arm throughout as if needing to be led.

Was she in her right mind? The thought of That Woman losing her faculties was terrifying. If it could to happen to Wallis, always so bright and sharp, sharper than any knife, it could happen to anyone. Elizabeth couldn't take her eyes off the widow during the funeral; Charles and Lilibet guided her through it as if she were a child. Elizabeth did not approach her at the burial either; she was torn between unaccountable sadness at seeing That Woman in this state and the need to be alone with her own thoughts. Because she was, inexplicably, awash in grief for them all. For Bertie, who had assumed the role that David had found too burdensome; for herself, who had seen her husband die too young as a result. For that pathetic, small little woman, who had once burned brighter than the sun.

For David. Whom she had once loved, perhaps still did. And what of it? What was wrong with loving? Surely one's heart could encompass all types of love; that was something she was learning as she aged.

When the casket was lowered into the ground near Frogmore Cottage, a location that David had picked out long ago, Elizabeth closed her eyes. Both the older Windsor brothers were gone now, those princes of her youth. Those kings. So different, and she was privileged to have loved them both and been loved by the better of them, darling Bertie. Perhaps she had been loved by David too. In his own way. If he had any love to spare once he met Wallis. For he had loved That Woman, and Elizabeth had known it back then, even if she didn't want to acknowledge it. But she did now. Whatever David's faults, he had been among the fortunate ones who had loved.

Wasn't that reason enough for one to forgive him, finally?

Following the funeral luncheon, Elizabeth—after a stiff belt of Scotch—decided it was time. Wallis was standing alone off to the side, watching them all in some astonishment—this family could be so inappropriately boisterous at funerals, one knew; Henry, now the only surviving child of King George V and Queen Mary, was arguing with Philip about which estate had the better shooting, Sandringham or Henry's country place, Barnwell Manor. Elizabeth started toward her enemy, legs a trifle unsteady, famous smile a tad uncertain. All the anger one had felt for so long—it had lost its edge, grown mushy, sloppy, and now it sloshed around in the pit of one's stomach.

"Wallis?"

The woman—so slight; would she even cast a shadow?—turned, and for a moment her face was as shrewd as ever, those blue eyes acknowledging who had addressed her. Disgust poured out of them, and Elizabeth took a step back, clutching wildly for her own disgust, which had deserted her.

"Elizabeth."

"I am so very sorry for your loss."

"How very charitable of you to say."

"Not charitable. I understand it, naturally. And mean it."

"Oh, yes—I mean—yes." Was that sympathy on the widow's face? She did wear *so* much makeup, and her face was *so* unnaturally tight, it was honestly difficult to tell. But Elizabeth was determined to be generous today.

"I know David loved you so."

Then the face changed; the eyes lost some focus, the mouth—always rather like a marionette's mouth, so wide yet unexpressive—drooped. Her lipstick, usually perfectly applied, smeared a little at the corners.

"David. David—where's David?"

"He's—do sit down, won't you? It's been such a long day."

"No." The head snapped up, the jaw was defiant. "No. I won't sit down with you. You broke his heart, all of you. You never knew how much he grieved for his country, how much he longed to return. You kept him out."

"With good reason. The country could not have two kings. He knew that when he chose to marry you."

"He was a fool," Wallis said, her voice full of bitterness. "A damned fool. I told him so—didn't I? Didn't I tell him what a damned fool he was?"

"I don't know—I hope not," Elizabeth replied, inexplicably sad. How tragic, if it was true. If David had not been loved after all. If he hadn't, then what was it all *for*?

Then she heard her elder daughter's voice from across the room. She turned to see Lilibet talking to Diana Cooper, still beautiful but so old now. They were all so old.

Lilibet looked dignified, assured, in her black suit. Like the Queen she had been for twenty years now. Twenty years since Bertie had died and Elizabeth ascended the throne. Her daughter had been Queen for longer than her husband had been King.

"I suppose," Elizabeth said, turning back to Wallis, who again grew vague and even smaller, if that was possible; her bones seemed on the verge of crumpling in on themselves, "I suppose it was all for the best, in the end." For it was. First Bertie, now Lilibet, had rescued the Crown from near ruin.

And neither one had done it alone, had they? Elizabeth knew her own role in saving the monarchy. It would be in her obituary when the time came.

"Have you seen David?" Wallis asked, heartbreakingly. Her eyes searched everywhere; she was wringing her hands and trembling, agitated. Elizabeth could only take her former formidable enemy by her fragile arm and lead her to a sofa. They sat down, side by side, and for a long while neither said a word. Elizabeth watched her children and grandchildren, a Queen and a future King among them. Yes, it had all turned out for the best.

Still, she was exhausted, and she decided to take advantage of one of the perks of old age. She beckoned to Charles to come replace her; she was in great need of another belt of Scotch and a lie-down. For she'd lost another friend today.

She'd said goodbye to a lifetime of anger.

Charles arrived, and she stood, took a step, then froze in her tracks when Wallis spoke again. Had she really heard what she thought she'd heard? Had Wallis really said it?

And, most important—

Did she *mean* it?

WHILE DAVID LAY DYING, Wallis was at first afraid she wouldn't be able to stand the ordeal. Never had she been able to cope with blood and fluid and the odors of *life;* she'd always preferred expensive perfume to the scent of real flowers. And from what the doctor had told her—she had a difficult time taking it all in; it really couldn't be true—that's what she was to expect: real life, at its agonizing end. David was in the final stages of the throat cancer that had been diagnosed only a year before.

She'd always told him cigarettes were a nasty habit. Why hadn't he listened to her?

But it turned out that the moment she heard his weak voice calling for her after he had been confined, for the last time, to his bed, she couldn't stay away. So she sat with him, for long nights and days. She didn't do any of the distasteful tasks; thank God for nurses. When they had to change his clothes and sheets or administer injections, she left the room. But only for the time it took to complete those tasks.

Despite his semiconscious state, David seemed to know who she was and why she was there, and he was grateful. So grateful, it made her realize that he hadn't expected this of her, this deathbed devotion. And he was right not to have expected it, although she knew that if it were different, if she were the one struggling for breath, delirious half the time, he would have been there for her. She would never have had to worry about that.

Penitence. Another missing link in their marriage for too long. Forged just in time.

But often as she sat next to him, her back aching, her head pounding, too agitated to eat or drink, she got confused. Weren't they supposed to be in Antibes by now? Why were they still in Paris at Villa Windsor? The timing seemed off, the world slightly tilted. When she tried to stand to go change her clothes or take a bath, she had to hold on to something, or someone.

Why hadn't David arranged all their travel details? Where were all the trunks and crates for the pugs? He was so very useful in this way; she used to tease him that he could run a travel agency and call it Windsor's Wanderings. But where *was* he?

She would awaken from this fog and find herself in the chair beside his bed, his small figure wasting away—he hadn't been able to eat solid food for weeks—his lungs rattling. And her hand covering his, trying to give him warmth, because he was cold, so cold.

Then she woke one night in her own bed—how had she gotten there? She was in her nightgown, although she didn't remember putting it on. And David's butler—the Black one, the one they'd brought back from the Bahamas, he was so polite and conscientious—told her, "The duke is gone, Your Royal Highness."

"Oh!" She gasped, ran across the sitting room to his room, and stopped in the doorway; his body was so small, so still. No more of that ghastly rattling. He was a boy again. A little boy, quietly sleeping. No. The King was dead. Long live the—

There was no one. No heir, no spare. Only Wallis.

And the ordeal of the funeral, in London of all places, the city she loathed in the country she could never understand, looming ahead.

SHE WAS TOO EXHAUSTED to accompany the casket right away; after she saw his body, the world tilted again, lights dimmed and bees buzzed in her head. She fell to the floor—marble was very cold and hard, she mused with a drowsy grin—and a doctor gave her an injection, and she slept for twenty-four hours, they told her later. While she slept, her maid must have had Givenchy whip up a black dress and veil because they were waiting for her when she woke, hanging on padded hangers on a dress rack, the first things she saw when she opened her swollen eyes.

She was a widow now.

She tried to sit up but her limbs were heavy and her head still fuzzy from the injection; what the hell had been in it? It wouldn't wear off. It refused to leave her body; like an unwanted houseguest it stayed and stayed in her system as she was helped into travel clothes, and it accompanied her on the flight to London—the Queen had sent a plane. How nice of her. No matter if she was in the air or on the ground, Wallis was shaky on her feet, and she couldn't always follow what others told her. After the short drive from the airport to London, she did register that she was being escorted into Buckingham Palace, finally, after all these years. But she couldn't muster any sense of pleasure or even triumph as she was helped out of the black car, the red-carpeted stairs looming up at her, footmen lined up like toy soldiers.

After Wallis was shown to her room, the Queen—Shirley Temple—said something about her attending Trooping the Color the next day with Cookie, how nice that would be, and when Wallis looked at her blankly, the Queen explained that Trooping the Color couldn't be postponed even for David's funeral. And then Wallis remembered it was that ridiculous thing they did to celebrate the monarch's official birthday, not the actual birthday, something she hadn't understood even when she wasn't under the lingering influence of that injection. And she shook her head. No, she couldn't attend. She couldn't expose herself like that, be on display with the rest of them—Cookie, Shirley Temple, Bertie, Queen Mary. She couldn't give them the satisfaction; no, they would not play happy family. Not now. *They* were the reason poor David was lying in a casket. Oh, yes, the doctor said it was the cigarettes. But Wallis would always believe he'd died of a broken heart, for in the end, she understood that he was more devoted to England than to "the woman I love."

But she did peek out one of the windows at Buck House during the ceremony, looking down at the courtyard where Shirley Temple—when did she get to be so big, so bosomy?—

was on a horse, all decked out in scarlet and black, receiving salutes from other people on horseback, and it all seemed so absurd. All that pageantry, all that show. For what?

The King was dead. Long live—

Nobody.

AFTER IT WAS OVER, all Wallis wanted was to go home. Back home to Villa Windsor, where David would be waiting for her—why hadn't he wanted to come again? After all, they were *his* family, not hers. She couldn't remember.

But Cookie stood in front of her and wouldn't leave.

"I am so very sorry for your loss," she said. "I know David loved you so."

David. Oh, David! Wallis's heart did the most unusual thing then; it turned over at the sound of his name for the very first time. Oh, he loved her, her David. Yes, he did.

"David. David—where's David?" she asked the woman next to her.

"He's—do sit down, won't you? It's been such a long day."

"No." Oh, it was Cookie! Cookie, looking a fright in her black tent of a dress. Cookie, who had been the cause of all of David's grief since the abdication. "No. I won't sit down with you. You broke his heart, all of you. You never knew how much he grieved for his country, how much he longed to return. You kept him out."

Oh, that's why he wasn't here! Why had he left England? He shouldn't have left; he should never have left, not for her!

But hadn't he been with her earlier?

"Have you seen David?" Wallis asked the woman—was it really Cookie? When did she get so old? The woman didn't answer, just took her arm and led her to the sofa, where they sat quietly for a while. Then she was beckoning to someone, a young man, to take her place. He looked nice too, and he reminded her of someone. The woman stood and started to go. "Where is he? I have to tell him, I have to tell him, whatever he does, *he must not abdicate*!"

The woman stopped and turned around. She looked at Wallis with so much sadness, so much regret, that Wallis decided she liked her. Whoever she was.

Turning to the nice young man—the Prince of Wales, yes, of course!—Wallis clutched his arm and told him again:

"You must not abdicate!"

CHAPTER
32

PARIS

OCTOBER 1976

AT LEAST THE FRENCH STILL WANTED HER. ELIZABETH THE Queen Mother had been invited for a state visit, just like old times, and for a real purpose: to improve relations between France and England, which had been at an all-time low since Vietnam. So she got the whole works: the official greeting at the airport from President d'Estaing and a procession through the streets of Paris, a state dinner at Versailles. She was to open a new British cultural center, something she could do in her sleep, so it was a nice little excursion as well as a refreshing change of routine. She'd brought her favorite staff, including Billy Tallon, who was as queer as they came. He told her all sorts of saucy stories and kept teasing that he was going to take her out to a very risqué boys' club in Montmartre. Which she had half a mind to let him do, except that Lilibet would be horrified. Although the grandchildren would probably approve.

She did enjoy gay men in her old age. They made her laugh, unlike the stuffy heterosexual men she knew, so earnest, so dull. Billy's partner was another member of her staff, so the two of them often came round for drinks in the evening if she didn't have engagements. They watched the telly together—

she adored *Happily Ever After,* especially the talking bird—and Billy and Reggie made bitchy comments and they all got rather snockered, but who cared? No one was going to scold the Queen Mum for having a wee bit more vodka than one should.

But on this trip she had to be Elizabeth the Queen Mother, not the Queen Mum. She assumed the mantle of majesty easily; it wasn't something one forgot. And Lilibet was awfully good about giving her work to do whenever she suspected her mother might be bored and always appointed her one of the counselors of state when the Queen was out of the country. So she kept up a royal schedule, but of course it was much lighter now and consisted mainly of opening supermarkets and visiting senior centers. She always joked that soon she'd be joining them; that was good for a jolly laugh or two and a quote in the papers the next day.

Everyone loved the Queen Mum!

But there was also plenty of time for gossiping with Billy and Reggie. Really, she was quite content with everything, with the exception of Margaret's upcoming divorce from Tony. Of course, she would be the first of the family to divorce! But one mustn't dwell on unpleasantness; this was Elizabeth's motto in her dotage. After all, she'd lived through the abdication and two World Wars. Hadn't she had enough unpleasantness to last a lifetime?

The grandchildren were growing up; Anne was married now, and it was long past the time when Charles should be. That boy! Such a dreamer. She'd encouraged that when he was young, but now he had to settle down and fulfill his duty lest he, like his great-uncle, wait too long, pick the wrong woman, and almost bring down the monarchy.

That would not happen. Not if Elizabeth Bowes-Lyon had anything to say about it, which she did.

Speaking of the wrong woman—

"Do you think," she asked Billy one morning in Paris when they were going over her schedule and she spied a gap in it, "do you think I should go visit *her*?"

"Who, ma'am? Not—*her*!" Billy gasped, looking horrified as only he could; his eyes were as big as eggs and he waved his hands as if warding off evil spirits. "Not *That Woman*! Perish the thought!"

"No, really. I've heard such sad things about her, you know. She was so confused at David's funeral, although when she returned home, she seemed to recover, at least according to Cecil Beaton, who visits. But Wallis has had a nasty fall, I believe—broke her hip or ribs—and I thought that while I'm here, I might bury the hatchet."

And score a nice little publicity coup in the process, one couldn't help thinking. The reconciliation, after all these decades. Before it was too late, and there was no one left with whom to reconcile.

"Bury the hatchet? In the middle of her back?" Billy grinned wickedly, and she had to giggle. Oh, he did go on!

"But I am serious, dear. Could you ask my personal secretary to put out inquiries to her staff?"

"You royals! Can't just pick up a phone and ring like the rest of us peasants!" And Billy bustled out of her room in search of the secretary.

Elizabeth went to the window of her suite at Le Meurice—her preferred hotel in Paris; the Ritz was altogether too busy and full of loud celebrities. Royalty stayed at Le Meurice, where one could almost feel as if one were at home with its lush appointments, priceless antiques in the suites, even butler service (although, naturally, one traveled with one's own staff). Looking out over the Tuileries Gardens—it was October, so leaves were turning, flowers fading in their neat little plots and rows, so very French—she allowed her thoughts to remain with Wallis.

Wallis. A woman much like oneself; a widow who had once been young, glamorous, who was now nearly forgotten. Well, not that much like oneself, really. Elizabeth the Queen Mother was most certainly not forgotten. She still regularly graced the cover of *Tatler,* although not as frequently as her daughters and granddaughter.

Still, Elizabeth could never forget Wallis's confusion after David's funeral, her strange cry of "He must not abdicate!" Wallis then had to return home to an empty seat at the dinner table—and while Elizabeth did know something about that and could never entirely forget that she and Bertie had only twenty-nine years together while Wallis and David had nearly thirty-five—her sister-in-law's plight tugged at the heartstrings, rather. Or at least, the sagging, aging heartstrings, especially when one had had that extra glass of wine, and the past had fewer defined edges.

Certainty was the privilege of the young.

Alone. Wallis was *entirely* alone. No children or grandchildren. No sisters or brothers. Not even a talking bird. No real friends, not the kind one could invite over at the last minute. Most of Wallis's friends lived elsewhere, not in Paris. So she was alone with only servants—and probably those messy pugs—and Elizabeth couldn't really imagine how entirely isolated that must feel, for she had never not been in the bosom of family.

And to be both ill *and* isolated—

Once, Elizabeth would have thought that Wallis had gotten what she deserved. No longer.

She determined that she would go and visit her sister-in-law; yes, it would be wonderful publicity, good for the cover of not just *Tatler* but maybe even *Hello!* But it would also be a good deed, and that was another thing one contemplated as one grew older: the chances of heaven versus the chances of hell. Gambling on racehorses was thrilling; gambling on one's eternal life was another thing entirely.

So Elizabeth the Queen Mother would go visit Wallis the Duchess of Windsor. After all, they were practically the only two people left who had been at the center of the abdication. They had shared memories, despite all their differences. They were the only survivors—it was rather like those gatherings of survivors from the *Titanic* or the *Lusitania*.

Strangers tied together for life because of tragedy.

WALLIS LAY IN BED, the curtains of her room pulled to block out the sun. The sun hurt her eyes, she remembered. Being outdoors hurt her lungs. Sitting up hurt her hips and ribs. Eating bothered her stomach. Her body, denied proper nourishment all these years in order to fit into those fabulous dresses (she must remember to make an appointment with Givenchy for a party she and David had been invited to), seemed to have gone on strike.

So she lay in bed and followed her mind down its wandering paths, forward and backward, only occasionally pausing in the present as if to catch its breath before roaming once more.

Troubled, troubled, troubled—that was what her mind

told her she was. Troubled because she had to go ask Uncle Sol for money; she remembered that safe in his office, how he kept the keys with him at all times, not even trusting his own kin. Family could be *so* petty, couldn't they? Win, his hands and his feet always aimed at her, a bottle in his hand, disgust on his face. Ernest, sitting alone in a corner while she danced with the Prince of Wales—imagine her, Wallis, dancing with the heir to the throne! Ernest looked so sad, so forlorn, but heavens, she was only doing it to help him, didn't he understand?

Men were so obtuse!

But it wasn't only to help him, was it? She didn't really care about Ernest's business; she'd never cared about him or anyone other than herself. Wasn't that what Uncle Sol had told her once? Or was it Win?

Or was it David?

David, David, David—the face she had known longer than any face but her own. The name she had said more than any name—but her own.

Wallis and David, the King and Mrs. Simpson—*he must not abdicate! He must not abdicate!*

Sometimes her own croaky voice roused her from these wanderings, and now she was awake, aware she'd spoken out loud. Aware there were other people in her room—oh, there were always other people lurking about! Spying and whispering and lifting her up, bathing her, clothing her; the only ones she recognized were the manicurist and hairstylist, both of whom still came every day. Someone else propped her up in the mornings and applied her lipstick, rouged her cheeks, and this made her both happy and furious. Why couldn't she do this on her own? Where was her makeup table? These idiots didn't know what to do, they always got it all wrong, and where were her jewels? Someone bring her her jewels—miraculous, they were! Appearing under armed guard a few years ago after she thought they'd been lost forever! They felt so cool against her skin, her precious baubles. David had picked them out, he'd designed them. For her.

But the sensation of being touched by human hands—even in this coldly clinical way—could make her cry sometimes. Because no one else touched her anymore.

Why didn't David? Where was he? He used to be so sloppily affectionate, too much; she remembered countless times she'd shrugged off his arms, turned away from his kisses. Why? Why on earth? She craved them now. She longed for his face, his touch. She couldn't bring herself to look in a mirror anymore, she hadn't in ages; looking into his face was the closest thing she had to peering into her own soul.

But David wasn't among all those people hovering around her now; they'd moved over to a window, those spies, those vultures. She could make out their sinister outlines but there were no faces. Nobody had a face anymore.

The Queen Mother, she heard. *Asks to visit. What do we say? She can't see her like this.*

The Queen Mother! Wallis searched her unreliable memory for a face. All those faces were so fickle now; they slipped in and out of shadows, they transformed from young to old to middle-aged, plump to thin, rosy to pale. *Elizabeth Bowes-Lyon,* whispered one memory—a cheerful young woman with dark hair and the creamiest complexion Wallis had ever seen—what she wouldn't do to have that complexion! The two of them, Elizabeth and her husband, so content together. Wallis would never be that content with anyone. Not even a prince. Not even a king.

Cookie, whispered another memory—a spherical riot in pink satin and lace, diamonds like tinsel on a Christmas tree. So chummy with the King and Queen. Freezing her out with that smile that fooled everyone. Everyone but Wallis. Whispering in her husband's ear, Winston's ear, Baldwin's ear, denying her—something. What was it? Once, she thought it was happiness.

Now she couldn't recall. So it really couldn't be that important, could it?

Tell the Queen Mother not at this time, one of the shadows hissed, and Wallis tried to sit up in bed; she propped herself up on one elbow, but the elbow failed her and she fell back, gasping with pain; her ribs burned so, they took her breath away.

"Tell the Queen Mother I would like to see her," she called out. After all, who was paying these idiots? David was. He was always so concerned with their finances. But David would like to see Cookie, wouldn't he? He missed her, he missed them all, even though he tried very hard not to let Wallis see.

But she did anyway. It was always there, her feelings of guilt. His unspoken accusation. They'd denied each other the things they most valued all their life together. But neither one could admit it to the other.

"Tell her to come," Wallis called out again. Very annoyed; when had the help become so insolent? She ought to fire the lot and hire new ones, but apparently she didn't pay enough. Someone had told her that once.

But none of the shadows seemed to have heard her. Soon they went away.

And Wallis was all alone with her memories.

He must not abdicate!

WHEN HER PRIVATE SECRETARY informed her that Wallis was too ill to see her, Elizabeth was startled by her disappointment. And it wasn't only because there would be no photo op, no magazine cover, no chance for the grand gesture of reconciliation.

She truly wanted to see Wallis. To see with her own eyes that she was being cared for; with no family, who was seeing to that? Was she being taken advantage of in her desperate state? And Elizabeth sincerely wanted to talk to her. She'd never attempted to understand the woman who had made her Queen. The woman who, in the end, had made David very happy. She had to believe that, for if he hadn't been, what was it all for?

But it was too late now, apparently. Another thing she was learning in her old age: Everything was finite. Even emotions—happiness, grief, despair. Anger. Everything had an expiration date. Even queens and kings. Something was always going to be left undone, unsaid.

Unforgiven.

"Don't fret," Billy told her with a sympathetic smile. "We'll make sure the press knows you tried. You did your best."

"Did I, though?" Elizabeth mused, then she gave herself a little shake. Well, one was certainly slipping, wasn't one? Voicing regrets in front of the staff, even if it was just Billy, was not behavior becoming a queen.

"Why don't you send her flowers?" Billy suggested, and Elizabeth had to laugh. Gay men always suggested sending flowers. She firmly believed it was a conspiracy, since every florist she knew was gay. But he had a point, and she nodded, then asked him for one of her cards so she could write a message to include with them. A large arrangement, she instructed Billy. But not too large—one mustn't go overboard. She was still stinging from the furor over her portion of the privy purse in Parliament not that long ago. Really! The government expected one to live like a peasant, it would seem.

Elizabeth sat at an antique desk in a gilt-trimmed room and stared at the thick blank card, embossed with a crown, for the longest time, so long that Billy discreetly withdrew and returned with a rather large gin and tonic, which she sipped while she stared and stared, thought and thought. What to say to the woman who had been her sworn enemy yet also her greatest blessing? For despite it all, Elizabeth couldn't imagine her life playing out any other way. Wife of a king, mother of a queen, beloved, and loved. She would not have to die alone in a ghostly mansion. She would not have to wonder if anyone would remember her after she was gone.

Elizabeth Bowes-Lyon had won. In the war between the Windsors, she was the victor, the last one standing. Sweet was this realization; as sweet as her favorite chocolates from Fortnum & Mason, as sweet as the honey harvested from her own apiary at Royal Lodge.

As sweet as the heather dear Bertie used to place on her pillow at night, often accompanied by a silly poem—*Ach, my lass, bide a wee, and when you dream, dream of me*. As sweet as the cocktails David used to mix at the Fort with a mischievous gleam in his eye and a smile he reserved only for his sister-in-law.

Once upon a time.

Those who have been loved could be generous, Elizabeth

decided. Not only could be generous, but *should* be. Especially toward those who were not so loved. Anger had once been her friend, and now the woman who had inspired it could be, for what was a friend, really? Someone who shared the same memories, who remembered the same songs, who had danced the same dances. Who had fought the same battles—and told the same lies.

Finally she picked up a pen and wrote, in a steady hand,

In Friendship,
Elizabeth

AUTHOR'S NOTE

Sometimes when I'm searching for subjects to write about, there are people or events that are so obviously perfect for a historical novel that I assume that it's already been written. This was definitely the case with the historically epic, gossipy, and juicy feud between Wallis Simpson and Elizabeth Bowes-Lyon.

I'd included this feud in my ever-expanding Word document titled "Potential Book Ideas" long ago. But there the two women remained, glaring at each other, while for years I chose to write about other subjects.

After I turned in my last novel, *California Golden,* I started two other novels before deciding they weren't right for me at that time. I also signed with a new agent, and when she and I first spoke on the phone as part of the mutual interview process, I mentioned—among many other ideas—this one, this royal feud. She said she loved it. I said that surely, someone else had already written it. How could this amazing story not have been turned into a novel yet?

I continued agonizing over what to write next, boring all my friends and family with my dilemma, and I mentioned this subject, again among other ideas, to my friend and fellow author Nicole Hayes. She might have squealed, and she definitely said something along the lines of "I would totally devour a book about them!"

I still wasn't convinced. We authors are stubborn folk and often slow to understand our strengths. Which apparently, in my case, is "gossipy high-society feuds." Because when I finally succumbed to the inevitable and wrote this novel, my editor declared after reading it, "You were born to write this book!"

So, as I had in *The Swans of Fifth Avenue,* I easily slid into the shoes of two amazingly complex but magnificently bitchy and sly people, Wallis Simpson and Elizabeth Bowes-Lyon. And, oh, what fun it was!

Each woman was, depending on the biography you were reading, either the most saintly woman of all time or an expert manipulator. The star of the most revered love story in memory or the long-suffering wife of an emotionally stunted man. A victim or a heroine.

Both women are still instantly recognizable and talked about today, of course. We can thank *The Crown* for that, as well as films like *The King's Speech.* That these two women from such different backgrounds changed history is unmistakable; there would have been no Queen Elizabeth II without both of them. What fascinated me most as I dived into the multitudes of books and television series and films about these two was how similar they actually were. Simply put, these were two strong, charming women married to weak men. Had they met under different circumstances, I've no doubt they would have been good friends. How they both loved to gossip!

But they met two brothers, one the dashing heir apparent,

the other the supposedly weaker younger brother, both sons of King George V of England. Thus there was no chance that an American divorcée and a pampered daughter of a Scottish earl were ever going to be friends, let alone companionable sisters-in-law. (You can draw your own parallels to current feuds between British royal sons and their wives; perhaps some things are destined never to change.)

There have been historical novels about Wallis Simpson before. She's a figure of fascination and the ultimate "Was she a victim or a predator?" conundrum. But what I finally realized was that there hadn't been a novel about the *two* of them and their royal Mean Girls trajectory before, and that's what finally pulled me in. It's fun! It's historical! It's tragic! There are castles and jewels and Nazis and the Blitz and scandal and designer clothes—and most of it actually happened!

I'm always asked what parts I imagine and what parts are real historical events in my novels. The easiest answer is that conversations, for the most part, are imagined. (Although in this novel there are some well-known quotes that I have included in dialogue, among them King George's fear that David would ruin himself and his hope that nothing would come between the throne and Bertie and then Lilibet. And, yes, Winston Churchill did downplay concerns over Mrs. Simpson at first, continually referring to her as the King's "cutie," and was an ally of the couple—until World War II.) The thoughts of these historical figures as they do the things we know they did are also the product of my imagination.

But we know the timeline of the abdication and it's pretty much as I've depicted it here. One detail that Wallis fans might object to is that I have Cecil Beaton taking photos of the duke and duchess on their wedding day; in fact, he took the photos the day before. We know what each couple did prior to and during the war, and the Duke and Duchess of Windsor did meet Hitler, the duke did express the opinion that it was good for his former subjects to be bombed if it brought about an end to hostilities, and the two were at least aware of Hitler's plan to put them back on the throne once he (Hitler) invaded Great Britain.

The person or people behind the theft of Wallis's jewels remains a mystery and has been explored in recent books. My interpretation of this event is my own.

To sum up, the private conversations, quarrels, manipulations—did Elizabeth really set the press on Wallis and David? Did David spread a rumor of Elizabeth's supposed illegitimacy?—are my own invention. We'll never know for sure. But based on my interpretation of these two women, after all my research, these conclusions make sense to me.

One enduring mystery about Wallis is unexplored in this novel; did she, as many claim, have an intersex condition? Specifically, did she have androgen insensitivity syndrome, a condition in which a person is born genetically male, with XY chromosomes, but presents as female? I didn't pursue that question; writing historical fiction means you have to focus on one narrative, leaving other stories unexplored. I believe that sex didn't mean much to Wallis except in terms of power and what it would gain her. Was sex painful, as it might have been if she suffered from that condition? Could she have conceived a child? Some claim she had an abortion at one point; others say the surgery she had was related to this intersex condition. Again, we'll never know.

(Elizabeth Bowes-Lyon was also the subject of some sexual

speculation, specifically about the use of a turkey baster, which I suggest you google if you want to know more.)

I'm so grateful that others helped open my eyes to the delightful fictional possibility of this feud. I'm an unabashed Anglophile; I've been to Buckingham Palace, the Tower, Windsor Castle; I devoured *The Crown* and other fictional portrayals. And I read *Tatler* every morning, first thing, with my coffee. The British royal family will always be good fodder for fiction; it has been since Shakespeare's time. Given the current cast of characters, I don't see that changing anytime soon. Once again, just like in 1936, there are valid questions about the need for a royal family in the first place. The Windsors' tendency to close ranks and protect the monarchy at all costs might well be the thing that destroys it.

So whether or not I was truly born to write this book, I'm awfully glad I did and I hope you have as much fun reading it as I did writing it. And researching it! Here is a partial list of books about the royal family that were helpful to me in various ways: *Royal Feud* by Michael Thornton; *Elizabeth the Queen Mother* by Hugo Vickers; *Yes, Ma'am: The Secret Life of Royal Servants* by Tom Quinn; *Queen Elizabeth: The Queen Mother* by William Shawcross; *That Woman* by Anne Sebba; *The American Duchess* by Anna Pasternak; *Wallis in Love* by Andrew Morton; *Power and Glory, The Windsors at War,* and *The Crown in Crisis* by Alexander Larman; *George VI and Elizabeth* by Sally Bedell Smith; *The Queen Mother* by Lady Colin Campbell; *George V* by Jane Ridley; *Matriarch* by Anne Edwards; *Once a King: The Lost Memoir of Edward VIII* by Jane Marguerite Tippett; and *The Heart Has Its Reasons* by the Duchess of Windsor. (Note: These last two, the memoirs, I take with a very large grain of salt, as I do most memoirs. They're never to be read as absolute historical truth; they're propaganda, written by those who are trying to shape their legacy in the most flattering way.)

And for your viewing pleasure, I recommend *The Crown* on Netflix, the film *The King's Speech*, and a vintage British miniseries, *Edward and Mrs. Simpson.*

ACKNOWLEDGMENTS

I'M SO GRATEFUL FOR THE ADVICE, PASSION, AND EXPERTISE of my fantastic editor, Susanna Porter, as well as my agent, Stacy Testa of Writers House. And that gratitude spills over to my entire Penguin Random House team: Kara Welsh, Kim Hovey, Jennifer Hershey, Karen Fink, Emma Thomasch, Caro Perney, Megan Whalen, Anusha Khan, Loren Noveck, and Tracy Roe. And my thanks to Sydnee Harlan and Tom Ishizuka of Writers House.

To my writing and publishing friends who put up with my endless agonizing over what to write every single time and who are patient and full of wisdom: Nicole Hayes (I believe this is the second book Nic made me write, after *Alice I Have Been*), Edward Kelsey Moore, Renee Rosen, Abbott Kahler, Bridget Piekarz. I'm forever in your debt.

My heartfelt gratitude to the book champions I've had the great fortune to meet and get to know: Suzy Takacs, Pamela Klinger-Horn, Mary Webber O'Malley, Stephanie Hochschild, Julie Slavinsky, and many more owners, managers, and booksellers of wonderful independent bookstores who have hosted me over the years. There are too many to mention, but here are a few: Anderson's Bookshop, the Book Stall, Book

Cellar, Lake Forest Bookstore, Unabridged Books, Barbara's Bookstore, the Bookstore of Glen Ellyn (all in the Chicago area); Warwick's in La Jolla, California; Pages in Manhattan Beach, California; Forever Books in St. Joseph, Michigan; Blue House Books in Kenosha, Wisconsin; Tattered Cover in Denver, Colorado; McLean and Eakin in Petoskey, Michigan; Diesel Bookstore in Los Angeles; the Best Bookstore in Palm Springs in Palm Springs, California—and so many more! Please support your local independent bookstore either in person or on Bookshop.org.

And to my family, as always—Dennis, Ben, Alec, Emily, and Mavis.

ABOUT THE AUTHOR

MELANIE BENJAMIN is a prize-winning novelist and the *New York Times* bestselling author of *California Golden, The Children's Blizzard, Mistress of the Ritz, The Girls in the Picture, The Swans of Fifth Avenue, The Aviator's Wife, The Autobiography of Mrs. Tom Thumb,* and *Alice I Have Been*. Benjamin lives in Chicago.

melaniebenjamin.com

Instagram: @melaniebenjamin_author

melaniebenjamin.substack.com

ABOUT THE TYPE

This book was set in Fournier, a typeface named for Pierre-Simon Fournier (1712–68), the youngest son of a French printing family. He started out engraving woodblocks and large capitals, then moved on to fonts of type. In 1736 he began his own foundry and made several important contributions in the field of type design; he is said to have cut 147 alphabets of his own creation. Fournier is probably best remembered as the designer of St. Augustine Ordinaire, a face that served as the model for the Monotype Corporation's Fournier, which was released in 1925.